ALSO BY EMMA SCOTT

Little Pieces of Light

LOST BOYS
The Girl in the Love Song
When You Come Back to Me
The Last Piece of His Heart

FULL TILT DUET
Full Tilt
All In

THE LAST PIECE OF HIS HEART

EMMA SCOTT

Bloom *books*

Copyright © 2021, 2026 by Emma Scott
Cover and internal design © 2026 by Sourcebooks
Cover design by Antoaneta Lisak/Sourcebooks
Cover images © Dmitri Toms/Getty Images, Lindrik/Getty Images, VeroRo39/Getty Images, EyeEm Mobile GmbH/Getty Images
Internal image © Viktoriya Klubovich/Getty Images

Sourcebooks, Bloom Books, and the colophon are registered trademarks of Sourcebooks.

All rights reserved. No part of this book may be reproduced in any form or by any electronic or mechanical means including information storage and retrieval systems—except in the case of brief quotations embodied in critical articles or reviews—without permission in writing from its publisher, Sourcebooks.

No part of this book may be used or reproduced in any manner for the purpose of training artificial intelligence technologies or systems.

The characters and events portrayed in this book are fictitious or are used fictitiously. Any similarity to real persons, living or dead, is purely coincidental and not intended by the author.

All brand names and product names used in this book are trademarks, registered trademarks, or trade names of their respective holders. Sourcebooks is not associated with any product or vendor in this book.

Published by Bloom Books, an imprint of Sourcebooks
1935 Brookdale RD, Naperville, IL 60563-2773
(630) 961-3900
sourcebooks.com

Originally self-published in 2021 by Emma Scott.

Cataloging-in-Publication data is on file with the Library of Congress.

The authorized representative in the EEA is Dorling Kindersley Verlag GmbH. Arnulfstr. 124, 80636 Munich, Germany

Manufactured in the UK by Clays and distributed by Dorling Kindersley Limited, London
001-359045-Apr/26
10 9 8 7 6 5 4 3 2 1

PLAYLIST

Everybody Knows // Concrete Blonde (opening credits)
Roots // Imagine Dragons
To Be Young, Gifted and Black // Nina Simone
The Most Beautiful Girl in the World // Prince
Hunger // Florence + The Machine
Let Me Blow Ya Mind // Eve (feat. Gwen Stefani)
Black Hole Sun // Soundgarden
Liggi // Ritviz
Heathens // Twenty One Pilots
Physical // Dua Lipa
Umbrella // Rihanna (feat. JAY-Z)
She Will Be Loved // Maroon 5
Skin and Bones // Cage The Elephant
Lightning Crashes // Live
Blinding Lights // The Weeknd (closing credits)

To my readers. You have taken these Lost Boys into your hearts and kept them safe. With my love.

CONTENT WARNING

Please note that this book contains content that may be triggering for some sensitive readers such as sexual assault and domestic violence (both off the page) and physical assault. It is my sincerest hope that I have treated these issues with the care they deserve. Intended for readers sixteen and up.

PROLOGUE

RONAN

"State your full name for the record."

"Ronan August Wentz."

"Age?"

"Nineteen."

"Do you know why you're here tonight, Ronan?"

Because it's the end of the road.

Two detectives waited for an answer. One was round and short—his badge said *Kowalski*. Harris was taller and had a mustache.

I folded my arms and stared back hard, pretending the white-walled holding room wasn't fucking suffocating me. On the table, Styrofoam cups of black coffee flanked a thick file with my name on it. A camera perched in a corner trained its black eye on us, recording everything.

The detectives exchanged glances at my stony silence, and then Harris got up and paced behind the short guy, Kowalski.

"Where were you on the night of July thirtieth around eleven p.m.?"

"My apartment."

"What were you doing?"

"Watching TV."

"Anyone with you?"

"No."

He nodded at my bruised knuckles. "How'd that happen?"

"Don't remember."

It was a shit answer, but the truth wasn't much better.

Kowalski smirked. "You don't remember?"

"Are you supposed to be asking me this shit without a lawyer?"

"Do you think you need a lawyer, Ronan?"

"We're just talking," Harris cut in. "Your hands are pretty banged up." He picked up my file off the table. "Lots of people find themselves 'banged up' around you, don't they, Mr. Wentz? Starting with your mother."

I stiffened, bracing myself.

"You grew up in a violent household is my point," the detective continued casually, flipping through my life story: behavioral write-ups, police reports from a stint in juvie, and ten years' worth of social workers' notes from my time in the foster care system. "Says here your dad beat your mother to death with a baseball bat when you were eight years old."

Inwardly, it felt as if he kicked me in the gut. Outwardly, I only nodded.

"He died in prison after a knife fight with another inmate?"

I crossed my arms. "He got what he deserved."

Wrong answer.

The cops raised their brows. Another knowing look passed between them: *Now we're getting somewhere.*

"You witnessed it, didn't you? Your dad murdering your mom?"

I winced as bloodstained memories instantly tried to claw their way up out of the grave. They wouldn't stay dead no matter how deep I buried them.

"Seeing something like that's gotta mess a kid up," Harris stated grimly.

"Did it make you angry, Ronan?"

"Angry enough to lash out?"

"They say that kind of violence runs in the family."

"In the DNA."

"Like father, like son."

The last words hung between us, sucking the oxygen out of the air. My worst fear spoken out loud. I shifted in my chair and said nothing.

"Back to the issue at hand," Kowalski said finally and took a turn with the file. "Says here on your first day at Central High, you broke Frankie Dowd's nose."

"He was harassing my friend."

"So you clocked him in the face without so much as an introduction?"

"Miller was fucking dying."

"Miller Stratton?" The cop read from the file. "He wasn't *your friend* at the time of incident. You didn't know him from Adam, isn't that right?"

He's my friend now, asshole.

I'd die for Miller Stratton. For Holden Parish.

For Shiloh…

Pain gripped my heart. Kowalski rapped on the table to jar me out of my thoughts.

"It's looking like you got a reputation for unprovoked violence. That true?"

I stiffened, said nothing.

I tried. I tried to do better. Be better.

"Let's take a walk down memory lane, shall we?" Harris consulted the file again. "In one year, you were suspended from Santa Cruz Central High no less than six times. Vandalism, assault… Two months ago, you had a physical altercation with Miller Stratton's stepfather. Dangled him over a two-story balcony."

I gritted my teeth. I didn't dangle anyone. I'd bent that fucker Chet Hyland over a railing to scare him away from Miller's mother. And it worked. But so what? These assholes weren't interested in the truth—it didn't match the story about me that was already written. Written in my mother's blood. And my father's. His blood flowed in my veins.

Like father, like son.

"Well?"

"Chet wasn't his stepdad," I muttered. "He was a deadbeat who hit Miller's mom. Not that you give a shit."

The cops exchanged glances.

"You got a problem with police?"

An old memory broke free—my mother, broken and bleeding, dragging herself into a corner, and my dad standing over her with the bat in his hand...

You failed Mom, and now she's dead, I thought, but was I aiming that at myself or the cops? They failed her, but so did I. I couldn't protect her.

Couldn't protect Shiloh either.

Guilt, rage, and grief—the three monkeys on my back—squawked and howled.

Kowalski gave me a hard look. "Answer the question, son."

"People need help," I said. "If they don't get it from you, I give it to them."

"Well, ain't that some vigilante shit." Kowalski rolled his eyes. "Threatening to toss a man over a balcony is *helping*?"

I sneered. "He left her alone after that, didn't he?"

"How about Frankie, two nights ago? Were you 'helping' then too?"

"I didn't touch him."

"You didn't see Franklin Dowd on the night of July thirtieth?"

I shifted in my seat. A bead of sweat crawled between my shoulder blades like an insect. "I'm not telling you shit."

"Come on, Wentz," Harris said. "Let's make this easy on everyone. We all know what happened."

Kowalski ticked off his fingers. "You got a

well-documented beef with Frankie Dowd. You broke his nose within seconds of meeting him. Fifty witnesses can say they saw you tackle him to the floor at a house party on September ninth of last year, and a few months ago, you were heard telling him that if he hurt anyone you cared about, you would, quote, *fuck his shit up*."

Harris crossed his arms. "Shiloh Barrera is someone you care about, isn't she?"

"Yes," I said. And that was the truest thing I said that night.

"And Frankie hurt her," Harris continued. "So you did just what you promised and fucked his shit up. Hard. Didn't you?"

"I told you, I—"

"He's in the hospital, Ronan," Kowalski said. "Fighting for his life."

Harris nodded. "That's called motive."

"And here you sit, your fists swollen and bruised all to hell. But this time, it wasn't you. Is that what you're saying?"

I tilted my chin. "That's what I'm fucking saying."

Harris heaved a sigh. "You're just making this harder on yourself, Wentz. This case is cut-and-dried. Confess and maybe they'll cut you a deal. If your victim survives, that is."

My aching hands made fists under the table. I was allowed a lawyer. A phone call. But what good would it do? I was guilty before they sat my ass in the chair.

Harris cocked his head. "You want to know what I think, Ronan?"

I already knew what he thought.
End of the road.
Like father, like son.
Shiloh, I'm sorry. I tried.
The detective leaned over me, his tone cold and final. Like a door slamming shut. "I think you're going to prison for a very long time."

PART I

ONE
SHILOH

ONE YEAR AGO

"Time to head out," I said, dragging my rolling suitcase into the lush family room of my aunt and uncle's house. "Got a plane to catch."

I hated stating the obvious, but if I didn't announce my departure, my mother—sitting in the kitchen—might ignore it altogether. Maybe reminding her that it'd be a full year before she saw her only daughter again would break down her cold walls and she'd show me some warmth.

No dice.

New Orleans bustled on the other side of the glass under a thick summer morning while Mama sat bent over the card table near the window, smoking her cigarette and doing the Sunday crossword. Aloof and distant. No different than how she'd been at the start of this visit six weeks ago—and every summer visit I could remember since I was four years old, when she gave me up to live with my great-grandmother, Bibi, in California.

Aunt Bertie—round and colorful in her purple blouse and matching slacks—made a pitying sound from her spot on the couch where she sat wedged between my uncle Rudy and their twenty-five-year-old daughter, Letitia. A Saints preseason game blared on the flat-screen.

"Already?" Aunt Bertie said and clucked her tongue. "Seems like you just got here."

For my summer visits, I always stayed at my aunt and uncle's Victorian in the Garden District. It was historically old and beautiful and richly decorated with Aunt Bertie's taste for jewel tones and velvet tasseled pillows. The front door's stained glass cast rainbows over the carpet.

I loved the house and the people in it, but I'd have traded it all to be with Mama at her little shotgun on Old Prieur Street in the Seventh Ward. She said it was too small, but I didn't care. I'd have taken the couch. The floor…

"The summer flew by, sugar pie," Aunt Bertie said. "The next time we see you, you'll be a high school graduate." She regarded me in my loose-flowing pants and tight white T-shirt that showed my midriff. "So beautiful, Shiloh. And growing up so fast. Isn't she, Marie?"

Mama made a noncommittal sound and didn't look up from her crossword.

Stay tough, I told myself, burying the pang of pain that tried to find its way to my heart. *You know better than to expect more.*

And yet my stupid heart never stopped trying to reach Mama no matter how badly it hurt.

"Before I go, I have something for all of you." I set my bag on the coffee table and pulled out four gift bags stuffed with tissue paper.

"You sweet thing. You didn't have to." A grin grew over Aunt Bertie's lips as she poked a finger inside one bag. "Are these, by any chance, Shiloh Barrera originals?"

I smiled. "Maybe."

"Hot dang," Uncle Rudy said, peeling his gaze from the football game. "Christmas come early."

I handed out the bags, one each to my aunt, uncle, and cousin, and one left over. For Mama.

Letitia took hers eagerly in her lap. Even on a Sunday, she was pure style in designer jeans, yellow heels, and a cropped top that showed off her toned abs. She'd expertly piled her braids on her head, a few trailing down around gold drop earrings.

"I already love it," she said.

I laughed. "You don't know what it is."

"You made it, so it's going to be beautiful."

I swallowed hard and risked another glance at Mama, unmoved from her spot in the kitchen.

Aunt Bertie pulled a turquoise brooch from her gift bag. I'd oxidized the silver filigree to make it look antique. She rested a hand on the shelf of her bosom. "Oh my stars, baby. This is the most beautiful thing I've ever seen. But why wait until the last minute to give us these treasures?"

I grinned. "So you only have to pretend to like it until I'm out the door."

"Pfft, it's gorgeous." Aunt Bertie pinned the brooch to her blouse and held her arms out for me to hug her. I bent over the table and was enveloped in her soft, perfumed embrace. "Such a talented girl. You're going to have that shop you keep dreaming about. I can feel it in my bones."

"Thanks, Auntie," I said, basking in her faith in me. Her love that she gave so easily.

"Ain't this something." Uncle Rudy turned over the pewter key chain pendant of the Saints' fleur-de-lis logo. "You *made* this? Wait till the fellas see. Thank you, baby girl."

His pride made the back of my throat tighten. I nodded with a faint smile and looked away. It was so much easier selling my jewelry online to strangers who didn't bring soft, uncomfortable emotions to the surface.

"Girl, *no way*," Letitia said, pulling from her bag a set of earrings, intricate silver twined around lapis stones in bright blue. She immediately took out the earrings she'd been wearing and exchanged them for mine. "Are you kidding? You got mad skills, Shi. My mama's right. You're going to take this all the way."

"Thanks, Teesh," I said, my fingers trailing over the handles of the last gift bag.

While Letitia and Rudy compared and crowed over their gifts, Aunt Bertie smiled gently at me. Pityingly. "Marie," she called to the kitchen. "Shiloh has something for you."

Mama couldn't ignore that.

She got up from her seat at the kitchen window and slowly made her way to me. My heart ached at the reluctance inhabiting her every movement.

Marie Barrera was young—only nineteen years older than me—and beautiful but heavy with sadness. Everyone said I was her spitting image, but my unknown father's DNA lightened my skin and muted our resemblance.

"At least that's no mystery," Jalen Jackson—my Louisiana friend with benefits—had bluntly stated in his bed the night before. "Someone put cream in your mama's coffee."

But the obvious fact that my father was white didn't fill the huge hole in my life where he belonged. He was a ghost, haunting the family through me. No one would speak of him. Least of all Mama. From what little I'd gleaned in seventeen years, I was the product of a one-night stand. Unexpected and unwanted. Mama had been on full scholarship to LSU with a bright future stretching in front of her until the pregnancy. Now, she worked part-time in a bank, her dreams of a job in marketing sidelined forever. Whoever my father was, she'd cut him out of her life and refused to speak of him ever again.

It made no sense. With a big family willing to help, why did Mama drop out of college? Why not put me up for adoption?

Why have me at all?

No one would tell me. But for all the mystery surrounding my father, one thing was crystal clear: Mama saw him when she looked at me, and she didn't like what she saw.

Her smile flickered like a dying bulb as I held out her gift bag. She took it slowly and hesitantly put her hand inside. "What have we here?"

"It's nothing. Just…something."

Mama pulled out the hammered copper cuff bracelet with a turquoise patina and held it up to the light.

"I wanted it to resemble something pulled from a sunken ship," I said, my normally strong voice wavering. "I know those have always fascinated you."

I watched her, breath held, as she turned it over and over. Tears filled her brown eyes—eyes like mine—and she really looked at me for the first time since the start of my visit. Then she dropped the cuff back in the bag as if it'd burned her.

"It's very lovely. Thank you."

Blinking her eyes dry, she gave me a brief, stiff hug. I wanted to sink into her arms, into her scents of cigarettes and jasmine perfume. But no sooner than I felt her arms around me, they were slipping away.

"Be good. Work hard. Give Bibi our love."

What about me?

I inhaled sharply, as if I could suck the thought back. Being weak and asking for what I wasn't given would never get me anywhere. I knew better than to even think it; I was stronger than that.

"Goodbye, Mama," I said.

But she had already retreated to the table, into her crossword puzzle and the haze of cigarette smoke. She set the gift bag on the floor at her feet, where it looked small and already forgotten.

"Let me drive you, sweetheart," Uncle Rudy said gently into the stony quiet Mama left behind.

"Thanks, Uncle Rudy," I said, mustering a sarcastic grin. "But I can't possibly pull you away from this very important yet meaningless preseason Saints game. I'll take an Uber."

Uncle Rudy grinned back. "Smart aleck, ain't ya?"

Aunt Bertie snorted. "An Uber? You going to get in a stranger's car? Pretty girl like you?"

In the kitchen, my mother flinched. Or maybe it was just a shiver from the air-conditioning.

"Thanks, Aunt B, but I'll be fine."

"Nonsense. Rudy will drive you, and that's the end of that."

My uncle shot me a wink, beaming perfect white teeth against rich dark skin. "You heard the boss."

"What would anyone want with her skinny ass anyway?" Letitia laughed and helped pull my luggage to the door. She arched her eyebrows and leaned in close with a knowing grin. "You say goodbye to Jalen already?"

I shot her a *keep your voice down* glare. "Last night."

She smirked. "I'll bet. You're going to break that boy's heart."

"Not possible. He and I have an agreement," I said, my voice low and my cheeks heating. I hated anything resembling gossip while my cousin lived on it. "No strings. No attachments."

"Your motto."

I glanced at Mama. *I learned from the best.*

"Going to miss you." Letitia ran her fingers over a handful of the hundreds of microbraids that fell softly down my shoulders. "You got someone in California who can duplicate my artistry?"

Letitia, not even thirty years old, was owner of her own beauty salon—The Studio—on Canal Street. She was my idol and an inspiration for my own ambitions.

"No chance."

"Great, then you'll have to come back and see me. And Jalen."

"Oh, hush up."

Letitia laughed and gave me a final hug.

Uncle Rudy joined me at the door and took hold of my rolling suitcase. "Let's hit the road, sweetheart."

Bertie and Letitia waved and offered safe travels and love. They wrapped me in it.

And then there was Mama, like a cold patch of air in the humid, cloying heat of New Orleans in August.

I shivered and went out.

My plane landed in California at one in the afternoon. An Uber ride later, I was hauling my rolling suitcase up the front walk of the cozy one-story house. The air in Santa Cruz was cooler and tinged with salt, and the trees spilled down from the mountainside to line our quiet street. A huge cypress shaded our front yard on one side, and on the other, Bibi's flower garden was a riot of color.

"Home," I murmured. I climbed the three steps to our tiny front porch and unlocked the front door. "Bibi, it's me."

"There she is," my eighty-year-old great-grandmother said from our lumpy, pillow-strewn couch. Her dark-brown skin was creased with wrinkles—mostly laugh lines—and her close-cropped hair was entirely silver now. Despite the summer warmth, she sat wrapped in a green-and-white shawl she had made herself. A pile of yellow yarn lay at her slippered feet, and needles clacked as she crafted another. Our lazy gray cats, Lucy and Ethel, were both stretched out on the back of the couch.

I left my rolling suitcase by the door and crossed our living room with its antique furniture that was too big for our little house—every available surface housing knick-knacks or stacked with old books Bibi was now almost too blind to read. Family photos covered nearly every inch of the flowered wallpaper, and Nina Simone crooned on the ancient stereo.

"How did it go?" Bibi asked. "Better than last year, I hope."

I flopped down beside her and rested my head on her shoulder. "Don't know about *better*. Bertie and Rudy are great, as usual. Letitia's like the sister I never had."

"But?" Bibi's needles *clacked*.

"But Mama is still Mama."

My great-grandmother patted my cheek with her warm, dry hand and sighed. "Oh, my darling girl. I wish it were better between you."

"I don't know why I keep going." Sudden tears stung my eyes, but I blinked them away quickly. Ethel jumped in my lap, and I focused on scratching her ears. "She doesn't want me around. That's not self-pity. Straight facts."

"She *does* want you there, honey," Bibi said. "She's showing you the only way she knows how."

"By ignoring me?"

"By asking you to come. Spending time."

"Not what I'd call quality time. It's like it's physically painful for her to look at me. I mean, I get it. I ruined her future. But why does she bother? Why do I?"

"Because there is love there, even if it's hard to see."

She didn't have to keep me.

The thought left me with a cold shiver in my heart, because no doubt, my mother must've had the same idea. Looking at her sometimes, I'd feel a strange, remembered vertigo, as if I'd once teetered on a razor's edge between here and oblivion.

"Don't go there, Shiloh."

Bibi might've been legally blind, but she saw everything.

"Can't help it," I said softly. "Why did she have me if it was going to be so hard for her?"

Bibi thought for a moment. "A woman's heart is not a single room with her feelings and choices stark on white walls, like an exhibit. It's a deep catacomb we spend our entire life mapping. Your mama is navigating her way, but it's slow and hard. Because she's lost."

I turned to face my great-grandmother, the woman who raised me, whom I trusted and loved more than anyone else. "What happened, Bibi?"

She heaved a sigh, her shelf of a bosom rising under her housedress. "I wish I knew, honey. But Marie is closed off to protect herself." She gave me an arch look. "Just like you."

After seventeen years, I was used to Bibi's gentle lectures on how I needed to open my heart to other experiences. But as wise as she was, she didn't understand. I had to work hard to make something of myself and prove that I was worth the choice Mama made to keep me.

Opening my heart is how the pain gets in.

"Did you see your boyfriend again this visit?" Bibi asked after a minute.

"Jalen is *not* my boyfriend. We have an understanding."

"An understanding. How *romantic.*" She frowned over her knitting. "I'd feel better if you came home crying over how you were going to miss that boy and wondering how you'd survive until the next time you saw him."

"Ugh, no thanks. I don't get mushy over boys."

My mother's rejection was enough to contend with, thanks very much. Bibi said a woman's heart was like a catacomb. Mine was more like a trashed hotel room I was trying to keep locked. No way was I going to let some guy move in and wreak his havoc too.

Bibi *hmphed.* "You two were careful, I presume."

"Of course."

Careful to use protection and careful not to let Jalen think I was about to get serious. But I didn't need to worry. He and I had known each other for years, our friendship growing into experimental messing around since we were fourteen. He was the quintessential friend with benefits: hot, smart, not interested in catching feelings. Just the way I needed him to be.

"Always careful, my Shiloh," Bibi said to her knitting. "Careful, driven, ambitious."

"You say that like it's a bad thing. And on that note, unless you need anything, I'm going to hit the garage."

"Already? You just got home."

"I have online orders waiting to fill."

She heaved a sigh. "Working day and night. My very own Tiana."

I grinned. *The Princess and the Frog* was another of Bibi's favorite themes. The cute Disney movie had somehow become a metaphor for my life.

"She got her restaurant, didn't she?" I said.

"She also learned to make room for love along the way."

"Might I remind you that Tiana was also—briefly—a frog. It's a fairy tale. This is the real world."

Bibi sniffed, needles hooking and poking. "Be that as it may, I don't like the idea of you in that garage all day, every day. It's not healthy and has to stop."

"Stop?" My heart dropped. Ethel felt the tension coursing through me and jumped off my lap. "But…I need the garage. It's where I work. It's—"

"Not good enough for you," Bibi said, smiling to herself. "Which is why I put an ad in the paper for a handyman. I'm going to hire someone to build you a workshop."

"A workshop. Where?"

"In our backyard."

I blinked. Aside from the vegetable garden and small patio, our yard looked like Northern California's version of a tropical jungle.

Bibi read my thoughts as she so often did. "This man can clear the overgrowth and build you a little place to work with your soldering tools and chemical polishes and what have you. I won't have you breathing in all those fumes another minute."

I sat back against the couch, envisioning it already: my own little space with a proper table that could handle a bench pin instead of the teetering old card table I had in the garage. I could get caught up on my Etsy orders while making the pieces that would eventually fill a brick-and-mortar shop in downtown Santa Cruz. That had always been my dream. Someday. Now, thanks to this amazing woman, *someday* just got a little bit closer.

Then the vision vanished like a mirage.

"Bibi, we can't afford it."

"Don't you worry about the money. I took an account of my savings, and there's plenty. And what am I going to do with it? Travel the world? I'm happy as a clam right here." She smiled. "It won't be a château, so don't get your hopes up. But you need it, Shiloh. You have incredible talent—that was obvious a long time ago. And while I tease you about making room for more in your life, I know how important your work is to you. This isn't some hobby."

"No," I said softly. "It *is* my life."

Her hand came up and found my cheek. "I want to do whatever I can—no matter how small—to bring you closer to your dreams. Even if it means I'll see you less than I do now."

I threw my arms around Bibi's shoulders. "I can't thank you enough. But I can help pay. The handyman or the materials—"

"I forbid it. You need every dollar for your shop. This is my gift to you, and I don't want to hear another word about it."

I hugged her tighter. "Thank you, Bibi."

"You're welcome, child. Now go. I know you're itching to get back to work. I can feel it running through your bones."

I laughed and kissed her cheek. "I love you."

"Love you, baby girl." She blew me a kiss and went back to her knitting, humming along to Nina Simone's "To Be Young, Gifted and Black," a knowing, satisfied smile on her weathered face.

I hurried to the garage where my materials were crammed into bins that lined one wall. A tiny worktable butted against Bibi's ancient Buick that was mine now. The single bulb wasn't enough light, but I hated working with the garage door open. I felt exposed, my business visible to anyone walking their dog or taking out the trash. Working in the privacy of my backyard would be a dream. A level up.

And the next level is my own shop.

I put in my headphones. Rihanna sang in my ear as I sat down at the table in front of my latest project. Before I'd left for Louisiana, I'd braided lengths of brass and copper for an eventual bracelet. Feeling at home on my stool, I slid the rough bracelet down a mandrel, then took up a rubber mallet. Hammering lightly, I shaped the coils of metal on the cylindrical rod until it was perfectly round and the size I wanted.

In minutes, I had another finished piece for a woman named Christine in Texas who'd ordered off my Etsy page. That website had been exactly what I needed to get my work out there and build some revenue for my eventual shop. By next summer even.

Thanks to Bibi.

Love for that woman filled me up, making me warm and erasing the vestiges of Mama's cold shoulder. Bibi was the only person I loved without reservation.

I turned over her words as I turned the new bracelet around and around in the light—her warning that I'd become closed off like my mother. Stuck behind a wall of our own making and lost at the same time. But what else could I do? Every brick in Mama's wall was one I added to mine.

It was the only way I knew how to survive the fact that my own mother hated me.

TWO
RONAN

"Ronan?"

I turned toward the sound of my name, scanning the baggage claim crowd, and there he was—Nelson Wentz. My only living relative.

My heart slammed in my chest at the resemblance.

Uncle Nelson was a preview of how my dad might've looked had he made it to middle age—mid-fifties, wearing old jeans and with a gut pushing out of his windbreaker. Nelson's dark hair was mostly gone, and his eyes were gray, flat, and empty. Like a shark's when they roll back for the kill. Same as Dad's.

Same as mine.

"Hey, Uncle Nelson."

"Just Nelson," he said. "So you're him, eh?" He scanned me up and down, taking in my torn jeans, black T-shirt, and the tattoos inking my skin as if I were cattle at auction. "Looks like they been working you hard on that farm.

Good. My back's not what it used to be. I'm gonna need you to do most of the heavy lifting."

I hefted my ratty backpack higher on my shoulder. "What for?"

"We'll get into that on the ride down." He jerked his flabby chin at the luggage carousel. "You got a bag?"

I nodded, trying to ignore the disappointment that bit at me.

So he's not throwing you a welcome parade. Get over it.

We waited in tense silence for a scuffed, oversize duffel to come around. I hauled it off the carousel, and we headed out the sliding doors toward the San José Airport parking.

When I turned eighteen in March, I aged out of foster care and was on my own. I did odd jobs to survive, the last at a dairy farm in Manitowoc, Wisconsin. The gig ended with the summer, and I would've been homeless, except my social worker called me with the news that after ten years, an uncle had finally made contact. My dad's brother was willing to take me in. I'd move to Santa Cruz, California, live with blood instead of with strangers. Maybe finish school. I'd have a family again.

I glanced at Nelson.

I have family again.

My instincts, honed from years of being on my own and trusting exactly no one, warned me to slow the fuck down. I had to be ready to let go at any time. Survival depended on it. But while waiting for the light to change, I took a second to breathe. Different air. Different sun somehow. It was only my fucked-up childhood talking, but Wisconsin's heat had been stifling, the winters heartless. Now I was in California. I could start over. Maybe leave the bloody ghosts of my past behind.

Nelson coughed and hawked a wad of phlegm onto the sidewalk. Beneath his bulk, Nelson had Dad's build. Tall with muscles lurking beneath the flab, large hands with calloused knuckles that could ball into huge fists…

So much for leaving the ghosts behind. I'm about to get into a car with one.

He led us out of the gold California sun and into the cold of the parking garage to an old Dodge pickup in faded red. I tossed my duffel in the flatbed filled with junk—stacks of musty coats, folding chairs, and a cardboard box that held a tennis racket, coffee maker, and chipped mugs.

"Eviction," Nelson said with a nod at the box. "You won't believe the crap they leave behind. You'll see."

I brushed balled-up tissues and fast-food wrappers off the seat and sat down with my backpack in my lap. More wrappers littered the dash, and plastic bottles of Mountain Dew rolled around my feet.

Nelson squeezed himself behind the wheel, and soon, San José Airport grew small in the rearview. The winding road—a sign said it was the 17—took us deeper through green forest, southward to Santa Cruz. Mountains rose up on all sides, looking like a miracle after the flatness of Manitowoc.

"You don't say much, do you?" Nelson asked after a few minutes.

"Not much."

"Fine by me. I don't need anyone jabbering my damn ear off." His shark-eyed gaze slid to me and back to the road. "You look like him. Russell. Not your mom so much."

"I know," I said through a tight jaw.

"Shameful what happened," Nelson continued. "A waste. Russ had so much going for him. Until he met *her*."

A red haze dropped over my vision, and I gripped the coarse material of my bag, making fists.

"Damn shame." Nelson shook his head, eyes on the road. "Women will do that to a good man. Fuck with his head. Make him crazy, and then *he* gets the short stick when it all finally blows up."

"He beat her to death with a baseball bat," I gritted out, my voice made of stone.

"Russ was no angel, but what did Norah say to piss him off? Wore him down is what she did. He didn't start out wanting to hurt nobody. That's what no one talks about these days. Takes two to tango, doesn't it?"

An image rose up like a flare: my fist flying, punching my mother's name out of Nelson's stupid mouth. I fought the rage—my dad's rage—that boiled up in me and turned away. The California scenery flashing outside the window was a blur. But in the window's reflection, I saw her. Crying and huddled in a corner of our shitty kitchen with its cracked tile and the dinner he didn't like splattered all over. Not one particular night. Could've been any night.

"You're not like him, Ronan," Mom whispered, her tears mingling with the blood on her cheek. "You're better than him. Remember that."

I sucked in a breath, forced my hands to uncurl from tight fists, and tried to believe her.

"We gotta talk about the terms of our arrangement," Nelson said.

"Okay."

I hadn't known there was an arrangement. I thought I had an uncle who wanted me. A chance at a family. A normal life.

I should've known better.

"I own two buildings, ten units each," Nelson said. "I live in the Bluffs Avenue complex. You'll be in the one on Cliffside."

I glanced over. "I'm not living with you?"

He frowned. "You're eighteen, aren't you? I was on my own and had a job at fourteen."

"But—"

"But nothing. You been in California for a hot minute and already dreaming about lazing around on a beach all day? Typical."

I gritted my teeth. I'd been working since I was eight— either on juvie work programs or doing chores for whatever foster family would take me in for a few months. The gig at the farm in Manitowoc was thirteen hours a day under a boiling sun and shit pay.

Don't talk to me about lazy, asshole.

"What's the job?" I asked.

"Apartment management. Maintenance. Handyman-type stuff. You ever do any carpentry?"

"When I was sixteen, I was placed with a family who owned a construction company. I learned a few things."

"Good. What about plumbing? HVAC?"

"Not much."

"Not much to know," he said. "I'll teach you. I like to do repairs myself. Keep costs down. Keeps me from being ripped off by overpriced, so-called professionals who don't know a quarter-inch pipe from a hole in the ground."

I shifted in my seat. My uncle wasn't interested in a family reunion. There weren't going to be any meals at the same table. No watching the game together. I was manual labor. Nothing more.

My stomach felt hollow, as if I hadn't eaten in years and wasn't about to anytime soon.

"What about school?"

Nelson frowned. "What school?"

"I got one more year."

He snorted. "Really?"

"I missed a grade when...all that shit went down. I want to graduate. Get a diploma."

"Take the test if it means so much to you. You're not going to have time for school. It's a lot of work. When someone moves out—or gets kicked out—then we got to clean up their mess and get it ready for a new tenant. We have to advertise a vacancy, vet the applicants. Then there's rent to collect, and that's a whole other ordeal. You'd think I was running a charity, the excuses I hear."

My uncle droned on while a memory surfaced. The last time I really talked to my mom, only three days before she died.

"Finish school, Ronan," she said, handing me a freshly washed dish to dry. "No matter what happens. Don't be like me. I dropped out, and it's been nothing but doors slamming shut in my face ever since. The end of the road." Her clear blue eyes turned shadowed, then she beamed at me. "You're smart. Don't let anyone tell you different, and don't let anyone take it away from you."

"Take what?" I asked, stacking the dish on the counter.

"Your future."

I turned to Nelson. "I want to finish school."

"That's not the deal."

"What *is* the deal? You want to put me to work."

"In exchange for a roof over your dumb head." He raised his brows at my stony silence. "You got other options? How about that farm, mucking cow shit and sleeping in a barn? If you want to go back, by all means, tell me to stop the car, and I'll let you out right now."

Like leaving a dog on the side of the road, I thought as every hope I'd had burned up, one after another. I was on my own again. So fucking be it.

"Pull over."

Nelson frowned. "Huh?"

"You heard me. I said, pull over."

"Now, hold on—"

"*Stop the fucking car.*"

Nelson flinched, his hands twisting on the wheel. He slowed and pulled over, trees rising on both sides of the winding road. "This is the middle of nowhere. Look, Ronan, maybe I spoke too soon—"

"Thanks for the ride." I climbed out and slammed the door behind me.

Nelson rolled down the passenger window and drove the car at a crawl to keep up with me, desperation in his voice. I guessed he needed me more than he let on.

"You going to leave all your shit in my trunk?"

"Yep."

"Be smart, Ronan. You got nothing here."

I'd always had nothing. I kept walking.

He leaned across the passenger seat, his tone softening slightly. "Look. I wouldn't have been no kind of parent to a little kid. But I'm here now, and we're family. This situation works for both of us. Right?"

Family. That damn word again. I stopped walking.

"There you go," Nelson said. "Now get in and—"

"She was going to leave him."

He blinked stupidly. "Huh?"

"You asked what Mom did to set Dad off," I said, turning my stare—flat and hard—on Nelson. "He came home after a night in jail for roughing her up. Because they never kept him long enough. Never protected her."

I didn't protect her.

I cleared the thickness from my throat. "She told him she was taking me and leaving. So he fucking killed her."

Nelson hunched his shoulders, his eyes anywhere but me. "Yeah, okay, okay."

"Don't talk about her ever again. Not her name. Nothing."

"Whatever you say."

"And I'm going to finish school."

Nelson's eyes widened. "Full of demands, aren't we? Watch yourself, boy."

I didn't move.

He spat another curse. "It won't work. You'll see. Hard for you and harder for me with the tenants."

I started walking.

"Okay, okay, if you insist, Einstein. Now will you get in the damn car?"

I climbed back in, my bag on my lap, and slammed the door.

"Christ," Nelson muttered under his breath as he pulled the car back onto the road. "When has anything been easy? Never, that's when."

At least we agreed on something.

My social worker, Alicia, had told me Santa Cruz was a smallish town, but it seemed huge compared to Manitowoc. Street after street of houses, shops, a huge university, and a boardwalk with games, rides, and a Ferris wheel that slowly turned in front of the Pacific. Lake Michigan was nothing to the endless blue green of the ocean that stretched along the coast. Turn around, and there were mountains covered in forests of green. Like a mirage after staring at the same hopeless landscape for eighteen years.

I glanced at Nelson, wondering how the hell he ended up here.

"Your grandma left me and Russell everything," he said, answering my unspoken question. "I got the properties she and Pawpaw invested in a million years ago, and your dad got the cash." He snorted. "Lucky me."

I nodded grimly, thinking of how Mom struggled to pay bills and keep food on the table with money she earned from two jobs while Russ drank and gambled the inheritance away on fantasy sports leagues and local poker games.

"This is you."

Nelson pulled the car into a cracked parking lot. It fronted a cement block of an apartment complex in a neighborhood filled with them. Wrought-iron bars covered the bottom windows. Peeling paint and exterior cement steps led to the second level.

He pointed at the top corner unit. "That one's yours for now. Grab your stuff. I'll show you the place."

I followed him up the stairs to the corner unit. A gold-and-black sticker that said OFFICE was stuck to the door.

"Typically, managers live on the ground floor," Nelson said. "But I got a lady in there with her two kids, begging me not to move her upstairs." He rolled his eyes as he unlocked the door from a ring of keys.

"Why doesn't she want to move?"

"The ground unit is bigger, of course. I told her it was up to you. If you want to kick the mouthy bitch out, be my guest."

My shoulders tensed. "I won't."

"Take the grand tour and say that again."

He shoved the door open, and I stepped inside a dark, shabby shoebox. A ratty couch, a table, and a single chair were the only furniture in the living room/kitchen area. The bedroom was tiny with a futon and a small window with a view of the street. The bathroom was a shower, toilet, and sink. A few dead bugs in the scratched, yellowing porcelain. I tried to picture a mom with two kids in here, and my stomach churned.

"Told ya," Nelson said, misreading my disgusted look. "The bottom unit's better."

"I'm fine here."

"Don't be stupid. If I were you—"

"I said, *it's fine*."

He sighed. "Suit yourself. Now let's get to work."

Over the next two weeks, Nelson had me meet the tenants of the Cliffside Apartments. The "mouthy bitch" on the ground unit below mine was Maryann Greer—a tired-looking woman in her mid-thirties. She had dark circles under her eyes, but there was a fire in them that hadn't gone out.

She reminded me of Mom.

Her twin girls, Camille and Lillian, looked to be around six years old. When Nelson introduced me as their new manager, they'd all stared at me with the same suspicion. I told Maryann I wasn't going to make her move upstairs. Even so, they shut the door on us quick.

"You were too nice to her," Nelson had said as we moved to the next shabby door in the shabby complex. "Don't make a habit of it. You gotta watch it with these tenants. Give 'em an inch, they'll take a mile."

As far as I could see, the tenants weren't getting much of anything. Nearly all of them had plumbing and heating issues, and their apartments were just as shitty as mine. Or worse. The whole building needed new paint, new pipes, new pavement in the cracked parking lot.

During those weeks, I did my best to fix what was broken—clogged drains, leaky pipes... On my iPhone—a gift from my social worker before leaving Wisconsin—I googled how to replace heating filaments. I paid for any repair materials out of my own savings, because Nelson was too slow, and he was even slower paying me back.

The work kept me busy. The first few days of school at Santa Cruz Central High came and went, but on Thursday, I was caught up enough to go. The school was in walking distance, thankfully, since I had no transportation.

Or a paycheck.

"You live rent free," Nelson had told me. "I'm supposed to pay you on top of that?"

"How am I—"

"You gotta get *a job*," he'd said, as if I were stupid. "Between work and keeping the units going, there's no time for school. I told you."

"I'm going."

He heaved a sigh. "For now. But if things start to fall apart at the complex, I'm yanking you out."

Try it.

Central High was like a movie. An open, outdoor campus with trees and classrooms that were cleaner and better lit than my apartment. I felt like an impostor. I was too old; I'd seen too much. I didn't belong with these students and their smiling faces and their fucking pep rallies. I felt the stares on my tattoos and heard the whispers that I was an escaped convict. A criminal.

Nelson was right.

But I thought of my mom and kept going.

In math class, Ms. Sutter—a sour-looking woman with dark hair and a pinched face—told us to get out our notebooks and pencils while she wrote out equations on an ancient overhead projector.

I tapped a pencil on the bare desk. I'd forgotten to buy supplies.

"Mr. Wentz, is it?" Ms. Sutter asked. "Where is your notebook?"

"Forgot," I muttered.

She pursed her wrinkly lips. "There is scratch paper by the window. You can use that. For today."

All eyes were on me as I got up and grabbed a few sheets of paper from an uneven stack on the shelf. I didn't give a shit what anyone thought about me, but the math equations on the projector didn't make any sense. Me being there didn't make any sense. I'd missed too much normal life and would never catch up.

Sorry, Mom. It's too late for me. Too late...

I grabbed my backpack and left the class, Ms. Sutter calling after me. I ignored her and headed down one of the cement paths toward the front walk. But the school was huge. When the football field came into view, I knew I'd gone the wrong way.

"Fuck."

I started to turn around when I heard voices and some kind of alarm clock going off.

"You don't look so good, Stratton. Gonna piss yourself again?"

I peered around the corner. Three guys were ganging up on a fourth in torn jeans, a jacket, and a beanie on his head. His watch was beeping, and he swayed on his feet as if he were drunk.

"Get the fuck out of my way," he said weakly to a scrawny red-haired guy wearing board shorts and a sick grin on his face.

"I'm good right here," the red-haired guy said, crossing

his arms and barring the way. "Kinda curious about what's going to happen next."

His two friends shifted nervously.

"Hey, Frankie, he really doesn't look so good," one said to the red-haired guy.

"Yeah, and he's got that alarm..."

"Nah, he's all right, aren't you, Stratton?"

The guy, Stratton, looked like shit—pale, sweaty, hardly able to stand.

Frankie gripped him by the back of the neck. "You still wearing that little machine stuck in your guts? What would happen if someone took it out? Just to get a better look?"

The fuck?

I strode into the small crowd just as Stratton threw a weak upward punch that caught Frankie under the chin. His jaw snapped shut with a *clack* and a spurt of blood.

"You fu-ther!" he howled. "I fu-thing bit my thung."

Frankie charged, fist cocked. Stratton was in my way. I shoved him aside and slammed my fist into Frankie's oncoming face. Bone and cartilage gave under my knuckles, and he staggered back, crying and cursing.

I could feel the others staring but kept my focus on Frankie, every muscle in my body itching to go if he wanted more.

I hoped he wanted more.

The vice principal, an oily fucker named Chouder, appeared behind us. "What's all this?"

"Fu-ther broke my nose," Frankie whined from behind his hand.

"Go see the nurse, Dowd," Chouder said and turned his hard stare on me. "Mr. Wentz. My office. The rest of you get back to class."

Stratton's beeping watch drew his attention and cooled the blood in my veins. He looked like hell. Maybe needed an ambulance.

"Are you all right?" Chouder asked, annoyed.

"Oh sure," Stratton said, lip curling. "Never better."

He staggered away toward a bank of lockers with a kind of tired stoicism. He didn't rat on Frankie or his friends. Didn't complain.

"He going to be okay?" I asked Chouder as we headed for the admin building.

"You broke his nose. A little late for concern, isn't it?"

"Not that asshole. The other guy."

"Miller will be fine," Chouder said, leading me through the offices of the administration building where counselors and staff talked or worked at their desks.

"Why were they fucking with him?"

"Watch your language, Mr. Wentz." Chouder indicated I should sit at the chair in front of his desk. "I suspect they were teasing Miller over the fact that he was briefly homeless and lived in a car with his mother several years ago." He bent to pull a file from a drawer and slapped it down, then frowned at my dark look. "I'm not telling you something you won't hear by lunch tomorrow. Let it go, Wentz." He tapped the file. "You have bigger problems. Your little stunt basically amounts to assault."

"That bullying prick deserved it."

"Hmm." Chouder arched his brows and consulted my file. "The apple doesn't fall far from the tree in the Wentz family, does it?"

I gritted my teeth.

"There are other methods, aside from violence, to achieve one's goals." Chouder folded his hands. "How about you take a three-day suspension to think that over?"

When I got out of Chouder's office, Miller Stratton was waiting for me.

"You didn't have to do that for me," he said, falling in step as I headed out of the school.

"I didn't do it for you," I said, not looking at him.

"Then why?"

Because he killed her, and I didn't stop him.

But who wanted to hear that fucked-up shit? I shrugged instead and kept walking. Miller kept walking with me. He was better now. Not so glassy-eyed or about to fall over. But he carried that same stoicism with him. Wore it like his ratty jacket that was as beat up as mine.

"Is it true you lived in a car?" I asked.

Miller's eyes flashed anger. "You've been on campus for all of ten minutes, and you heard that already? A new record. Yes. A long time ago. No one seems to be able to forget it."

"Then make them forget."

"How?"

I flexed my fingers that ached a little from clocking Frankie. *Not my way. Don't be like me. Like* him.

Miller peered up at me. He was a few inches shorter than my six two. "The guy you punched? His dad's a cop."

A sneer curled my lips. "Fuck them both."

"What do you have against cops?"

I thought of the dozens of late-night visits from police that ended with my dad "cooling off" in jail for a night, only to come back the next day, more pissed off than ever. Restraining orders that he wiped his ass with like toilet paper.

That was shit you couldn't tell a total stranger, but it felt like, with every step we took on that same path, Miller was less and less strange.

We walked in easy silence until I got to the corner of the building I managed. I'd turned on the TV before I left that morning. We could hear it droning.

"That you?"

I nodded.

"I'm a block down." Miller stuffed his hands in the pockets of his jacket. "You need to get home?"

"Home." I scoffed. I didn't know what that word meant anymore. "No."

Miller nodded. His dark-blue eyes looked like they'd seen their fair share of shit too.

"Follow me."

Miller walked us down a path that started behind a parking lot with an abandoned utility shed. It led to the beach, away from the boardwalk with its lights and roller coasters and laughing tourists, and toward the cliffs that gave our neighborhood its name.

The way was rocky and hard; we climbed over large rocks where the coast crumbled and spilled into the ocean. Just when I thought we'd have to turn back, it got easier. The water receded, and Miller led us around a huge boulder that blocked our path. On the other side was a small fisherman's shack, weather-beaten and old but still standing.

"Found it four days ago," Miller said. "Been coming here every night since. After work."

"Yeah?" I examined the small space that had a wooden table, a bench, and a window cut into one wall. "Where's work?"

"The arcade, down at the boardwalk."

I nodded and sat on the bench. "You can see the ocean."

Miller jammed his hands into his pockets again. "Yeah, it's nice. A good place to just..."

"Get the fuck away from everyone?"

"Precisely."

"You looked sick earlier," I said. "What's with the watch? That part of it?"

"It's an alarm. My blood sugars were low." Miller lifted his shirt to show me a small white device stuck on his abdomen. "I have diabetes."

I nodded, and then an old childhood memory—one of the rare decent ones—came back to me. I covered a smile so Miller wouldn't think I was making fun of him.

Too late.

"Something funny?" he asked, a suspicious edge to his voice.

"I knew a girl when I was a kid…five years old," I said, and then the laughter came at me like a wildfire, taking me off guard. "Her aunt had diabetes. The kid called it dia-ba-titties."

Miller stared at me, and then the laughter spread to him too.

"No one corrected her?"

I shook my head. "Would you?"

"Hell no."

We lost our shit over that stupid word, like it was the funniest thing we'd ever heard. But I hadn't laughed in ages, and I bet Miller hadn't either.

"Shit, haven't thought of that in years," I said when we could breathe again.

Miller wiped his eyes. "That's a winner. Dia-ba-titties. Sounds like something my mom's new boyfriend would call it. On purpose."

I caught the subtext instantly. Our laughter vanished. "He's one of those?"

"Yeah. One of those."

I stared out the small window to the ocean crashing over the sand again and again, leaving it smooth. A fresh start. That's what I'd come here for, and I'd nearly given up school on day one.

I could keep going. For me and Miller too. I touched the owl tattoo on my right shoulder. Mom would want me to watch out for him.

I'll help him. Because I'm not like my father. I'm fucking not.

"They won't fuck with you anymore."

Miller frowned, confused, then suspicion swarmed back over his face. "You going to be my bodyguard or something? Forget it. I can take care of myself."

I cocked my head, waiting. He wasn't used to people doing shit for him without a price either.

"Okay," he said finally, and with that one word, something settled between us. Became solid and real. He gathered up his stuff. "I gotta get to work. Stay as long as you want."

It's yours now too.

He didn't say it, but I heard it in his voice. Miller Stratton was like me. A loner who'd been dealt a shit hand. But he didn't bitch and moan. He handled his business and got on with it. I respected that.

I stayed until the sun set. I didn't want to leave, but it was getting dark. Old pieces of driftwood lay scattered around. I dug a shallow pit in the sand with my hands and tossed in the driftwood. Next time, I'd bring lighter fluid. Then I could stay as long as I wanted.

Except I needed to eat. Eventually.

I dragged myself away from the shack, back to the parking lot and my empty apartment. I heated up a frozen dinner while the TV blared sports news and scanned a local paper's want ads. I made a few calls and lined up a couple one-time gigs—and one longer job building a work shed in an old lady's backyard. The timing was good; I'd caught up with the tenants' requests and had three days of suspension to kill.

I ate the dinner and watched a football game, then sports talk about the game, and still, it was only 11:00 p.m.

But it was a new town. A fresh start. Maybe I could sleep like a normal person. Maybe it'd be okay.

I curled up on the shitty futon and eventually dozed off.

The nightmare was waiting.

The thud of his bootsteps across our kitchen. The slide of her jeans against the linoleum as she tried to back away. The bat, rising and coming down.

Again.

And again.

And again.

I woke up to my own screams, the sheets drenched in sweat, the reverberations of the bat still running through me like aftershocks.

I sucked in deep breaths until I felt steady, then threw on some clothes and laced up my boots.

So much for fresh fucking starts.

Outside, I stared into a dark, quiet night and began to walk.

THREE

SHILOH

That Friday, the end of the first week of school, I woke at 5:00 a.m.—like usual. Dawn had just begun to creep into my bedroom that was impeccably neat yet completely full of everything that was me.

Bibi called it my nest.

"You're like a magpie, collecting beautiful, shiny things."

My best friend, Violet, called it a reflection of my creative energy. My full-size bed was tucked in one corner to make room for shelves filled with books about metalwork, gemology, crystal energy, artist biographies, and poetry collections. Collages hung on every available wall space along with mandalas I'd drawn in black ink and a few watercolors from my brief foray into painting. Pencil sketches and doodles were stacked in neat piles on my desk under the window beside planners and notebooks full of to-do lists—each with every item scratched off.

I flipped on the multicolored lights hung where the wall

met the ceiling. Their soft glow gave the room a dim but colorful ambience I loved.

I put on some Prince and sat at my desk to draw, and in twenty minutes, I had a rough sketch for a new piece. A ring where thin strands of metal—copper and silver, probably—coiled around a semiprecious stone like a vine. This afternoon's work in the garage. I smiled.

I make my own shiny things.

Of all my creative outlets, making jewelry pulled me the strongest. The work was difficult; it required a lot of skill, materials, and time. Early mornings, late nights, and weekends. If I didn't give it everything, the *nothing* feeling would swoop in, whispering I was a mistake my mother never wanted.

I held up the drawing of the ring. It wasn't curing cancer, but it was what I had to give. To put something beautiful in the world that wasn't there before.

The clock read six thirty. I exchanged the headscarf I slept in for a shower cap, showered, then ran through my morning hair care routine. *My cousin Letitia is an artist herself*, I thought as I sprayed shea butter moisturizer on my scalp and along the hundreds of perfect little braids that fell softly around my shoulders. Not for the first time, I considered taking her up on her offer to fly back to NOLA in six weeks for a touch-up at her salon. Maybe I'd barge in on Mama and demand answers. About her. My father. Maybe then, the hollow feeling inside would be filled up with the truth.

Maybe you don't want to know the truth.

The warm smells of breakfast seeped into my sanctuary, dispelling cold thoughts. I dressed in a sundress in yellow and strappy sandals. A half-dozen coppery bracelets slid down my wrists, and I slipped on a silver-and-turquoise ring I'd made earlier that summer. Before I stepped out, I checked my horoscope desk calendar with its prediction for the day.

Be prepared for something unexpected.

I scoffed. Nothing was unexpected. I planned and prepared to make sure of that.

I joined Bibi in the kitchen where she was at the stove, presiding over pancakes and bacon. She shuffled around the small space in a white housedress and slippers, her robe sweeping over the old linoleum.

"Morning, Bibi," I said, pecking her cheek.

"Good morning, honey pie. Grab a seat. There's fresh cantaloupe."

I sat at the too-big dining table tucked between the kitchen and living room. A bowl of sliced melon sat amid the ceramic tea set in the center. Bibi made her way from the stove with two plates in her hands and joined me. In her own house, it was nearly impossible to tell her vision was all but gone. Or that she was eighty years old.

She set a plate in front of me while I refilled her teacup from the ceramic pot.

"How was your first week as a senior?" Bibi asked. "Anything new and exciting on the horizon for this year?"

"Not much," I said. "There're a couple of new guys in our grade this year. Roman or Roland Somebody. He's in my history class. Allegedly. So far, he's been a no-show. The other guy, Holden Parish, is rumored to be a billionaire."

"A billionaire. My, my."

"I don't know if that's true, but he's a stone-cold hottie, and the girls are throwing themselves at his feet. Which is hilarious, because I'm ninety-nine percent sure he's gay."

Bibi grinned over her teacup. "And how is Miss Violet? Is she throwing herself at this handsome new gentleman?"

"Not remotely. She has a grand plan to date the star quarterback of the football team and lock Miller in the friend zone permanently. Meanwhile, poor Miller is still playing guitar and singing love songs to her every night." I sighed. "New year, same story."

My best friend had met Miller Stratton when we were thirteen. He'd been homeless then, living out of a car with his mom, and his situation had gone straight to Violet's soft heart. A beautiful friendship grew between them, though "beautiful friendship" was Violet's phrase. It was obvious to everyone—me mostly—that what they had went a lot deeper than friendship.

"A shame," Bibi said. "What is she waiting for?"

"She has her reasons for keeping things where they are. I don't agree with them, but I respect them."

"Just as you have your reasons for not letting that young man in Louisiana be more than a *summer fling*."

"It's different with Violet and Miller. It's so obvious they belong together that them *not* being together doesn't make sense."

Bibi lifted her teacup. "I'm going to remember you said that so one day I can hold it against you."

I laughed. "You're like the auntie from that matchmaking show, trying to get everyone a happily ever after."

"No, dear. Just you." She set her cup on its saucer with both hands. "What else? What's the news?"

"Chance Blaylock is throwing his annual back-to-school rager tomorrow night."

"Are you going?"

"I have too much work to do. Orders to fill."

Bibi *hmphed*. "New year, same story."

"I see what you did there."

"Shiloh, you were in the garage until nearly midnight last night. I love that you give so much of yourself to your work, but don't get FML."

I choked on my orange juice. "FML?"

"Isn't that what young people say when you don't want to feel left behind?"

"FOMO," I said, laughing. "Fear of missing out."

"What does FML mean?"

"I can't tell you. It's inappropriate for your young ears."

Bibi snorted and swatted my hand. "At the very least, go to the party to spend time with your best friend."

"Violet and I are fine."

I doubted the words as they left my mouth. Even before my trip to New Orleans, I wasn't seeing her as much as I used to. Evelyn Gonzalez, the queen bee, and her crew had taken Violet under their wing. My shy bookworm friend might even get herself nominated to the homecoming court.

"Anyway, you know that alcohol makes me violently ill." I shot her a grin. "So does listening to shitty house music."

Bibi sighed. "I can't argue. Here I am, building you a better workspace. What do they call that? An enabler. I've become your enabler."

I laughed and took our plates to the sink. "Which reminds me, don't let the handyman come in the house until I get home."

"Nonsense. I'll be fine. Which reminds *me*, Detective Harris came by yesterday."

"Again?" I waggled my eyebrows. "Did he bring a guitar and sing you love songs too?"

"Wouldn't you like to know?" she shot back with a sly smile.

I grinned. My great-grandmother knew everyone in the city, and they all loved her.

Because she practices what she preaches. Her heart is open.

Mine was too, I argued as I rinsed the dishes and put them in the washer. I loved Bibi. I loved Violet. I'd lay down my life for either of them. What more did I need?

"I want you to be careful out there, Shiloh," Bibi said as I dried my hands and packed up my school bag, her tone suddenly grave. "Detective Harris told me one of the officers at his precinct had to be disciplined again. Mitch Dowd. I believe his son is in your grade."

"Frankie," I said. "He's a little prick."

"His father's a big prick. He's got something of a bad temper, I hear. A short fuse and an excess of pride. The worst combination."

"Sounds like a real winner."

"Harris used the word 'psychotic.'"

"Christ. And he's still on the job?"

"Likely not for much longer. But, Shiloh, if Dowd pulls you over…"

"I know what to do, no matter who pulls me over." I pecked her cheek. "I gotta run. You'll be okay?"

"Of course."

"Call me if you need anything."

"I will. And, Shiloh?" she called when I was at the kitchen door that led to the garage. "I might not agree with your boundaries, but I respect them."

I smiled, warmth filling my chest. "I love you, Bibi," I said, the words coming easily. Without hesitation.

There is nothing wrong with my heart, I thought in the garage, climbing into the boat of a Buick. *It's open for exactly the right people.*

At school, I kept my earbuds in between classes. "Hunger" by Florence + The Machine filled my head while the rest of the school populace bustled around me, talking and laughing, full of new school year energy that'd wear off in a week.

I caught sight of Miller Stratton trudging across the quad alone, head down, shoulders hunched. He met my eye and gave me a wave. I waved in return. The boy looked like he carried the weight of the world on his back. I wished Violet would help him carry the burden a little. But then, who was I to talk? I carried my own shit and was just fine.

But when Violet joined me in history—our last class of the day—her dark-blue eyes were heavy and had *Miller Stratton* written all over them. She was miserable and beautiful at the same time.

This is why I don't get involved with boys.

"Hey," I said. "You okay?"

She put on her Violet McNamara Everything's Fine trademark smile. "Sure. You look pretty, Shi. As usual. That's stunning." She reached over and touched the turquoise-and-silver ring on my index finger. "A Barrera original, I presume?"

"Free advertising."

"You're a genius."

"And you're deflecting in a *really* complimentary way. What's going on?"

Violet was saved from answering. Our history teacher, Mr. Baskin, a heavyset guy with a graying beard and large glasses, took the podium at the front of the class. We all grew quiet as he called roll. He got to the W's and frowned.

"Wentz? *Wentz?*" No answer. "Oh, that's right. Suspended."

He made a check in his roll book, then restarted the

movie on the whiteboard that we'd begun last time: a documentary on the Russian Revolution.

When the room was dark and the movie rolling, I leaned to Violet. "Okay, Miss Friends-with-TMZ. Who is this new guy who keeps not showing up?"

"Ronan Wentz," she whispered back. "Evelyn says he's suspended for punching Frankie Dowd. Broke his nose."

"My hero. That shithead had it coming."

The heaviness in Violet's eyes deepened. "He was giving Miller a hard time. Again."

"Frankie's psychotic. Gets it from his dad, I'm sure." I gave her the rundown on Mitch Dowd from what Bibi had told me that morning. "If this guy Ronan broke Frankie's nose, his dad is going to be out for blood."

Mr. Baskin glanced up from his desk and shot us a warning look. Violet and I pretended to watch the film, though I could practically feel the angst wafting off her like perfume.

After a few minutes, she leaned back to me. "Did Miller mention to you about his mom having a new boyfriend?"

"No. He's been pretty quiet lately. Why?"

"I think he's not a good guy. Miller won't tell me much, and I don't think he's coming over anymore. I think…"

"What?"

Violet started to speak, then changed her mind. She forced another smile. "Nothing. You're so lucky, Shi. You know who you are and what you want. You're going to open your own shop the minute we graduate, and you won't let anything—or anyone—stand in your way."

My brow furrowed. "You're going to med school, Vi. To become a *surgeon*. No one works harder than you."

"I know, but sometimes I feel like I'm missing something fundamental that's putting me off-balance. But you're so...whole." She smiled faintly and waved a hand. "Never mind me. I'm just being silly. PMS, probably."

Mr. Baskin cleared his throat, shooting us another look from his desk. Violet took notes on the film while her words churned in my head. I had no idea who my father was, and my mother's love for me was like a dimmer switch, flickering on the lowest setting. If I was whole, it was because I was holding myself together with a patchwork of glue—my art, Bibi, and my ambition to prove to my mother I wasn't a mistake.

Not that I ever told any of that to Violet or confided my fears to her the way she did me.

Someday, she's going to get tired of spilling her guts when I never give her anything in return.

I leaned over to Violet and touched her arm. "Hey. I'm here for you. Anytime. You know that, right?"

She smiled softly and clasped my hand. "Of course. Thanks, Shi."

But her hand slipped off mine, and I couldn't help but feel she was slipping further away from me too. By the time class was over, I'd decided to bite the bullet and take Bibi's advice.

Ugh, this is going to suck, but Vi's worth it.

"You still going to Chance's party tomorrow night?" I asked as we headed back out into the sunshine.

Her face brightened instantly, and then Evelyn Gonzalez swooped in. She looked like Ariana Grande—perfect makeup, tight black clothes, and a ponytail that swept her shoulders.

"Of course she is," Evelyn said. "And so is a certain quarterback. There will be alcohol and my infamous version of seven minutes in heaven. It's going to be lit."

Violet blushed up to her hairline. "That's a yes," she said to me. "Why? Are you?"

"Nah, just wanted to make sure you weren't going to be there alone," I said quickly.

Evelyn took Violet's hand in hers and swung them as if they were in elementary school. "I'll never let her out of my sight. Except when she and River Whitmore need their alone time in the closet."

I smiled thinly. "Great."

"You sure you won't come, Shi?" Violet asked.

Evelyn was watching me, her smile not touching her eyes.

"I have too much work to do," I said. "But go. Have fun. Be safe."

"Yes, *Mom*," Evelyn said with a laugh and pulled Violet away.

That afternoon, I came home from school to find Bibi in the kitchen squeezing lemons from our tree. Sprigs of mint and basil leaves, also from our garden, lay on the cutting board.

I hugged her from behind and rested my chin on her shoulder. "Your famous fancy lemonade. What's the occasion?"

Bibi reached up and patted my cheek. "No occasion. The young man out back needs a break. He's been weeding that mess for an hour."

I groaned and retrieved a bottle of seltzer water from the fridge while Bibi added sugar to the lemon juice. "I told you not to let him in while you're here by yourself."

"No one wants to hurt a harmless little old lady like me." She poured the seltzer and the lemonade over ice in two mason jars, then added the mint and basil leaves.

No, they just might rob you blind. Literally.

"Besides," she continued, stirring the jars, turning the delicious concoction a pale green. "I have good instincts about people. This boy is quiet. Respectful." She handed me the glasses. "One for you, one for him. See for yourself who's building your shed, and then tell me he's not a perfect gentleman. Shoo."

I obeyed, mostly because I wanted to confirm she hadn't invited a *respectful* serial killer into our home.

I strode to the back of the house and stopped short at the screen door that led to our large, overgrown backyard. A tall guy—six feet, if not more—with short dark hair was bent over a rake, clearing weeds from a patch of land next to the patio. He wore jeans with a black tank, revealing powerful arms and several tattoos. The muscles of his back and shoulders slid and moved under smooth, if pale, sweat-slicked skin. A hyperrealistic owl—inked in all black and white except for stark orange eyes—watched me watching him.

I stood like a dope while the guy paused in his work and arched his back, revealing a profile straight out of an artist's manual—high cheekbones, thick brows, a long straight nose, and luscious mouth with full lips.

Okay, so he's a beautiful serial killer.

I clutched the mason jars to my chest as I opened the screen door. The guy turned at the sound and leveled intense gray eyes on me. Eyes that—had I been that type of girl—would have knocked me on my ass. Cold and flat like slate, they warmed instantly at the sight of me. His mouth that had been a grim line fell open a little.

Then he shut it all down, his gaze turning hard and stony as he watched me cross the patio. Shields up.

Right back at you, pal.

"Hey," I said, keeping my voice as steady as my eye contact. "From Bibi."

"Thanks," the guy said. His voice was deep and masculine. A man's voice. He accepted the lemonade with relentless eye contact of his own, taking me in and not letting me go.

I tilted my chin, unwilling to break first. "I'm Shiloh."

"Ronan."

I blinked. *Damn it.*

"Ronan…Wentz?"

He nodded, taking a sip of the sparkling lemonade.

"You're in my history class," I said. "Your name's in the roll book anyway."

Another nod. A bead of sweat trickled down the axe blade of his cheekbone, down to his square jaw.

I cleared my throat. "Where have you been?"

"Work. And now suspension."

He said it simply enough. Everything about him seemed simple: his clothes that had seen better days, his scuffed boots, and the way he moved—directly and deliberately. Except for his eyes. There was depth there.

The kind you'd get lost in if he let you.

I snorted at my own ridiculous thoughts. Now that Ronan had his lemonade—and I'd confirmed in all likelihood he wasn't a serial killer—I should've left him to it. But he wasn't the want-ad handyman I'd expected. He was a high schooler, even if he didn't look like that either. His eyes were hooded, almost haunted. Whatever they'd seen had set him apart in some intangible way. It gave him an aura of intense loneliness that hung over him like a shadow.

I didn't like it.

And I didn't like that I didn't like it.

It won't kill you to be friendly to him. New kid and all.

Only this guy was no kid. He was a man in every sense of the word. Something in his past had rushed him into adulthood, and a not-so-small part of me needed to prove I could be in his space and not melt into a puddle at his feet.

"Bibi said it's break time." I nodded at the small

wrought-iron table with two chairs in the middle of the patio. "You want to have a sit for a minute?"

"Sure." He sounded less than thrilled.

He lowered his tall frame of lean muscle into a chair at the table and went at the sparkling lemonade, downing huge gulps that made his Adam's apple move under the sweat-glistened skin on his throat.

I brushed a cluster of braids off my shoulder. The afternoon suddenly seemed hotter.

"So you're new to Santa Cruz?"

He nodded.

"Where did you move from?"

"Manitowoc, Wisconsin. Got here a few weeks ago."

"How do you like it here so far?"

He shrugged. "It's better than where I was."

Holy shit, I felt the weight of the subtext in those six words as if he'd packed his body with muscles to carry it all.

And to fight back.

"I heard you're suspended for punching Frankie Dowd."

Another nod.

"My friend Violet said you were protecting Miller Stratton."

"You could say that."

"I didn't realize you and Miller were friends."

"We are now."

I furrowed my brow. Talking to this guy was like walking a maze and hitting only dead ends. I had to keep turning to keep the convo going.

"Well, I'm not glad you're suspended, but Frankie's been a dick to Miller for years, and Miller can only fight back so much."

Ronan's gray eyes hardened. "Why? The diabetes?"

"That, but also he's a musician. Plays guitar. If his hands get banged up, he won't be able to play."

He nodded again, almost to himself. "He doesn't have to worry about Frankie anymore."

"That's heroic of you, but Frankie's dad's a cop."

"So I heard."

"So he's not going to be happy that you broke his son's nose."

Ronan shrugged.

"Bibi says he's a psycho. You're not worried about payback?"

He inhaled through his nose, chin tilting up. "No."

I pursed my lips. Maybe he wasn't an intense loner after all. Just a typical alpha male, flexing his muscle to show how tough he was.

Yawn.

But those muscles...

Against my will, my gaze went to his spectacular arms and the tattoos inking his skin. A half sleeve on his right arm—wrist to elbow—showed a clock face with roman numerals surrounded by lilies. At quick glance, the time read a little after ten.

On his inner left forearm, a right hand stabbed the left straight through the palm with a medieval-looking dagger.

A drop of blood hung off the tip and dripped onto the words *HANDS REMEMBER.*

Remember what?

His right pectoral bore a quote that I couldn't read—his tank covered most of it, and I sure as hell wasn't going to ask. But the owl on his right shoulder was so realistic it looked like it could take flight at any moment.

I tore my gaze from it to see Ronan watching me. "How old are you anyway?"

"Eighteen. Nineteen in March." His eyes dropped to his lemonade glass, his low voice laced with bitterness. "I know. I'm too fucking old for high school."

"I wasn't going to say that. I only asked because most guys in class don't have ink yet. Not to mention you seem young to be taking on Frankie's dad."

Ronan's gaze came back to me. "I can handle it."

And this time, there was no bravado. Only a kind of resignation. I got the feeling that a pissed-off Mitch Dowd wasn't the worst thing Ronan Wentz had ever contended with.

"What about your parents?" I asked, letting my tone soften slightly.

"I don't live with my parents," Ronan said. "I live…with my uncle. Over at Cliffside."

"Miller lives in that neighborhood." I shot him a dry smile. "But I'm sure you know that, seeing as how you two are besties now."

Ronan's lips twitched in what passed for his version of a smile.

A short silence fell, but it wasn't a bad one. Ronan didn't seem itching to get out of the chair anymore. He glanced around the large, overgrown yard and at the house behind me with longing in his gray eyes.

"It's nice here," he said. He nodded at his empty mason jar. "And that was good."

Without thinking, I pushed my untouched glass to him. Suspicion flooded his expression.

"You need it more than I do," I said. "Working in this heat, I mean."

"Thanks." He made no move to touch it.

The conversation had sputtered to a halt, but apparently, I wasn't in a hurry to leave the table either.

"How is it? Living with your uncle?"

"It is what it is."

"Any brothers or sisters?"

"No."

"Same. I'm a loner too. Just me and Bibi."

"Your grandmother."

"Great-grandmother. My grandmother's mom. She died before I was born."

"What about your parents? Are they dead too?"

"Are they..." I crossed my arms. "That's direct. Where are yours?"

"Dead."

I stared.

"My mom when I was eight," he said. "My dad a few years later. I only asked because...never mind."

"Because why?"

"Forget it."

This guy is so damn frustrating.

But my ire was already flaming out. I couldn't stay irritated at someone who'd lost both parents at such a young age.

"To answer your very blunt question," I said, "my mom's in New Orleans with the rest of our family. As for my dad, I have no idea if he's alive or dead. Only Mama knows that, and she's not talking."

"Do you talk to her much? Your mom?" Ronan asked, his voice low.

"Not much," I admitted. "We're not close."

To put it mildly, I thought, and it suddenly struck me how much I'd shared with this guy, a virtual stranger. Ronan's brand of honesty—rough and unpolished and unapologetic—had done more in a few minutes to dismantle my privacy than anyone else had done, including Violet.

"Anyway, I'll let you get back to work—"

"You're the one I'm building the shed for, right?"

"For my business. I make jewelry. Now I work in the garage, but Bibi doesn't want me breathing in fumes or burning the house down."

Ronan's gaze went to the ring on my finger and the bracelets on my arms, then lingered on my skin, skimming up to my neck, my chin, my mouth. I imagined I could feel his gaze wherever it landed, sending little shivers…

Nope, I'm out.

I stood abruptly. "Speaking of which, I have work. I should get back."

Ronan stood at the same time and pulled a piece of paper from his back pocket. "This is what I was thinking about for the shed if you want to take a look. Since it's going to be yours."

"You drew up plans?" I asked, impressed he was taking this gig seriously.

He clearly mistook my surprise; his eyes turned flatter if that were possible. "Because it's so hard?"

"No, I just meant..." I gave my head a shake. "Never mind. Let me see."

I reached across the table for the paper. On it was a finely rendered work shed, the measurements reading ten feet by twelve feet. It had a slanted lean-to roof, double doors, and even a window on one side.

"Wow," I said. "This looks..." *Perfect.* "...expensive."

"I'll stay within budget," Ronan said, sitting on the edge of the table, arms crossed. The scent of shower soap—plain and generic—and the heat of his skin wafted over me. His hand came up, his finger tracing a line on the paper. "This is where you can run electricity for lighting and your tools. I'm not certified. You'll have to hire another guy for that."

"No need," I said. "And no budget. No matter what Bibi says, I'm not letting her drain her savings for me. My hand torch runs on batteries, and I'll run an extension cord for my soldering stick."

"A decent camping lantern should work too if you're out here after dark."

"I will be." I looked over the plans again. "This looks great, Ronan," I said and immediately regretted saying his name. An inexplicable flush of heat swept over me as the sounds rolled off my tongue.

I raised my eyes to his; Ronan towered over my five foot seven. My heart stuttered at how close his square jaw and full lips were to mine. The hard, stony gray of his eyes was now smoky and soft.

"Yeah, so thanks," I said, clearing my throat and stepping back from him.

"Yep." He held out his hand.

"What?"

"The plans."

"Oh. Right." *Jesus, girl.*

Ronan stuffed the paper into the back pocket of his jeans and turned away from me to pick up the rake.

I took his empty mason jar, leaving the other for him. He could drink it or not. What did I care?

But against my will, I glanced at him over my shoulder. My heart tripped to see he was stealing a glance at me too. We both looked away, and I hurried into the house.

No, no, no. I do not get flustered.

Bibi was on the couch knitting, Lucy and Ethel curled around her feet.

"Well?" Bibi asked, not looking up. "Can we keep him?"

I coughed. "Yeah, he's…fine. Goes to Central, turns out."

"Oh?" Bibi's needles flew. "Isn't that something? I thought he seemed pretty young for a serial killer."

"Right. So…I'll be in the garage."

I put the glass in the sink and hurried to the safety of my workshop to throw myself into my work—the ring I'd sketched that morning. A piece for my eventual shop.

I rummaged in a bag of semiprecious gemstones I'd ordered from a wholesaler that had cost me a semiprecious fortune. I imagined the coils of metal would hold something vibrant and rich. Malachite, maybe.

I found myself reaching for the smoky quartz instead.

"Stop," I scolded myself. "He's hot. There. You admitted it. Now get back to work."

But Jalen Jackson was hot too, and he'd fallen out of my thoughts the minute I left New Orleans.

Ronan Wentz was…

Something unexpected.

And I was going to have this guy at my house, in my class at school. Every day. Inescapable.

Nothing can stand in your way. Not one thing.

I put the gray stone back in the bag.

FOUR
RONAN

I dragged the rake through the weeds as Shiloh started back for the house. I snuck a final glance as if to convince myself a girl like that was fucking real and not a mirage or an Egyptian queen in the flesh. Hundreds of black braids fell around the light-brown skin of her shoulders that glowed in the late-afternoon sun, that light glinting off the bracelets and rings she'd probably made herself.

Christ, she was beautiful, her dark eyes soft but sharp with intelligence. And guarded. She didn't give anything away for free. You had to *earn* this girl's time and trust…and would probably feel like a fucking king if you did.

My stupid heart stopped as she glanced back at me. Our eyes met, sparking a jolt to my chest. We both looked away quickly, and she disappeared into the house, her dress sliding like water over her body.

I hacked at the ground mercilessly.

"Fuck my life."

I didn't need this torture. The house, the yard, the goddamn lemonade. It was already too much. And now Shiloh…

Forget her. No more conversations or asking personal shit. No more nothing.

Because *nothing* was what I had to offer a girl like that.

I finished up for the afternoon and grabbed my old fleece-lined denim jacket from the back of the patio chair. The scent of fresh-baked cookies hit me before I even touched the screen door.

"Ms. Barrera?" I called. The old lady was mostly blind. I didn't want to scare her.

"In here, darling."

I stepped inside, making sure to wipe my boots on the porch mat first so my footprints wouldn't dirty their floors. A plate of chocolate chip cookies was cooling on the kitchen counter.

My stomach growled, and so did that old hunger that went deeper than flesh and bone. The Barrera household was a goddamn buffet. Cozy and warm and crammed with photos and antique furniture, glass cabinets of old-lady knickknacks, and trees made out of wires and beads. Traces of homecooked meals lingered in the air. The entire place felt like a kind of wealth I'd never known or understood. Not in money but in every other thing that mattered. It was hard to believe this house—this home—and my crappy, empty apartment existed in the same town.

Ms. Barrera sat knitting with the two gray cats curled

next to her on the couch. Shiloh was nowhere to be seen, thank God. I stank with sweat and needed to get the fuck out of there.

"How is it out there? Not too hot, I hope."

"No, ma'am."

"You met my great-granddaughter?"

"Yes, ma'am."

"I hope she didn't give you a hard time."

"No, she's…fine."

She's a work of art.

"Good. She can be rather direct."

Which I liked. Too much. There was a lot about Shiloh I liked too much.

I cleared my throat and pulled a second folded paper from my pocket. "This is the supply list. I called around to a bunch of places to make sure you got the best prices."

I handed it to her and quickly backed off.

"Aren't you a doll? My eyes aren't what they used to be, but I trust this is just right. I'll have Shiloh place the order today."

"Yep. Same time tomorrow?"

"Nonsense. Tomorrow is Saturday. The weekends are for fun, though I wish someone would tell that to my great-granddaughter." Her eyes widened with a sudden thought. "Shiloh tells me you're in her senior class at Central."

"Yes, ma'am."

"There's a party tomorrow night with one of your classmates. A real *rager*, I hear."

I coughed. "Okay."

"Wouldn't it be marvelous if you and Shiloh attended together? You could get to know your classmates and get Shi out of that garage." She beamed in my direction. "What do you think, darling?"

The woman had to be more blind than I thought if she wanted *me* to take her granddaughter anywhere.

"I don't think so, Ms. Barrera."

"Please. Call me Bibi." She smiled into her knitting. "Too bad. I just figured since you go to the same school and all." She chuckled. "Shiloh worried you were a cold-blooded killer."

I stiffened, Chouder's words coming back. *The apple doesn't fall far from the tree.*

Bibi sensed a shift in the air and looked up, finding me with her hazy brown eyes. "I didn't mean to make you uncomfortable, dear. Shiloh would screech to hear me meddle in her affairs." She smiled gently. "There are fresh cookies on the counter. Please help yourself before you go."

For a second, I thought about Maryann Greer's twin girls in the apartment below mine. Kids loved cookies. But there was no way in hell I was going to take anything out of this house. I already felt like an invader, barging in their perfect home and sullying it with my presence.

"No, thanks. I should go."

"Suit yourself, but next time, I'll insist. See you Monday, darling."

"Yep."

I went out, closing the door behind me. Closing it on

Ms. Barrera's mothering smile and her "darlings" and her great-granddaughter who was the most beautiful goddamn thing I'd seen in so many ugly years.

She's a cathedral while I'm a broken-down strip mall.

As if to prove it, I walked to the Cliffside complex. The cement block of apartments looked even poorer after the Barrera household. My own place was like a bad joke. I'd scrubbed it clean when I first moved in, but the grime of poverty and solitude infiltrated every corner. I tried to imagine Shiloh here.

Not going to happen. Ever. And you know it.

Yeah, I knew that.

Uncle Nelson had hung a box for maintenance requests outside my door. "*For when you're playing school and someone needs you,*" he'd said with an eye roll. The tenants all had my cell number too, for emergencies. But the box was empty and my cell phone quiet.

I fired up a frozen dinner and scrolled my phone while I ate, waiting for the night to be over. Around seven o'clock, the door banged shut downstairs. Maryann Greer's daughters squealed and laughed, tearing around while she started dinner.

They deserved a house like the Barreras'. Warm and safe with chocolate chip cookies from a decent oven, not delivered by the weirdo who lived upstairs.

They're making the best of it.

I showered, changed into boxer shorts and an undershirt, and lay down on the lumpy futon in the bedroom that smelled like old piss and tried to make the best of it.

The next afternoon, I fixed a nasty clog in 2C's toilet, and then the rest of the day and night unrolled in front of me like an endless stretch of hours with nothing to fill them. The old hollow hunger had started to hit me when I remembered the shack. Unless Miller was there, I'd still be alone, but it was a better kind of alone. Cleaner.

I hit the convenience store for lighter fluid and beer. The young guy behind the counter didn't card me. The tattoos helped, but I didn't look eighteen anyway. I didn't *feel* eighteen. When my dad picked up that baseball bat, he beat my childhood out of me too.

Miller showed up at the shack an hour after I did, carrying a banged-up guitar case. He sat down on a small boulder in front of the firepit and laid the case over his lap.

"I caught Chet fucking with it," he said, answering my look. "I'll have to bring it everywhere from now on. Here. To school. Fucking asshole."

My skin grew hot at the thought of his mom's lowlife boyfriend messing with that guitar. I remembered what Shiloh had said about Miller needing his hands to play. To make something of himself. There wasn't much I was good for. No talents or special skills. But Miller was fucking smart, and he thought about what he said before he said it. I nearly asked him to play and handed him a beer instead.

We shot the shit for a few minutes, and then I caught

him taking in my tattoos the way Shiloh had. Except when she did it, there'd been more than curiosity there. I felt it wherever her brown eyes landed on my skin, had noticed her lips parting just a little…

Cut it out.

I buried thoughts of Shiloh and told Miller my story. I said the words that tasted like blood. But the shack was a place where you could be yourself, no matter how fucked up.

Still, I waited for Miller to decide I must be too much of a psycho to hang out with anymore, but he let it be and said nothing. What could he say anyway? Nothing that would change what happened. Nothing I could do either. My chance to stop my dad had passed, and I'd never get it back.

When I returned from gathering more driftwood for the fire, Miller was messing with his guitar.

"It's about time," I said.

"I don't play much for people."

"Why not?"

"Don't know. Besides, you don't want to hear the shit I've been writing."

I dumped the wood over the smoldering remains of the first fire I'd lit. "How the fuck do you know that?"

"What kind of music do you listen to?"

"Heavy stuff. Melvins. Tool."

"Yeah, what I play is not that. Mostly, I've been writing songs for a girl."

"A girl." I popped another beer and handed it over. "Now I really feel bad that you can't get drunk."

"Amen," he said, and we clinked beer bottles. Thanks to his diabetes, Miller was stuck with a two-beer maximum.

"What's the story?" I asked.

"You'll just call me a pussy, tell me to fuck someone else and get over it."

"Yeah, maybe I will."

He laughed, but it collapsed into a sigh. "It's hopeless is what it is. She's perfect and rich, and I'm a poor bastard without a working pancreas."

I snorted a laugh.

"Her name is Violet," Miller said, his eyes on the fire. "When I was thirteen, I passed out in her backyard, pissed myself, and woke up in the hospital to see her sitting there, looking like a mess. Crying over me. Because she cared, you know?"

I didn't know. I'd never had a girl cry over me. Couldn't imagine it.

"That was the moment I knew she was it for me. Always." Miller's voice turned bitter. "And the same day we swore a blood oath to stay friends. Violet's idea." He took off his beanie and ran a hand through his brown hair. "So there you go."

"Yep. You need to fuck someone else and get over it."

I was going to stay out of his business like he'd stayed out of mine, but I remembered all the times my mother was ready to take me and get the hell away from Dad and never did. And then one day, it was too late.

"Nah, that's bullshit," I said. "You need to tell her."

Miller frowned. "She's hell-bent on us being friends. She thinks it'd ruin us if we tried to be more."

"So? Tell her anyway."

"I can't. She'd shoot me down, and things would never be the same. Though I guess they're pretty fucked already."

"So don't talk to her," I said. "Just...I don't know. Kiss her."

Shiloh's perfect lips rose in my mind. I took a sip of beer to wash the imagined taste of her out of my mouth.

"No way," Miller said.

"Why the hell not?"

He made a sour face. "Uh, fucking *boundaries*, for one thing. She's told me how she feels explicitly. Friends. I have to honor that."

I snorted and finished off my beer.

"What can I do?" Miller asked miserably. "I told you, we swore a blood oath."

"When you were *kids*. Does she suspect you like her?"

"Not exactly."

"Where is she now?"

"I don't know." Miller kicked at the sand at his feet. "There's a party tonight. She'll be there."

"So go to the party and tell her."

"I just said—"

"You gotta fight, man," I said. Practically shouted. "You fight, because if you don't, it'll be too late. And too late is fucking *death*."

Miller stared, shocked. I looked away and forced my

hands to unclench, waiting for him to tell me to take my crazy shit and get the fuck out.

But he didn't.

"She needs me to be her friend," he said after a minute. "She needs…me."

"So you're her pack mule. You carry all her shit and try to make life easier on her because you care about her. But what about you?"

Miller started to answer but then grew quiet. Thinking. Finally, he put his guitar back in its case and stood up.

"You want to come?" he asked. "I mean, it's probably going to be a bunch of drunk jocks playing beer pong to shitty house music."

"I'm coming," I said, kicking sand over the fire. "I told you. I got your back."

"Why?"

I stared. After everything he knew about me, he wanted to know why *I* bothered to hang out with *him*.

"You don't annoy the living shit out of me," I said gruffly. "Good enough?"

He grinned. "Good enough."

I turned to grab my jacket so he couldn't see my face.

The party was just what Miller had said it would be. Chance Blaylock, the center for the football team, invited half the school to his place at the start of every year. His team was wasted and playing beer pong in the kitchen while a sound system blasted popular music all over the huge house. We pushed through a crowd of dancers, Miller searching for Violet among the faces in the dark.

I realized I was searching the crowds for a face too.

Leave her alone.

We made it to the patio outside where lights were strung up. The crowd was thinner; people were talking and drinking in smaller groups by the pool.

"I don't see her," Miller said, taking a seat on a lounger. "This was a stupid idea."

I caught a flash of a red dress in the kitchen and nodded my head. "There."

Miller looked, and the way his entire face softened to see Violet made me lower my gaze. Like I shouldn't be seeing something so private. Or unfamiliar.

He heaved a sigh. "Here goes nothing. Watch my guitar?"

"Yep."

Miller made for the kitchen, and I glanced around in search of beer. A cooler was set up by the pool, green necks poking up from hunks of white ice. I grabbed Miller's case and headed over, but a guy drunkenly stumbled there first. He grabbed a beer, then blinked up at me stupidly.

"Holy shit, are you the bouncer?" He cackled in my face. "Hey, look! Blaylock hired a bouncer."

"Fuck off."

"But for real," the guy slurred. "Did you escape from jail or what? I heard—"

I took the beer bottle out of his hand and gave him a shove. His arms pinwheeled, and then he fell backward... straight into the pool. Everyone on the patio laughed as the guy sputtered to the surface.

"*Dude*... What the fuck?"

I tipped the beer his way in salute and headed back to the lounger, ignoring his curses. A few minutes later, a cheer went up from inside, and then Miller returned, looking like someone had pissed in his Cheerios.

"Well?"

"I acted like a possessive asshole, insulted her, and now she's going to play that stupid closet game where River fucking Whitmore is going to kiss her. Maybe...more."

"So it went well."

He scowled at me.

"The night's not over yet. Play the game too."

Miller snorted. "Hell no."

"You won't play, but you'll torture yourself by watching." I tipped my beer. "Solid plan."

"Fuck off. I have to stay and make sure she's okay."

That, I understood.

Miller grabbed his case and headed back inside. He took a seat in a corner of the living room in a circle of weed smokers, his guitar in his lap. I stood over him like a sentinel in case that prick Frankie showed up. Against my will, I scanned the crowd, my gaze snagging on a slim girl with bracelets sliding down her arms as she danced. My heart thudded dully, but the girl moved into a slant of light, showing pale skin and light-brown hair.

"Dumbass," I muttered.

"Hi!" A skinny blond with long hair and a long dress plopped down beside Miller. "I'm Amber."

"Miller," he muttered.

"Are you going to play something for us?"

He ignored her, his eyes on the center of the living room to where some chick named Evelyn announced a seven minutes in heaven game. I followed Miller's hopeless expression right to his Violet. Pretty girl. Sweet face. My chest ached for him as she went into the closet with the king of the jocks, River Whitmore.

"So that's that," Miller muttered.

I squatted on my heels beside him. "It's just a game. Tell her when she comes out."

"She'll kiss him in there," Miller said miserably. "Her first kiss."

"Then kiss her better. But don't let her go."

He narrowed his eyes at me. "You have a girlfriend? Someone in Wisconsin?"

"I don't do girlfriends."

He frowned, and I knew what he was thinking—I was being awfully fucking chatty with the relationship advice. But just because I couldn't have something real and good didn't mean he shouldn't.

Violet came out of the closet with a strange smile on her

face. She shot a pained glance at Miller, and he immediately pretended to give a shit about the skinny blond beside him.

"Well?" Amber put her hand on his arm. "Do you know how to play that guitar, or is it just for decoration?"

I wanted to hear him too. I had a feeling whatever Miller had in him was better than the bullshit playing over the sound system.

Miller glanced around the living room. Violet wasn't there anymore. The closet game had broken up, and everyone had followed their football king into the kitchen.

"Uh, yeah," he said, a pained look on his face. "Yeah, I'll play. Why the fuck not."

Amber clapped her hands. "Yay!"

The small group around us went quiet as Miller sang Coldplay's "Yellow." Not my jam, but holy fuck, the guy could sing. He turned the song into something else, made it his own. Every damn lyric told the story of him and Violet.

A smashing of glass cut through the noise of the party. A guy with silver hair and fancy clothes stood on the dining room table, a broken bottle at his feet. I'd heard some people talking about him earlier by the pool—his name was Holden, and he was new to the school, like me.

"*Everyone shut the fuck up!*" Holden bellowed. His drunk, watery gaze was focused on Miller. The rest of the house followed his lead.

Miller didn't miss a note as the entire house went quiet, listening. Violet came tearing in from the back and stopped short, recognition on her face.

Because this is their song.

Miller's eyes met hers, and he sang straight to her.

"For you, I'd bleed myself dry."

That could've been my motto. To bleed myself dry for those I cared about. It was too late to save my mother, and all that was left was the grief and anger. Anger that was the same as my father's, coursing through my veins like it had in his. It flared and burned, and I wished it would flame out altogether, but it never did. The only thing I could do was use it to protect those who needed protecting. Like Miller. He poured his love out of his guitar, straight to his girl.

Violet, crying now, ran for the exit. Miller stopped the song with a *twang* and got up to follow her. Someone stopped him at the door.

"Well, lookit who crashed this party. Where you running off to, Stratton?"

Frankie Dowd.

My anger flared like fire when gasoline hits it. I shook out of my jacket and cracked my neck left and right.

Let's go.

"Back off, asshole," Miller snarled at Frankie.

"Or what? You going to have your convict bodyguard coldcock me again?"

I snorted. The dumbass hadn't seen me. I moved in front of Miller and crossed my arms, cold and stony, while inside, the fire raged.

Frankie wore a bandage over his nose, and his eyes were

rimmed with bruises. They widened in fear. "You're fucking dead, dude. You have no idea who I am."

"I know who you are," I said. "I know exactly who you are."

The cowardly, punk-ass bitch who tried to keep my friend from his medicine.

A handful of seconds passed, the air tightening with every breath, until a bellow sounded from the adjacent dining room.

"Dude! What the fuck are you doing?"

All eyes went to Holden, who was tap-dancing on the mahogany dining table, grinding shattered glass into the wood and drunkenly crooning "Singin' in the Rain" while Chance Blaylock stared wide-eyed at the damage.

"My parents are going to fucking kill me," Chance seethed. "Someone get over here and help me get this prick off the table."

River Whitmore emerged from the kitchen, and the two of them made grabs for Holden, who easily danced out of reach despite looking as if he'd drunk half a keg all by himself.

"You're dead, fucker," Frankie snarled, drawing my attention back to him. He pulled a police-issue Taser from his board shorts.

Miller held up his hands. "Whoa, hey…"

Frankie lunged. I dodged right and swung my left arm up, knocking the Taser out of his grasp. I gripped him by the front of his shirt and drove him away from Miller. The crazy fucker with the silver hair had danced his way to the living room coffee table, but he barely registered. The rage was free now, flowing through me and into Frankie. He stumbled and went down, and I went down with him, both of us grappling and throwing punches wherever we could. I reveled at the burst of pain when one of his fists connected, almost more than when I got one in on him.

Which was more often.

It wasn't a fair fight; I could beat the shit out of the scrawny guy…

How far are you taking this? a voice whispered in the chaos. *You going to kill him? Like father, like son.*

Then Chance hauled Frankie away. River tried to do the same with me, but I jerked free and gave him a rough shove.

"Fuck this guy," Frankie screamed, wrestling out of Chance's grasp, his nose leaking red again. "You are so dead." He grabbed the broken beer bottle off the coffee table and leveled it at me. "I'm going to kill you, motherfucker!"

Frankie took a tentative swipe at me, and the crowd gasped. Pain flared at the top of my left forearm, igniting the fire burning through my veins for a second time.

I glanced down at my skin that was split and bleeding, then back to Frankie. "That was a mistake."

His eyes widened, and he took a step back at the deadly calm in my voice, the bottle trembling in his hand.

Don't be like him, my mother pleaded from somewhere far away. But she was dead. Dead because I'd done nothing.

No more doing nothing…

My fists were coiled and ready, but suddenly Holden was there between us. He wore a long coat and an expensive-looking shirt that he ripped open, sending buttons flying. His eyes were wide and crazy as he bared the left side of his chest to Frankie.

"Right here," he hissed and tapped his heart. "Put it right here. Go on. Do it. *Do it.*"

I stared at this guy who could not look more different from me but mirrored my chaos. Like watching an out-of-body experience. For a split second, I thought Frankie would take Holden up on the offer.

No! Me. Not him.

I reached to pull Holden to safety, but Miller was faster. He stepped into our small circle of psychopaths and took Holden's arm, talking soothingly.

"Hey, man. Come on. Hey…"

Holden jerked from Miller's grasp, closed his coat, and put a cigarette in his mouth. He grinned. "Anyone got a light?"

"What the…" Chance blinked stupidly, then his mouth twisted in rage. "Get out. You three. Get the fuck out of my house."

Holden pretended to be offended. "*Rude*, right?"

A laugh burst out of Miller, and I suddenly felt crazily close to laughing too.

"Get out!" Chance roared.

Miller and Holden made a run for it, cackling like idiots. I moved more leisurely, grabbing my jacket and giving Frankie a warning stare that promised pain if he fucked with either one of them. On my way to the door, the yellow Taser caught my eye. Without breaking stride, I snatched it and tucked it in my jacket pocket.

"You're dead, Wentz," Frankie screamed after me. "You're fucking dead!"

Outside, Miller and Holden were lying on their backs on the front lawn, laughing at the sky and getting acquainted.

"I don't believe we've officially met. Holden Parish."

"Miller Stratton."

They shook hands, and Holden tilted his chin up at me. "And who's the Brute Squad?"

"Ronan Wentz," Miller managed through his laughter.

Holden jerked his hand straight up. "A pleasure."

"Crazy bastards," I said, which only made them laugh harder. While they pulled their shit together, I kept an eye on the front door. A warm trickle of blood flowed down the back of my hand, and I wiped it on my jeans.

"How did you do that?" Holden was asking Miller.

"Do what?"

"Play and sing like you did. Like…a fucking miracle."

"Nah. Everyone's heard that song. It's a million years old."

Holden shook his head. "They've heard the song, but you put your heart and soul out there. That's not something people hear every day."

Amen. I didn't have the words to tell Miller the truth, but Holden did. He spoke for both of us.

The front door banged open, and the football team poured out.

"I said, get the fuck off my property!" Chance raged.

Miller and Holden scrambled to their feet, and that was when I heard it. Police sirens. Distant but growing closer. A cold sweat broke out over my body as that day came surging back, ten years old but as clear as yesterday.

My mother on the kitchen floor. The blood…

There was so much blood, and she wasn't moving, and then the sirens came. The sound of help. Too late, too late…

I stood on the grass, hardly able to move. Dimly, I noticed Amber giving Miller his guitar case and then Holden flying at us.

"Time to go."

Feeling drunk, I followed him and Miller to a black sedan parked across the street with a uniformed driver waiting in the front seat.

"Good evening, James," Holden said as we climbed in the back, him wedged between Miller and me. "Would you be so kind as to remove my friends and me from the immediate area?"

The car doors closed, and the siren sound was cut in half but still coming. I turned my head to the window and shut my eyes, wanting to see nothing but black. Not her. Not the bloody bat rolling across the bloody floor…

"Home, sir?" James asked, driving fast and taking us away from the scene.

Soon, the sirens faded in the distance, and I let out a breath.

"Fuck no," Holden said. "Thoughts, gentlemen?"

Miller leaned over to shoot me a look, a question in his eyes. There was only one answer. I nodded.

"My place," Miller said and told James the address.

At his shitty complex that looked exactly like my shitty complex, James parked the car, and we climbed out.

Holden eyed the building. "Cozy. After-party at Chez Stratton?"

"Not quite," Miller said. "How long will he wait?"

"As long as I need him to." Holden lit a cigarette. Cloves, judging by the sickly-sweet smell. "Fear not, James is being well compensated for his time."

Miller shot me another look. I nodded.

"Okay. Let's go," he said, and we took Holden to the shack, because it was his now too.

FIVE

SHILOH

The weekend rolled around with no word from Violet. My texts went unanswered. Phone calls went to voicemail. At history class on Monday, she was late. Violet was never late. Fear and guilt that something terrible had gone down at the party racked me.

Baskin called roll.

"Watson?"

"Here."

"Wentz?"

"Here."

I froze as the single syllable dropped into the air behind me, spoken in that deep, unpolished voice. Somehow, I'd missed him coming in. A shiver danced up my spine.

You are not this ridiculous.

Yet I couldn't keep myself from peering over my shoulder, like Molly Ringwald's character in *Sixteen Candles* stealing a peek at Jake Ryan. Ronan was slouched in the corner seat, last row, arms crossed, eyes flat and guarded at all the attention. I wasn't the only one who'd turned to stare.

Ronan's gray gaze met mine. When I offered a small wave in greeting, he glanced away.

Okay. Good talk.

Baskin finished calling roll, and Violet hurried into the room. I breathed a sigh of relief. She looked like herself, if a little tired.

"McNamara…" Baskin intoned.

"Sorry!" She caught sight of Ronan as she hung her bag on the back of her chair. "He's real," she whispered to me.

You can say that again.

"He's also the guy Bibi hired to build my work shed," I whispered back. "Which you would know if you had answered my texts this weekend."

"Yeah, sorry. I was…really tired, recovering from the party. But for real? He's working at your house?"

"Forget him," I said, wishing it were that damn easy. "I was worried about you."

"I'm fine, promise," Violet said. She glanced at Baskin, who was still at his desk organizing his notes and muttering to himself. "But the party got crazy. The new guy, Holden, caused a major scene. He smashed a bottle on the Blaylocks' dining table and then tap-danced all over it."

"I like him already."

"Chance doesn't feel the same." Violet giggled. "And you'll never believe it, but Miller played for the first time…to an entire houseful of people. He sang our song.

'Yellow.'" Her deep-blue eyes swam for a moment, and I knew instantly what she was recovering from. "According to Evelyn, it got even crazier after I left. A knife fight or something."

"A *knife* fight?"

"Between Frankie, Holden, and your new handyman."

It took everything I had not to steal another glance at Ronan. Even rows away, I swore I could feel him—his presence, solid and strong behind me.

A small voice wondered if he was hurt.

Oh, stop. If anything, it's Frankie you should be worried about.

"Sounds like I missed all the action."

"You could say that. River asked me to homecoming."

I frowned at Violet's unsure expression. "That's good, isn't it? Part of your grand plan?"

She smiled faintly. "Yes, exactly. My grand plan."

Baskin took the podium at the front of the class. I faced forward, thinking about my own grand plan that had no one in it.

"Your first major assignment of the year is a paper on the Russian Revolution," Baskin said. "I'll leave the exact focus to you, but the paper must be ten pages, minimum. Typed, single-spaced."

The class collectively groaned.

"A warning. This paper will account for 50 percent of your first-semester grade." He eyed us over his glasses. "So it had better be good."

After class, we headed out quickly. I needed to get away from Ronan Wentz and all the unsolicited thoughts that came with him, and Violet had to get to the Whitmore house where she was a patient care volunteer. She'd been assigned to help take care of River's mom three afternoons a week through the medical program at UCSC.

"Nancy has liver cancer," Violet said as we made our way to the student parking lot. "It doesn't look good."

"Oh God, I'm so sorry to hear that," I said. "It sounds like a lot to handle. You up for it?"

"I have to be. I'll never make it as a doctor if I don't do all the hard things." She gave me a hug. "Call me tonight, and let's catch up. You can tell me all about Ronan. I saw him hanging with Miller earlier today. I guess they're friends now. Holden too. Evelyn calls them the Lost Boys."

"Evelyn needs a hobby."

"I'm just glad Miller has someone. Or someone's… friends."

"The so-called Lost Boys can't replace you. Your friendship is special, and Miller knows that."

She smiled faintly, unconvinced. It was on the tip of my tongue to tell her she could turn her friendship with Miller into something more with one word, but it was none of my business. Not to mention I was completely unqualified to give advice on relationships.

You have to believe in them first.

We parted ways—her to her white SUV that was manufactured in this decade and me to Bibi's Buick that was...not.

On the drive home, I cranked "Let Me Blow Ya Mind." Violet and I used to go nuts over the song when we were kids. She liked to say she was the Gwen Stefani to my Eve.

I can't replace her either.

But she might be replacing *me* with Evelyn Gonzalez. I vowed to call Violet and tell her all about Ronan building my shed. Maybe I'd even share that I'd been thinking about him a little bit this weekend.

A little bit.

Apparently, the universe was testing me. A tall, dark-haired figure came up on the right side of the road wearing jeans, boots, and a plain white T-shirt. A denim jacket with fleece lining around the collar was hooked on his finger and slung over his shoulder.

Shit.

Ronan Wentz walked casually but not slowly. Steady. Eyes straight ahead. I got the strange impression he was a hitchhiker on an endless cross-country trip, waiting for someone to pick him up but not expecting anyone would.

Then I realized he was probably on his way to *my* house.

Shit again.

"Do all the hard things," I muttered and pulled over a few feet ahead of Ronan. I turned down the music and cranked the passenger side window down. "Hey. Do you need a ride?"

Ronan stopped, stared. A peculiar expression came over his face, his thick brows furrowed. "I don't need a ride."

"How about do you *want* one?"

He considered the road in front of him.

"You're going to my house, right?"

He nodded.

"So how's it going to look if I arrive home and you walk in twenty minutes later—in this heat—and I didn't give you a lift? Bibi's going to think I'm a major asshole."

Ronan hesitated for a second more, then climbed into the car. Immediately, the space was filled with *him*. The scents of his generic soap and, fainter, campfire smoke. The sheer masculinity of him washed over me, and I gripped the wheel tighter.

I thoroughly regret this decision.

"Thanks," Ronan said.

"It's more a favor to me. I'd prefer my great-grandmother *not* think I'm an asshole."

He didn't smile. Didn't look at me at all.

"You care if I roll down the window?" he asked after a minute.

"Be my guest."

He used the hand crank—nothing automatic here—wearing a small smirk.

"Something on your mind?" I inquired, brows arched.

"Sweet ride," Ronan deadpanned. "What is it? An '82?"

"It's an '84, if you must know, and still going."

"Pretty sure I was walking faster."

A shocked laugh burst out of me. It didn't seem possible that Ronan Wentz had a sense of humor, but there we were.

"Did you just dis my vehicle?"

"Yes."

I shot him a stern look, trying not to laugh. "You'll have to take up your complaints with Bibi. This *sweet ride* is hers, technically, though she's not allowed to drive it anymore."

"Because it belongs in a museum?"

"Hilarious. You didn't have to accept a ride if my boat is so offensive to your automotive sensibilities."

"Yeah, I did. So Bibi doesn't think you're an asshole."

"So you did it out of pity."

"There's nothing pitiful about you."

Ronan stiffened as if the words had escaped him without thinking. A sudden tenseness filled the car, killing the light mood, even as a warm glow bloomed in my chest against my will.

I quickly put my eyes back on the road, but a maroon slash of dried blood on the top of Ronan's left forearm caught my eye. The cut was nearly six inches long and curved like a hook. Two Band-Aids were laid clumsily over it, like bridges over a thin red river.

He's hurt.

I gave myself a mental shake for being so soft. It was probably just the type A personality in me demanding I take care of him.

It. Take care of it. Not him.

"I heard the party got a little crazy on Saturday," I said.

"You could say that."

I nodded at the cut. "Is that a souvenir?"

"It's nothing."

"Doesn't look like nothing. And it's getting red around—"

"It's *nothing*," he said. "Forget it."

I expected my hackles to rise, but the aura of loneliness I'd noticed the first time we met lurked beneath his rough tone. Like he wasn't used to people giving a shit.

I let it go and pulled into my drive. We entered the kitchen from the garage, Ronan behind me.

"Bibi, we're home. I mean…I'm home. With Ronan."

God, girl…

No answer. I crept down the hall and saw Bibi's bedroom door was closed, which meant she was taking a nap. By the time I came back to the living room, Ronan was already in the backyard raking a smooth space where he'd torn up all the weeds.

I needed to get my ass to work too and focus on what mattered—my eventual business. But Ronan's raking was kicking up dust and dirt, and my eyes couldn't stay off that cut on his arm with its smears of dried blood and its sad little Band-Aids.

"The big dummy didn't even clean it properly," I murmured.

Without letting my old guards and protections talk me out of it, I grabbed rubbing alcohol, cotton balls, gauze, medical tape, and antibiotic ointment from my bathroom. In the yard, I dumped the supplies on the patio table.

Ronan stopped and narrowed his eyes at me. "What's all that for?"

"Your cut's getting infected."

"You don't have to, Shiloh," he said in a low voice.

"I don't *have* to, but why wouldn't I?"

He didn't seem to know what to do with that. He set the rake aside and sat down reluctantly, stiffly. I sat beside him and gently peeled off the dinky Band-Aids.

"So what happened?"

"Some shit went down at the party."

"To put it mildly." I scooted my chair closer to his and upended the bottle of rubbing alcohol, soaking a cotton ball. "Violet said you got in a knife fight."

"No knife. Frankie Dowd took a swipe at me with a broken bottle."

"How did it start?" I shot him a smirk. "Did you insult his ride?"

He almost smiled. Almost. "He was being a dick to Miller. Again."

I laid one hand on Ronan's forearm and gently dabbed his wound, trying not to notice the striations of muscle moving under his skin.

"I hope you didn't kill him," I said, and he winced. From the sting of the alcohol, I guessed.

"No," he said in a low voice. "Holden caused a diversion."

"Holden the billionaire?"

"Holden the crazy motherfucker," he said, but the affection in his voice was obvious.

"The Lost Boys," I said, wiping away dried blood. "That's what Evelyn Gonzalez is calling the three of you."

Ronan didn't comment, but I thought he didn't mind the name so much. He was quiet for a minute, then said, "I looked for you."

My hands on his skin jumped, and my cheeks heated in an actual blush.

He looked for me?

"I…I didn't go. I can't drink, and that's pretty much the main point of a rager."

"Why can't you drink?"

"I have some weird allergy to alcohol," I said. "Even a sip of beer can make me drunk as hell and instantly hungover."

"That's fucked up."

"Those kinds of parties aren't my scene anyway."

But he looked for me.

I gave my head a shake and focused on the work, not those words or how his low voice sounded when he said them.

"Same. I was there for Miller."

I'd finished cleaning the cut and took up the antibiotic ointment. Ronan watched me smear the greasy stuff on his wound, though he was capable of doing it himself. And we both knew it.

"I'm beginning to think I should've been there for Violet."

"Yeah?"

"We've been BFFs since we were kids. But I don't know. She seems to be doing okay with Evelyn."

"She and Miller—"

"Are complicated." I opened the gauze and moved Ronan's arm closer to me on the table. "But we shouldn't talk about it behind their backs. They need to figure it out themselves."

"He's in love with her," Ronan said.

My head snapped up at the softness in his rough voice. His gray eyes met mine, and he shrugged. "He is."

I quickly averted my gaze to concentrate on my work. "I know. And she loves him too. But she has her reasons for keeping things as they are. To keep herself safe. I can appreciate that."

"Why?"

I raised a brow. "Are you always this direct?"

He shrugged. "Not a fan of bullshit."

"Neither am I, actually."

"So?"

"So I can appreciate Violet's caution, because I don't want to get involved with anything or anyone that distracts me from my goals either," I said. A declaration of independence that needed to be said in Ronan's presence.

"Your goal is the jewelry," he said.

I nodded. "I'm going to open my own business. Which isn't easy for a woman and even less so for a woman of color. So I work really hard, not just to make it happen for myself but to prove to everyone I can do it."

Mama's face rose up in a curl of smoke, but I waved it away.

"Anyway," I said, laying strips of tape on the gauze to hold it in place. "I feel for Miller, but I get where Violet is coming from." I glanced up at Ronan to find him staring at me with an unreadable expression on his face. "You don't agree?"

He shrugged.

"So you're a romantic?"

"No," he stated flatly. "I don't like to see him suffer."

"Ah, a big softy then."

"I'm not that either."

I set the tape down and looked him in the eye. "What are you?"

I needed to know. The pragmatic side of me needed to know what in the hell it was about Ronan Wentz that was messing with my head. Sex appeal was the easy answer, but there was more to him than that. He was radioactive, his presence rearranging my atoms, turning me into someone I didn't recognize. Someone who got flustered, unsettled, who *blushed*, for God's sake.

"I'm nothing," he said.

"No one is nothing."

"I was eight when my parents died. I was shuffled around foster homes for ten years before my uncle showed up. Been trying to figure out a lot of shit ever since."

"*Ten years* in foster care?"

He nodded.

"God, I can't imagine it," I said. He stiffened, and I could see he didn't want to imagine it either. "But I know what you mean. A little. My mother…" I waved a hand. "Never mind."

He didn't say a word but watched me, the message clear in his eyes. *You can tell me.*

"I was just going to say that Violet's parents were best friends, and now their marriage is falling apart. She's never seen a healthy relationship. And neither has Miller. And neither have I."

"Same," Ronan said.

"So you're not nothing," I said. "We're all just…I don't know, refugees of broken marriages."

"Broken," he said, a slight curl to his lips. "Yeah, you could say that."

I raised my eyes to his. Talking to Ronan felt like tugging a thread—pull too hard and it would snap. Against my better judgment, I wanted more of him. I wanted to know he'd had something good at least once.

"Did you ever see your parents happy?" I asked gently. "Before they died?"

His arm under my hand stiffened, and his gray eyes went hard and flat again.

"No. Never."

"I'm sorry. It's none of my business." I glanced at his arm, freshly bandaged. "And my work here is done."

But he didn't move, and neither did I. Both of us watched my hands that were still touching him. Without thinking, I turned his arm over, revealing the tattoo of one hand stabbing another with a dagger.

"*Hands remember*," I said. "What does it mean?"

"It's part of a quote," he said. "*Hands remember what the*

mind forgets. It means shit happens, and we want to forget it. Move on. But we can't. It burrows into our damn cells. Our blood."

I was still holding his arm. "What kind of shit?"

What happened to your parents, Ronan?

Our eyes met, and I lost a few seconds in the depths of his gaze that weren't flat and hard now but miles deep and cloudy with memories. The kind that stabbed like a dagger.

Ronan's large body seemed to sink deeper into my touch without moving. His eyes cleared and became intent on me, roaming over my face, my chin, my mouth…

Then he blinked like a man coming out of a trance. The thread snapped. He snatched his arm from me and stood up. "Never mind."

I sat, slightly shell-shocked, as he picked up the rake and scraped it over the ground that was already clear.

"I shouldn't have come," he said after a minute, his back to me.

"Why?" I said, striving for casual as I gathered the first aid supplies.

"I can't do anything else until the building materials get here."

"How long will it take once you have them?"

"A few days."

A few days and he's done.

"They're due to arrive tomorrow morning."

"Then I'll come back tomorrow."

"Sure," I said just as stiffly. "Whatever."

A crash sounded from inside. Ronan whirled around, and we glanced at each other, wide-eyed. He tossed the rake to the ground, and the supplies fell out of my hand as we both rushed into the house.

"Bibi?" I cried, my heart in my throat.

"Here, dear. Darn my butterfingers."

Bibi was holding hard to the kitchen counter. At her feet, the ceramic teapot lay in shards.

I rushed to her. "Are you okay? What happened?"

"I'm fine," she said, smiling weakly. "It's silly. Just got a little dizzy."

"Come sit down." I gently put my arms around her, shooting Ronan a panicked look. His mouth was a grim line of worry.

"It's nothing, I promise," Bibi said as I led her to the couch. "When you're my age, things break down, dear. My eyes aren't what they used to be. I misjudged the distance to the counter, and the teapot fell." She shook her head. "A shame. I loved that teapot."

"You said you were dizzy."

"I'm eighty years old! It happens."

I exchanged another glance with Ronan.

"Where's the broom?" he asked, the solidity of his presence helping to calm me.

"Back of the kitchen door."

Bibi frowned. "Ronan is here? Oh my, I'm afraid I'm even more embarrassed. I didn't see you there, darling."

"It's fine," Ronan said and went to fetch the broom.

Bibi leaned into me. "He's a good boy, isn't he?"

He's stubborn and frustrating.

"Yes," I said. "He's a good guy."

He returned a few minutes later. "You're set. Do you need anything else?"

"Not a thing."

"Then I'll go. I was telling Shiloh there's no work for me to do until the supplies get here."

"Understandable," Bibi said. "But I made a fresh batch of cookies, and this time, I insist that you take a few."

"Ms. Barrera—"

"I *insist*."

I arched a brow at Ronan. "She insists."

He narrowed his eyes at me, and I grinned. The tension between us loosened.

"There are paper bags by the toaster," Bibi called as he went back to the kitchen. "Fill one up. Or two. You're a big man. You need your energy."

"Bibi," I hissed, my cheeks enflamed.

"It's true, isn't it?"

Ronan returned holding a bag that couldn't have had more than a few cookies in it. "Thanks for these. You going to be okay?"

"Are you addressing me?" Bibi said. "My goodness, what an angel. I'm fine."

Ronan shifted his gaze to me, same question.

I nodded. "Thank you."

"Goodbye, darling."

Ronan made a sound that might've been goodbye, then turned and went out.

"He didn't take many cookies, did he?" Bibi sighed when the front door shut. She shook her head. "I've seen his type before."

"His type?"

Please tell me his type. Tell me what to think about Ronan Wentz.

"He's the type who gives but hates to take."

"Sounds about right." I took Bibi's hand in mine. "Are you sure you're okay?"

"I'm fine, baby girl." She patted my cheek. "In fact, I'm famished. How about we order pizza?"

"Sounds good. And maybe a movie?"

"What about your work in the garage?"

"I'm taking the night off."

I had Etsy orders to catch up on, but there was no way I was leaving Bibi alone for the rest of the night. Not for one damn second.

"My, my," Bibi said. "I should have a little dizzy spell more often."

"No, you should not," I said, shivering. "You're not allowed, ever again."

"I'm getting up there, Shiloh. I don't ever want to be a burden to you but—"

"You're not," I said fiercely. "You never will be. You took me in, Bibi. If anyone's the burden, it's me."

"Never think that, Shiloh. Not ever. I'd do it a hundred

times over." Her tone softened. "But we don't get to say how long we have, my dear. We can only make the most of the time we're given. And I cherish every minute with you."

Hot tears sprang to my eyes, but I blinked them back. "Me too, Bibi. Every minute."

Bibi patted my cheek, then smiled brightly. "Now, how about some Madea?"

"Again?" I sniffed a laugh. "Which one?"

"The first one, of course."

"You've seen it a hundred times."

"Then it must be really good."

"Can't argue with that."

As if I'd say no to her anyway.

I ordered pizza and curled up next to Bibi on the couch, my eyes straying from the movie to the door where Ronan had gone, taking his quiet strength with him. As Bibi cackled at Tyler Perry's antics, I tried not to think about the time when that laugh would be forever silent. The pain would break me into a thousand pieces.

And I'd have no one to put me back together but me.

SIX

RONAN

Saturday afternoon, Miller and I lugged a tall wingback chair from the parking lot nearest the path to the beach, all the way to the shack, hauling it over boulders and sweating under a relentless sun.

His Lordship directed and guided us along, not breaking a sweat. Once there, Holden wedged the chair inside the little cabin and flounced into it, grinning at us.

"Perfect, right?"

Not remotely. It was too fucking big, for one thing, but since we'd brought Holden to the shack last week, he'd wasted no time filling it with upgrades. Like a mini fridge and a generator to run it. The fridge stored my beer and Holden's vodka, but I knew he'd bought it for Miller's snacks and juices to keep his blood sugars even.

Holden had also brought a trunk big enough to store Miller's guitar so he wouldn't have to haul it around wherever he went.

What was a chair to that?

Miller smiled gratefully at Holden, likely the same thoughts running through his mind. "The chair's not so bad." He shouldered his backpack for his job at the arcade down at the boardwalk. "I'm off at ten."

"We'll meet you," Holden said, and I nodded.

Most nights, the three of us walked the boardwalk, getting stares and whispers from Central High students. None of us gave a shit. Since the night of Chance's party, Holden had become one of us, and now our weird circle felt complete.

That night, around the bonfire, he'd told us a little about his past. About some "wilderness camp" his parents had sent him to in Alaska when he was fifteen. Whatever the camp was, it had fucked him up. Hard. He'd spent a year in some fancy Swiss sanatorium to recover, but the effects stuck with him. Holden wore coats, scarves, and sweaters no matter the weather. As if whatever happened had been embedded into him like a permanent frost.

I made sure to keep the bonfire high for him from then on.

That afternoon, he sat in one of the three beach chairs around the pit while I gathered wood.

"What about you?" he asked after Miller had gone. "Do you work?"

"I do odd jobs."

"You're a freelancer."

"Sure."

"And you live with your uncle?"

I didn't look at him but concentrated on the fire.

"The reason I ask," Holden continued, "is because I also used to live with my parents and now live with my aunt and uncle. We're twinsies."

I could've laughed. Holden was a billionaire, had an IQ over 150, and wore clothes that cost more than anything I'd ever owned in my entire life. We could not be more different…until I remembered him baring his chest to Frankie and daring him to stab him in the heart.

"Shit happened in Wisconsin," I said. "I had to get out of there."

Holden nodded, thinking, and raised the ever-present vodka flask to his mouth. The knuckles of his left hand were wrapped in white bandages. Automatically, my fingers went to the cut on my arm that Shiloh had cleaned up. She'd done a good job; it was healing fast. I hoped it'd leave a scar to remind me. Not where Frankie had cut me open but where Shiloh had put me back together.

"What's that all about?" I asked, taking a seat and nodding at Holden's hand.

"Oh, this?" He waggled his injured fingers. "Or are you wondering why today is a vodka day?"

"Seems like every day is a vodka day." Along with the cold that racked Holden in seventy-five-degree heat, he also seemed to have a pretty solid drinking problem.

"True. Today's been extra special." He glanced at me, unsure. "You want to hear this?"

"If you want to tell it."

He looked to the ocean that crashed on shore a good twenty yards from us. "Alcohol keeps me warm because Alaska stole something from me. It stole something and left me with nightmares—memories—to remind me I'll never get it back."

"The camp?"

He nodded. "It fucked me up, and I wasn't entirely solid to begin with. There were seven of us. It broke us down until we were nearly dead. Or wanted to die."

I listened, my jaw tight.

"Anyway, that's why most days are vodka days. And why I sometimes put my fist through bathroom mirrors." He coughed. "Or why I dare people to stab me in the chest at parties."

He glanced at me again, doubt in his eyes. The same doubt I'd had when I told Miller my story. As if Holden was afraid I'd kick him out of our group. I didn't have the words to tell him that would never happen.

But I could give him something back.

"I don't live with my parents because they're dead."

Holden had started to sip from his flask. His hand dropped into his lap. "What happened?"

I told him. He listened, hardly moving, though I kept the details to a minimum.

"I was pretty messed up," I said, watching the fire. "I had to repeat fourth grade and did ten years in foster care. Eventually, social services tracked down my dad's brother. That's how I ended up here."

Holden was quiet for a minute, then said, "I'm so sorry about your mother, Ronan."

I nodded, and we didn't say much for a while but watched the sun sink toward the ocean.

"Well, aren't we a jolly pair," Holden said just at the right time, before the quiet got too heavy. "Tell me something good that happened to you today, Wentz. Anything. Before I throw myself into the ocean."

Shiloh Barrera happened.

I tossed a rock into the fire. *Cut that shit out.*

Impossible. I remembered every damn word of our conversation, which was longer than any I'd had with anyone in years. I remembered every glance of her brown eyes and where they skimmed over me. I remembered every time she touched me and where. I could feel her gentle fingers on my skin and the sting of alcohol while she cleaned my wound. Like her—sharp and soft at the same time.

She was something good, but I had to leave her alone to make sure she stayed that way.

"I didn't get suspended," I said finally.

"Hey, there you go! A two-day streak."

Holden offered his noninjured hand in a high five. I hated high fives. I slapped his palm hard, and he hissed with pain, laughing.

"Easy, tiger."

"Your turn. Something good."

"Hmm, don't know that it's *good* so much as *doomed and hopeless* but…" Holden sighed dramatically. "There's a guy."

"Okay."

"I can't say who, so don't ask."

"I wasn't going to."

"Of course you weren't. That's one of your most endearing characteristics. Anyway, there's a guy, and I don't *want* there to be a guy. Not one that I might…"

"Want to fuck?"

"That's a given."

"Care about?"

"Exactly. And I can't care about anyone. Bad for me, worse for them." Holden shook his head, watching the fire struggle against a breeze that had picked up. "It's stupid. And too soon. I didn't come here to immediately have my every waking thought hijacked by someone I've only known for a few days." He laughed at my wide eyes. "No, it's not Miller. And I hate to break your heart, but it's not you either."

"So what's the problem?"

"The problem is that the guy in question is not my type, to put it mildly. An all-American good boy. Warm, gooey, everyone loves him. He's the human equivalent of a grilled cheese sandwich."

"So?"

"So? It doesn't make sense. Yet I can't stop thinking about him and feeling guilty, because…I may have said some things I shouldn't have."

"I'm shocked," I said into my beer. Holden was a smart-ass with zero filter.

"Oh, shut up," he said. "But yes, I stirred up some shit for him that I had no business stirring. I even gave him my number in the event he wants to talk. To *me*. As if I could actually *help* somehow." He snorted a laugh. "It's impossible."

"Why?"

"I'm not one hundred percent positive that he and I are on the same page, if you catch my drift. I need to leave it alone. Leave *him* alone."

I rolled my eyes and hurled a rock into the fire.

Here we go again.

Both my friends were hell-bent on being miserable instead of making a stand for what they wanted.

Holden read my scowl. "You disagree?"

"If you care about him—"

"Let's not go that far."

"—then tell him."

"That proves difficult, since he specifically asked that I never speak to him again. And even if by some miracle he is gay, nothing good can come of something with me. Except for sex. I can do meaningless sex." He narrowed his eyes at me. "That's not an offer, by the way."

I snorted a laugh. A short silence fell, and Holden shivered a little as he took a sip from his flask. I sprayed more lighter fluid over the embers until they flared in a wall of light and heat.

"Is that what they stole from you in Alaska?"

Holden's head whipped to me. "What?"

"You said nothing good could come of you being with that guy," I said. "Is that what they taught you? That you're no good?"

"Yes," he said slowly. "But it began earlier with my parents. And it's more complicated—"

"It's bullshit is what it is," I snapped. "Whoever made you think that, no matter when it started, it's bullshit."

I finished my beer and strode to the shack to get two more. I stood over Holden, offering. He looked up at me, gratitude in his eyes, and took one. The flask went into his coat pocket.

We drank our beers while the sun sank lower, and then Holden turned to me, his voice more subdued than I'd ever heard it.

"What was it like? Seeing something like…what you did?"

Instantly, my body stiffened. "What the fuck do you think it was like?"

"I have no idea," Holden said. "I can't fucking imagine it, actually. As much as I loathe the sentient viruses in human form that are my parents, to witness something like that…" He shrugged. "I guess what I'm really asking is are you okay?"

I shot him a glare, and he held up his hands.

"Don't bite my head off. It's a valid question."

I held my stare, but the defensive anger was melting away as I realized no one apart from my social worker had ever asked me about my parents. She'd told me most people wouldn't—that they'd be afraid bringing it up would remind me of my mother's death. As if I'd forgotten all about it until they said something. As if I didn't walk around with it all day, every day.

Or relive it in my nightmares every night.

I nearly told Holden to fuck off, but no one asked me if I was okay either.

"I don't know," I said to the fire. "I'm doing my best, I guess. And I'm done talking about it."

Holden smiled—a rare, soft one with no sharp edges. "Fair enough. Let's talk about something only slightly less painful and traumatic."

"Like?"

"Girls. Not my preferred subject, *obviously*, but I confessed to you the depressing state of my love life. If you wish to unburden yourself likewise, I'm all ears."

Shiloh's perfect face with her smooth skin and full lips rose up in my mind. I recalled the intelligence in her eyes as she focused her attention on whatever job was in front of her. Like patching up a criminal like me. That was the gossip at school—Miller was the outcast, Holden was the vampire, and I was an ex-con posing as a high school student.

They were right, in a way. The stain of my father's crime was all over me. Just standing in Bibi's house or sitting on the patio with Shiloh felt wrong. Good but wrong. As if I'd broken into their perfect life and left bloody fingerprints all over it. But when I tried to hold back, stay quiet, and get to work, Shiloh drew me out of myself. I didn't want to move so long as she was sitting across from me.

Holden was waiting for an answer.

There's a girl, and I don't want there to be a girl.

"Nah," I said tipping back my beer. "There's no one."

At ten, Holden and I met Miller at the arcade. He got off his shift, and we walked the boardwalk, stopping for slices of pizza and to play a few carnival games. After, I walked home.

I walked everywhere. Luckily, the school, the shack, Shiloh's place, and my apartment were all close enough to each other that I didn't need a car. But it would've fucking helped.

I climbed the exterior cement steps up to my corner place, reaching for my keys. But the door swung open at the slightest touch, revealing a wedge of black that was deep and dark.

"Nelson?" I asked, my hand creeping toward my jacket pocket for the Taser I'd swiped from Frankie. "You here?"

I reached to my right, feeling along the wall to flip on the light when I sensed it. Him. Someone waiting…

The dark came to life, breathing and moving. I lunged blindly, and something heavy whacked my wrist. The Taser went skittering across the linoleum in the kitchen. Big hands gripped me by the neck and shoulders, and a cannonball of pain exploded as a knee drove up into my gut.

Another blow from out of the dark split my lip, and then I was shoved to the ground.

I was still trying to get my wind when the light flipped on.

A huge guy loomed over me, his back to my busted door. He looked to be middle-aged, wearing track pants, a T-shirt that stretched over his bulk, and a blue windbreaker. His reddish hair was thinning on top, and he had pale-blue eyes stuffed in a ruddy face.

I scrambled to my feet, rage burning up the pain and shock.

"You want to try that shit again?" I snarled. "With the lights on?"

"I wouldn't if I were you," the guy said when I took a step toward him. He moved his blue windbreaker aside to reveal a holstered pistol at his waist.

His smile sent shivers down my spine. It was the same kind of sick smile my dad wore when he announced that my mother was "in trouble."

"Ronan Wentz, right?" the guy said. "My name is Mitch. But you can call me Officer Dowd."

Mitch Dowd. He looked and sounded deadly casual, but I could feel the readiness tensing in him, waiting for me to make a move.

"I could have you arrested for breaking my son's nose, but I prefer to handle things personally."

"Fuck you." I spat a wad of red onto my carpet at his feet. "And fuck him too."

Mitch chuckled, though his gaze grew flatter. "I read your file, Wentz. You're a criminal. A degenerate, just like your father." His eyes went to the Taser lying a few feet away. "A thief too, who steals police property. I believe that belongs to me, son."

Christ, he *sounded* like my dad.

"I want you to go over there and hand it to me. *Slowly. Slowly.*" He rested one hand on the butt of his pistol, one hand outstretched, waiting.

I retrieved the Taser from the kitchen and crossed the small space to him, our eyes locked. Every muscle in my body was coiled tight, ready to spring. But something besides adrenaline zipped along my nerves like an electric current.

Fear.

He looked nothing like my dad, yet the resemblance was uncanny, catapulting me to another time. My breath came short. Mouth dry. I put the Taser in his left hand. It touched skin, and the blue of his jacket blurred as his fist slammed into my eye in a blow I should've seen coming.

My head rang, but I took the hit with a grunt and answered by throwing a right hook that connected with his mouth. It would've knocked another guy flat, but Mitch hardly flinched. I took a shot to the kidney, another to the gut, and then he was hurling me across the room. I crashed, shoulder first, into the cheap wooden coffee table that splintered under me like kindling.

With a satisfied smile, Mitch ran his thumb under his lip, wiping a trickle of blood.

"This was a warning, Wentz," he said, heading for the door. "You only get one."

He went out, and I lay for a minute in the wreckage of the table, feeling drunk on pain and bloody memories.

Slowly, my head cleared, and I hauled myself to my feet just as Maryann Greer from downstairs poked her head inside.

"Ronan? Oh my God…"

I waved her off, but it was too late. She rushed in and put gentle, steadying hands on me as she guided me to the kitchen table.

"What in the hell happened? I heard a crash and saw a man leaving. Big one."

"It's nothing," I said, slouching into the chair, keeping a hand over my eye that was already swelling shut. "You should go."

If he comes back…

"Go?" Maryann stood over me, her blue eyes studying me. She wore jeans and an old sweatshirt, her dark-blond hair in a messy ponytail. "Fat chance. I'm calling the police."

"He was the police."

Gently, she moved my hand from my eye. "Sweet Jesus, what *happened*? And don't say nothing."

"It's over. He came to settle a score. That's it."

"You have scores with cops?" Maryann rummaged in my freezer, found it empty, and checked out the fridge. "You have no ice. Hardly any food either."

"I'm fine."

"My ass. Stay right there," she said, going to the door. "Don't move."

"Maryann..."

But she was already gone.

A flare of anger in me wanted more fight—a fair fight—but shame washed it away. A single fluorescent bulb lit my dim apartment. My coffee table was a heap of busted wood. A splotch of blood stained the carpet.

Sorry, Mom. I'm trying.

Maryann came back with a bag of frozen peas. Instead of handing it to me, she stood over me and pressed the bag to my eye, her other hand gently holding the back of my neck. For long moments, I just sat there with Maryann and her peas, her worry and concern wafting over me in warm, motherly waves. She smelled like lemon dish soap.

I closed my eyes and let myself have that for a minute, then stiffened to push her away.

"I got it, thanks." I took the bag and held it to my eye. "You can go."

Maryann pursed her lips, then sat in the chair across from me and rested her arms on the card table in a way that said *I'm not going anywhere*.

"You're young, aren't you?" she asked. "You go to the high school?"

"When I can get there."

"Who takes care of you? Not your uncle," she said darkly. "He doesn't take care of sh—" Her mouth snapped shut, her eyes anxious. "I mean no disrespect."

"It's okay. He's an ass."

"What can I do?" she asked. "Because this"—she gestured at the smashed table—"is *not* okay."

I knew Maryann Greer worked her ass off at an accounting company and took online classes to get a degree. To get a better job and make a better life for her girls. Weariness was written in every line of her face that made her look older than she was.

"I don't need anything."

I'm not taking anything from you.

"I disagree. Ronan, I—"

"Mommy?"

Lillian and Camille, her six-year-old twins, were peeking their heads inside, sleepy and curious.

"I told you both to stay in bed," Maryann said.

"We couldn't sleep," said one.

"Yeah, it was loud up here," said the other.

They had Maryann's blond hair and blue eyes. Both wore little nightgowns with butterflies on them and an initial, C or L. They looked at me and then at the smashed table, eyes wide.

"They shouldn't see this," I said to Maryann in a low voice.

"Agreed. But this isn't over yet," she said and rose to her feet. "Girls…"

Too late. The twins had already rushed into my place and surrounded me at the table. Their energy filled up my small dark space and made it brighter.

"Are you okay?"

"Why do you have peas on your face? Is your eye all gross under there?"

One peeked under my T-shirt sleeve. "You have an owl on your shoulder! Ew, yucky bruise too."

"Were you in a fight? Is that why?"

"Ronan was…wrestling," Maryann said.

Instantly, the girls' faces lit up, and they exchanged excited looks.

"Really?"

"No way!"

Maryann leaned into me. "They love WWE women's wrestling. Just go with it."

"Yeah, I was wrestling," I said. "Practicing for a match."

"That is so cool!"

"Did you do a pile driver? That's my favorite."

"I like it when they fly off the ropes." Lillian glanced around with a frown. "I don't see any ropes…"

Maryann held up her hands. "Okay, Cami, Lily. Let's leave Ronan alone. Back to bed."

They both sagged with disappointment. And so did I. A little.

The bag of cookies from Bibi I'd taken the other day was still on my kitchen counter, untouched. "Do you guys like chocolate chip cookies?"

Their little faces lit up again while Maryann shot me with a *Don't you dare* look in her eyes.

I pretended not to see it.

"A lady made these," I said, keeping the peas on my eye as I grabbed the cookie bag. "She's a grandma, so you know they're good."

I handed the bag to Cami, who immediately pulled out a cookie, gave it to her twin, then took one for herself. "They look so yummy! Can we, Mommy?"

Maryann crossed her arms, shaking her head ruefully at me.

"They're from one of my jobs," I said. "Good people."

She relented with a sigh. "Okay, but just *one* each."

"Yay!"

"What do you say?"

The little girls flew at me, hugging me around my bruised ribs, though I hardly felt it. I held my arms up, not daring to touch them until they let me go.

"Thank you, Mr. Ronan!"

"Thanks a lot!"

"Okay, okay." Maryann herded them to the door, shooting me a puzzled look over her shoulder. "Go back down, girls. I'll be there in a minute." She watched them descend the stairs to make sure they got in safe, then turned back to me. "They like you," she said.

"Must be the wrestling."

"Or the chocolate," she said with a dry smile. "You sure you're going to be okay?"

"Fine. It's over, I swear," I said, even as I wondered what would happen if Frankie decided to test me and fuck with Miller again. Or Holden.

I'd beat his ass if he touched either of them.

But I'd already brought Mitch Dowd here once, too close to Maryann and her girls.

Fuck.

Maryann read my dark expression. "Put those peas back in the freezer, then get some sleep. Use it again tomorrow. You have something for the pain?"

"I'm good."

She nodded slowly, then reluctantly moved to the door as if she didn't want to leave me alone. "Good night, Ronan."

"Yep."

The door closed behind her but wouldn't stay shut. The locking mechanism was busted. Dowd must've pried it open somehow. I tossed the peas in my freezer and dragged one of the cheap kitchen chairs to the door and wedged it under the knob. After Lily and Cami, the silence in my place was thick and heavy.

I went to the bathroom and inspected the damage. My lip was split—not too bad—but my right eye looked like hell. Swollen, blue, the cheekbone puffed and dashed with a small cut where he must've got me with his ring.

I lifted my shirt and sucked in a breath. Already, my torso was a patchwork of bruises. My right shoulder, which took the brunt of the table, was stiffening up, and more bruises colored my skin beneath the owl tattoo. It stared at me in the mirror as if to say, *What did you expect?*

I couldn't go to school like this, and I sure as shit couldn't go to the Barreras', even though Shiloh needed that shed. If my eye wasn't better Monday, I'd wait, then work twice as hard and fast to get it done for her.

Then you won't be over there anymore, interfering in their lives.

It was early yet, not even 1:00 a.m., but I was too stiff and sore to walk and no good to anyone anyway. I lay down to sleep, knowing the nightmares were going to be worse and tinged with real pain.

And I was right.

SEVEN
SHILOH

I was right about Violet. Not only did she make homecoming court, she'd been voted queen, stealing the crown right out from under Evelyn Gonzalez. Not that Violet had been trying to steal anything. Her genuine surprise and humble attitude were why everyone loved her.

To support her, I went to the football game on Saturday and the parade after with Miller. Or maybe it was to support *him*. We took our places on the aluminum bleachers and watched our Central Capitals destroy the Soquel Saints. Miller scowled every time River Whitmore completed a pass or threw for a touchdown.

Which was frequently.

My gaze kept wandering from the field to scan the faces in the crowd. Ronan hadn't been at school for the last week and was a no-show at my house too. Bibi said he'd called in sick. As the football game droned on that morning, I found myself on the verge of asking Miller if Ronan was okay.

Because that's allowed.

But the words stuck in my throat. Asking about Ronan's well-being—putting it out there for someone else to hear—might somehow make the unsettling thoughts and feelings I'd been having about him finally *settle*.

And then I'd have to look at them.

After the game, Violet and River—still in his uniform—sat on the back of a convertible as the homecoming parade tooled around the track. Violet was radiant in black, her smile wide as she waved at the crowd or when she beamed up at River.

Miller's scowl collapsed, and then he just looked sad.

"Why do you do this to yourself?" I asked gently.

"Sorry?"

"Watch her be with someone else."

"I need proof that she's okay with him. That he'll take care of her. Or I'll sic Ronan on him."

A shiver danced up my arm. I cleared my throat. "River's unproblematic. At least there's that."

Miller's expression darkened. "Speaking of *River*, did Vi mention that she and I kissed?"

My jaw fell open before I could catch it, and Miller quickly looked away.

"I'll take that as a no."

"I haven't seen her much lately. But no, she didn't say a word." I touched his arm. "I'm sorry. I always knew something was going on there."

"Don't be sorry. Just confirms everything she's been telling me for years."

"Is that why you asked Amber to the dance? To get over her for real?"

Amber Blake had flown at me at school the other day, her blue eyes lit up as she told me Miller had asked her to homecoming. For a second, I thought she was joking; I couldn't imagine Miller giving another girl the time of day. He hadn't once in four years, since he'd met Violet.

I guess everyone has their breaking point.

"I have to try," Miller said. "Maybe something could happen with Amber. Maybe if I gave her a chance, I could move on and be the friend Violet wants me to be."

"Uh-huh. Amber is a friend of *mine*. A real flesh-and-blood human. Not a blow-up doll to take your frustrations out on."

"Jesus, I know that."

I sighed. "I know. You're a good guy too."

"Try telling that to Vi."

"She already knows. That's why she's fighting so hard. In her mind, things are either falling apart or they're standing still. Never becoming something beautiful." I turned my gaze to the field, but in my mind, I was in my backyard, Ronan's arm under my hands as I traced a line from his tattoo down to his wrist where his heartbeat pulsed. "She's trying to hold the two of you still so you don't fall apart."

So she doesn't fall apart. So things stay the same. So they don't go deeper. So she doesn't spend every waking moment wondering if you're okay and driving herself crazy with worry.

I gave myself a shake. Being indirect and wishy-washy wasn't me. If I wanted to regain myself, I needed to *be* myself. I turned to face Miller. "You, Ronan, and Holden are friends now, right?"

"Yeah," Miller said absently.

I plucked an invisible piece of lint off my loose-flowing linen pants. "Ronan's been building a shed for me in our yard. My great-grandmother hired him from the want ads."

"Oh yeah?"

"Yeah. He didn't mention it?"

"Not a word. But that's how he rolls."

I nodded and irritably brushed a cluster of braids off my shoulder. "Well, he hasn't been around the last few days…or at school. We have a monster paper coming up in history."

Miller tore his gaze off Violet, his brows drawn down with concern. "He hadn't been hanging with us either lately. Then he showed up the other night with bruises on his arm and a pretty good shiner."

My eyes widened, and suddenly my heart felt twice as heavy. "Bruises? From where?"

"Don't know. His uncle maybe."

"God, do you think?"

Miller shrugged. "He won't say."

"Well, did you *ask* him?"

"Of course," he said with a frown. "Holden and I both asked him. He told us to fuck off. That's Ronan for you. When he doesn't want to talk, he won't." Miller nudged my arm. "Hey. He's okay."

I realized I'd been gnawing my lower lip. "Good. I mean...what?"

"You just looked a little worried there for a second."

I sat up straighter. "I'm not completely *heartless*."

My voice quavered on that word, but Miller didn't notice. He'd resumed his miserable vigil, watching Violet talk with River. The parade had ended, and the preparations for the dance had begun.

"Let's get out of here," I said.

"Good idea," he said grimly, and we made our way down the bleachers with the rest of the students and parents. "What about you? Going to the dance tonight?"

"No. I've had a few offers, but..." I shrugged. "I love dancing but not dances. They're kind of silly."

I'd had that stance for years and never gave it a second thought. Now I was questioning everything.

Why? What's different?

Ronan tried to crowd my thoughts, but I pushed him out. It was senior year. There weren't going to be any more dances. It was nostalgia, that was all.

Miller sighed. "Holden and Ronan are ditching me too."

"Oh? They're not going?" My voice was three octaves higher than usual.

He shook his head. "I mean, with Ronan, it makes sense. Can you picture him at a dance?"

Not dancing, no chance. But holding a girl, enveloping her in his arms, keeping her close...

Jesus, I need an intervention.

"But Holden, that fucker, could've backed me up," Miller said.

We'd reached the parking lot, and I patted his arm. "Sorry, my friend. Do you need a ride? So you have time to get ready?"

"No, thanks, Shi. I need to walk. Clear my head."

I gave him a short hug, and we parted ways without me saying anything else that would help him or give him a boost. I had nothing.

When I arrived home, Bibi was making her mint-basil lemonade in the kitchen.

"Hello, baby girl. How was the game?"

"We won," I said, pecking her cheek and eyeing the lemonade suspiciously. "This is for…"

"Ronan. Our boy's feeling much better now."

I went to the kitchen window. *Our boy* was in the backyard looking every inch *the man* as he stacked plywood from the shipment of supplies that had come the other day. He wore his usual uniform—jeans, boots, plain T-shirt. Even from the kitchen, I could see the bruises darkening the skin beneath his owl tattoo and another around his right eye.

Anger flared hot in me, taking me by surprise.

"I'll bring this to him." I grabbed the mason jar and headed out.

On the patio, I plunked the glass on the table and strode to stand right in front of Ronan.

Up close, the bruising around his eye was turning green, which meant it was a few days old.

Which meant it had been so much worse.

"Who did that to you?" I demanded.

Ronan frowned down at me, taken back by the fire in my tone. "No one."

"It was Dowd, wasn't it? For Frankie?"

"Doesn't matter."

"Of course it does," I said, incredulous. "It matters to me."

We both froze. Ronan's gaze on me softened. We were standing so close. Close, like we were about to dance or…

I stepped back, my cheeks flaming. "I mean…it's not right. First your arm and now this."

"Forget it."

"I don't want to forget it. I want to press charges."

"No."

"Ronan—"

"It's *over*, Shiloh," he said harshly, though his gray eyes looked more sad than angry. "I don't want to talk about it. I don't want to fucking *think* about it. Just…leave it alone."

"But…"

But nothing. Ronan had shut down, turned away, and resumed his work on my shed, leaving me gaping after him in the middle of the yard like a dope. I turned on my heel and strode back into the house.

"Shiloh, what's wrong?" Bibi asked.

Everything. Because nothing is what it's supposed to be.

I sucked in a breath. "Nothing. Everything's fine."

"Hmm," Bibi said, wiping down the counter with a cloth. "Are you sure?"

Bibi probably hadn't seen Ronan's bruises, and I didn't want to worry her.

"Yeah, sorry. It's just been a weird day." I forced a smile that she'd hear in my words. "I'm going to the garage. Holler if you need anything."

Lying to Bibi was high on my list of things I never do, but then again, so was losing control. I sat at my dim workstation and concentrated on my work, refocused my attention, and calmed my beating heart. It was slow going at first until I thought of my mother sitting in Aunt Bertie's kitchen, smoking over a crossword, and not looking at me.

It went faster after that.

Yellow twilight was slipping under the garage door when I finished. Everyone at school would be getting ready for the homecoming dance, taking pictures and going out to dinner. I'd completed a bracelet that would go in my eventual shop. That was something.

I expected—hoped—Ronan would be long gone, but he was still in our yard, working. The base of the shed had been laid, and he was hammering a nail into one corner. More nails stuck out of his mouth, his thick brows furrowed in concentration. The muscles of his arms flexed with each *whack* of the hammer.

I quickly turned and joined Bibi on the couch where she was listening to *Law & Order* on the TV and knitting.

The cats, Lucy and Ethel, lay stretched out over the back like throw pillows.

"Well?" Bibi asked. "Feeling better?"

"Yes, thanks. I'm sorry. I…" I sighed out the rest of my words, not sure what I'd have said anyway.

"It's getting late," Bibi said pointedly. "That boy is going to work until dark if we let him. Will you go tell him it's quitting time, or shall I?" She smiled and patted my hand. "Don't want you to get flustered after all."

I gaped. "What? I'm not… I'll tell him."

I ignored Bibi's snickering and went out to the patio.

"Hey," I said when there was a break in the hammering. "Bibi says it's time to quit."

"I can stay longer," Ronan said without looking up. "Need to catch up."

"Bibi won't allow it. Besides, we have that big paper due in history next week. You've missed a lot of class."

"I'll figure it out."

"Okay, but you have two days to figure it out and no notes to work from."

"What's it to you?" Ronan asked, though his tone was more curious than defensive.

"Nothing," I said too quickly. "But it's a huge part of our grade. So I was thinking…" I swallowed hard. *Jesus, what am I thinking?* "I was thinking I could grab some dinner for us and Bibi and then maybe study a little. You can borrow my notes."

Ronan didn't say anything but watched me, a conflicted expression on his face.

I coughed. "Or not."

"Okay," he said.

"Okay?"

"I can't fail history. Or any class. I made a promise… Anyway, yeah. Thanks."

"Great," I said and went back in the house, wondering who Ronan gave his promises to.

EIGHT
RONAN

I FOLLOWED SHILOH TO THE LIVING ROOM WHERE SHE explained her dinner plans to Bibi.

"Sounds marvelous," Bibi said. She was on the couch with a pile of yarn on her lap. Two gray cats watched me through slitted eyes. "Do you like ribs, Ronan? Tony's makes the best plates with slaw, biscuits, and extra-crispy onion rings."

"Sounds good," I said. Much better than my usual frozen dinner or fast-food takeout.

"Shi, why don't the two of you walk downtown, and you can introduce Ronan to Tony?"

"Walk?" Shiloh said, looking alarmed. "It'll be faster if we drive. In fact, I can just hop down there and back...alone."

"There's no rush, dear."

Shiloh bit her lip. "The food will get cold..."

"Nonsense. It's a lovely night for a walk. Don't you agree, Ronan?"

I coughed. "Sure."

Shiloh glared at me. Wrong answer.

"If you're into that sort of thing," she muttered. She grabbed an oversize cardigan from a chair near the door, tied it around her waist, and kissed her great-grandmother's cheek. "Be back soon."

"Take your time, you two."

We headed out, Shiloh facing forward, not looking at me. Clearly, she was regretting her casual dinner invite.

Or being alone with me.

"Shiloh, take the damn car if you want. I don't care."

"No, it's fine."

"Fine," I said, strolling with my hands in my pockets. "Uh-huh."

She frowned. "It's no big deal."

"*It's no big deal*, but you're going to be pissy the entire time."

Shiloh glanced up at me. "I am not *pissy*."

"Then what are you?"

"I'm just…walking."

I chuckled, which only irritated her more.

"Pardon me if I don't want my great-grandmother's food to get cold before she eats it. Bibi deserves the best."

I smirked and shook my head.

"You disagree?"

"No, I one hundred percent agree your great-grandmother deserves the best."

That's why she has you.

"Well?"

"Well, you're stubborn as hell."

Her eyes—fringed with long, soft lashes—widened. "Me?"

"It's not a bad thing. It means you want what you want."

"I do," she said, her tone softening a little. "It's hard to compromise, especially where Bibi's concerned."

"How is she?" I asked. "Any more dizzy spells?"

"None, thank God." She shivered a little, though it was still warm out. "But it's scary, you know? She's eighty and… Never mind. I don't want to talk about it. Like inviting bad stuff in."

"Yeah, I get that."

She gave me a small smile, and the tension evaporated. Or maybe it just changed. Shiloh was wearing high-waisted, flowing white pants and a short white T-shirt with the beige cardigan tied loosely on her hips. The T-shirt revealed her midsection. Bracelets and rings—all her own making, I guessed—decorated her slender arms and hands, and her ears were pierced a dozen times, the rings and studs visible when she pushed her braids off her shoulders.

I couldn't keep my eyes off her, and my hands wanted to touch all the different textures of her. Hard metal and soft skin. Her hair where it was braided and where it frayed at the ends into soft waves.

So much for keeping my damn distance.

The walk to downtown from Shiloh's neighborhood took about fifteen minutes. Her quiet street gave way to rows of galleries, restaurants, coffee shops, and bars. We passed a tattoo place with a Chinese dragon on a screen hanging in the window.

"What makes you decide to get a tattoo?" Shiloh asked with a nod at the shop. "There are an infinite number of designs or quotes to choose from. How do you pick?"

"You narrow it down to the most meaningful or important. Something you want to wear forever," I said and thought of my owl. "Most times, they pick you."

As if she were reading my mind, her dark eyes went to my shoulder—to the Indian eagle-owl. In life, they were brown and gray with black stripes along their stomachs and long earlike tufts over bright-orange eyes. My tattoo had no color but for the eyes. Shiloh looked like she was going to ask about it but changed her mind. She did that a lot, I noticed. Like tonight, letting herself get personal, then retreating.

I couldn't blame her. Something in her pulled something out of me too. I had to keep reminding myself who I was.

The son of a murderer.

"Sooo, do you have an idea about the topic of your paper?" Shiloh asked. A neutral subject. "Like probably half the class, I picked the Romanov assassinations."

"I was thinking the Khodynka Tragedy."

"What's that? Baskin hasn't talked much about it."

"It occurred about twenty years before the revolution."

Shiloh arched a brow. "And? Don't leave me hanging."

I jammed my hands in my pockets. "I don't know. Maybe it's dumb."

"I'm sure it's not dumb." She nudged my elbow with hers. "Tell me."

"Okay, so…at the coronation of Nicholas II, there was a big banquet held in a field for the citizens. But five hundred thousand people showed up—more than anyone planned. A rumor went around that the beer and souvenirs were going to dry up, which started a stampede. Fourteen hundred people were killed."

"Holy shit…" Shiloh breathed.

"Yeah. And the fucked-up thing was Nicholas knew about it. As he rode in, he saw wagons of the dead being carted out. But he went on with the celebration anyway. Making speeches. Business as usual."

"Sounds awful. What made you want to write about that?"

"Because it set the tone for the revolution," I said. "Really terrible shit happens to regular people, and the ones who're supposed to be watching out for them don't."

Shiloh was staring at me as if she was seeing something that hadn't been there before. Then she blinked and looked away. "Sounds like you know what you're talking about, paper-wise. Not sure how I can help."

"I checked out some books from the library, but I'm still really fucking far behind. You might have notes for a better topic."

"I don't think you need a better topic. I think it's perfect."

I looked down at her, and she looked up at me, her

features soft and unguarded for a split second, then she faced forward again. Drawing close and retreating, like a tide.

We walked in silence for another minute or so, then Shiloh stopped at an empty storefront that used to be a tiny laundromat. The place was cleaned out, paint peeling off the walls, and two small front windows were plastered with GOING OUT OF BUSINESS signs.

"This one," Shiloh murmured, almost to herself. "Perfect location. Perfect square footage. Perfect everything."

"For your own shop."

She nodded and heaved a breath. "My own shop… I can feel the weight of the responsibility just saying the words. Excitement too, though maybe that's just anxiety and self-doubt in disguise."

I glanced down at the intricate ring on her finger, easily imagining it on a display in her shop.

"How did you get into jewelry making?"

"When I was about ten years old, Bibi showed me how to make trees by twisting copper wires into a trunk, then branching them out and hanging little plastic gems off them for leaves."

"Yeah, there're a few in your living room. You made those?"

She nodded. "I was obsessed. Bibi thought it'd pass the time for a few afternoons, but I wanted to make more and more—trees with green leaves, with gold and orange leaves for autumn, pink and white for cherry blossoms. A whole forest of them."

I nodded, thinking of those trees differently now, knowing that Shiloh made them.

"I loved making something beautiful, but I didn't like that they just sat in a case. I started wrapping coils of copper around my fingers and wrists, adding the little gems, and that was it. As I got older, my designs became more difficult and required real work and tools. Bibi wasn't too keen on the soldering iron or the hand torch at first, but she trusted and supported me every step of the way. This is now her dream too."

Shiloh turned her gaze on the empty laundromat, populating it in her mind with displays of her art. I'd never seen anything as beautiful as that girl in that moment, drenched in twilight, her future in her eyes.

And my fight with Dowd had slowed everything down.

"Sorry I missed so much work."

"I don't care about that. I care more that you got hurt." She glanced up at me, her eyes soft. "I mean…of course that's more important."

In that moment, the tide of her attention and warmth flowed in as she looked up at me, her face open, her lips parted. The air thickened, and my heart was a hammer in my chest. My eyes roamed but kept coming back to her mouth. Fuck, her mouth was perfect—round and ripe like fruit I wanted to bite and suck.

Shiloh held still, as if she were waiting. Her pulse jumped in the hollow of her throat. I felt myself draw in to her, her small, lithe body dwarfed by mine. Then my shadow fell over her. I caught our reflection in the glass of the shop she wanted. Me in black, tattooed and bruised, and her glinting gold…

She is beauty. I'm everything ugly.

My head reared back, and I took a step away from her. I gave a jerky nod to the laundromat. "So…you going to make a bid for this place?"

"Oh, uh…no," Shiloh said, retreating. Her open face reverted to its usual focused, no-nonsense expression. "I mean, yes, I'd love to. But I'm not ready yet, and it'll be a miracle if it's still available this summer."

"*This* summer? How old are you?"

"Eighteen in December. I want to be the youngest entrepreneur in town," she said as we continued our walk. "Not that that means anything. Mostly, I just don't want to waste time. I know what I want, and I'm working really hard to get there, so I see no reason to wait."

"Seems like a lot of work."

"It will be, but that's what I love. While making the copper trees, I became addicted to the satisfaction of doing difficult things." She smiled dryly. "I can't drink booze, so I have to get my buzz elsewhere. Plus, I'm not getting sidetracked with marriage or kids. Not for a long time anyway. Or maybe ever."

"Why not?"

"I don't think I'd be good at the whole mom thing. I'm a workaholic, type A kind of person. And my own mother hasn't exactly set the best example. I told you we aren't close, but that's putting it mildly. Sometimes it feels like she can hardly stand to look at me."

I couldn't imagine it. But maybe that was because I couldn't *stop* looking at her.

"Bibi says she's lost," Shiloh continued. "Her mom died when she was young, her dad about ten years ago. Our family is all broken up. Only my aunt and uncle are solid. I guess that's why I go and visit. To see what a real family looks like. That's a terrible thing to say, like I'm ungrateful for Bibi when I'm not. But sometimes I feel cut adrift. I don't know who my dad is. Don't know who *I* am. So I work really hard at my jewelry, wanting to make a name for myself. An identity." She hunched her shoulders. "Sorry. That was a lot."

"I get it."

"You do?"

I nodded. "I know what you mean about feeling cut loose from everything. I feel the same. Adrift."

"Because your parents died so early?"

"Yeah. Something like that."

Shiloh stopped and faced me. "I never said I was sorry about that. When you told me on the day we met, I was too busy being defensive. But I am. I'm sorry."

"Don't be. Not for him. For her maybe…" My throat tightened.

"What happened?" Shiloh asked gently.

"You don't want to hear it."

"I do. But if you don't want to tell it, I understand. Talking about the past can suck. How about the future instead? What do you want to do after we graduate? College?"

"Doubt it. I'm just trying to get through this year. It's kind of like a reset, to leave a lot of bad shit behind. Try to be better."

Mitch Dowd lurking in my apartment clouded my thoughts.

Trying and failing.

"I just want a normal life," I said. It seemed like it wasn't too much to ask, yet it was everything.

"Normal. Like…having a family?" Shiloh asked. "Kids?"

I shook my head. "No. I didn't have the best role model either."

Understatement of the fucking year.

Shiloh was watching me, wanting to know more. Willing to listen. But telling her about my parents wasn't like telling Holden or Miller. The three of us were fucked up in our own ways. Telling Shiloh would be like smearing mud over a beautiful painting.

We started to walk again, and the cardigan slipped off her waist and hit the ground. I made a grab for it and shook it out. Night had fallen, and she shivered under a streetlight. I wanted to wrap the sweater around her, protect her from the cold. From anything that would hurt her.

Remember who you are.

I thrust it at her. "Here."

"Oh. Thanks." She looked away as she slipped it over

her slender arms. The yellow Tony's sign blared above us. "Aaand, we're here."

Tony's BBQ had a line out the door. We waited in it, neither saying a word. When it came time to order, I tried to pay, but Shiloh waved me off.

"It was my idea."

"Shiloh…"

"Your money's no good here, Wentz. I got this. I insist."

I scowled. "I'll get the next one."

"The next one?"

Shit.

We walked back to her place, and Bibi—moving like a sighted person—set the table and dumped a pile of napkins in the center.

"If it's Tony's, we'll need every single one," she said, beaming in my direction.

I was going to be eating dinner with them…at their table. Like a normal person. But now that I was about to have a taste of normal, I didn't know what to do. I was going to fuck it up. Say or do something and embarrass the shit out of myself.

"I could just take mine out back and keep working," I said and turned to Shiloh. "Maybe I could take a look at your history notes later."

Shiloh glared. "*What?*"

"Absolutely not," Bibi said. "Come. Sit."

There was no getting out of it. I took a seat opposite Shiloh while Bibi sat at the head of the table. The barbecue was better than anything I'd eaten in a long time, the sauce spicy and sweet.

Like the girl sitting across from me.

Bibi asked me harmless questions and made small talk until I no longer felt like an intruder. It snuck up on me, that feeling of belonging. Mostly because I didn't recognize it. Shiloh and her great-grandmother teased each other, finishing each other's sentences and sharing their inside jokes.

Bibi was in the middle of telling me how five-year-old Shiloh once caught a tadpole in the pond up the road and had plans to raise it in the toilet when a hard pounding on the door jolted all of us. The cats darted off the couch and disappeared down the hall.

The warm feeling of belonging evaporated, and for an instant, I had the crazy thought that I'd brought my own bloody past right to the Barreras' doorstep.

Mitch Dowd…

"Sakes alive," Bibi said, her hand on her throat. "Who could that be?"

The pounding came again, and I got up and strode to the door. I threw it open to a bored-looking delivery guy in a brown uniform, a package in his hand.

"I need a signature," he said. "Mrs. Bibi Barrera."

"You gotta pound the door like that?"

"Hey, man, this is my last delivery of the night." He glanced up to see me looming over him and took a step back. "You don't look like a Mrs. Barrera."

"I'm here," Bibi said, pushing me gently aside. "Thank you, Ronan, I got this."

I went back to the table, grabbed my denim jacket, and threw it on. "Thanks for dinner."

Shiloh stood up. "You're leaving? What about the history notes? The paper is due in a week."

"I'll be fine."

"But—"

"I don't need your help, Shiloh," I said and gestured at the remnants of dinner. "I don't need…any of this."

My stomach was full, but the hunger had returned, gnawing with sharp teeth. This wasn't my house. Wasn't my life.

Bibi had returned to the dining table with a package in her hands. "Well! I hope this is worth scaring us out of our wits…" She cocked her head, sensing tension. "Everything all right?"

"Fine," I said, taking the sharp edge out of my tone for her sake. "I'll be back Monday to work on the shed."

I shot a glance at Shiloh. *And that's all.*

Shiloh's soft expression hardened, and she tilted her chin up. "Great," she snapped. As if to say, *fine by me.*

I mumbled more thanks to Bibi and headed out into the night that was cold and dark.

NINE
SHILOH

For the next week, instead of going home where Ronan was working every day in my backyard, I holed up in the school library with my history paper that was due that Friday. I pored over Romanov facts, thoughts of Ronan breaking my concentration every other minute. I wondered—worried—how he was doing on his paper and then reminded myself for the millionth time he didn't want my help.

I made progress, but I felt like a coward. I never hid. I faced things head-on and dealt with them quickly. Always.

Like you do with Mama? a voice whispered.

That was a whole other galaxy of pain. It was unbearable enough that she hated me. Knowing *why* might wreck me altogether. Ronan Wentz, I told myself, was merely a distraction. The best way to deal with him was to…not.

Ronan must've had the same idea. I didn't see him except for history class, and he wasn't talking either. Hell, he barely made eye contact.

Good, I thought, ignoring the twinge in my chest…and the memory of us standing on the sidewalk outside the old laundromat. How his gray eyes weren't hard like stone but soft like smoke as he looked down at me, his gaze lingering on my mouth. Close enough I could smell the campfire scent of him. For a split second, I thought he was going to kiss me. Not just kiss but devour…

Wrong. Sit in your wrongness and be wrong, I told myself, still feeling Ronan's presence all those rows behind me. *No complications. No drama.*

But that damn twinge wouldn't go away all week. It burrowed deeper until it resembled an ache.

On Thursday afternoon, I finished the paper. Not my best work, admittedly. Hopefully a solid B. I drove home around five and parked the Buick in the garage. The much emptier garage. My worktable and all my tools and supplies were gone.

"Bibi?" I called, hurrying in through the kitchen. "I'm home."

"Out here, honeypie," she called from the patio table in the backyard. Behind her was the finished work shed.

I froze, my eyes glued to the simple little shed. Green with white trim, it had double doors and even the window Ronan had shown me in his sketches.

Bibi clapped her hands. "It's incredible, isn't it? Go and see what he did."

Moving slowly, I pulled open the doors. Inside, it smelled of cut wood and fresh paint, clean and new. Ronan had moved my table from the garage and had stacked my plastic supply bins neatly on one side. Shelves lined two walls, and on them sat all my tools. Ronan had spared me countless trips back and forth from the garage.

I ran my hand along one perfect shelf and inhaled deep. I could almost smell the campfire scent of him under the fresh wood and paint. Faint and fading fast.

"Our boy did a marvelous job, didn't he?" Bibi asked when I came back out.

Our boy.

Tears sprang to my eyes.

"Shiloh?"

"It's silly," I said, blinking hard. I did *not* cry. "I'm getting emotional for no reason."

"Not for no reason," Bibi said gently.

I sank into the chair beside her. "It's really perfect and will help me so much. I guess that's why…"

"That must be it," Bibi said, patting my hand.

"Thank you, Bibi." I reached to hug her. "Thank you so much for this."

"You're welcome, honey. I know you're going to make beautiful creations in it. Will we be seeing Ronan anymore now that it's done?" she asked, light as a feather.

"No," I said. "Why would we?"

"Oh, child." She briefly laid her hand on my shoulder, then got up and went inside.

I hugged my elbows, feeling like she'd just passed judgment on me and found me guilty of a crime I didn't commit. Ronan had made it clear—the other night and in class with his stony silence—that he didn't want anything more to do with me. Even if that stung somewhere deep in a place I didn't want to look at, there wasn't anything I could do about it.

I studied the shed, still not believing it was really mine. I was going to work so much better—so much harder—in that space. That was all that mattered.

"Might as well start now."

I got busy organizing everything the way I wanted it. It didn't take long—Ronan had set everything up as if he knew exactly how I'd need it for maximum efficiency. I worked fast in fresh, clean air and sunlight instead of a dark, grungy garage.

By the time I was finished for the day, there was no trace of Ronan left at all.

"Let's have 'em, folks," Mr. Baskin said the next day in history. "Pass your papers to the front of the class."

Violet and I exchanged glances. "I don't have a good feeling about this," she murmured. "This paper was written under extreme duress."

I smiled gently back at her. The entire school was buzzing about how River Whitmore had stood Violet up at the homecoming dance. To add bitter insult to injury, she'd then witnessed Miller in a very NC-17 hookup with Amber Blake.

And I wasn't there for her.

Instead, I'd been wasting my time with Ronan, getting

barbecue, my absurd imagination pretending he'd almost kissed me.

"You got this," I said to Violet. "You write this stuff in your sleep."

Her smile slipped. "If only I could sleep."

The guy behind me tapped my shoulder and handed over the stack from our row. I added my report in its neat folder to the others like it, noticing that one paper was only stapled pages, the edges torn, as if it had been ripped out of a spiral notebook.

Ronan…

I passed the stack forward and bit my lip. Baskin had specifically said the papers had to be typed. Hopefully, he wouldn't notice today. Maybe he'd only dock Ronan a few points. Maybe it wasn't his at all…

Baskin shuffled through the stack, his brow furrowed behind his thick glasses. He held the handwritten report and squinted at it.

"Ronan Wentz." He peered over the class until he found him in my row, last seat. "I specified more than once that this paper must be typed."

My skin heated with anger that he'd call Ronan out like this. The rest of the class was turning to look. I kept my gaze forward, unwilling to add to his embarrassment.

"Mr. Wentz? Do you have a response?"

"I don't have a computer," Ronan said, his voice low, and in that moment, I hated Baskin.

"That's what the school library is for," Baskin said. "There is no excuse for not completing the paper as specified." He walked down the aisle past me to Ronan and dropped his paper on his desk. "I'm going to give you a chance to remedy the situation. Get this typed up and returned to me. I'll dock you one half-letter grade for every day it's late."

"Today's Friday," Ronan said.

"Then it had better start out as an A paper."

Baskin resumed the day's lesson, but I could hardly concentrate. When the bell rang, the class poured outside and dispersed. I lingered by the door.

"Heading home?" Violet asked.

"Um, not yet. Call me this weekend?"

"Sure."

I gave a handful of braids a tug in frustration. My best friend was walking away alone because I was waiting for a *guy*. I was about to come to my senses and chase after Violet when Ronan exited the classroom, his expression stormy. Baskin probably kept him in to berate him more for not being prepared.

Ronan didn't look up at me but strode fast down the walk, head down.

"Hey," I said, falling in step with him. I practically had to jog to keep up.

Ronan grunted in greeting.

"What Baskin did is utter bullshit."

"He's right. It was supposed to be typed."

"But he didn't have to call you out in front of the whole class. Let's go to the library. Right now."

"What for?"

"We'll get your paper typed up and get it in Baskin's box before he leaves today."

"It won't work."

"Why?"

"Because I can't type that fast." He looked out over the campus, anywhere but at me. "It's fucking embarrassing but...I've never had a laptop or computer. Never stayed one place long enough to learn."

That's what he said, but what I heard was that surviving ten years of foster care had taken up his time and energy. The ache in my chest deepened.

"I'll type it for you."

"Why would you do that for me?" he asked, suspicion hard in his tone.

Because I want to.

And because Ronan made a promise to someone to get through this year. But I knew he wouldn't accept either answer. He'd think it was charity, and he'd already been embarrassed enough for one day.

"To thank you for the shed. It's beyond perfect."

"Bibi thanked me. That's what the money was for."

"That was from her. This is from me." I gave the cuff of his denim jacket a tug. "We don't have much time. If we're going to beat Baskin at his own dickish game, we have to move fast."

Ronan hesitated a moment more, then nodded. "I guess."

"Try to contain your enthusiasm," I said with a grin. "This will work."

We hurried to the library, and I jumped on one of the computers while Ronan stood stiffly behind me, arms crossed tight.

"Paper," I said, holding out my hand like a surgeon asking for a scalpel.

Ronan pulled the paper from his backpack. "Fuck it," he muttered, then handed it over.

The first thing that shocked me was how long it was. More than the ten pages Baskin required.

Worse, it was really damn good.

Damn it. Ronan looks like he does, and he's smart as hell. I'm being tested. The universe is testing me.

As I typed, Ronan's intelligence came through loud and clear, though in an understated way. Simple but powerful sentences. His empathy for the nearly fourteen hundred people who died in a stampede thanks to poor planning bled through too. It was more than a paper on a tragic event but a convincing argument that Nicholas II's time as emperor was doomed from the start.

"How did you get so fast?" Ronan asked after a few minutes.

"Practice," I said, eyes on his paper while my fingers flew. "I don't like things that slow me down."

He made a sound that might've been a chuckle. "I guess not."

For the next ten minutes, I typed as fast as I could,

conscious that the clock was ticking and that Ronan was behind me, relying on me to help save his grade.

"What's this say?" I asked, holding up the paper where his pen ink had smudged a word.

"*Commemorative*," he said. He rubbed the back of his neck self-consciously. "Shiloh…you don't have to do this. It's not worth it."

"Yes, it is," I said. "Your spelling could use work, and your commas are a disaster, but the paper itself is really damn good. And if Baskin can't see that, he's an asshole."

"But…"

"Hush. I'm working."

Ronan snorted a small laugh, and twenty minutes later, I was done. I hit Print, and we dashed from the library to the admin building.

Inside, office staff were at their desks or talking in small groups. We hurried to Ms. Oliveri, the front desk administrator.

"Is Mr. Baskin still here?"

"I'm afraid not. He's gone for the day."

"Shit."

Ms. Oliveri arched a brow.

"Come on, Shiloh," Ronan said. "Let's go."

"Never give up. Never surrender." I looked at Ms. Oliveri. "How long ago did he leave?"

"Not long. A few minutes—"

"Parking lot," I said and grabbed Ronan's hand. It was large and strong, calloused from work…like my shed. I tugged him outside the admin building and was still holding his hand as we reached the faculty parking lot.

"Oh, sorry." I let go quickly and gave him the paper instead. We scanned the lot. "There."

Baskin was just unlocking the door to his brown Hyundai, juggling keys, a portfolio, and a coffee thermos.

"Mr. Baskin! Wait!"

He watched us approach, a frown under his mustache. Ronan offered the paper to Baskin, who took it with narrowed eyes, his gaze taking in Ronan's worn-out jacket and the tattoo peeking from under the sleeve. He scanned the pages; the more he read, the more the stern lines in his face softened. He glanced up, unable to keep how impressed he was off his face. Then his judgy frown returned.

"How much help did you give Mr. Wentz?"

"No help. I typed it. A little proofing. That's it."

"I wrote it," Ronan stated.

Baskin's eyes narrowed again. "Plagiarism is a very serious offense, Mr. Wentz."

I gaped. "He didn't…"

"*I* wrote it," Ronan repeated.

Baskin pursed his lips. "Teachers have methods of knowing if that's true or not." He tucked the paper under his arm. "I'll see you both on Monday, unless there's anything else?"

"Nothing else," I said tightly.

Baskin shot us a final dubious glance. We stepped back, and he drove away.

"What an asshole," I burst out when he was gone. "That paper is excellent. It's smart and strong and…deep. It's one hundred percent *you*." I felt Ronan's eyes on me and realized what I'd said. A flush of heat burned my cheeks. "I mean… anyway, whatever, we did it."

"You did it," Ronan said. He was looking at me like he had the other night, and the parking lot—the entire planet—suddenly felt very empty. Just him and me…

"It was nothing," I said.

"You probably saved my grade. That means a lot."

The moment caught and held. Me, who planned and prepared to the nth degree, had no clue what was going to happen next. The feeling was woozy and exhilarating at the same time. And completely unacceptable. I was getting in too deep. Too invested in whether this guy passed history.

Too invested, period.

"I gotta go," I blurted. "Lots of work."

Ronan stiffened. "Yeah, me too."

We both turned and went our separate ways, from being alone together to just being alone.

Monday afternoon, Violet was absent from history. She'd texted me that she'd been up late studying for the SAT and AP tests. But I knew she was hurting to have to go to school and see Miller holding hands with Amber Blake.

Like a knife in my heart, said her text.

I wished I had something to say to make her feel better, but my own heart was twisted in knots, and talking to Violet about my feelings felt silly compared to everything she was dealing with.

In class, Baskin passed back our Russian Revolution papers. Mine had an A-minus in red ink on the cover page.

"All in all, I'm very impressed," Baskin said, almost grudgingly. "Some of you picked *interesting* topics indeed." He seemed to look at Ronan when he said this.

I itched to know what grade Ronan had received. Not because I cared all that much, I told myself. But to make sure my efforts hadn't been in vain.

After class, I waited outside. "Well?"

"B-minus," Ronan said.

"*What?* That's bullshit. Your paper was better than mine."

"I passed. Thanks to you."

"Nah, I told you. It was nothing."

"It wasn't nothing. I appreciate it. A lot." His gray eyes met mine. "Thank you."

I started to make a joke—my usual defense. Instead, I said softly, "You're welcome."

Ronan glanced around and rubbed the back of his neck like he was nervous. It was a strange look on him…and sweet.

"So listen, I was thinking. There's this place…"

I held perfectly still, my pulse counting down the seconds until his next words.

"It's on the beach. Out of the way, right where the cliffs come down. Miller, Holden, and I hang out there a lot after school and on weekends. Make bonfires, shoot the shit, drink beer."

"Okay…"

"So maybe…if you wanted to come and hang out with us sometime, you could. If you wanted."

"You want me to…" My stomach and heart both felt like foreign objects, fluttering with butterflies and beating faster in ways they'd never done with a guy. I struggled to keep my tone casual. "You're inviting me to the secret hideout of the infamous Lost Boys?"

"Basically." He looked to the ground, then back to me. "So…you want to?"

Yes!

The thought was so loud, he must've heard it. But it was drowned in the sirens and alarms going off, the ones that blared I was already getting too close. And how hurt Violet would be.

"Miller would be there?"

"Of course."

"Then I can't. Violet's my best friend."

Ronan frowned. "So?"

"So she and Miller are barely speaking." I shook my head, disappointment biting hard. "The girl he hooked up with the night of the dance is a friend too. It's all a big mess, and I… I can't go. I can't do that to Violet."

"I get that." He rubbed his chin; his boot scraped the

ground. "Yeah, maybe it's better anyway… Okay. See you around."

"Oh, wow…okay," I said as he walked away without another word. "I guess that's that." The sudden end of our weird acquaintance or friendship or whatever it was between us.

Nothing. There is nothing between us.

I watched Ronan blend in with the students at school and disappear.

"I'm better off," I said out loud, ignoring the pang in my heart that told me that was a lie.

TEN
RONAN

Thanksgiving Day, there was a knock on my door. I opened it to Maryann and the twins. The girls pushed past their mom's legs and hugged me.

"Ronan!"

"Hi, Ronan!"

"Look what we made!"

Lily and Cami hustled me away from the door, excitedly holding up Thanksgiving turkeys made out of brown construction paper, traced from their own little hands. Each finger was a colorful feather, with googly eyes glued to the thumb.

"We made these in class," Cami said proudly.

Lily nodded. "We got to do arts and crafts and eat popcorn instead of do math."

I smiled. Over the past few weeks, I'd learned to see the difference in the twins after spending more time with them. Like when I went down to replace the batteries in their smoke detector or when they came up to visit me for no reason at all. Separately, it was difficult to tell them apart, but together, it was easy to see the differences in the girls' faces. Their mom, of course, knew who was who without a glance.

Maryann gave me a small smile and a shrug as she shut the door behind her. "I hope we're not bothering you. They've been talking all morning about when they could come over."

"They never bother me," I said. Just the opposite. I'd babysit if Maryann ever needed me but never offered. Didn't want to come across as a perv. I just liked having them around.

The girls pressed their paper turkeys at me.

"They're for you!" Lily said, and Cami nodded vigorously.

"For me?" My damn throat felt tight. The papers felt small and light in my big hands.

"Because today is Thanksgiving," Cami said. "We're going to Auntie Colleen's house for a big dinner."

"You can come with us," Lily said. "If you want."

I went to the kitchen and rummaged in a drawer for a roll of Scotch tape. "That's nice of you, Lil, but I'm going somewhere already."

"You are?" Maryann asked sharply. "Where? If you don't mind me asking."

I smirked. If Maryann was going to ask a question, she asked it.

"I'm going to Nelson's," I said, taping the turkeys to my refrigerator door. "He's my uncle," I told the girls.

Cami made a face. "We know."

Lily wore the same sour expression. "Mommy says he's a son of a bitch."

"Lillian Angela Greer!" Maryann cried. She shook her head at me, her eyes wide. "I'm sorry. I never…"

I chuckled. "It's all right." I sat on my heels in front of the girls. "Your mom's right, but don't say those words in front of him."

"Why not?"

"It's not polite," Maryann interjected.

"And they're bad words," Cami added.

"Right. And they're magic words," I said. "If you say them to his face, he might turn into an ogre."

The girls' eyes were wide. "Really?"

I nodded. "That's why grown-ups never want kids to say bad words in front of other grown-ups. You never know if it'll turn them into a monster."

"How do you know so much about it?" Cami asked, the skeptic of the two. "Have you seen a monster?"

"I sure have." I felt Maryann's eyes on me and gestured at the turkeys on my fridge. "What do you think? Do they look good there?"

"Your fridge needed them," Cami said seriously. "There's nothing on it."

Lily agreed. "Our fridge is covered in our artwork and when we do good on a project."

"Do *well*," Maryann corrected gently. She stood between the girls, stroking their hair. "So you're having dinner with your uncle?"

I stood up. "Heading over at two."

That, at least, wasn't a lie. It was true I was going to visit Nelson but only because he needed me to drop off some invoices from a plumber we'd hired last week.

"That's great," Maryann said. "Hold on a sec."

She hurried out, leaving the girls with me. It wasn't too cold of a day; I was wearing a T-shirt, showing my tattoos—their favorite subject. They never got tired of looking at them.

"That looks ouchy," Lily said of the dagger tattoo on my left arm.

"The clock says 10:05," Cami said, inspecting the sleeve on my right. "We're learning about time in class."

"What happened at 10:05?" Lily asked.

She was pronounced dead. Right there in the kitchen. Because I couldn't stop the monster…

"When I was a kid in school, we had recess at 10:05," I said. "That was my favorite time of day."

"Then you could go out and play with your friends?" Cami asked.

"Yep. Exactly."

"That's my favorite time too," Lily said.

Maryann returned holding a box from a local bakery I passed on my walk to Central every day when I wasn't suspended or working odd jobs.

"For you and Mr. Wentz." She set the box in my hand. "Surprise! It's pumpkin."

"That's the pie we were going to bring to Auntie's!" Cami said.

"You said our job was to bring the dessert," Lily added.

I started to hand the box back. "I can't take this."

Maryann stopped me. "Yes, you can. I'm trying to imagine the feast two bachelors may have cooked up." She smiled softly, though her forehead was creased in worry. "Please."

"What about Auntie Colleen?" Lily asked.

Cami nodded. "She's going to be *pissed*."

I shot Maryann a look. "Yeah, what about Auntie Colleen? She's going to be pissed."

The girls busted up, giggling.

Maryann smirked and rolled her eyes. "We'll stop at the store and pick up something else," she told her daughters. "Tell Ronan bye-bye."

Again, I was surrounded, two pairs of little arms hugging me around the waist. I didn't know what it was with those girls and hugging.

"Bye, Ronan!"

"Byeeee!"

"Thanks for the turkeys," I said, then to Maryann, "and the pie."

She smiled. "Happy Thanksgiving, Ronan."

They left and, as usual, my place felt a little darker and emptier. At quarter to two, I grabbed the invoices and the pie and waited for the bus. The complex Nelson managed—the

Bluffs—was at the very edge of my walking range and in an even worse neighborhood than where Miller and I lived.

The iron railings were rusted, and cages covered every lower window. The entire complex was painted a dark green not long ago. Nelson said it cost him a "pretty penny," but why spend the money fixing the cracks when you could cover them with paint?

My uncle's place was on the lower level, corner unit. I knocked and waited. A kid on a tricycle pedaled in circles in the cracked and pitted parking lot, watching me.

"Yeah?" Nelson called from inside.

"It's me."

"Come in."

His apartment was larger than mine but seemed smaller. Stacks of newspapers, garbage bags filled with God knew what, and piles of old clothes were heaped all over. Not quite ready for *Hoarders* but getting there.

My uncle was watching football from a dark-green upholstered chair that matched the building's exterior. Slashes of yellow stuffing puffed out where the old fake leather had dried up and split. A TV tray table sat beside him with three empty beer bottles and an ashtray overflowing with pistachio shells. He had the footrest on the chair kicked up; the carpet beneath—a ruddy-orange shag—was littered with more shells, more newspapers, and empty soda bottles. The entire place reeked of solitude. The kind that has settled so deep, you don't care anymore who sees your place, even when it looks like shit.

"Here are the invoices," I said. "And pie."

"Toss 'em on the table."

The kitchen table was just as bad, covered in fast-food wrappers, a month's worth of junk mail, and coupons cut out of mailers. I cleared a space and set the pie and invoices down, wondering if they'd get lost in the sea of crap and not get paid.

"Have a seat," Nelson said.

The only other chair in the living space was an old throwaway he'd salvaged from the curb. It had once been white. I sat on the very edge, resting my elbows on my thighs.

"Our team's playing," Nelson said. "Green Bay versus Dallas. Packers up by ten."

"Sweet."

We watched the game for a few minutes. The place smelled of sour sweat and old beer. I wanted to get the fuck out of there yet couldn't stand the thought of leaving him alone.

"You're doing a good job with the building," he said after a minute.

"Thanks."

"The tenants like you."

I nodded.

"That's fine so long as they don't walk all over you."

"They don't," I said, thinking of Maryann's twins. *They climb all over me.*

"Good. See that they don't."

"The Cliffside building needs a new roof," I said slowly.

Nelson let out a shout. "There it is! First down, hot damn."

"Nelson..."

"I heard you. I'll think about it."

I left it alone. That was more than I expected.

The game went to commercials, and Nelson looked at me for the first time. "Did you say you brought pie?"

"Yeah. A gift from one of the tenants. Maryann Greer."

"For me?"

I nodded.

His lips pursed and he *hmphed*. "Go figure. Well, I got two turkey dinners. You may as well stay. Since you're here."

I nodded, stunned. "Two dinners?"

"They're in the freezer," he said, his eyes on the TV. "Beer's in the fridge."

The freezer was frosted over, but I pried two dinners from the white cave. Sliced turkey, peas, mashed potatoes and gravy, and a square of some kind of dessert that looked like it might've been an apple tart.

Each one took eight minutes to cook. While Nelson's was rotating in the microwave, I cleaned up a little. I found cheap plastic plates in a cabinet and put the meals on them—minus the apple shit—so they wouldn't look like TV dinners but more like real food. I grabbed silverware and two beers from the fridge. Nelson had cleaned off his TV tray and showed me where a second one lay folded against the wall.

We sat with our food in front of us and watched the game, neither saying much except to talk stats and Green Bay's prospects for the rest of the season.

"I may live in Cali, but Wisconsin's in my blood," he said.

"Yeah," I said, thinking of my dad. *Mine too.*

After we ate, I cleared our plates and cleaned up until the counters and kitchen table looked a little better. A little more normal. I served up the bakery-fresh pumpkin pie.

"This is good stuff," Nelson said, forking a bite. "Not bad, right?"

I thought about Miller and Holden, my friends I was going to meet later tonight at the shack.

I thought about how things were okay in my classes. Not failing any at least. Frankie Dowd still gave me the stink eye, but it seemed like the score had been settled.

I thought about Shiloh Barrera.

We'd only spoken a handful of words since I'd asked her to come to the shack. As close as I'd get to asking her out. Another moment of weakness. I'd had a hundred around her, always saying yes—to barbecue or help on a paper—when I should've been saying no.

Shiloh said no.

The right answer. You shouldn't have fucking asked at all.

Now we only saw each other coming or going in history. She'd whisper with Violet, glancing at me sometimes as if I were vaguely familiar. Someone she used to know.

The nameless hunger in me grew sharp teeth then, but it was still my favorite part of the day.

And I thought about Shiloh with her grandmother, probably sitting down to their own Thanksgiving dinner at that moment. Safe. Happy.

"No," I said to my uncle. "Not bad at all."

That night, after hanging with Holden and Miller at the shack, I had a small hope that the nightmares wouldn't come. Because being with my friends was always good, and dinner with Nelson hadn't been half bad.

I was wrong.

I woke to my own ragged screams tearing out of my throat, to the bloody kitchen in Manitowoc slowly fading to the dark of my empty apartment in Santa Cruz.

"*Fuck.*"

I tore the covers off and sat on the edge of my bed, holding my head in my hands. My heart pounding, blood rushing in my ears, blood staining the floor…

The cheap clock radio said it was a little after 3:00 a.m. I gave up on sleep for the rest of the night, dressed, and headed out. After months of walking, I had a route now. Maryann first. I paused at her unit, listening. All quiet. The door closed and locked, I hoped.

Then I set off for Miller's complex. All the windows were dark. Quiet. No trouble out of his mom's boyfriend.

Next, I walked to the Bluffs, back to Nelson's place. The TV was still on, droning through the open windows. I imagined he'd fallen asleep in the same chair where we'd eaten our version of Thanksgiving dinner hours before.

I kept walking.

No matter how hard I tried to pry it out of Holden, he wouldn't tell Miller or me where he lived, so I didn't have him on my route. Probably up in the Heights where the rich people were and too far from my shitty neighborhood. I'd still have walked it.

But Shiloh…

Her and Bibi's house was in between my place and Central. In ten minutes, I was in her tree-lined neighborhood of small one-story cottages. Had to be careful here; if there was a neighborhood watch, I'd get busted, easy. No one would believe me if I told them what I was doing there. Or why.

The Barreras' house was quiet and dark. Secure. No one suspicious or threatening out on the street.

Except for me.

I made the rounds three times—between Nelson, Maryann, Miller, and Shiloh—until dawn broke in the east behind the forested mountains. Then I returned to my complex and checked on Maryann once more before heading upstairs. I didn't bother to change out of my clothes; I'd only get an hour or two of sleep if I were lucky.

I lay down in my bed, exhausted, and closed my eyes.

They're all safe, Mom, I thought, and only then did sleep come.

Black, merciful nothing.

ELEVEN
RONAN

The sky darkened with rain as I walked home from Central on the Monday after Thanksgiving. I wasn't far from the school when the first droplets fell, and all I had was my denim jacket.

"Shit."

I walked faster, and then I heard it. The groaning, creaking sounds of a car that had a huge engine but no horsepower. I bit back a smile as Shiloh's pale-green boat pulled up alongside me, the passenger side window already cranked down.

Shiloh gave me a look, eyebrows raised. "In about ten seconds, it's going to get bad."

The sky rumbled as if to prove her right.

She rolled her eyes at my hesitation. "Will you get in already? Otherwise, this time, it'll be Bibi thinking I'm an asshole for letting you get pneumonia."

I ignored the warm feeling in my chest and climbed in.

"That wasn't so hard, was it?" Shiloh asked, shooting me a dry look. "You can even make fun of the Buick if it makes you feel better."

"No need," I said. "It speaks for itself."

"Oh my God..." She socked me on the shoulder with an incredulous laugh.

I chuckled too. I couldn't help it; it felt too good to be in this girl's space, inhaling the same air. She smelled like flowers and rain and was so damn beautiful...

I shouldn't be here, and I can't fucking say no.

"So..." Shiloh wasn't driving yet. We sat in the quiet car, watching the rain come down on the other side of the windshield. "It's been a while. How was your Thanksgiving?"

"Good," I said. "Yours?"

"Good."

A silence fell.

She huffed a sigh. "Well, that was riveting."

"Shiloh—"

"You want to go somewhere with me?" she blurted suddenly.

Christ, no one took me off guard like Shiloh. Fucking no one. "Where?"

"I don't know. I feel restless. Unsettled. Craving... something." Her gaze darted to me and then quickly turned away. "I want a doughnut."

"A doughnut."

"Yes. Suddenly, I'm in desperate need of a doughnut. I know a great place. The best in Santa Cruz."

Say no. Say no. Say fucking no.

"Sure."

Shiloh drove us to a street filled with coffee shops, a burger joint that kids from school liked to hang out in, and Bob's Doughnuts. The rain had become a drizzle as she found street parking a block away in a space big enough to dock the Buick.

She shot me a warning look.

I held up my hands. "I didn't say anything."

She narrowed her eyes, and I chuckled again.

"You're like this kid I knew in kindergarten," I said. "He used to tattle on me for 'thinking bad thoughts about him.'"

"I'm going to tattle on you to Bibi for all your Buick slander, spoken or otherwise."

She gave me a last knowing smirk and climbed out of the car. We hurried along sidewalks slick with new rain. Clean.

The doughnut shop consisted of one giant display, a coffee station, and a handful of grimy little booths, all of which were empty.

"There's no Bob," Shiloh said, leaning in to me as we waited in line behind the only other customer. She pointed to the squat, dark-haired guy behind the counter. "That's Francisco, the owner. He's always in a bad mood and will disappear in the back if you take too long deciding what you want. I love him ever so much."

"Next," Francisco barked.

"Powdered jelly, please," Shiloh said.

Francisco jerked his chin at me. "You?"

"Chocolate bar," I said and glanced down at Shiloh. "Coffee?"

She reached for her bag. "Sure, but let me—"

"I got this," I said, my tone final.

A small smile spread over her lips. "So this is *next time*."

"Yeah, it is," I said, glancing down at her. She was small and slender; I towered over her, sheltering her. And now I was paying for her food. Taking care of her. It wasn't much, but the moment felt big. And maybe she felt it too. The way she was gazing up at me…

Something's happening.

Except that wasn't true. Something had been happening since that first afternoon in her backyard.

"You want coffee or not?" Francisco demanded, inching toward the back room.

"Two coffees," I said.

I paid cash, and Francisco handed us the doughnuts in a paper bag and two coffee cups and nodded in the direction of the coffee station.

Shiloh and I sat in a booth as the rain picked up. I watched her take a bite of her jelly doughnut, powdering her lips with sugar. She started to take another one but stopped and stared, looking almost angry as I took a bite of my chocolate bar.

"What did I do now?"

"*That*," she said, flapping her hand at my doughnut.

"I'm eating."

"Yes, exactly. You're eating. With that mouth of yours."

"What's wrong with my mouth?"

"Absolutely nothing. That's the problem. Your lips should be illegal." She huffed a sigh. "Look, I'm going to be blunt, because being wishy-washy just isn't my style. I don't peddle bullshit to anyone, least of all myself."

"Okay." I reached for my coffee. "This allowed?"

She made a frustrated sound that was cute as fuck. "I'm being serious."

"So am I."

"You're too damn cheery—your version of cheery—when I'm trying to spill my guts to you."

My smile fell, and the levity between us collapsed. "Don't, Shiloh."

"You don't know what I'm going to say."

"I know but…" I muttered into my coffee, "This was a mistake."

"Yes, exactly!" she said. "It's one hundred percent a mistake, yet it keeps happening. And for weeks, nothing happened, and that was even worse. Not…seeing you. Or talking to you."

I nodded. "I know."

She inhaled, then let it out. "I miss you."

The words hit me hard, then sank in, because they were the last thing I'd expected a girl like Shiloh to say to someone like me.

"I mean…I miss hanging out with you," she added quickly. "Even though you're stubborn and surly and frustrating as hell. For some crazy reason, I haven't been able to stop thinking about you. And maybe it's simple hormones because you look like…how you look. I'm honest enough to admit that there could be some plain, old-fashioned sexual attraction going on here."

I sat back in the seat, my blood heating. I took a sip of coffee, not tasting it.

"I feel like I'm playing Ping-Pong with myself," Shiloh continued. "I go back and forth, wanting to keep my distance, focus on my work, because I don't do drama or messy relationships or *feelings*. But then something happens, and suddenly I'm asking you over to dinner or out for doughnuts. Do you see where I'm coming from?"

I nodded.

She glanced down at her food, toyed with her napkin. "So…am I alone in this? Am I crazy?"

"No," I said quietly. "You're not crazy."

Her head whipped up, and that feeling came back—of something deep passing between us.

"Well," she said, swallowing hard. "What do we do?"

"I don't know, Shiloh."

She leaned in, her deep brown eyes intent on me. "I'm going to need more than that, Ronan."

"I don't have more than that. Nothing to offer." She started to protest, and I talked over her. "I'm not like everyone else, Shiloh."

I'm not normal.

"I know," she said softly. "That's why I'm here, sitting

across from you, instead of at my beautiful workspace—that *you* built—working on my future."

"No, you don't get it," I said. "Shit happened in Wisconsin, and it fucked me up pretty bad. It's just better for you…to not have to deal with it. The repercussions."

"What repercussions?"

Nightmares, fights, the anger that's the same as his…

When I didn't answer, Shiloh looked unsure of herself, uncharacteristically vulnerable. She tore little pieces off her napkin, not meeting my eyes.

"I kind of put myself out there just now," she said. "I never do that."

"I know."

"You asked me to hang out with you at the shack."

"I shouldn't have. Sometimes I forget who I am." She raised her eyes to mine. I shook my head slowly. "You don't want to know. Believe me."

"But I do, and that's entirely my problem," she said. "I pride myself on being levelheaded, and instead I'm…"

Perfect. You're fucking perfect.

But I couldn't say that to her. She didn't need to hear it from me but someone better. Someone who could give her everything she deserved. And my silence sealed the deal.

"Fine." She took a last bite of her doughnut and a swig of coffee. "Let's go."

Frustration and longing—that hunger—roared. I wanted to grab her, haul her to me, and kiss her. Drown in her. Pretend for a second I was in another life. One where I wasn't fucked up. Where my mom was still alive because my dad hadn't fucking *murdered* her, staining my every waking thought with blood. Where I didn't see it happen every time I closed my eyes. Where I didn't feel the heat of his rage burning in me and the fear whispering I was just like him. Where I didn't walk all over town in the middle of the night to make sure the people I cared about were safe. A pitiful penance that would never be enough. Never bring her back.

Shiloh would think I was a psycho if I told her all that.

Better to let her go. Keep her safe.

I followed Shiloh out of the shop, but the rain was coming down hard now. She ducked under the shallow awning.

"Shit."

I slipped off my jacket and held it over her, keeping her dry while the rain pelted me.

Shiloh's expression softened, and then her eyes darkened, her gaze moving over my face, watching the trails of water.

"Here we are," she said. "Again."

I nodded absently, not hearing her, because her lower lip was dusted with powdered sugar. "You have something…"

"Yes?" She inclined her head, defiant of her own protections she kept up at all times. Except with me.

I leaned in, entering the shelter of the jacket. Shiloh made fists in my T-shirt, drawing me against her, her eyes locked on mine, daring me. Our mouths inches apart, our noses bumping, I angled my head left, then right, savoring the moment before I took what I shouldn't have.

"Ronan," she breathed and then whimpered as my tongue swiped the sugar from her lip.

Oh fuck.

One small taste, and I was already fucking gone. A short inhale, a heartbeat, was all that stood between right and wrong. And suddenly, I didn't give a shit. There was only her.

My hand snaked up into her hair and grabbed a fistful of braids as I crashed my mouth to hers.

TWELVE

SHILOH

I froze as the first sensations found me, and then I melted.

Ronan's kiss infiltrated my mouth with a taste that was so purely masculine and perfect, it stole my breath and lit up my insides with a fire I'd never felt before. The want I'd been suppressing since the moment we met awakened, impossible to deny anymore. Like trying to hold back a tidal wave.

I gave in.

I moaned softly into his kiss, letting him take my mouth. Letting him shield me with his strong body against the cold and the rain. I surrendered to his hands, his lips, his biting teeth. Kissing Ronan was everything I thought it would be and nothing I expected. Rough and raw but with a strange softness beneath. Reverence. He plundered my mouth with hard, needy possession, but I felt worshipped at the same time.

His. I'm his.

But I was no one's. I belonged to myself, yet suddenly there I was on that street, daring myself to throw my grand plan into the fire and burn with Ronan Wentz.

My hands surged into his damp hair, along his back, taking their fill as he pressed closer. Damn, the power in him… I felt every hum and vibration in his body, tense with want but holding back. His hand in my hair tightened, and the lick of pain was enough to elicit another moan. I gripped him around the waist, wanting him on me and over me.

Inside me. I want him inside me.

"Oh God," I breathed and wrenched myself away from Ronan, coming back to myself and where we were. "Not here."

"Where?" Ronan said gruffly. "You want to go somewhere and…"

Do anything. Everything. Last summer with Jalen had felt like ticking off a box on my to-do list. A job that needed doing. I was going to start a business right after graduation and wanted to jump into adulthood with both feet, nothing left in my way.

But kissing Ronan Wentz felt monumental. A seismic shift in my carefully constructed world that made my rules and protections feel flimsy and weak.

Ronan was pressed against me, waiting for me to tell him what came next, breathing hard, his eyes dark and dilated. The rain slid in rivulets down his cheekbones, down the sharp cut of his jaw, droplets falling from his lips… Then his gaze flickered to something down the street, and he pulled abruptly away from me.

"Let's go."

His sudden, cold tone felt like the rain, dousing the heat between us. He kept his jacket over me as we hurried to my car, but I got the impression it was more to hide me than to keep me dry.

We climbed in the Buick, me behind the wheel and him in the passenger seat. He glanced around, water dripping on the white upholstery.

"What was that?"

"Nothing," he said. "Let's just go."

Ronan gave the address of his place, and I drove us in silence to the complex near the Cliffs, not far from my house.

"Which is yours?"

"Upper left."

"Can I see it?"

"No."

The word dropped, final and hard. Humiliating. Like a cold slap to the face after the perfect heat of his mouth on mine. Worse, my heart ached as if it had been slapped too. Hard.

That's it. I'm done making a fool of myself.

"Fine," I snapped. "See you around some—"

The words were stolen from my mouth as Ronan closed the space between us and kissed me again. With both hands, I shoved him back, ready to spit fire. But in the space of one heartbeat, I fell into the smoky haze of his eyes, and in the next, I was straddling him on the seat and bending my mouth to his.

Damn him.

He leaned back against the seat, bringing me with him and kissing me deeply now, languidly, his tongue tasting every corner, indulgent and slow. My arms wrapped around his neck, my hands in his hair, cradling his head as we kissed, savoring the taste and touch and wet heat of his mouth.

Finally, I came up for air. I traced the line of his cheekbone, down to his cheek, to his full lips. Taking my time, examining every inch of that face that interrupted my minutes, and gazing into those gray eyes that were miles deep.

Don't fall in, a tiny warning voice whispered, then was burned up in the small space between Ronan and me, in the car that was humid and hot.

"Put your hands on me," I breathed.

His eyes widened and then darkened again. His hands that had been resting on my thighs slid up the loose linen, up to my waist, higher. With a feral grunt, his kiss turned raw and savage. His hands went under my sweater, found my breasts over my bra, cupping them and pinching my nipples while his mouth moved down my neck, leaving biting kisses that set fire to my skin.

Beneath me, I felt the iron hardness of his erection pressing through his jeans against the soft material of my pants. I ground down on him, and he answered by sliding his hands to my hips and doing it again. Moving me on him.

"My God," I whispered, my head falling back. Ready to give him everything.

Then Ronan froze. He wrenched his mouth from my neck, his eyes on the street through the windshield behind me.

"What?"

I heard the squeal of tires and turned in time to see a flash of a white car swerve around and drive away.

"What was that?" I asked.

Ronan didn't seem to hear me. "I'm so stupid," he said, his voice heavy. "So fucking stupid…"

His words trailed, and he gently but firmly removed me from his lap and pushed me away.

I blinked, still feeling him everywhere, my mouth swollen and raw from his kisses, my body aching from his sudden absence.

"I can't do this. We can't do this. *Fuck.*" He carved a hand through his hair. "I'm sorry, Shiloh," he said, his tone gritty.

"What? Why? What is happening right now?"

But Ronan was already reaching for the door. "I'm sorry," he said again. "I'm so fucking sorry."

Feeling as if I were in a bad dream, I watched Ronan get out of the car, shut the door, and walk heavily to the shabby complex without looking back. He went up the stairs to the corner unit and vanished inside.

The rain came down steadily, the windshield fogged from our kisses. It was reminiscent of Mama's cigarette smoke. The gaping pit in my stomach reminded me why I didn't let anyone get close. Because of *that* feeling. That hollow, hopeless feeling of sitting alone and watching a door close between me and what I wanted.

Stop it. It was only a kiss.

Except it didn't feel like *only* anything.

Tears blurred my vision. Or maybe it was the rain. Because I didn't cry. Not over a guy. Not over anything.

I turned on the windshield wipers and drove away.

THIRTEEN
RONAN

"Fuck me," I muttered and slammed my door shut behind me. I crossed to the kitchen in two steps and grabbed a bottle of beer from the nearly empty fridge.

I could still taste Shiloh—the sweetness of sugar and strawberries and her own clean warmth beneath. Kissing her was better than I'd imagined. My entire body had woken up, wanting her so goddamn bad I could hardly keep my hands from tearing at her clothes. To get at more of her skin, the heat of her…

I bit out a curse and took a long swallow of beer.

They followed us.

Outside the doughnut shop, it was Frankie Dowd and Mikey Grimaldi I'd seen leaning on Mikey's white Jeep Rubicon parked in front of the burger joint. They'd nudged each other, watching us, smiling in a way I didn't like. With an agenda. And then they did a drive-by as Shiloh and I went at each other in her car.

"Because they fucking followed us."

If it were only Frankie and Mikey, I wouldn't have given a shit. I could beat their asses one at a time or both together. But Mitch…

This is who you are. The criminal.

Outside my apartment, I heard a metallic scrape and footsteps. I strode over and threw open the door, ready to go, Mitch Dowd or not. Instead, I scared the shit out of Louis Maroney from 2F. The wiry, middle-aged guy shrank at my menacing glare.

"Rain's pretty bad. There's a leak in my ceiling, so I was putting in a maintenance request." He nodded at the metal box affixed to my door. "But it can wait."

"No, it can't," I said. "I'll handle it."

"Thanks. Uh, thank you," he said and practically ran back to his apartment.

He was right; the rain was coming down hard now, but I needed to wash Shiloh off me. Kissing her had been a mistake. Taking what wasn't mine in one reckless, selfish moment.

She wanted you too, I thought, remembering how she'd silently dared me to kiss the sugar off her mouth. How she'd been in the car, straddling me, grinding against me…

Didn't matter. Frankie's knowing sneer reminded me who I was. What I could bring right to her doorstep.

I threw on a cheap rain jacket and went to the locked shed out back. I found a few decent pieces of plywood among the rough materials Uncle Nelson salvaged from other jobs. I grabbed nails and a hammer and set the tall ladder against the side of the building.

The rain was relentless and showing no signs of stopping. I climbed up one-handed and hurled the plywood onto the roof ahead of me.

In one of the better foster homes I stayed at when I was a kid, we watched movies on Friday night. *Forrest Gump* was Janet—the mom's—favorite. I trudged across the roof, stepping over broken or missing shingles, the wind and rain buffeting me, and thought of Lieutenant Dan in that movie. How he'd dared God to finish him off during the storm that battered Forrest's shrimp boat. Because he'd lost everything.

"Go ahead," I muttered under my breath as I struggled over the slick shingles beneath my boots. "I fucking dare you."

I found the hole over Louis's apartment. I knelt on the roof that was mostly flat and sealed the opening. It looked like shit and probably wouldn't do the trick if the rain kept going. The entire roof needed replacing. The tenants paid their rent—they deserved better than cheap plywood and some nails.

I climbed down to find Maryann Greer in a raincoat, arms crossed, glaring at me from under her hood.

"Just what the hell are you doing?" she demanded.

"What's it look like I'm doing? Fixing the roof."

"Don't get smart with me. Are you aware that it's raining cats and dogs? That you could have slipped and broken your damn neck?"

I was very aware of that.

Maryann flapped a hand. "Never mind." She turned on her heal and stomped back around the building, presumably back to her apartment.

I returned the tools to the shed and went back to my place. I was shaking out the useless rain slicker when a knock came at the door.

Maryann opened it before I could, a mug of something hot in her hand. "Hot cocoa," she said in a slightly softer tone than earlier. Slightly. "The girls are bundled up watching a movie. We had extra."

"Maryann…"

"Look at you. You're drenched." She shook her head and set the cocoa on the table.

Too tired to argue, I shut the door and joined her, slouching heavily into the chair.

"Why did you do that? Did you stop to think for a second how dangerous that was?"

"Louis had a leak that needed fixing."

"So he puts a bucket under it until tomorrow," she said. "Wouldn't be the first time. We're used to waiting for your uncle to fix anything."

"It's done."

"Yeah, but—"

"Who else was going to do it?" I snapped, that old pain burning a hole in my stomach. "There's no one else. So I did it. I did *something*."

Maryann's worried frown deepened. "Ronan…"

"If you call for help and there's no fucking answer...or they finally show up and it's too late, what're you supposed to do?"

I ran a hand through my damp hair and looked up to see her watching me, her lips a thin line.

"I don't know what—or who—you're actually talking about, Ronan, but I know it's not about a hole in the damn roof. I'm not going to push it, though I'd like to have a word with whoever failed you so badly."

"What for? Done is done."

"True. But that doesn't mean it was okay. And I think you need to hear that."

Her words punched me in the chest. The smell of warm chocolate and her concerned expression—her kindness—dragged me back years, to when I still had a mother. A feeling of disorientation, like déjà vu, came over me. The past and present mixed in that dingy apartment, awakening feelings I'd buried with Mom—the day I'd known I was on my own.

"I don't need to hear anything," I said gruffly. "I don't need your lectures or your fucking cocoa. I don't need a damn thing."

"Is that right?"

"Yeah. That's fucking right." I heard my tone grow low and stony. "What are you doing here anyway? Always up in my business. You're just a *tenant*."

I made the word sound like an insult and half expected Maryann would slap me across the face for being a dick and then walk away.

She did neither.

"Are you done?" Maryann smiled gently. "It's okay. I get it. I'm something of an expert at being let down myself. You get to the point where you've been alone for so long, you don't trust anyone. Not even yourself. It gets so bad that it's almost scary when someone offers to help. Right?"

The fight drained out of me. I nodded.

"I can take being let down," she continued. "But my girls…" She slid her thumbnail along the card table, her eyes shining. "My ex, their dad…he left us in the middle of the night. Never said goodbye. So I promised the girls they will *never* not have me. Because that's what they needed to hear. To know that someone would always be on their side."

"I get that."

"I know you do. You're on everyone's side but your own." She cocked her head. "Did something happen today?"

I kissed Shiloh. And it was the best and worst fucking thing I could've done.

But I was done talking. "No."

"Hmm. I don't believe you, but I've meddled enough for one day." She got up and went to the door, shooting me a final stern look with a smile behind it. "Don't go up on that roof again in the middle of a storm. Not ever again. Promise?"

"Yeah."

"Ronan?"

"I promise."

"Not sure I believe that either, but…" She sighed. "Get some sleep."

If only.

When she was gone, the only sound was the rain smattering against the windows and the water dripping off my clothes onto the kitchen floor. The cocoa was cold. The past faded away, and there was only now, bleak and empty.

I took a hot shower to burn the cold out…and to wash the scent and feel of Shiloh off me. But going up on the roof hadn't done it; I didn't know why I thought the shower would be any different. She had seeped into my skin, my bones, and wouldn't leave. I didn't want her to.

But she has to.

I remembered Frankie and Mikey's knowing sneers. The malicious fucking glee in their eyes at seeing us together, like eager dogs who'd found a new toy. I had nothing to offer a girl like Shiloh. I'd already given her everything she needed, building her that shed. Kissing her was a stolen minute—something good and fucking perfect but not mine to keep.

At school the next day, I crossed the quad, heading toward the long, low wall that separated the upper and lower sections of the campus and where Holden, Miller, and I hung out between classes. Shiloh was coming from the opposite direction, wearing a long skirt that brushed the ground, a tight-fitting top, and earbuds in her ears. The sun after yesterday's rain made everything seem brighter, including the glint of copper, silver, and gold on her arms, her neck—her skin where I'd touched her. She looked sexy as fuck—even more *because* I'd touched her.

Her head came up, and our eyes met. For a split second, her expression softened, then turned passive. Not pissed off but worse. As if I were inconsequential.

I deserve that. And it's better this way.

As if to punctuate the fucked-up futility of it all, Frankie Dowd and Mikey Grimaldi called out to me and approached. Frankie was scrawny next to the bigger football player. Mikey usually hung out with his friends on the team but slummed it with Frankie now and then. Holden said it was their mutual lack of brain cells that brought them together.

"Trouble in paradise, Wentz?" Mikey pretended to check his watch. "It hasn't been twenty-four hours, and you fucked it up with Barrera already?"

"Yeah, Wentz." Frankie cackled. He looked like an underfed hyena. "What did you do to piss her off?"

I stopped, leveled both of them with my flattest stare as they approached, while inside, my blood was rushing, muscles coiling.

"It's probably for the best," Mikey said casually. "She's a little out of your league, don't you think?"

"*A lot* out of his league," Frankie said. "But I hope you got some of that sweet ass before she came to her senses—"

His words choked off as my hand shot out and gripped him by the collar of his shirt. I hauled him to me until we were nose to nose. Frankie's pale-blue eyes lit up with fear but were manic with a wild energy too.

"Don't fucking talk about her like that," I seethed. "Don't talk about her, *ever*."

"Or what?" Frankie managed. His grin was full of yellowed teeth.

My fist twisted and tightened in his T-shirt, and we stared, locked in the moment where I battled with the urge to punch the smug smile off his face, to beat any thought of Shiloh out of his head…

"Go ahead, Wentz," Frankie said. "What are you waiting for? You know you want to. Or are you scared of the consequences?"

"Fuck you."

I wasn't afraid. Not for me.

You're not like him, my mother's voice whispered.

But what if I was?

My grip on Frankie loosened.

"Well, well, well, what do we have here?" Holden sidled up beside me in a long coat and scarf, though it was warm out. He put his hands in the pockets of his slacks and rocked back on his heels, casually taking in the scene. "Two nocturnal discharges about to have their asses handed to them by my dear Ronan." He grinned. "And it's not even noon."

I released Frankie with a rough shove. He staggered back, relief flashing over his face, quickly replaced by a sneering grin.

"That's what I thought," he taunted. "Chickenshit."

"This is an unexpected turn of events," Holden muttered, shooting me a confused look.

"No, it isn't," Frankie said. "Wentz turned into a giant pussy." His sneer sharpened. "Or maybe my dad broke you. Was that it?" He cocked his head. "I think that was it. He broke you like a dog."

"A dog." Mikey laughed. "Good boy, Wentz. Who's a good boy?"

When I didn't take the bait, he and Frankie high-fived each other and walked away, still chuckling. I inhaled through my nose, forced my fists to uncurl.

I felt Holden's eyes on me.

"Leave it alone, Parish," I said and strode to our space on the low wall.

But Holden couldn't leave it alone if you paid him. He joined me, leaning casually against the cement bricks.

"You feeling okay? Feverish? Delirious? The Ronan Wentz I know wouldn't walk away from a chance to beat Dowd's ass." He narrowed his eyes. "Your name *is* Ronan, isn't it?"

"Fuck off," I said dully and glanced down at my calloused hands with their scarred knuckles. "I don't always fight. Do I?"

Like father, like son.

The teasing tone fell out of Holden's voice instantly. "No. But when you do, it's for a good cause. Like defending Miller and me at the Blaylock party."

"You jumped in front of me when Frankie had the broken glass."

"That was nothing. You were ready to take one for the

team when Frankie pulled out the Taser. You did it out of pure honor, whereas mine was more of a psychotic death wish."

I glanced over at him. "You still have a death wish?"

"Life and I have called a truce. For now."

"Keep it that way."

"What's the fun in that?" Holden waved a hand. "Forget me. I heard what Frankie said about Shiloh. If I didn't know how you are about things like 'talking,' my feelings would be horribly wounded that you haven't shared whatever's going on there."

"Nothing's going on."

Holden coughed, "*Bullshit*," into his fist. "I know what you're thinking."

"What am I thinking?"

"That you need to stay away from her. For her sake. To heroically protect her from whatever you think it is she needs protecting from while sacrificing your own needs and desires, blah blah blah." He rolled his eyes.

"I *do* have to protect her."

"From Frankie fucking Dowd?"

From his father. And mine.

I didn't answer.

"You haven't brought her to the shack."

"I asked. She said no."

Holden blinked. "Oh."

I raised a brow. "So it *is* possible for you to shut the fuck up."

"Don't change the subject."

He started to speak again, but I cut him off. "Stay out of my business, Parish."

Holden sulked, then nodded his chin at something across the quad. "Oh look. Here comes my other dumbass friend, being miserable instead of being with his one true love."

I looked to where Miller walked with Amber Blake. They'd hooked up at homecoming. He felt he owed it to her to stick around while trying to get over Violet at the same time.

It wasn't working.

Amber went to kiss him goodbye and got only a peck on the lips. She snapped at him, tossed her long blond hair behind her, and stormed away. Miller's shoulders slumped, and he joined us at the wall.

He frowned at our silence. "What?"

"We were just admiring you and Amber," Holden said. "The very picture of relationship bliss. Blinding, really, how radiant you two are in your happiness."

I shot Miller a commiserating glance. "He's in a fucking mood."

"I can tell," Miller said with a small smile, then sighed. "Not today, Holden. You either," he said to me, since I usually gave him just as much shit for staying with Amber.

"Ronan is in no position to talk," Holden said. "The two of you are the poster boys for pointless self-sacrifice and deprivation."

Miller frowned. "What's he talking about?"

"No idea." I cocked my head at Holden, my stare hard and pointed. "Seen any good football games lately?"

His mouth shut with a *clack*. "Assholes, the both of you," he said and walked away, his coat flaring behind him.

Miller's brow furrowed. "What was that about?"

"It's Holden," I said with a shrug. "Your guess is as good as mine."

I waited to see if Miller would buy it.

Holden had confessed to me that he'd been responsible for River Whitmore ditching Violet at homecoming. *"I ran interference,"* he'd said. I could only guess what that meant, but it was clear that River was the guy Holden had told me about earlier. The one he had feelings for. Neither one of us kept shit from Miller, but the situation with Violet was messed up enough already. No need to add Holden into the mix.

Miller was nodding heavily, his thoughts full of Violet. As usual. He didn't believe it, but they'd make their way to each other eventually. I'd heard him sing to her at the party, and I'd seen her reaction. He'd poured himself into that song, and she'd felt every word.

Because he has something to offer.

Jealousy stabbed me in the gut, the same old hunger. I pushed it down, buried it deep where it couldn't hurt Shiloh.

It wasn't much, but it was all I had.

That afternoon, I did a job for a guy who needed some shelves built for his garage. Turned out I was getting pretty good at putting things together, doing something with my hands that was building instead of breaking.

At home, I fired up a frozen dinner, watched some TV, then took a shower. I was drying off when my phone rang. My phone never rang unless it was for a job or Nelson calling to bitch orders at me. The number was local but no one I recognized.

"Yeah?"

"Ronan, it's Shiloh." Her voice sounded breathy and tight. "I'm sorry… I got your number from Bibi's papers, from when she hired you. I don't know why but…you're the first person I thought to call."

I'd never heard her so undone. So scared.

Frankie fucked with her. Or Mitch. He got Mitch to harass her.

"Shiloh, what is it?"

"Bibi," she said, swallowing down her panic. "God, Ronan, it's Bibi."

FOURTEEN

SHILOH

I PACED THE WAITING ROOM, HUGGING MYSELF IN MY CARDIGAN. Hospitals were always so cold. I remembered when I had my appendix out. Twelve years old and scared to death and shivering under a thin blanket before surgery. But Bibi was with me the whole time, holding my hand, stroking my hair, and telling me they were going to "fix me up, good as new."

A sob rose in my throat, but I swallowed it down.

She's going to be okay. She has to be.

I paced and gnawed my lip. A string was unraveling at the cuff of my sweater. I felt like I was unraveling too, waiting for the doctors to finish their tests. Helpless. No plan, no checklist to tick off that would get me through this.

Then Ronan strode through the door.

He didn't stop at the front desk but came straight to me. I didn't have to say anything; he enveloped me in the safety of his arms, and I closed my eyes and clung to him, letting him hold me up. I couldn't remember the last time I'd shared a burden with anyone. Ronan took it wordlessly, and for a few precious moments, I stayed in the shelter of him. He smelled fresh from a shower and clean. Warm. His heartbeat in my ear was steady.

When I stepped back, the fear and anxiety swooped in, but I felt more like myself and ready to face whatever lay ahead. As if Ronan had loaned me some of his strength.

"What happened?" he asked as we took a seat in the waiting area.

"We were watching a movie," I said. "She seemed fine. But when she got up to go to the kitchen, she stumbled a little. I jumped up and tried to hold her steady, but she kept falling slowly, slipping out of my grasp." Tears gathered in the back of my throat. "She fainted or…collapsed. I don't know. Her eyes were fluttering, and she was mumbling a lot. I called an ambulance, and now I'm just waiting. God, the waiting…" I dragged my hands over my hair, my elbows on my knees. "If something happens to her…"

I closed my eyes, unwilling to think of a future without Bibi.

Not yet. Please. I'm not ready yet.

Ronan said nothing, but when I looked up, his face was drawn with worry, his lips a thin line.

"I know why I called you first," I said. "Because you care about her too. And because I was kind of falling apart, and I knew you'd hold me together."

"Shiloh…"

"I never do that. Let anyone help. Thank you for being here."

He started to speak, and then a tall doctor with dark hair and a kind face stepped in from the double doors. "Barrera?"

I shot to my feet...and so did Ronan.

The doctor strode forward in blue emergency room scrubs and a white coat. "I'm Dr. Fenton. I understand Bibi is your grandmother?"

"Great-grandmother. How is she?"

"She's doing fine. Resting now."

A sigh of relief miles deep gusted out of me, and I tipped sideways into Ronan. His arm went around me, reassuring and strong.

"What happened?"

"She's had an episode of hypotension or low blood pressure," Dr. Fenton said. "We've run some tests and have ruled out any adrenal or heart valve issues. We're going to recommend a change in diet and fludrocortisone to boost blood volume. Overall, she's in good health, and I'm optimistic she won't need further treatment. But we'll want her to see someone in a few weeks and regularly after that just to be sure."

I nodded, taking in every word, clutching tightly to *optimistic* and *good health*. "Whatever she needs. Whatever you need me to do, I'll do it."

The doctor smiled. "Bibi speaks highly of you, Shiloh. She said you take excellent care of her."

Not good enough. Tears threatened again, but I willed them back. "Can I see her?"

"She's stable now and sleeping. Better to let her rest and come back in the morning."

"But she's alone…"

"And sleeping," Dr. Fenton said gently. "Which is what she needs."

I nodded reluctantly. "Okay. Thank you. I'll be back first thing in the morning."

"How are you getting home?" Ronan asked.

"I drove. I followed the ambulance. They wouldn't let me ride with her. God, that was the worst drive of my life. Not knowing…"

I shivered, and his arm around me tightened and then let go.

We walked to the visitor parking. I fumbled my keys out of my bag with shaking fingers, and they dropped to the concrete. When I bent to get them, Ronan was there. His large hand closed over mine.

"I got it."

I managed a smirk. "You think you can handle her?"

He didn't tease or poke fun. "I got it," he said again.

Everything about him was steady and solid. He walked me to the passenger side and opened my door, then went around and got behind the wheel. I sank into my seat, his competence and quiet capability putting me at ease. There was something inherently masculine about a man behind the wheel that even in my exhausted, wrung-out state I appreciated. Ronan handled the Buick as if he'd driven it a hundred times, expertly maneuvering the huge car out of the parking lot.

At my house, he pulled into the garage and was at my side before I could even step out of the car. I wondered if I were about to throw every feminist sensibility out the window and let him carry me inside, caveman-style.

Ronan led me into the house and stopped in the kitchen, unsure. "You want to rest on the couch or…"

"In my room. I'm about to pass out. Being terrified is fucking exhausting."

He nodded. Now that the immediate danger was over, I was acutely aware of how alone we were. Our kiss came back to me, a kiss unlike any I'd ever had before. One I could feel somewhere deep inside me.

But he'd broken it off suddenly and left me alone in the car, cutting me loose.

"You don't have to stay," I said. "I'm fine."

"You sure?"

"I'm sure," I lied.

"Okay," he said slowly. "Good night."

He started to go, and the fear swept back in. A night alone stretched in front of me.

"Wait."

He turned.

"I…I…" My jaw worked soundlessly. I had no idea how to tell him I needed him. I'd never said the words before.

Ronan nodded as if he'd heard me, and his hard expression softened. "You want some water?"

"Now that you mention it…"

"Go lie down, and I'll bring it," he said, and I knew what he was doing. Sparing us the awkwardness of walking into my bedroom together.

In my room, I turned on the rainbow lights; they gave a soft glow that was soothing after the harsh hospital fluorescents. I sank heavily on my bed and kicked off my shoes. My strength was draining out minute by minute. I tipped over and curled up on my side, head on the pillow.

Ronan came in, a glass of water in hand. His inherent sexiness that was raw and potent was made beautiful by the multicolored lights.

He set the glass on the nightstand next to a photo of Violet and me when we were kids. His gaze swept the room, taking in my art and scribblings and ceramics, his hands in his pockets as if to keep from touching anything.

I pushed myself to sitting and took a long pull of water. I set the glass down with a shaky hand and nearly knocked it off the table. Ronan's hand shot out and steadied it.

"Are you sure you're okay?"

I curled back up. "I don't know," I whispered. "I don't think so."

He nodded again and took off his jacket, revealing a black T-shirt. In the dim light, he was mostly black—shirt, hair, the tattoos that inked his perfect arms. He sat on the floor beside my bed, his jacket tucked behind him like a pillow.

"What are you—"

"I'm staying until you fall asleep."

I studied his profile, his lips that had been on me, my mouth, my skin…

A pleasurable shiver slipped through me, then faded out. Something had spooked him that afternoon we kissed. His own baggage maybe. Stuff he wouldn't tell me.

"I'm no better," I muttered, my thoughts getting ahead of my tired brain and escaping.

Ronan's head turned to me. "What?"

"I didn't tell you everything. Back at the hospital."

"You don't have to tell me anything."

"I know. Neither one of us are very good at this—talking about our stuff. I need to, but I can't if you're all the way down there on the floor."

"What do you mean?"

"I mean, I'm not going to ask anything of you, Ronan. We're not…compatible," I said with an ache in my chest. "Or maybe we have too much stuff in the way, but…I'd like you to come up here. No kissing. I know you think that was a mistake."

He stiffened. "Shiloh…"

"It's okay. It was. Because I'm kind of a mess, though no one knows it. But I want to come clean a little. Okay?"

He hesitated, then nodded. I scooted over until my back was touching the wall, and Ronan sat on the edge of my full-size bed. His weight made it dip, my heart dipping with it, my stomach fluttering. He took off his boots and then maneuvered his large body to lie down next to me on his side so that we were face-to-face in the dark.

This close, the masculine beauty of his face resting on my pillow was almost overwhelming. I shut my eyes.

"I didn't think it was possible to be this tired."

"You should sleep."

"Then I'll be alone. And I'm so tired of being alone."

Ronan said nothing for a moment, then sighed, his breath warm and clean. "Me too."

"It's my fault though." I forced my eyes open and nodded at the photo of me and Vi. "We were so close. She used to tell me everything. But you can only do that for so long without getting anything in return. I mean, my first call in the hospital should have been to my best friend, right? But it was you."

Ronan's voice was low and rumbling in the dark. "I'm not sorry about that."

Another dip in my stomach, as if I were drunk or on a kiddie roller coaster at the boardwalk. "Me neither." I inhaled, then exhaled. "A few hours before Bibi fell, I walked in on her talking on the phone with my mother."

"Okay."

"I knew it was Mama because Bibi gets this look on her face when she's on the line. A look I never see her wear, like she's nervous. Bibi was upset. Angry even. She kept glancing at me and finally took the call out to the yard."

"What was it about?"

"She wouldn't tell me. Mama is the only dead zone between Bibi and me. A place where our honesty breaks down. I begged and then practically demanded to know what was going on. Bibi said Mama had been drinking, and it was all nonsense. But I don't think that's a hundred percent true." I swallowed hard. "But I do know whatever they talked about, it didn't include Mama wanting to talk to me."

Ronan didn't deny that or try to comfort me with scenarios that he couldn't possibly know were true or not. He was just there, listening. And that was all I needed.

"She hates me, Ronan," I said, my throat tightening. "My mother hates me."

"That can't be true. All moms love their kids."

I shook my head against the pillow. "Not her."

"Then she's not your mom, Shiloh," Ronan said. "Not really. And if she's not, then what does it matter what she thinks? It's her loss. She's the one who's missing out. Not you."

I let his words settle around me like a blanket. "Easier said than done. To stop caring, I mean."

"I know."

"Were you close to your mom?"

He rolled onto his back and stared up at the ceiling. "Yeah, I was." He swallowed; I heard the *click* in his throat and watched his Adam's apple bob. "I couldn't save her."

"Save her? I thought you said you were eight when she died."

"Yeah, but I was there and I... Never mind."

"You can tell me."

He shook his head. "This night isn't about me. You need to rest."

"You're a good guy, Ronan," I said. He started to protest, but I talked over him. "You are. I'm not good for anyone. I'm closed off. Bibi says so, and she's right. I hate this. So helpless against what I feel about her and…"

You.

He turned to look at me.

"I worry about you too," I said. "Don't like it."

"You don't have to."

"But I do. It's like my mom. I don't want to keep caring and getting hurt, but I do. And it's nearly wrecked me. My bandwidth is stretched to breaking, and I have nothing left to give." I shook my head against the pillow. "I can't hurt anymore. I can't. And that's why it really sucked when you got out of the car yesterday, but I think…" My voice faded to a whisper. "I think it was the right thing."

"I get it, Shiloh," Ronan said. "I really do. The only thing I care about is that you're safe. And happy."

"Why does that make me so sad?" A great welling sorrow drowned the tingling, pleasurable anxiety of having Ronan in my bed.

"Because we can't always have what we want. Sometimes it's better—safer—to walk away."

"Safer? For who?"

"You, Shiloh. Always you."

I shook my head. I was losing the thread of our conversation to exhaustion. My eyes wouldn't stay open.

"When I wake up, you'll be gone," I said from under closed lids.

"Yes."

"And that's better. For both of us, right? I can't give... enough. Don't want to hurt you..."

I was babbling now, but I felt Ronan nod. Felt a shift on the bed, felt him press a soft kiss into my hair.

"Good night, Shiloh."

I started the slide into sleep, but that kiss and the emotion breaking through the cracks in his hard tone made me fight to wake back up. A feeling of making a terrible mistake gripped me, but I was falling down a deep, dark hole, scrabbling for purchase and failing.

When I woke up, the bed was empty. The pillow still smelled like him. Light was streaming in through my window, and the clock read a little after 7:00 a.m.

"Bibi."

I kicked off the covers. Since I was still dressed, I drew on my shoes and sweater and hurried for the garage.

At the hospital, I rushed into Bibi's room to find her surrounded by nurses and a few doctors. She said something, and a round of laughter rippled through them. I was not laughing.

I pushed through the crowd and threw my arms around her neck.

"There, there, sweetheart. I'm going to be just fine." She stroked my hair. "Everyone, this is my amazing, brilliant great-granddaughter, Shiloh."

I straightened, conscious that we were surrounded. I pulled my sweater around me tighter, feeling naked and fragile after talking to Ronan last night. But Bibi was all that mattered.

The doctors dispersed, and one nurse told us she'd be back in a bit to help get Bibi ready for discharge.

"So you're okay," I said, dropping into a chair beside her.

"Oh, baby girl. You look so tired. Yes, I'm fine. The docs say my blood pressure is a tad on the low side. But they got me fixed right up with a new pill to add to my repertoire and some ugly old compression stockings they say I need to wear. On the bright side, Dr. Fenton tells me I need more salt in my diet. So what do you say about getting some french fries when we clear out of here?"

"What were you arguing about with Mama?"

Her smile collapsed with a sigh. "Nothing important, I promise you."

"But, Bibi…"

"If I believed for one second that anything I could say would make you feel good, I would say it. But I told you, honey. She'd had too much to drink. It's not worth giving another thought."

I looked down at my hands, twisting in my lap. "There's just so much I don't know. I hate this feeling, like I'm being excluded from my own life."

"I know." She patted my cheek, then cocked her head, studying me.

"What?"

"I can't see much, but I feel like there's a new softness in your eyes."

Ronan.

I sat back in my chair. "I'm just tired. Like you said. You being in the hospital will do that to a gal."

"Are you sure that's all?"

Ronan's words came back to haunt me with their finality. *Sometimes it's better—safer—to walk away.*

"Yeah," I said. "That's all."

Bibi was discharged a few hours later with a new prescription and a web address for a site that sold medical compression socks to keep the blood from pooling in her legs. The rain had begun again as I drove us home.

I got Bibi set up on the couch, ordered her the socks, and went back out to the pharmacy. Then I called Aunt Bertie, filled her in, and reassured her Bibi was okay.

"If you need anything, Shiloh, you tell us, okay?" Bertie had said. I could hear the subtext—Bibi was eighty years old. We were slowly morphing from her taking care of me to me taking care of her.

After a few hours of hovering, Bibi shooed me away with good-natured teasing and a kiss. I went to the shed in our backyard. The rain had been coming down pretty hard, yet not one leak. Ronan's craftsmanship was like him—solid and strong.

This is my *refuge*, I thought as I worked. *This is what will save me. Building a future that is just mine. And nothing Mama says—or doesn't say—can take it away from me.*

I had Etsy orders backing up, and whatever Ronan and I had started was officially over, but I let my hands reach for what they wanted. I fell into my work, not surprised that it was taking the shape of something masculine. A pendant I knew wasn't going in my shop.

Around one in the afternoon, a text came in on my phone, pulling me out of the zone. I smiled at the short, straight-to-the-point text.

Bibi?

She's good, I typed back. Home.

Good.

I bit my lip. Thank you for last night.

No answer. And as the minutes stretched into days, I knew there wouldn't be.

PART II

PART II

FIFTEEN
RONAN

MARCH

"Happy birthday, dear Rowww-nennn," Holden belted in an off-key tenor. He stood in front of the bonfire at the shack, arms spread. Miller sat to my right, accompanying him on his guitar and laughing his ass off. "Happy birthday tooo...yooooo."

Miller strummed a flourish, and Holden bowed deep, sweeping his long coat behind him.

I gave a slow clap. "That was…"

"Miraculous?" Holden offered as he sat down hard in his beach chair. "Divine? Inspired?"

"I was going to say like a geriatric cat in heat."

Holden pretended to be offended. "Jeez, tough crowd."

"Why are you singing instead of him?" I pointed at Miller.

Miller toyed with the frets on his guitar. "Maybe later."

Holden rolled his eyes. "Ever so modest, our Stratton. The musical program for the evening has only just begun."

I hoped so but didn't push it. Miller had crazy talent. Listening to him made everything seem better, even if the song was a sad one. Which it usually was. But he wasn't a show-off. He played when he felt like it.

"I'm starved," he said. "Let's eat."

We had a strict, unspoken "no gifts" policy when it came to birthdays and Christmas. Miller and I were broke as shit, while Holden could buy up an entire mall's worth of stuff if we let him. Only food and beer for celebrations, and Holden could go crazy. It didn't feel as weird if the spread was for all of us.

That night, he brought hot Italian sandwiches, sides of pasta, and vegetables we'd probably skip. Miller provided pretzels and chips. I brought the beer.

I glanced around the bonfire at these guys I'd fucking die for. They filled empty spaces in me, but lately, it was getting harder to ignore the nameless hunger that had taken shape and wasn't so nameless anymore.

Shiloh.

I tried to push her out of my thoughts, that night and every damn waking minute of my life, since the morning we'd called it quits. But the promises I'd made to her that day were starting to feel old and stale, while the hunger for her grew ravenous.

"I propose a toast," Holden said, getting to his feet. He held up his vodka flask, swaying slightly. "To Ronan, the quintessential handyman."

"Uh, thanks?"

"Shush, I'm not done yet. You take broken-down shit and put it back together, no matter if that broken-down shit is a shed or a shelf or a shell of a man. Such as myself. You, Ronan Wentz, greatly improve the lives of everyone you know."

"Hear, hear," Miller said, lifting his beer.

I scowled at him, but he shook his head as if to say, *You're not getting out of this one.*

"Okay, that's enough," I said and took a pull of cold beer to douse the warm feeling spreading across my chest. It was nice, what Holden had said, but not true.

Shiloh's life is improved by not *having me in it.*

We ate and drank, and then Holden went inside the shack and returned with a bag of gourmet, sugar-free chocolates for Miller and a German chocolate cake, both from a bakery downtown with a French name.

"Who's got candles?" Holden asked. "We need to sing again."

"Hell no," I said. "You're done."

"I think that's your cue, Stratton."

Miller pulled off his beanie, ran a hand through his hair, and then settled his guitar on his lap. His preshow warm-up. "I know you like heavier shit," he said to me. "I tried to work out something from Tool—"

"Something romantic," Holden put in, dumping a huge piece of chocolate cake on a paper plate and handing it to me. "Like 'Stinkfist.'"

Miller chuckled. "Right. But it doesn't translate to acoustic very well, so I arranged something else. Hope you like it."

I concentrated on my food. Miller playing was a big deal by itself, but having him play *for* you was fucking priceless.

He strummed the first few notes, and it took me a second to recognize the song. Then Soundgarden's "Black Hole Sun" came pouring across the fire in the dark night.

Chris Cornell had a once-in-a-lifetime voice. Miller's take on his song turned it into something completely different and yet somehow paid respect to Cornell at the same time.

Holden listened the same way he had that night at the Blaylock party—riveted and silent. I set my food aside, wanting to do nothing but listen too. Miller sang about walking sleep, and I thought about my nightly treks to keep the nightmares away. To make sure those I cared about were safe.

"In my youth, I pray to keep heaven, send hell away," Miller sang, and my hand went to the words tattooed on the right side of my chest. When I was a kid, I prayed every day for the hell that was my father to go away. When he finally did, it was too late.

A quiet settled when Miller's last note faded out. I didn't know what to do or say. Thankfully, Holden broke the silence before things got awkward, rising unsteadily to his feet.

"Fucking hell, man," he said, clapping hard. He looked at me, bewildered. "How is he not famous?"

"It's only a matter of time," I said.

Miller shook his head, and I shot him the same look

he'd given me: *You're not getting out of this one.* He smiled gratefully. He wanted nothing more than to make it big and rescue his mother from poverty and her asshole boyfriend. His music was all he had, and he worried it wasn't enough, while everyone around him had no doubt.

We drank a few more beers, all of us laughing our asses off when it became Holden's karaoke hour. Miller accompanied him—or tried to—with numbers like "Karma Chameleon" and "I'm Too Sexy." A little before midnight, we called it a night.

"Who needs a ride?" Holden asked. Lord Parish had a car with a personal driver—James—who took him wherever he wanted at all hours.

"I'll take one," Miller said.

"Wentz?"

"I'm good. I'll stay awhile, put the fire out."

"Good idea," Holden said with a strange smile.

After they left, I found out why. I went into the shack to stow the uneaten food in the mini fridge and lock up. There was a large black shoebox tied with a dark-purple ribbon sitting on the wooden table.

"Fucking hell, Parish."

Inside the box was a pair of heavy-duty black leather work boots from a brand name that screamed *money*. A note was tucked inside one.

Happy Birthday, my friend. I was going to get you a set of nunchucks or maybe a flamethrower, but Miller said no. DO NOT try to give these back, or I'll never speak to you again.

Love,
Holden

My jaw tightened. My old boots were falling apart—no thanks to my nightly walks. I slipped on the new pair. They felt sturdy and high quality.

I took the shoebox and tossed it in the fire, destroying the evidence of Holden breaking our rule, though his note made it sound like Miller was in on it too.

"Assholes," I murmured. The four or five beers I'd drunk must've given me a good buzz, since I felt warm all over.

Almost content.

I kicked sand over the fire and took the route along the coast back to the old parking lot with the abandoned utility shed. Trying to sleep now would ruin the best birthday I'd ever had. I'd walk and let the night air sober me up.

I made my rounds in a little over an hour. The new boots were fucking good; I'd never owned anything so nice.

But it was still too early to try for sleep. I kept going until I reached the outskirts of downtown. The streets were empty, the shops dark, streetlamps casting cones of yellow light. I passed the doughnut shop where I'd kissed Shiloh. It seemed a lifetime ago, but the hunger that flared was immediate and sharp.

I passed the Burger Barn and was at the driveway that

led to its rear parking lot when I heard a girl crying. Then a guy's voice.

"Kimberly, wait. Come on..."

Mikey Grimaldi. I pressed myself into the shadows and peered around the corner. Kimberly was facing me, hugging her elbows in a short skirt and rumpled shirt. Her blond hair was messy, falling in her face.

What the fuck am I looking at?

But I knew. My fucking guts churned until I thought I'd puke up beer and birthday cake, because I knew.

"It's cold out," Grimaldi was saying, cajoling from behind, big and beefy in his letterman jacket. "Get back in the car."

"Home," Kimberly said. Her voice sounded small. "I want to go home."

"Yeah, sure, of course." Mikey led her back to his white Jeep Rubicon, the only car in the lot. When she was safely in the passenger seat, he jogged around to the driver's side, chuckling and shaking his head.

The Jeep's engine roared to life, and headlights filled the driveway as he came tearing out of the parking lot, passing in front of me. I caught a glimpse of Kimberly's face in the passenger window, her eyes staring at nothing. The Jeep made a right and peeled out in a screech of tires, leaving me alone on the quiet, dark street.

I'm too late again. Too late.

I gave up the rest of my route and went back to my place. The nightmares were as bad as I expected.

I was almost glad.

It took a week for what I'd suspected to be confirmed. On Friday at Central, senior girls were huddled together, whispering and talking. Mikey Grimaldi hurried past a group of cheerleaders, his shoulders hunched against their angry and tear-filled stares.

"What's all this about?" Holden asked, leaning with me at our spot on the wall.

"Nothing good," I said with that same stomach-churning feeling as the other night.

"I must know," Holden said. "BRB with the intel."

Holden crossed to the nearest group of girls. They watched him approach warily, but within moments, he'd charmed his way into their circle. A few minutes later, he reported back, his face grim.

"Well?"

Tell me I'm wrong.

"Kimberly Mason isn't coming back to Central."

My stomach dropped. "Why not?"

Holden rubbed his chin, subdued. "She was out Monday night with that walking hemorrhoid, Mikey Grimaldi. Everyone else left. She and Mikey stayed."

"And?"

"The shit swizzler took things too far, if you catch my drift."

"Fuck me."

He nodded grimly. "But her friends say she's not pressing charges."

"Why the hell not?"

"Probably because she's fucking scared," Holden burst out angrily, wearing a look I'd never seen him wear. "I'm sure it's humiliating to report that shit and get questioned on every last thing you did or didn't do. Like being forced to strip naked and parade around while that asshole stays fully clothed."

My damn heart thudded dully as I looked at my friend. There was a story there I wasn't sure I wanted to hear. "You got all that from what those girls told you?"

"Yes," Holden said too quickly and looked away. "Anyway, that's the deal. She's leaving town, and Grimaldi's going to get into college, play pro, and go about his life like nothing happened. The American dream."

"Fuck that."

"That sounded like a threat," Holden said. He gave me a strange, hopeful look that sort of broke my heart.

"Because it was."

SIXTEEN
SHILOH

MONDAY MORNING, I'D JUST MADE IT TO THE PARKING LOT at Central when my phone chimed a text from Amber Blake.

Did you see this???

A photo popped up of a white Jeep with the word *RAPIST* spray-painted in red along the entire length of the passenger side.

I climbed out of the Buick and hit Call. "Is that Mikey Grimaldi's Jeep?"

"The brand-spanking-new Rubicon he got for his birthday last summer? It sure is," Amber said, sounding breathless. "He was at the Burger Barn on Saturday night with Frankie Dowd and some people. They say he drove all over town like a dumbass before noticing. Must've happened while he was eating."

"Holy shit." I bit my lip. "For Kimberly."

"Yep. Whoever did it is a hero in my book."

Amber was waiting for me at the parking lot's chain-link fence entrance to the school. She looked pretty in a long, flowered skirt, similar to the flowing white one I wore that day.

"Crazy, right?" she said as I joined her.

"Maybe something good will come out of it," I said. "He might not go to jail or have his future tainted forever like hers is, but he didn't get away with it either. That's something."

"Agreed," Amber said. "I wonder who did it. Kimberly's brother, maybe? No, he's at NYU."

The quad was bustling before first bell. All three Lost Boys were headed to their usual spot along the short wall. My gaze was stuck on Ronan, his long legs striding purposefully, inked arms striated with muscle. He was dangerously beautiful in my eyes, and suddenly I knew Ronan had spray-painted Mikey's car. I'd have bet my future shop on it.

I reached into my oversize embroidered bag for the necklace in the side pocket that I'd started all those weeks ago. I'd finally finished it and had been carrying it around wherever I went, waiting for…I didn't know what. Ronan and I had agreed that it was best to go our separate ways, but something in me couldn't let go.

Amber tucked a lock of her long blond hair behind her ear with a sigh, and I realized she was staring at a different Lost Boy.

"How are things with Miller?" I asked, though I already knew the answer.

"Terrible. As usual. Don't know why I stay. Don't know why *he* does."

Because he's trying to do the right thing.

I had a hand in that when I told Miller not to treat Amber as if she were disposable, and I stood by it. But I hadn't expected the dummy to stick with her for *months*.

Amber led me behind the flagpole in the center of the quad. "Watch this." She tapped out a text.

Are we hanging out today or not??

Miller slowed his steps, peered at his phone, and visibly sighed. He did not reply.

"See?"

I didn't know how to comfort her without the truth—and my loyalty to Violet—bursting out. I needed a change of subject. Clusters of kids were huddled together, all of them watching the Lost Boys and whispering.

"God, this place is a gossip mill today," I said.

Amber made a sour face. "Evelyn Gonzalez put Miller on her vlog, and it's going viral."

"No shit?"

She nodded. "I keep waiting for him to sing to *me*, but he never does. He's a jerk."

This has gone on long enough. And not just the mess with Miller and Amber.

I couldn't take my eyes off Ronan and didn't want to. These last months had been like suffering through a forced diet. I was starving for him. To be touched, kissed, to have those gray eyes darken with want for me. But why? I was strong. I could protect myself. Back in Louisiana, Jalen and I'd had no problems keeping it casual. Why couldn't Ronan and I do the same?

I caught up to Miller at the start of the lunch hour. He was sitting on a large rock near the lunch tables, giving himself an insulin shot in the upper arm. With his beanie and plaid flannel tied around his waist, he was the perfect image of a rock star in the making.

If Shawn Mendes and Dave Grohl had a love child.

"Hey, Mr. Famous."

"Yeah, right," he scoffed, but I didn't miss the glint of hope flashing in his eyes. "What's up?"

"Ronan mentioned his birthday was this month."

"It was on the twentieth."

"Shit." I'd missed it by a week.

"Why?" Miller put his kit away and reached for a brown paper sack lunch.

"Nothing. I have something for him. It's no big deal. At all."

He smiled, a rare sight. "Yeah? I didn't realize you two even knew each other."

"Your friend isn't exactly the super-chatty type. We have history together."

Miller nodded, his smile not going anywhere. "Well, if you want to find him, he spends most lunchtimes in woodshop."

"What for?"

"Beats me. Why don't you go and see?"

I rolled my eyes. "Don't get cute, Stratton."

He laughed, and I started to go.

"Shiloh?"

I turned. "Yeah?"

"Thanks for thinking of him."

Oh, the irony. I couldn't stop.

The industrial arts building—or woodshop—was a huge shed on the east side of the campus next to the gym. It was crammed with tools along the walls and workstations, some with table saws embedded in them. The gardeners stored the riding mowers there too; the place smelled green and woodsy.

I found Ronan alone in the far left corner, bent over a worktable. The *whack* of a hammer reverberated in my chest, my heart pounding to keep time. He was working on a small cabinet of shelves made from stacks of spare wood leaning against the walls.

It was a little bit scary how happy I was to see him.

When there was a lull in the hammering, I cleared my throat. Ronan turned, his eyes widening to see me by the light of the industrial fluorescent bars running along the ceiling. He glanced around quickly.

"What are you doing here?"

"Hello to you too," I said, my confidence slipping. I trailed a finger along the side of the cabinet. "Is this a woodshop assignment? Impressive."

Ronan's craftsmanship was amazing. Smooth lines, even shelves. Simple but sturdy.

"Not an assignment," he said. "It's for a tenant in the building I—in my building. My uncle's the manager. I help him out sometimes."

"You use your free time to make stuff for your neighbors?"

"They need it," he said with a shrug. "Nelson...my uncle, doesn't always want to spring for repairs."

My eyebrows rose. "Doesn't surprise me, actually. You, doing good things—kind things—for others. Like Kimberly Mason." I cocked my head. "It was you, wasn't it? Grimaldi's Jeep?"

He was a split second too late denying it. "No."

"It was you. I know it was you."

"Doesn't change what happened to her." His mouth was a grim line. "I was too late."

I shook my head. "It helps to know that he didn't get away with it. Maybe he'll think before he tries shit like that again."

"He'd fucking better."

"Thank you for doing that. For Kimberly. For womankind too, but especially for her."

The space between us warmed, grew smaller. I didn't know if he moved closer to me or me to him, but I was standing in front of him now, close enough to smell his clean scent, mixed faintly with sweat and wood. The bottom of his owl tattoo showed from under the short sleeve of his black T-shirt. A part of me wondered if Ronan had more tattoos on his body I couldn't see. And if I'd ever find out.

Somehow, my hand was on his forearm. I ran my fingertips along the sleeve of ink, over the face of the clock. "What does this mean?"

"It's for my mom. They're all for her."

I nodded, tracing the flowers surrounding the clock.

"What are you doing?" he asked, his voice gruff, watching me.

"I don't know. I just…miss you." I gave my head a shake. "I've said that before. I didn't like it then, and I don't like it now. Missing you."

He nodded. So close to me, I could feel the warmth of his skin.

"So I've been thinking," I began, marveling at how steady my voice sounded. "About what we said that night Bibi went into the hospital. You said it's safer to walk away."

"That's right. It's better for you, Shiloh. Trust me."

"I've thought a lot of things were better for me, and they weren't." I tilted my head up to him; he was so tall, I barely brushed his chin. "There's something happening here, right? An attraction?"

"Yeah," he said roughly.

"But neither of us do relationships, right? So let's…not."

"What do you mean?"

"Let's just keep it casual."

"Casual."

I glanced down at my hand that looked small and delicate on the muscles of his forearm, dark with ink. "I don't trust myself to be in charge of someone else's heart. I'm not doing a bang-up job with my own, to be honest. So let's skip the part where we get tangled up in feelings and just...see what happens."

He swallowed, and I could see him thinking over my indecent proposal. His gray eyes were lidded, his body looming over me, ready to give in.

Then he shook his head. "I don't want you to get pulled into my shit, Shiloh. Not now. Not ever."

My stomach dropped. I'd gotten it all wrong. He'd meant what he said about walking away, and here I was, bartering for a little piece of him. Any scrap he'd toss me. Heat rushed through me—the burn of humiliation.

I snatched my hand away.

"Never mind. Forget I said anything. I gotta go."

Ronan's hand closed on my arm, gently but firmly. "Shiloh." The intensity and gravity of his voice pulled me back to him almost as much as his grip. "I want what you want." His hand came up, brushing fingertips over my face, tracing my lips. Then he shook his head like a man coming out of a trance. "But it's not safe. If Grimaldi knows it was me who tagged his car, shit could get ugly."

"For who? Me?"

"Maybe."

"Did he see you?"

"Not sure. But I'm not taking any chances."

The protective undertone to his words was unmistakable, sending shivers over my skin. I smiled weakly. "You're like a superhero, worried that his enemies will hurt him by getting to those he cares about."

"Something like that."

"I doubt that coward is going to try anything. But it's fine. I don't do mushy romance or hand-holding or PDA. We don't have to show off in school if that makes you feel better."

"The shack," he said, still watching me with heated eyes. "Come to the shack. It's private."

"That offer still stands?"

He nodded and slowly, his eyes never leaving mine, pressed the back of my hand to his mouth and inhaled. "Let's go today. Or…right this fucking minute."

God, I'm a dead woman.

His lips were brushing my skin, and I struggled to keep from falling into those damn eyes of his that were swallowing me whole. "Can't," I said faintly. "Have a date with the library. This afternoon?"

He nodded, and we lingered a moment in each other's nearness. I thought he was going to kiss me. I was desperate for him to kiss me. But his gaze darted to the entrance, then back to me, as if daring himself to break his own promise.

He released my hand. "I'll text you."

"Okay. Great."

I shouldered my bag as he got back to work, and I left quickly, my heart pounding louder than his hammer.

I was in the school library about an hour after last bell, muddling distractedly through algebra, when I got Ronan's text to meet at an abandoned utility shed overlooking the ocean, a mile or so west of the boardwalk. He was waiting for me in the parking lot, weeds growing out of cracks in the pavement. I climbed out of the Buick, shielding my eyes from the sun that was sinking behind the horizon.

"You okay getting those wet?" he asked with a nod at my sandals.

"Now you tell me," I said with a grin. "There's no turning back now."

A smile flickered over his lips, and then he wordlessly led me down a short path to the beach. Eastward, the shore was rocky and narrow before giving way to more sprawling beaches leading to the boardwalk. Ronan led us westward, toward what looked like an impassable stretch of shore where the cliffs had begun a slow crumble into the sea.

I shouldered my bag and hiked up my skirt, stepping over rocks and shivering as cold water lapped at my feet.

"You do this a lot?" I asked, stumbling slightly as the boulders were growing bigger, the ocean closer.

Ronan, walking a few paces ahead of me, reached back and offered his hand. "Most nights."

His fingers closed around mine, large and rough and warm. I held on because the way was difficult. Then it grew easier, but he didn't let go, and neither did I. He led me around a huge boulder, and on the other side was a fisherman's shack. The ocean had retreated, crashing at the shore some twenty yards away. A bonfire pit with three beach chairs faced the horizon.

"So this is the secret hideout of the infamous Lost Boys."

"It's the shack," he said, but I could tell it was so much more. A sanctuary for him and Miller and Holden. To be invited here meant something.

Ronan led me inside the small wooden structure, and I peered around, distracted by his hand still wrapped around mine, his thumb running back and forth over my skin.

"Is that a *generator*?" I asked of the little machine whirring in the corner. "Ah, for the mini fridge, no less."

"Lord Parish has standards." Ronan smirked, but his affection for his friend was obvious.

"I'm assuming that ridiculous chair is his?" I said about the white wingback against the wall near the window.

Ronan nodded, moving closer to me, towering over me. He wasn't smirking now. Whatever hesitation or caution he'd had in the woodshop was gone. He backed me against the edge of a long wooden table that wasn't new but weather-beaten and salt worn. His hand came up and cupped my cheek, holding me in his strong grip as if I were something precious.

My lips parted, like an invitation, and in the next instant, his mouth captured mine in a searing kiss.

God, this...

This was what I'd been starving for. Him. His mouth hard and hot on mine. His body pressed to me so that I could feel the power coursing through him, vibrating like electricity. I clung to his shoulders, then slipped my hands in his hair. His tongue invaded me, then pulled back to let his teeth graze my lips before pushing in again. Until I was dizzy. Overwhelmed in the best way, lost in everything that was him. The taste of him, the sounds he made as he kissed me—hungry sounds of want, as if he'd been just as starved for me as I was for him.

We wasted no time making up for the months we'd spent doing nothing more than stealing furtive glances at each other in history class. His hands were everywhere, reacquainting himself with my body and me giving in. Molding myself into his touch to get closer. Always closer.

"You're not shy, are you?" I whispered against his lips as his hand slid up my shirt, over my bra, squeezing.

He reared back, his eyes searching mine. "Too much? I'll stop..."

"Don't you dare."

I kissed him, hot and wet, while his rough hand cupped my breast, his thumb rubbing over the hard nipple, making it ache for his mouth. I let my own hands roam, slipping under his shirt, fingertips tracing the tight lines of his abs that contracted tighter under my touch.

With a grunt, he lifted me effortlessly and set me on the table. I pulled him in, wrapping my legs around his waist. How easy it was to fall into him, how good he felt and tasted. My hesitations and self-preservation burned up in the heat of his want for me. So potent I could taste it.

A hand slid into my braids, gripping and angling me to the side for better access to my mouth. The other was still under my shirt, kneading my small breast under my bra now, flesh to flesh. His lips moved hotly down my neck, then back up, toward my ear. Tongue flicking and teeth biting until my skin was tingling everywhere.

"God, Ronan," I breathed and slipped a hand over the front of his jeans. The hard length of him was straining against the denim, huge in my palm.

"Just me," he growled into my ear, his tongue slipping between the earrings, his teeth tugging at one small hoop. "No one fucks you but me."

A moan escaped me, his words shocking and thrilling me at the same time.

"That's presumptuous," I managed and hissed a breath as his mouth clamped down on my neck. "*We're* not even fucking."

"Our agreement or whatever this is…no one else touches you." He pulled away to meet my eye. "*No one.*"

The possessive heat in his gaze stole my breath. I'd never had anyone look at me the way Ronan did. There wasn't one thing casual in his hard stare or the softness behind it. A softness no one saw, not unless they were close to him like this.

"No one else." I tilted my head, striving not to melt under that heated gaze. "The same goes for you."

He frowned as if the idea of being with someone besides me made no sense, and I worried my *casual* plan was in serious fucking trouble.

"No one else," he said, and then, as if to seal the pact, his hand slid between my legs, palming me completely. Staking his claim.

My body arched into his touch instantly, giving in to him. I whimpered as his fingers rubbed against my underwear, now damp, and found my clit. His other hand joined the first under my skirt, his thumbs meeting and rubbing circles while he took me in a rough, raw kiss.

"I want to put my mouth on you," he stated. Matter-of-fact. Direct.

"Here? Now?"

He backed away. "We don't have to..."

I pulled him back in. "I want to."

God, I wanted to. I wanted everything with him. I wanted too much. A lone rational thought—a refugee from my old practical self—stopped me.

"Will the guys be here soon?"

"In a few minutes," Ronan said, hotly against my lips. "I only need two."

The possibility of getting caught added to the intensity building in that small shed. I held my breath as he bent between my legs, my skirt bunched up around my waist. He pulled aside my underwear, and I tensed. I'd never been naked like this in broad daylight. Before the self-consciousness could dig in, he licked his lips and inhaled.

"You're so beautiful," he murmured, almost to himself.

"Jesus, Ronan—" I began, then gasped as his mouth descended. Every nerve ending flared to life, an ache of pleasure that deepened with every lick of his tongue, every graze of his teeth. When he latched on, sucking, I let out a cry. One hand gripped his hair, the other, the edge of the table, holding on for dear life as Ronan went at me.

He was wrong. It took one minute, not two.

In seconds, my entire body tensed, my breath catching in my chest and starbursts going off behind my closed eyes as the orgasm rocketed through me, flaring hottest where his tongue met my flesh. Ronan didn't relent but coaxed me through it until the end, lapping at me in dirty, raw strokes that threatened to bring me to the brink all over again.

"No more," I breathed, pushing him away and sitting up. "Oh my God."

Ronan emerged from under my skirt, his face flushed, chin wet. "Good?"

"I can't feel my legs, so...yes."

He smiled a little, and I wondered how beautiful he'd be wearing a full, genuine smile.

His happiness isn't my responsibility, I reminded myself. We were friends with benefits. Casual. I pulled away and jumped off the table, but Ronan was there. He caught me and kissed me again. Sweetly, though I could taste myself on him.

He's sweet and dirty at the same time. Soft and rough.

The humming between my legs hadn't diminished in the slightest; I could still feel Ronan's mouth there, and

I wanted more. But his kiss that lingered on my lips was even stronger. The way he'd looked at me, held my face in his hands...

I wanted more of that too.

I cleared my throat and reached inside my bag. "In all the intrigue of vigilante justice, secret hideouts, and mind-blowing oral sex, I nearly forgot. I have something for you."

Something I spent two solid weeks making because... casual.

I took Ronan's hand and dropped the pendant in his palm. "Happy birthday."

Ronan glanced at me, then at the necklace in his hand. It had turned out pretty well, I thought. A sleek silver North Star with four short and four long points radiating from the center, each one sharp. I'd carved little sigils of lines and ovals in a repeating pattern around the star and then ringed the entire pendant with a ropelike design to give it a sailing, compass-like look.

"For when you feel adrift," I said softly.

Ronan frowned, then looked up at me, confused. Touched. I took the two ends of the silver chain and reached around his neck to clasp them. The pendant lay against his chest, heart level.

"I've never had something like this." He was holding the pendant but looking at me.

My heart thumped too hard and broke a little at the same time.

"Now you do."

SEVENTEEN

SHILOH

Male voices sounded from outside, rescuing me from a moment that was growing too soft. Miller and Holden had arrived, and I was suddenly nervous, as if I were about to go in for an important job interview.

"It's cool," Ronan said. "They knew you'd be here."

I nodded, smoothing down my skirt and watching as Ronan tucked the compass pendant under his T-shirt. A twinge nipped at me until I reminded myself we'd agreed not to show each other off.

Ronan's just following the rules.

Except he read my expression and explained, "It's fucking perfect, but I don't like people in my business."

Or not.

I turned away before he could see the flush in my cheeks.

Outside, Miller and Holden stood near their beach chairs, talking. They both looked up, and Holden beamed like a proud parent. He approached me, hand outstretched.

"You must be Shiloh Barrera," he said cheerfully. "Ronan has told me almost nothing about you."

I laughed. "Sounds about right."

Up close, Holden was devastatingly handsome in a completely different way from Ronan. Elegant, refined, with dyed silver hair and piercing green eyes that glinted with intelligence. Ronan had street smarts; Holden looked as if he had a hundred libraries behind his eyes and smelled of expensive cologne, clove cigarettes, and vodka. Like what I imagined a Parisian department store might smell like.

"Make yourself at home," he said with a bow. "And might I add, it's about damn time. Now if we can get Miss Violet here…"

"I'm on the job," I said and joined Miller where he sat tuning his guitar.

He gave me a dry look. "That must've been some birthday present."

"Oh hush. Are you cool with this? I don't want you to feel like your private space is being invaded."

"It's fine, Shi. I'm really glad you're here. With him."

My cheeks flushed all over again. "Right, well…will Amber be coming tonight?"

"No," he said, his expression darkening. "Please don't tell her about it either, okay?"

"I won't," I said slowly, my brows furrowed. "I just thought since you've been together for months…"

"She's never been here. This place isn't for just anyone."

The implications smacked me in the face. Ronan had asked me to come here months ago. After homecoming.

Miller was watching. I cleared my throat. "What about Violet? Is this place for her?"

He stiffened and looked about to protest. Then he nodded, his voice thick. "Yeah, it is."

I'd hung out at the shack a few more times that week, telling myself it was to pave the way for Violet more than it was to be with Ronan as much as humanly possible. But mostly, it was just nice being there. I'd lived in Santa Cruz for fourteen years and hadn't appreciated the ocean in this way before. Just sitting with it, listening to the waves crash while a bonfire warmed my face. I understood implicitly why the guys loved this place.

Holden regaled us with crazy, hilarious stories from when he'd spent a year in a Swiss sanatorium. He wouldn't say for what, and I wasn't about to pry. Sometimes Miller played his guitar and sang for us. I'd catch him watching Ronan and me, a wistful look on his face.

Finally, Violet agreed to come with me. Miller was still technically with Amber, but all three were miserable, and something had to change. The friendship between Miller and Violet was worth salvaging, if nothing else.

That night, after a rocky start, they took a walk and came back looking more at ease, and I felt hopeful that they'd each found their way back to the other.

The guys ragged on each other, Miller played for us, and the hour grew late, the fire burning low. From the other side of it, Violet and Miller were a bundle on the sand under blankets, sleeping.

Holden, alone and drunk, staggered to his feet. With a finger to his lips, he warned us not to wake them, then stumbled away.

"Will he be okay?" I whispered.

Ronan shrugged, his mouth grim. "I don't know. He's drunk a lot. I don't know what to do for him."

"You're here," I said. "He knows that. You have his back."

"Always," Ronan said, then nodded at Miller. "Him too." He looked down at me. *You too.*

He didn't need to say the words for me to hear them, and I immediately felt like crap for working so hard to prove that Ronan and I weren't an item.

"I'm sorry about earlier," I said. "When I was short with you."

"Which time?" Ronan asked and smiled into his beer. "I started to lose count."

I nudged his arm. "Every time. When you offered to open my soda. Violet was watching us, and I hate that feeling."

"What feeling?" Ronan asked with a dry smirk. "Being helped?"

"*Yes*, smart-ass. It's like you said, I hate people being in my business. Even if that person is my best friend."

"It's better if she doesn't know about us," Ronan said. "She's friends with Evelyn Gonzalez, right?" He drained his last beer of the night. "If Evelyn finds out, the whole damn town will know."

"True." I studied Ronan's profile. In the firelight, his eyes looked silvery, his jaw cut to sharper angles by the shadows that danced over his face. "You're really serious about that, aren't you? Keeping me safe from Dowd or—"

"*Yes.*" Ronan turned to look at me then, his voice low and intense. "Yes. I'm really fucking serious about that."

I sat back, a flare of heat sweeping through me at the dangerous glint in his eyes. Not for me but for whoever he thought might want to hurt me. Heat pooled between my legs, wanting him, while my heart was craving something else entirely. Something it shouldn't.

We've already come so far beyond casual, it's not even funny.

I jumped to my feet and brushed sand off my pants. "I have to get back. Bibi's starting to wonder if I still live there."

Ronan nodded and packed up his stuff.

"What about them? Think they'll be okay?" I whispered with a nod at Miller and Violet, sleeping tangled up in each other. She was tucked under his chin. His arms held her close.

"Yes," Ronan said. "They're finally okay. Thanks to you."

"I just gave them a push."

I wish someone would do the same to me.

Half of me wanted to throw my precautions and

protections to the wind and let myself fall for Ronan. It would be so easy.

The other, stronger half wondered if I'd survive the crash if he decided I wasn't worth catching.

The night was dark and the moon hidden behind silvery clouds, yet Ronan led me back along the coast safely, as if he could do it with his eyes closed. We arrived at the parking lot just as the sky was showing the first hints of dawn.

Even before climbing in the Buick, Ronan reached for me, but I stiffened.

He pulled back. "You okay?"

"Fine. Just tired."

A weak excuse. I hadn't been tired all the other mornings we welcomed the dawn from the back seat of my car, practically attacking each other. Fogging the windows in heated, grasping embraces, clothing askew but never removed. Ronan was holding back, slowing things down for my sake. We were supposed to be keeping things on the surface. Friends with benefits. No grand gestures or declarations of feelings required. Or wanted.

But even without sex, Ronan was unraveling me, stripping me naked with each passing day, until one day, I'd be exposed. He'd see all of me, and then what?

Then he'll leave.

I fumbled in my bag for my keys and managed to get the car door open. Ronan held it open for me instead of going around to the passenger side.

"You don't want a ride?"

"No," he said. "I'll walk."

"You sure?"

"I'm sure."

I crossed my arms. "Well…are you mad? I'm just tired. That's allowed, right?"

Dawn had only just begun to climb from behind the mountains in the east. Ronan's expression was unreadable.

"I just feel like walking, Shiloh," he said, his voice low, and I immediately felt like shit.

"Okay. Good night."

"Yep."

I climbed behind the wheel. Ronan shut the door for me and then waited, watching to make sure I left safely. He grew small in my rearview, then I turned a corner, and he was gone.

Bibi was awake and bustling in the kitchen when I came in.

"Sorry, Bibi. I fell asleep at the beach."

She smiled to herself as she reached into the fridge for a glass pitcher of orange juice. "You smell like campfire. And Ronan."

"Bibi!"

"I am merely stating the obvious." Her grin turned sly. "I was eighteen once too, you know."

"Oh my God."

"And anyway, I'm glad. I love him for you."

"Don't...say things like that. We're keeping it casual."

She pursed her lips and poured me a glass of orange juice. "So you keep saying. Yet you've been out with him most nights this week. *Late*."

"It's not just us. We're hanging out with friends," I said. "Violet too. I managed to get her to come tonight to reconnect with Miller."

"Good for you! Little cupid, aren't we? Now if only you could aim that bow and arrow at yourself..."

She swatted me on the butt and cackled a laugh.

"You are in too good a mood for this early in the morning. Any mail come for me yesterday?" I asked, desperate for a change of subject.

"Not yet, honey."

"Damn."

I had turned in my applications for business operation and seller's licenses and was now waiting to hear back from the city. If approved, I'd be one step closer to my own shop.

"It'd be nice to know if I got my permits before someone rents that old laundromat space."

"It's been available this long, so it must be destined for you," Bibi said. "But that old place is so run-down. Wouldn't it be nice to have someone who could help you make it beautiful?"

I tensed and then eased a breath. "I don't need Ronan—or anyone else—to help me. I'm doing this on my own. I've come this far." I smiled to take the harshness out of my words. "I'm going to take a shower."

"Shiloh—"

A knock came at the front door.

Bibi squinted at the clock in the kitchen. "Who could that be? At this hour?"

She watched from the dining room table as I went to find out.

I opened the door to my mother.

My breath caught in my throat, my heart dropping as I clutched the jamb, not believing my own eyes.

"What…what are you doing here?"

"I flew in late yesterday," Mama said, her gaze darting everywhere and finally landing on me. Taking me in. She took a fortifying breath and stood taller. "To talk to you, Shiloh."

"You came all this way to talk to me? It's seven in the morning."

"You're eighteen now, and I think it's time," she said, her hands gripping and twisting the strap on her purse. "I waited eighteen years, and suddenly, I can't wait another minute."

I fell back from the door to let her in, staring. She wore blue jeans and a red sweater under her coat. A yellow headband kept her curls back.

Blue, red, and yellow. The primary colors… I thought and wondered if I were losing my mind.

"Hello, Marie," Bibi said warily.

"Hello, Bibi. How are you feeling?"

"That depends," she replied pointedly.

Bibi moved to the couch and sank down with a heavy sigh. I couldn't take my eyes off Mama, afraid she'd disappear if I blinked.

"What's...what's happening? Is Bertie okay? Uncle Rudy?"

"They're fine. I told you, we need to talk." Mama clutched her bag like a shield. She looked younger somehow than she had this summer. More fragile. She wasn't in her territory now but mine. "Now that I'm here...I don't know if I made the right decision."

"Marie," Bibi warned and shook her head.

"No!" I cried. "I'm glad you're here." I drew her inside and shut the door behind her. "I want to talk to you. I always want to talk to you."

Mama came in reluctantly, her gaze clashing with Bibi in a way I didn't understand.

"Do you want some juice? Or coffee?"

I heard the desperation in my own voice, but Mama was *here*. She wouldn't have bought a flight and flown six hours for a conversation that could happen over the phone. This was *it*. She was here to tell me who my father was and what happened between them. Everything.

"No, thank you. Maybe we can speak privately?"

"Of course. The patio?"

Mama immediately headed for the back.

Bibi took my hand. "Shiloh, wait..."

"It's fine. I want to hear this. More than anything."

Even if it scares me to death.

Her grip tightened. "Listen to me, Shiloh. You know who you are. Whatever she says, whatever she tells you can't change that."

"That's just it," I whispered. "I don't know who I am. She's going to tell me. Finally."

Bibi closed her eyes for a moment and let go of my hand. "I suppose this day had to come eventually."

Her resignation that something awful was about to happen squeezed the knot in my stomach, but I hurried to join my mother in the backyard. On the patio, sprinklers had left the wrought-iron chairs and table wet with droplets like glass beads.

"We could go to my room?" I suggested.

"We don't have to sit," Mama said. Indeed, she looked like she was ready to bolt. "How is Bibi? Any more dizzy spells?"

"None. She's doing great."

"She's getting up there, and I know her vision is declining."

I squared my shoulders. "Are you afraid you might have to take me back?"

Mama flinched and looked beyond me to the shed. "That's new."

"Ronan built it," I blurted.

"Who is Ronan?"

"He's…" I realized I didn't know how to answer that, and an ache panged in my heart, adding to the boulder that sat on my chest to see my mother—a stranger in my own backyard.

"It's nice," she said.

"It's for my work," I said. "It's what I do, Mama. I make jewelry until my eyes water and my fingers burn. I work instead of doing almost anything else."

"So you can open your own business."

"Yes, for that. But also..." I swallowed down a jagged lump of pride. "To prove myself to you. Make you proud. But it doesn't feel like that's possible."

Her dark eyes met mine, and she was quiet for long moments.

"Mama?"

"Do you know the origin of your name, Shiloh?"

My brows furrowed. "Bibi said it means 'tranquil.'"

"That's very *Bibi* of her to tell you that."

"What's that supposed to mean?"

She ignored my sharp, protective tone or didn't hear it. She wandered the patio, touching the delicate pink and purple fuchsias hanging in a pot from the corner of the pergola.

"Our ancestors fought in the Civil War. The First Louisiana Native Guard. Did you know that?"

"Yes," I said slowly. "Uncle Rudy has a framed sketch of Captain Andre Cailloux on the wall of his study."

Mama nodded. "My daddy—your grandpa—used to tell me the stories *his* grandpa told him. He said the Battle of Shiloh was one of the bloodiest of the war."

"Was our family involved?"

"No. Black soldiers never fought in that battle, but the

name stuck with me. Because deciding to keep you or not… that was a battle."

The backyard was suddenly airless. Still.

"And?" I asked tightly. "Did you win, Mama? Or did you lose?"

She said nothing, but it was all there in that silence. In her eyes that couldn't look at me.

The ground under my feet swayed as if I were on a sinking ship; I gripped the back of a chair to keep from falling.

"Oh, Shiloh. I was nineteen. In love." She scoffed weakly. "As if I knew what that was. I had a promising future ahead of me, and I gave it up. For him. Biggest mistake of my life."

I thought I was the biggest mistake of your life.

I nearly said the words, but she was so close to letting go of the truth at long last. I held my breath, my heart pounding in my chest.

Mama's eyes shone, her lips parted, she inhaled…and then she stepped back from the edge, stuffing it all back down.

"I shouldn't have come," she said, her voice steady again. Cold. "I'm not ready. Bibi knows that. It's why I'm not welcome here." She smiled ruefully. "She knows me better than I know myself."

"What… No! Please, Mama." I leaned over the chair, gripping it so hard the cold metal dug painfully into my fingers. "Keep talking to me. Who is he? My father…tell me—"

But it was too late. Only the patio table stood between

us, but she may as well have been back on the other side of the country. On the other side of the world.

"You don't have a father, Shiloh," she said stiffly. "*I* lost the battle, but you're the casualty, and I'm sorry. I'm so sorry." She moved around the table and raised her hand to my cheek; her fingers were cold on my skin. "Nothing is your fault. Remember that. Not one thing. I only wish I were stronger. For your sake. I tried but..."

Her hand fell, and she turned for the door.

"You're leaving?" I stared, my breath coming hard. "You just got here. You haven't told me anything. Only cryptic... *bullshit*."

She acted as if she hadn't heard me. At the patio door, she turned. "I'm not enough of a mother to give you advice. I haven't earned it, but I'll give it anyway. Be careful, Shiloh. Be very careful. Love will make you do stupid things."

"Like me," I said, my voice wavering. "I'm the stupid thing you did."

She didn't answer me but went into the house, leaving me alone on the patio, her silence the only reply.

The backyard blurred as if I were underwater. Slowly, I made my way inside. Bibi was on the couch, stroking one of the cats. Mama was already gone.

"What just happened?" I said.

"Oh, honey. Come sit."

I sank down beside Bibi, staring at the door.

"What did she say to you, Shiloh? Did she..."

"Tell me the truth? No." I turned my head on a stiff

neck. "*You* have to tell me, Bibi. Tell me everything you know."

"I can't—"

"Do you know who my father is? Do you know what happened between him and Mama?" I felt tears gather in the back of my throat. "I'm the battle she lost, Bibi. That's what she came to tell me."

Bibi's eyes fell shut. "Lord, baby, I'm sorry. I'm so sorry."

"So is she. Everyone is sorry, but no one will tell me anything."

"It's not my place," she said. "It's up to your mother to unlock her heart for you or not. I'm angry with her for showing up out of the blue when I knew she wasn't ready. Saying things that would only hurt and confuse you." She shook her head grimly. "Foolishness."

"I hate feeling this way," I said quietly. "With her but with you too."

"I know. But it can't be helped. I made a promise. And keeping one's word means something."

"Even if it hurts me?"

She shook her head, her warm face that I'd turned to for comfort a thousand times now stiff and unmovable, her tone firm. "I'm sorry for that, Shiloh. But I also made a promise to myself. To only ever do what I think is best for you. To protect your happiness."

I understood her meaning, and the dread sank heavier in my stomach. *Telling me the truth is worse than keeping me in the dark.*

I pushed off the couch. "I didn't get much sleep last night. I'm going to lie down. Do you need anything?"

"No, honey, but wait…"

I did something I'd never done before; I ignored her and went to my room. My heart, already cracked wide, cracked again for the rift between us. I curled up on my bed and didn't go to school that day. Or the next.

Or the one after that.

My phone chimed with texts until I put it on silent without looking at them.

On the third afternoon I'd spent lying on the couch in sweatpants and an old T-shirt, watching her programs with her, Bibi stood over me, hands on her hips.

"You just going to lie around for…how long? You're missing a lot of school."

"I'm taking a few personal days."

"This isn't like you, Shiloh."

Isn't it? Who's to say? I don't know who I am.

She sighed at my silence and sat down next to me, her hand gentle on my shoulder.

I couldn't resent her for keeping whatever promise she'd made to Mama, but it had taken these three painful days to get us back to where we'd been—about the same amount of time for the shock of my mother's sudden visit to wear off.

But the hangover wouldn't quit.

A pain had lodged deep in my chest or heart…or maybe deeper than that. A knife stab in my damn soul. I thought about Ronan's mother. It was horrible he'd lost her, but maybe that was better than having her alive and walking the earth, thinking her own kid was a battle she'd fought and lost.

The sun was turning a twilight gold when my phone vibrated with an incoming call.

"You going to get that?" Bibi asked.

"No."

On TV, Judge Judy scolded a man for not remembering the basic facts of his own case.

"It's Ronan, isn't it?" Bibi said. "He's probably worried sick about you."

"He doesn't want anyone to know we're seeing each other."

"That doesn't sound like him."

"He has his reasons. And we're *casual*. Because I have my reasons too."

The phone buzzed again from the coffee table.

"*Shiloh*." Bibi wasn't messing around.

I heaved a sigh and reached over to pick it up. I had two missed calls and a half-dozen texts.

Are you okay?
Shiloh?
WTF??

"It is Ronan." I closed my eyes for long moments, then set the phone back down.

"Talk to me, baby," Bibi said, her tone gentle now.

"Come on. I know your mama didn't do right, but I'm getting scared."

"I'm sorry," I said, hauling myself to sitting. My braids were getting rough, my sweatshirt stained. "I hate myself like this. Mama hates me, period."

"She doesn't, honey. But I hate that she makes you feel this way. So you think being alone is the only way to be strong."

"Because it's true. I can't open my heart and be strong at the same time. I can't...be in love and still be in control." I gestured at my nest on the couch. "Look at me. Mama was here for ten minutes, and it wrecked me for three days." I shook my head. "I have to be alone. I have work to do."

"You choose to be alone because it's safe. Because your mother hurts you terribly, and I'm so sorry for that, Shiloh. I'm sorry you feel the need to protect yourself. But Ronan... He's a good man, yes?"

I nodded, my hands twisting in my lap. "But how long before..."

"How long before what, baby?"

"Before he sees what Mama sees? How long before he decides he doesn't want me either?"

"Oh, sweet girl." Bibi gathered me to her, held me tight.

God, I felt so pathetic. So weak. My chest torn open. Exposed. My heart bleeding for my mother and beating for Ronan. The tears tried to come, but I willed them back and shook my head.

"Never mind," I said, gently extracting myself from

Bibi's embrace. "I'm going to school tomorrow. I'm going to get my shop. That's my only goal. It's where I should put my energy. Not in silly boy drama that I promised I'd *never* get involved in. Because I was right. It's just a distraction."

A beautiful, sexy, intense distraction that I can't stop wanting.

"No, Shiloh." Bibi's voice was back to firm. "Marie coming here is the distraction. Don't let her words poison you. Not against Ronan and especially not against yourself."

I smiled for Bibi's sake. "I'll try," I said, but it felt too late. Mama's rejection had burrowed down, planting roots that had gone so deep I didn't know how I'd ever tear them out.

We ate a quiet dinner, and soon after, Bibi went to bed. I stayed on the couch in the dark; the only light was the glare of the TV. *The Simpsons* was a too-bright blare of yellows, blues, and reds.

I must've dozed off, because I was jolted out of my skin when a hard rapping came at the door. The night was deep and dark when I peered through the peephole. Ronan was angrily pacing our front walk, rain drenching him.

I threw open the door. A square of light from the house fell over him, illuminating his face that was hard and angry. His dark hair was plastered down over his forehead and cheeks.

"What are you doing here?"

"Are you all right?" he demanded.

"Of course I am. What—"

"Good." He practically spat the word, then turned to go. He took two steps and whirled around, whipping wet hair out of his eyes. "I mean…what the fuck, Shiloh?"

I recoiled, crossed my arms over my chest. "I stayed home for a few days."

"You can't answer a damn text?"

"My phone was off. I was trying to rest. So you show up at my house and… What are you doing here?"

"Nothing. Making sure you're okay."

I hugged myself tighter, scared of how badly I wanted to throw myself into his arms. The fear put ugly things in my mouth to push him away.

"Why? What is your crazy obsession with me? Being safe? From whom? What the hell do you think is going to happen?"

"I don't know," he said, frustrated. "I… Fucking hell. Never mind. Forget it."

"We are not together. You don't want to be seen with me."

"I know what I said, but—"

"And I told you, I don't have anything to give. We set up…rules. You can't just come here and break them."

"And you can't just fucking disappear!" he shouted, making me flinch. His gray eyes shone silver in the rain and moonlight. Like steel. "You can tell me to fuck off, but you can't just *vanish*."

The hurt behind the anger was palpable, slamming into my chest and sinking into my heart that was already bruised and bleeding from my mother's visit.

We stood in silence, the rain smattering the pavement the only sound. He carved a hand through his drenched hair. His stormy expression softened, his eyes trailing over my face.

"Shiloh…"

I shook my head, unwilling to break. I didn't know how to break down in front of him. I had no idea what would happen if I did.

He nodded, resigned, and turned and walked away. The words to call him back stuck in my mouth, Mama's warning whispering in my ear.

I watched him go until the dark swallowed him up, and then I went back inside and shut the door.

EIGHTEEN
RONAN

"Fuck."

I slammed the door to my apartment shut and tore off my jacket that was drenched from the sudden, cold rain.

"*Fuck.*"

The look on Shiloh's face when she answered her door was going to stick with me for a long time. Part shock, part anger, part fucking *fear*.

She thinks you're a psycho.

I went to the bathroom to shower and warm up, and the reflection in the mirror agreed. Hair sodden, eyes hooded and ringed with dark circles from so many sleepless nights. So many tired hours spent walking away from nightmares that came anyway when I finally collapsed into bed.

"She's better off," I told the reflection.

But I'd known that all along. Shiloh was too good, too beautiful, too *whole* for someone like me—shattered into pieces until there was hardly anything left but this shit apartment, school (when I wasn't suspended), and odd jobs that didn't make a future. I hung out at the beach at night drinking beer, and I walked around town until my old boots were full of holes, for what? To make up for a day ten years ago that could not be given back.

Shiloh had plans and dreams. *She* had a future. What did she need with pieces of me?

The next morning, after waking with screams in my throat and the futon sheets soaked with sweat, I dragged myself into the shower again. To get ready for school.

Because I'm trying, Mom. It's pointless and stupid, but I'm still trying.

I threw on my jacket and was nearly at the door when a knock came. Maryann was there looking unsure and nervous. Not herself. She was dressed for work in a plain brown skirt with a blazer that more or less matched.

"Hi, Ronan, glad I caught you… Oh, but you're heading to school, right? I don't want you to be late."

"It's fine," I snapped, last night's anger and failure still bitter in my mouth. I exhaled. "Everything okay?"

"We can talk about it later. This afternoon."

I could see whatever she had to say would kill her to keep inside until this afternoon. I opened the door wider and stepped back to let her in.

"Okay, yeah, I should stop acting like a chickenshit and just come out with it." She huffed a breath and thrust a small envelope at me. "This month's rent."

"Oh, right." I'd forgotten it was the first already, which meant a trip to Nelson's after school.

"It's short a couple hundred bucks," Maryann said in a rush. "I'll have it later, but I don't have it now." Her eyes fell shut. "I'm sorry. I don't know—"

"Hi, Ronan!"

Cami and Lily rushed in, and both wrapped their arms around me. They were dressed in matching denim skirt overalls, Lily with a yellow shirt, Cami in blue.

"Today is picture day at school!" Lily said.

"Mommy says we're not allowed to touch anything," Cami added. "So we don't mess up our clothes, but that's the whole reason for overalls."

Their mom looked sheepish. "I didn't plan this. A cute offensive."

"It's okay," I said, feeling a little lighter with the girls running around my nearly empty living area.

"It's *not* okay." Maryann blinked back frustrated tears. "God, I hate this."

"Hate what, Mommy?" Cami asked.

"Being in traffic?" Lily turned to me confidentially. "Mommy says a lot of bad words when we're in traffic."

"That's a pretty necklace, Ronan!" Cami exclaimed. "Let me see."

She tugged my hand until I squatted down, and then she and Lily took turns examining the pendant Shiloh had given me. Had *made* for me.

"It's so pretty!"

"And pointy. Where did you get it?"

"A friend made it for me."

"Really? That makes me love it more!" Lily said. "Do you love it?"

Fuck.

"I...like it a lot."

"Okay, girls, we're going to make Ronan late," Maryann said, the worry lines rushing back in to crease her face. "Your uncle?"

"I'll handle him."

"How? He never lets this stuff slide. Last time, the late fee nearly killed me, and he told me I might not get a second chance if it happened again."

"*Maryann.* I'll handle him."

Her eyes filled with tears.

"Why are you crying, Mommy?" Cami asked.

"Because it's not often we get to see true kindness," she said, not bothering to hide it. "You're a good man, Ronan. And that pendant is beautiful. Whoever made it for you obviously cares about you. A lot."

A flare of hope went up in my chest, warm and bright, then flamed out just as fast. Wanting what I couldn't have never got me anywhere.

"Thank you, Ronan," Maryann said, herding the girls to the door. "Thank you so much."

"Don't mention it."

They left, the girls waving enthusiastically, and I went to my bedroom. I lifted a loose board in the floor and reached for the small metal lockbox hidden under it. I didn't have a bank account; I rarely had money long enough to keep one.

The box held a little more than seven hundred dollars, saved up from odd jobs on Craigslist. More than I'd had in a while. I counted out ten twenties, tore open Maryann's envelope, and put the cash in with her check.

The day dragged until history. Shiloh had finally shown up after three days of absence but didn't look my way once. From my vantage four rows behind her, I did enough looking for both of us. Her eyes had dark circles, and her foot tapped in her sandal nervously all during Baskin's lecture on the Cold War. A war without weapons, only tension and silence.

When class got out, I headed straight back to my place, walking over rain-slicked pavement, thinking (hoping) every car on the road was the creaky, chugging Buick, slowing behind me.

None were.

I went to my place, grabbed the rest of the rent checks left in my manager's box, stuffed them in a manila envelope, and headed back out again.

Somehow, the Bluffs complex looked even more shitty since last I'd seen it. The roof was in worse shape after a rainy winter, and the cheap, dark-green paint was already chipping off in huge chunks.

I knocked on my uncle's door.

"It's open."

I stepped inside, mentally preparing myself for the claustrophobia of his crammed apartment. It was worse.

There was a second small coffee table in his living room with a foldable bed frame stacked on top of it. A brand-new mattress, still in its plastic, leaned against one wall. The TV was on—I wondered if it ever got a break—with Nelson parked in front of it. The scent of microwaved ravioli hung in the air.

I nodded at the furniture. "What's all this?"

"Tenant eviction," Nelson said. He was wearing a stained undershirt, boxers that brushed his knees, and black socks pulled up his pale legs that were crisscrossed with bulging veins. "But the mattress is new. Figured you could use it."

"This is for me?"

"You had a birthday, right?"

My birthday was weeks ago. Usually it came and went, uneventful. Except this year, I'd had Shiloh's pendant, Holden's boots, and Miller's song. And now a real bed instead of that shitty futon.

Maybe I'll sleep.

"How did you know?" I asked.

"That social worker, Alicia, called me. Made me promise not to forget, but I did. Hey, better late than never, right? She sends her regards."

Alicia Marquez was one of the few people who'd ever shown me kindness over the years, going above and beyond the duties of her job to make sure I was okay. Hell, even after I turned eighteen, she found Nelson.

Except that didn't make sense.

I hadn't thought about it at the time; I was just happy to get the fuck out of Wisconsin and be with family. But Alicia had been searching for a blood relative since I was eight years old, and Nelson showed up after I aged out of the system?

I turned the thought over and over in my mind, like the envelope in my hands.

"That's the rent?" Nelson held out his hand. I gave it to him. "Any issues?"

"No. What's our late fee policy again?"

He frowned, peering into the envelope. "Seventy-five dollars for the first week. One fifty for the next. If they're late more than once, they're out."

"Seems kind of rough."

"Rough? That's the rules."

"Do you ever let it slide?"

"Why the hell would I do that?"

I shrugged. "Shit happens. Circumstances."

"Not my problem. I got my own *circumstances*. Don't need to deal with someone else's." He narrowed his eyes. "Why?"

I shrugged again, not looking at him.

Nelson snorted and hauled himself out of his recliner to hobble to the kitchen. He didn't look well. His skin had a yellowish tinge to it, his hair thin and brittle. The strength under his bulk that had reminded me of my father was just bulk now.

"You're doing a good job," he said, poking his head

inside the fridge so I barely heard him. "Better than I expected."

"Thanks."

"Keep it up. Don't get soft just because you know the tenants now. And their *circumstances*."

Too late.

"What about you?" I asked.

"Huh?"

I raised my voice. "How are you?"

His head popped out of the fridge. "What's it to you?" Nelson emerged from the kitchen with two beers. "Here." He thrust one at me and clinked his to mine. "Happy birthday."

We both drank, and then Nelson sank down heavily in his chair. I sat in the other, toying with the bottle. The TV blared a commercial for a local used car dealership.

Maybe it was last night's fuckup with Shiloh—another good thing in my life that had slipped through my fingers. Or maybe it was that I knew, even with a decent bed and a real mattress, the nightmares would still find me because they were in my blood. My blood that was *his* blood, while hers had been splattered all over the kitchen floor so I was alone for ten fucking years…

I couldn't let it go.

"Alicia called you?" My voice sounded tight.

"That's what I said."

"And she found you last summer? When I was at the farm in Manitowoc?"

He grunted what might've been a yes, not looking at me.

"Nelson."

"What? Christ, I'm trying to watch my show…"

I concentrated on peeling the label off my beer bottle. "Alicia's job ended when I turned eighteen. But she worked her ass off for ten years before that. Looking for you."

"Yeah? So?"

"She found you, didn't she?" I said, peeling. "But you waited until I was eighteen to come forward."

He shifted in his recliner. "You're asking this now?"

"I'm asking."

His eyes went back on the TV, not answering.

The label came off. I crumpled it up in my hand. My voice was low. Stony. "I did ten years in foster care, Nelson."

"So?"

"*So?*"

"That's what I said. We all got tough luck stories. You think you're special?"

"No, but—"

"Good, 'cause you aren't. Remember that."

The old anger boiled up in me and spilled over. I chucked the balled-up label on the floor where it joined the rest of the trash. "I remember. I remember being a scared little kid, shuffled around from house to house. No family. No *nothing*," I said, my voice rising. "Just where the fuck were you?"

Nelson's head jerked back and swiveled to me, his eyes wide. "Beg your pardon? You talk to me like that when I'm trying to do something nice for you? Well, shit, I learned my lesson, didn't I? Never again. You get nothing else from me if that's how you're going to act. Spoiled brat…"

I barely heard him, the bloody memories washing over me. "I was eight years old when he killed her."

"Here we go again."

"You knew. You fucking knew what happened, and you stayed away. *I was in the system for ten fucking years.*"

Ten years of foster life. A soul-crushing weight I carried every day on top of losing my mother. Abusive guardians or negligent ones that used me for a paycheck. Beatings, locked closets, hunger, and cold, harsh words and violence. It all pressed down on me until I couldn't breathe, until I wanted to hit something until my bones broke. To feel anything that wasn't *that*.

"You knew I was out there…and you let me fucking rot until I could be useful to you. Free labor. Not family."

"Boo-fucking-hoo," Nelson snapped back. "You look all right. You survived."

I put the naked beer bottle down before it shattered in my grip.

"Look," he said into my silence. "I wasn't ever going to be any kind of a parent. Can you see me with a kid? Doing what…cooking you breakfast? Sack lunches? Making sure you did your homework?"

You could've tried, I wanted to say, but I was done asking for anything from anyone. Even if that ask was ten years too late.

"Besides," Nelson said, turning back to the TV. "We're here now, aren't we?"

The anger gusted out of me. That was as good as it was going to get. My hand went to Shiloh's compass pendant.

For when you feel adrift.

I closed my eyes for a moment, held it tight, inhaled. Then I let go, exhaling. Calmer now.

"Yeah," I said dully. "I'm still fucking here."

Nelson let me borrow his ancient pickup truck to take the furniture back to my complex. Maryann poked her head out of her unit when I pulled into the parking lot, as if she'd been watching for me.

"Hey," she said, walking to meet me, her hands twisting. "How'd it go?"

I unlocked the truck bed. "Fine. Nelson said you're good. He'll waive the late fee."

"Really?" Her brow wrinkled. "That doesn't sound like him."

I shrugged. "I must've caught him in a good mood." Her eyes narrowed, and I busied myself hefting the mattress onto my shoulders. "I could go back and ask him to reconsider if you want."

She waved her hands. "Ha, no. Thanks. Thank you, Ronan. It won't happen again."

"Yep."

She said something else, but I pretended not to hear it. Her gratitude made me sick. Where the fuck were the people who were supposed to take care of her? They left her so alone…so *adrift*…that she needed *my* help? Was that the point of life? A lucky few would make it unscarred while everyone else was on their fucking own?

Bullshit.

The new coffee table was just as old and plain as the first one—chipped wood and stains on the surface. But my living room looked more like a living room. The bed was a real bed. The futon went straight to the dumpster, and I lay down that night on an actual mattress.

The nightmares came anyway.

NINETEEN

SHILOH

Did you hear? Violet's in the hospital.

I FROZE, AND THE PHONE NEARLY FELL OUT OF MY HAND. It was a little after 10:00 p.m. Bibi and I had been watching a movie when my phone chimed a text from Annika Shaw, a girl on the soccer team who I'd been closer to in middle school.

My fingers trembled as I jammed out a reply.

What happened???
Head injury at practice. She's at UC Med. Blacked out.

"Holy shit."
Bibi's head turned to me. "Shiloh?"
"It's Violet. She's in the hospital."
"Oh dear. Is she all right?"

"Don't know."

My fingers flew. How bad is it?

I waited for a reply while tears burned the corners of my eyes at the sudden rush of fear I felt for my best friend. I blinked them away angrily. It shouldn't have to take losing someone to realize how much you loved them.

Oh God, Miller...

There was still no reply from Annika, and I remembered why we weren't close friends anymore.

Flake.

Panicked, I called the hospital. Dispatch put me through to the nurses' station on Violet's floor—only to be told they couldn't tell me anything.

"I'm going up there," I said to Bibi as I ran to the kitchen for my car keys and sweater that hung on the hook on the door. I threw on my cardigan, then typed a text to Miller.

> I just heard. Violet's at UCSC Medical. Head injury. They won't tell me more.

His reply was almost instant. On my way.

"Send Violet my love," Bibi called. "But drive carefully, Shiloh."

"I will. Promise. I'll call you when I know something."

On the way to the hospital, it took everything I had not to push the Buick as hard as it could go, and I reminded myself of my promise to Bibi.

Reception at UCSC Medical Center told me Violet was

on the fifth floor, neurology, room 504. Miller was already there, sitting against the wall outside her closed door in his usual uniform—worn-out jeans, T-shirt under a plaid flannel, beanie. His guitar case lay across his lap.

Because he ran to her.

"Hey," I said, hurrying to him.

He looked up, his face a mask of tense, tight worry. "Shi…"

I sank down on the floor beside him, hugged him. "What's happening?"

"She's okay. I guess. Her parents don't like me much. They won't let me in to see her."

"Screw them. Violet likes you a lot. That's all that matters."

"I guess. But fuck, Shi. They say she lost consciousness. They're keeping her here overnight."

"Probably just to be on the safe side."

A nurse strode by, giving us a perplexed look.

"I talked to Amber this morning," I said. "She told me you broke up with her."

He nodded miserably. "Last week, the morning after Violet came to the shack. Amber wanted me to give her time before I told Violet. So I did. I waited too damn long. A few days and four years too long."

"You're here now."

"What if I'm too late, Shi?" Miller said, his voice gruff. "What if she gets worse? What if—"

"You can't think that way," I said, even though my own

imagination was running away on the same terrifying tangent. "What-ifs will drive you crazy."

He nodded grudgingly, and I rested my chin on my drawn-up knees. A short silence passed, and then Miller shook his head, speaking almost to himself.

"Never again. If she's okay, I'll never let it get to be *too late* ever again. Ronan was right."

I tensed, every part of me at attention. "What was he right about?"

"He said *too late* is death. I think he was talking about his mom."

"Yeah? I know that she died when he was little. Both his parents died, but he only ever talks about her."

Miller nodded grimly. "That's because his dad killed her."

I stared, the blood draining from my face. "What? He *killed*… Oh my God." I clapped a hand to my mouth, my heart beating hard and breaking for Ronan. "How?"

"Don't know. But I think he saw it happen."

"He did," I said, remembering. "He told me he was there. He said he couldn't save her. Oh my God…"

Miller's head snapped up, eyes wide at my horrified expression. "Shit, maybe I shouldn't have told you. He's a good guy."

"Of course he is. Why would you say that?"

"Because he's my friend and I don't want you to think badly about him. He's been a lot happier since you've been around."

"He has?"

"Ronan's version of happy. But yeah."

My head fell back against the wall. "He never told me."

"He's self-conscious about what happened," Miller said, running his fingers along the edge of his guitar case. "I think he thinks he's damaged or something. Like what his dad did poisoned him too."

I nodded. "He told me what happened in Wisconsin messed him up and he didn't want me to deal with the repercussions."

My heart cracked again, thinking of Ronan going through all that alone. And thinking it might hurt *me* somehow.

Because he wants to protect me. Always. Even from himself.

"God…" I ran my hands over my braids, giving them a tug to keep myself from crying.

"You haven't been to the shack lately," Miller said in a low voice.

"I know. I…wasn't feeling well."

"But you're better now?" He was looking at me like someone who could see into people's hearts and then write songs about what they saw.

"Not really," I admitted, thinking of my mom's visit. "But I'm working on it."

He smiled faintly. "That's all we can do, right?"

I nodded and rested my head against his shoulder. Time dragged. My butt was getting numb from sitting on the cold linoleum floor. Finally, the door beside us opened, and Vince and Lynn McNamara emerged.

I'd known them since I was a kid, in better times, when they'd been happy and in love. Now they looked tired in rumpled business clothes, like lawyers fighting on opposite sides of a case.

Vince smiled wanly as we got to our feet. "Hey, Miller. Shiloh. It's great of you to come."

"But it's late," Lynn said. "Violet needs to rest."

"Is she okay?" I asked. "What happened?"

"She crashed into another soccer player at practice and suffered a concussion," Vince said. "But they say she's going to be fine. Keeping her overnight is just a precaution."

I sagged as relief gusted out of me. Miller stood ramrod straight.

"I'm not leaving," he stated, his voice hard. "I want to see her."

Lynn sighed. "It's late…"

"It can't hurt," Vince put in. "A few minutes. They came all this way."

His wife glared daggers at him. "It's not even visiting hours. They can come back—"

"I'm not leaving," Miller said again. "I don't care what time it is. I'll stay here all night if I have to, but I'm going to see her."

The protective tone in his voice reminded me of how Ronan spoke to me.

And Miller loves Violet.

A strange sensation flooded me, something between euphoria and nausea. I fumbled my phone out of my bag to give myself something to do. I called Bibi and told her that Violet was okay.

"I'm so glad, honey. But it's getting late. I'd feel better if you came home."

I checked the visitor situation: Lynn McNamara wasn't going to budge, but then Miller wasn't either. Violet was in good hands, and I was suddenly exhausted. Drained.

"I'm leaving now. Love you, Bibi." I hung up with her and turned to Miller. "Bibi wants me home. You going to be okay?"

"I've never been better," he said. "For the first time in a long time."

I smiled. "I'll be back in the morning. Tell Violet I said get well or else I'll kick her ass."

Visiting hours began at 11:00 a.m. I knocked on Violet's door and peeked my head inside. My heart swelled to see her awake, a strange but beautiful smile on her face.

"You decent?"

Her serene expression morphed into a huge grin to see me. "Shi!"

I laughed at her enthusiasm. "They must be giving you some strong drugs."

"Miller is here. He just went to the cafeteria for coffee."

"Ah. That explains it." I bent over the bed and hugged her as tight as I dared. "You're okay, right?"

"I'm okay. Better than I have been in a long time."

"Miller said almost the exact same thing last night," I said, dropping into the chair beside her.

Violet beamed, her cheeks pink. "Did he?"

"I take it you two got everything sorted out?"

"Finally. It's funny, everything's falling apart with my parents and my college fund, but I feel like I'm exactly where I'm supposed to be. With Miller. And I'm so happy."

A twinge of jealousy tightened my stomach.

"I'm glad, Vi. Truly. And I won't even say I told you so, even though I've been saving it up for four solid years."

Violet laughed, radiant even in a hospital bed. "It's been a journey. You'll never believe it, but right before I got whacked in the head, River Whitmore asked me to prom." She braced herself for my reaction. "And I said yes."

I smacked my own forehead. "Girl…"

"I know!" she said, still laughing. "Just as friends. But I didn't know what was happening with Miller, and I was so tired of feeling like I had no control over my feelings."

"I get that," I said with a tight smile. "Does Miller know?"

"He knows. We told each other everything, and it's like I can breathe again."

Jealousy rumbled in my guts, stronger now. *Violet is so much braver than I am.*

My friend grinned knowingly. "So. Been to the shack much lately?"

"Come again?"

"You heard me. Maybe it's that I'm deliriously happy and want you to feel the same, but…you and Ronan?"

"Umm…"

She glanced down, plucked the hospital blanket. "I know you don't like to talk about this stuff. In all the years I've known you, you've never mentioned a boy."

"I never told you a lot of things going on with me, Vi. And I'm sorry about that."

"Don't be sorry. I just figured you're a private person. I respect that. But sometimes, I wonder if something…bad had happened to you. With a boy."

"No, nothing bad. God, Vi. I'm sorry for making you think that. I've been a shitty friend."

"No…"

"*Yes*. You keep saying I know who I am and what I want. How I'm whole. But the truth is just the opposite."

"Tell me."

It was my turn to toy with the blanket. "I don't know what to say. Because I don't know what I feel. Or *how* to feel."

"About Ronan?" Her voice softened. "Do you love him?"

I didn't know how to answer except that a little voice whispered I could love Ronan Wentz if I was brave too.

"I…don't know."

Violet smiled gently. "You can't lie to someone in a hospital. It's a rule."

I tried to smile back and failed. "What's wrong with

me started long before Ronan. With my mom." I heaved a breath. "Every summer, I go to New Orleans. All those visits I don't tell you about? They're to see her. But she hates me, Vi. I work hard trying to make something of myself, as if I have to prove my worth. But it doesn't matter what I do. She regrets having me."

I'm the battle she lost.

God, that truth was like a knife straight through the center of me, a wound that wouldn't close, and I didn't know how I could be good for anyone until it did.

"Oh, Shi."

"I've been putting on the appearance of strength, hoping if I pretended hard enough, I could just *be* strong. So that I'd look like I have my shit together. But I'm an impostor. So when Ronan comes along…"

"You're scared."

My automatic reflex was to deny. I nodded instead. The image of Ronan on my doorstep in the rain came back to me, and my chest tightened, trying to squeeze out a lifetime's worth of tears.

"Mama taught me it's better to be alone than left behind," I said, hardly a whisper. "It's better to be the one who shuts the door. To not risk being hurt. Because I already hurt. Every day."

Violet took my hand and just held it, saying nothing but being there.

I heaved a breath. "This is stupid. I should be the one comforting you."

"You are," Violet said. "I love you, Shi. You're my best friend, but I've never felt as close to you as I do right now."

"I wish I'd told you everything sooner."

"We have from now on." Violet smiled. "It's not too late."

I squeezed her hand. "I'm so grateful that it's not."

Because too late is death.

They discharged Violet several hours later. Her parents came to pry her away from Miller and me and take her home.

I hugged her goodbye and went straight to the shack.

TWENTY
RONAN

"Hey."

I looked up from where I was sitting in Holden's huge chair, staring at nothing. Shiloh stood at the rough-cut entrance to the shack, looking insanely beautiful in a long white skirt and tight white T-shirt. Her braids fell over her shoulders and frayed softly at the ends, blowing in the breeze off the ocean. The sun was setting behind her, glinting off a copper bracelet coiled around her upper arm. She looked like a fucking queen.

You really thought you had something with her?

I stood up and reached to unclasp the compass pendant. Shiloh's eyes widened. "What are you doing?"

"I figured you wanted it back. Isn't that why you're here?"

She quickly moved to me, grabbed my wrists. "It's yours. No matter what happens between…us."

Us. I'd never used that word before.

Shiloh read my hard expression and let go of me. She leaned back on the edge of the table and crossed her arms.

"I didn't come here to take anything from you," she said. "I came to... I don't know. Talk." She cocked her head, her face soft. "You look tired."

"Shiloh, don't," I said, going to the mini fridge for a beer. We were out of beer. *Shit.*

"Am I not welcome anymore?"

I sank back in Holden's chair. Too many sleepless nights—years' worth—were dragging me down. I didn't have the energy to feed the useless hope that sparked in my chest that she was here. I shut my eyes. If I could only sleep, I could think better. Could say the right things to change everything.

Be better for her.

"You can do what you want," I said tiredly.

"Ronan..."

"What do you want me to say, Shiloh? We ended... whatever it was. Again."

"You're right," she said, her voice heavy. "I shouldn't have come. I just thought... Never mind."

I heard the shuffle of her sandals on the wood plank floor, making to leave. I should've let her go. I was *supposed* to let her go. But like tossing out a lifeline, my hand shot out in the dark and found her wrist. I closed my fingers around her warm skin and opened my eyes, keeping my gaze where I held her. I brought my other hand up and slid it against her fingers, trailing over the rings in gold, silver, and copper.

She moved closer, her skirt brushing my knees. I looked up to see her eyes on me, the same apprehension on her face that lived in my heart.

"I don't know what I'm doing," she said softly. "I've never…been here before."

"Me neither."

"A week ago, my mother came to see me."

My hand tightened on hers automatically. She squeezed, then gently let go, her fingers slipping out of mine as she hugged herself.

"What happened?"

"Nothing," she said with a grim smile. "I thought she'd tell me the truth about my father. Instead, she said some horrible shit and left. It spun me out, I guess, like a mini breakdown. So I ignored you."

"I get it."

"I'm sorry."

"So am I. That she did that to you."

Shiloh huffed a shaky sigh. "You always do that."

"Do what?"

"Put things simply. Cut through all the complicated crap and make me feel…"

I held my breath, waiting.

"Better," she said finally. "Being around you makes me feel better, Ronan. And, since we're being honest, turned on." She smiled weakly, then shook her head. "But it also brings up all the fears and self-doubts I've been trying to bury for years. It's enough to make a gal seasick, Wentz."

"What do you want to do about it, Barrera?"

She laughed. "I don't know. What do you want to do?"

"Right now? I want to make you come."

Her eyes widened, and an astonished sound burst out of her. "Jesus…" She cleared her throat. "We've already established we're good at the physical stuff, thanks. But be serious. What do you want long-term?"

I leaned back in the chair. "I can't see that far. Most of my life has been day by day. Just getting through one to the next. Surviving." I lifted my eyes to her. "And I *was* being serious. I want you. But I shouldn't say shit like that. That's just me being greedy. It's better for you if we don't have a long term."

"You keep saying that, and I keep freaking out, yet we both keep ending up here."

"I don't want you to get hurt."

She arched a brow, dubious. "You'd hurt me?"

"*Never*," I said. "But it might not be up to me."

"I don't understand." Her voice softened. "Does this have to do with what happened to your mom?"

My head whipped up.

"Miller told me."

I spat a curse. "He shouldn't have done that."

"It slipped out. He cares about you."

"He still should've kept his mouth shut."

"What happened?"

"You don't want to hear this, Shiloh."

"I do. If we have a prayer of…anything, we have to be

honest with each other. I've been pretty open about my baggage, all things considered."

"I know."

When I said nothing more, she nodded, the hope falling away. "If you really want me to go, I'll go. But if I walk out of here, that's it. No phone calls. No texts. No showing up at my door in the rain…"

Her eyes shone for a moment, but she blinked hard. Christ, it took all I had not to hurl myself out of that chair and grab her and kiss her until the past was someplace distant and couldn't touch us.

But it always comes back.

Then something worse unfolded in front of me. A future without Shiloh in it.

"I was there," I said, spitting out the words hard and fast. "Mom threatened to leave him for good, so he took a baseball bat and made sure that could never happen. That she couldn't go anywhere ever again."

Shiloh's hand flew to her mouth. "Jesus…"

"My dad did that," I said. "His blood is in my veins. I'm his son. Stints in juvie. Fights. The rage of it all… How fucked up he was… That's *in* me. And the very last fucking thing I want to do is bring that ugliness to you."

Her hand dropped, her face soft. "I don't see anything ugly in you, Ronan. I see someone who protects his friends from bullying assholes, calls out rapists… Someone who walks in the rain to make sure that the dummy who won't answer her phone is okay."

Christ, if she knew I walked every night to make sure she was okay...

She cocked her head, still trying for tough while the soft vulnerability in her eyes bled through. "Well?"

I got to my feet, towered over her. "No one can know," I said. "If we do this, no one can know at school. It may seem fucking stupid, but I need that, Shiloh. At least for a little while. Until after graduation maybe."

She smirked, but her breath was turning fluttery. "I told you, I'm okay with that. This is like a do-over. We'll keep things…"

"Casual?"

"That word just doesn't stick. But I can't make any promises either. This is all new to me, and I'm scared I'll fuck it up." She cast her gaze down. "I don't want to hurt you either."

No one had said anything like that to me before. No girl had ever stood in front of me and bared her soul like Shiloh. Or given a shit about my feelings. Because I'd never let myself have any.

She heaved a breath, her hands sliding up my chest, her fingers toying with the pendant. "So how about no labels? No rules. We'll just do our best and maybe land somewhere between you coming to my house in the rain and me answering your texts." She raised her eyes to mine, dark and rich. "Sound good?"

There wasn't a word for what I felt in that moment. Not one I recognized. All I could do was nod, my hands going around her waist, holding tight. That was what you did with good and precious things. You held them tight and took care of them. I could do that. I could keep her safe and have her too.

"That sounds good," I said and bent to kiss her. Softly. My eyes falling shut, savoring the taste of her.

Don't fuck this up. Jesus, God, don't let me fuck this up.

She moved in closer, molding to my chest. I could feel her heart, and it was beating fast. She smiled against my lips.

"Something funny?" I asked, my hands roaming her back, soft and warm, her hair brushing my wrists.

"Not funny. Just good. Today's light-years from earlier today when I was at the hospital visiting Violet. It feels like a lifetime ago."

"What happened?"

"She had a crash at soccer practice. Concussion."

"Is she okay?"

"She's okay. Miller's with her now."

"About time."

"Agree, but those two are giving me an ulcer. *Literally* hours before, River Whitmore asked Violet to prom. As friends. And Violet said *yes*."

"Doesn't mean anything," I said. "If Miller's with Violet now, he won't let her slip away again."

I won't let you slip away again either.

"I just wonder what River's endgame is."

"River asked her to prom as a friend, right?" I shrugged.

"Maybe that's what he needs. A friend." I held her tighter. "And maybe it's none of our fucking business."

Shiloh smiled. "Good answer."

Now we were pressed together, my forehead to hers, breathing her in, inhaling her scent.

"We're doing this now?" she asked, her voice hardly more than a whisper.

I nodded and lifted her onto the table. Her lips parted in a little gasp, her eyes never leaving mine as her fingers trailed up my arms. She spread her legs, bringing me in, holding me tight to her as I bent her over the table.

"Ronan," Shiloh breathed, kissing my chin, my lower lip, my upper. "Is this when you make me come?"

The words went off like a flare in me. I crushed my mouth to hers, my hand in her braids, holding her in my kiss. Devouring her. Shiloh moaned and kissed me back, just as ravenous and ready. I wanted to crawl on top of the table and take her, but a whiff of clove cigarettes and expensive cologne infiltrated my red haze of desire.

I stood up. The window showed no one, but reality flooded in like a sobering slap to the face. Casual or not, Shiloh deserved better than a splintery table in an old fisherman's shack that was splattered with gull shit and seaweed. Where Holden or Miller could walk in on us at any time.

"Come on." I offered Shiloh my hand, helping her off the table.

"Where are we going?"

"I don't know. Out. Are you hungry?"

She arched a brow. "Are you taking me on a *date*?"

"Maybe. You want to? Or is that against the rules?"

She looked like she was going to clap back with something smart-ass. Instead, her smile softened. "I could eat."

"Good." I realized I hadn't been on an actual date with a girl since…ever. All my "dates" had been sex in rough places. Drunken hookups. Quick fixes. Shiloh was not that.

"But where to?" she asked as we left the shack and walked the path along the coast. "Not downtown Santa Cruz, I presume."

"Not downtown. Any ideas?"

"Yes, actually. Ever been to Scotts Valley?"

"I haven't been anywhere that's not in walking distance from my place."

"Ever have Thai food?"

"Also no." I helped Shiloh over a good-size boulder.

"Unacceptable." She jumped off the rock, the ocean water washing over her sandals as she stood on tiptoe to kiss me. "Stick with me, Wentz. I'll take care of you."

Scotts Valley was a little town tucked into the redwoods, just north of Santa Cruz—built on rolling hills with views of the forest in every direction. Shiloh maneuvered her Buick into a parking space on the main drag next to an art gallery.

"The restaurant I'm thinking of is on the other side of

town," she told me as we climbed out. "But it's turning into a beautiful night. I thought we could walk."

I nodded and marveled as her hand slipped into mine. We walked as the sun dipped behind the trees, and I could almost pretend I was a regular guy, living a normal life, going on a date with his girlfriend.

Slow the fuck down. She said no labels.

Still. The moment felt good, and I let myself have it.

"You come up here a lot?" I asked as we passed shops and restaurants.

"Bibi and I used to come once a month or so. I've been so busy preparing for my shop, it's been a while."

"How's that going?" I asked. It seemed strange to think of her opening a business straight out of high school, but if anyone could do it, it was this girl.

"It's in a holding pattern," she said. "I've applied for all the permits and licenses, and now I'm just waiting to hear back. But that's not the worst of it. If I get the licenses, the next step is a meeting with a bank for a small business loan. Which should be fun since I have no collateral to speak of and it'll be a cold day in hell before I let Bibi put up the house."

"She offered?"

"She sure did," Shiloh said, her voice turning thick for a moment. "But it's far too risky. Most new businesses fail within the first three years, according to basically every article I've read on the subject. Bibi's retired, and the house is paid off. I'm not about to wreck that for her."

"Maybe she doesn't feel like it's wrecking anything but helping you build something instead."

"That's what she said too." Her smile lingered, and then she shook her head. "But I need to do this on my own. If I fail, I'm not taking anyone down with me."

I couldn't imagine her failing at anything but kept my mouth shut. God knew life had a way of fucking shit up for good people. Like my mother. Or Maryann. I didn't want to jinx it for Shiloh.

"What's Wisconsin like?" she asked as we walked up and down the hilly streets, the night quiet.

"I'm not the right person to ask."

"Why not?"

"Because I've got nothing good to say about it."

"Was it hard? All those years in foster care?" She gave her head a shake. "Stupid question. I'm sure it was hard."

"It was more than hard."

"Do you want to talk about it? You don't have to."

I nearly said no and then realized that I wanted to. I felt close to Shiloh, and I wanted to keep feeling that way.

"Some of the placements were okay. Some were not."

"Were you moved around a lot?"

"Thirteen homes in ten years."

"God." She squeezed my hand. "I don't understand how people can do that. Take a kid in and then kick them out again."

"Some people do it for the money. Those are the worst. The good ones are rare, and only so many are looking to adopt. Thanks to my history, I wasn't a good candidate."

"Then your uncle found you?"

I looked straight ahead. "Yeah. But I'd already turned eighteen."

"Bad timing."

To say the least.

"But you're with him now," she said. "That's a good thing, I hope."

That was the time to tell her the truth, that I lived alone. But I liked feeling like a normal person too much to wreck it just yet.

"He's okay," I said. "But yeah, it's good to have family. Even if it's just one person."

Shiloh nodded as we waited at a light to cross the street. Only a few cars were out; the town was sleepy.

"I feel the same. I love my aunt and uncle, and my cousin, Letitia, is the best, but I got lucky with Bibi. She's my person. When my mom decided she didn't want me anymore, Bibi was there."

"How old were you?"

"Four. Old enough to remember crying when she dropped me off at Bibi's house. Old enough to remember feeling like I'd done something wrong." Her voice grew thick again. "I remember that."

"Why did she wait until you were four?" I asked after a minute.

"I don't know. I guess she was trying to be my mom, but she couldn't do it."

"I'm sorry, Shiloh."

She smiled tightly. "It's fine. I mean, it's not *fine*, but it's what happened. And when bad shit happens, we figure out how to cope, right?"

I nodded, thinking of night walks and watching bonfires burn.

"My brilliant solution to deal with her rejection was to keep to myself. I figured if people didn't get to know me—including my best friend—they wouldn't have any cause to get rid of me." She glanced up at me. "These are all new revelations, by the way. And do you know when they began to arrive?"

"No."

"Roughly the exact instant I met you."

"Is that good or bad?"

"Both," she said and resumed walking. "Kind of pathetic, isn't it? But I can't help it. She's my mom. She's supposed to love me. It's in the contract."

"It's not pathetic. It's survival. Like you said, you do whatever you can to keep your shit together."

"What do you do to keep your shit together?"

"I walk."

"Walk?"

"All over town," I said, shocking myself by telling her the truth. At least the part that didn't sound crazy. "I can't sleep. Bad nightmares. So I walk around until I feel tired enough to hopefully crash out."

"God, you have nightmares that bad every night? Does it work?"

"Not really. But it's either that or drink myself stupid." I shrugged. "Seems like a better alternative. For now."

We arrived at a small restaurant called Thai Heart. It seemed like Shiloh wanted to ask something else, but I held the door for her, ready to leave all my fucked-up shit outside.

The restaurant was simple but nicer than I was used to. Little knickknacks from Thailand—Buddhas, temples, elephants, and brightly colored strings of beads were displayed in glass cases or hung from the walls. The hostess gave us menus and a table by the window with a view of the street, and a waiter hurried over and took our drink order. Shiloh ordered milk tea. I asked for a beer.

The menu made me feel stupid. I'd never heard of any of the dishes.

Shiloh read my face. "You want some recommendations? Do you like spicy food?"

"I've had hot sauce on Mexican food. That's about it."

I waited for Shiloh to ask me what rock I'd been living under, but she only smiled.

"Well, there's hot and then there's *Thai hot*. Proceed with caution."

I imagined kissing Shiloh, my mouth hot with Thai spice and her mouth like sweet milk, soothing the burn...

I cleared my throat and surreptitiously adjusted my crotch under the table.

When the waiter returned, Shiloh ordered something called panang curry. I ordered pad kee mao.

"Drunkard's noodles," the waiter said, smiling. "Excellent."

"There's booze in it?"

"No, but it's very spicy."

I glanced at Shiloh across from me. *Good.*

When the waiter left, it was just her and me.

"The moment of truth," Shiloh said, sipping her tea.

"What is?"

"The waiter is gone. We can't attack each other, sexually speaking. We're either going to start talking and hit it off, or…not. The moment of truth."

"Okay." I toyed with the chopsticks on my napkin. "You want to know all the pointless, boring shit about me?"

She laughed. "Are you saying you don't want to know all the pointless, boring shit about *me*?"

I doubted there was any such thing. "I don't like small talk."

"You told me. When we first met. And neither do I." Shiloh stirred the ice in her drink with her straw. "It's funny though. We're kind of doing it all backward. We've talked about heavy shit, we do all the kissing things, but we skipped the basics."

"Basics?"

"The easy stuff. For instance, what kind of music do you like?"

I shrugged. "Not much. Older bands. Tool. Soundgarden is pretty good, I guess. You?"

"All kinds. From all over the world." She pulled out her

phone. "Check this out. His name is Ritviz, and he's from India. He's an EDM artist."

"EDM?"

"Electronic dance music. Listen."

Shiloh gave me one of her earbuds and put the other in her ear. A second later, I was listening to Indian EDM music in a Thai restaurant. Shiloh, even in her seat, danced to the electronic beats and the lyrics that were more rapped than sung.

"You know what he's saying?"

"No clue," she said, her smile radiant. "But it's not about that. It's about how it makes you feel."

I liked the music okay, but it was Shiloh who made me feel everything. I watched her move, closing her eyes, getting lost right there at the table.

She grinned. "Good, right?"

Incredible.

"You like dancing?" I blurted like a jackass. "I mean…I see you at Central a lot, listening to music, but you didn't go to homecoming."

She shot me a wry smile. "I was out getting barbecue with you, if you recall."

As if I could forget.

"I love dancing," she continued. "I just don't like school dances. The social scene in general doesn't interest me. Not like I'm above it, but more like I'm running parallel on a totally different vibe, trying to get through it. Like I want my childhood to be over with."

"Why?"

"Maybe because I feel like if I'm an adult with my own business, then what my mother thinks of me becomes irrelevant. I won't be a kid anymore, needing her." She waved a hand. "I know it doesn't work that way, but it's just something I do. To cope."

I nodded.

Shiloh rested her chin in her hand, watching me. "We're not doing a very good job of sticking to the basics. Quick, ask me something easy."

"Uh…what's your favorite movie?"

"Good one. I should say something deep and profound to impress you like *The Color Purple* or *Citizen Kane*, but I love *Coming to America*." She chuckled. "Just thinking about it makes me happy. Yours?"

"*Citizen Kane*."

Shiloh burst out laughing and chucked her napkin at me. "But for real."

"I don't know… My mom and I used to watch *The Wizard of Oz*, so I'll say that."

"I love that," Shiloh said softly.

And so did I—being able to talk about my mother's life instead of how she died.

"My turn," Shiloh said. "What's your favorite color?"

"Seriously?"

She arched a brow at me.

"Black. Yours?"

"Yellow." Shiloh smiled, and she was positively fucking

luminous. "Look at us. We are *slaying* the basics. Okay, one more. If you could go anywhere in the world right now, where would you go?"

"Nowhere."

Shiloh frowned. "Oh, come on. Don't quit on me now. We were doing so well…"

"There is nowhere else I'd rather be than here with you."

The words landed between us, stark and naked, and I inwardly cursed.

Too much. It's too much.

Shiloh's smile slipped, and her lips parted in a way I was coming to know meant I'd said or done something that stole her breath.

"Ronan Wentz," she murmured and turned to look out the window. "I'm in more trouble than I thought."

The food arrived, and I ate a pile of noodles that scorched my mouth but didn't come close to filling me up. I insisted on paying the bill, and we left.

Out on the sidewalk, Shiloh smirked at me.

"What?"

"That wasn't enough food for you, was it?"

"Not remotely."

She laughed and tucked her arm in mine. "Come on. There's a Mountain Mike's Pizza up ahead. Let's get you a slice or two."

I stopped her before she could take a step and kissed her. And I was right; Shiloh tasted sweet and soft from the milk tea. Her tongue slid coolly against mine, and then she pulled back, breathless.

"Ronan, you taste like fire." Her arms ringed my neck, and the kiss deepened, became the kind that wanted to lead to more.

"I don't need pizza," I said when we came up for air.

"You sure?"

"I'm sure."

"Thank God."

TWENTY-ONE
SHILOH

We walked in silence back to the car. The air between us buzzed like electrical lines; I could still taste Ronan on my lips.

My heart was pounding as my car came into view. Because tonight was different. I'd been fighting to keep Ronan at arm's length and failing at every turn. He smashed down my walls and, in turn, trusted me enough to tell me about his own brutal childhood. Each moment spent with him drew us closer together, like the tide that stopped for nothing and no one.

Therefore, sleeping with him is a bad idea.

But when I stripped it all away, all that remained was that I wanted him in every way.

We climbed into my car, and I sat facing forward, my heart clanging madly in my chest.

"Do you want to go home?"

"No," he said, his voice rough. "Do you?"

I shook my head. "There's a really pretty lookout not far from here. Great views. Want to check it out?"

"Yeah, I do," Ronan said, not even bothering to hide his intentions; they rumbled through his words, slipping under my skin and raising goose bumps.

Somehow, I managed to drive the car without getting us in an accident, every part of me humming and attuned to Ronan beside me. I pulled onto the overlook that was off the main road and killed the headlights. The valley unrolled a dark carpet of forest under a half-moon and a sky full of stars.

We enjoyed the view for all of ten seconds and then reached for each other, crashing together hard. We kissed in heated, desperate need, our hands greedy. But after the third time I whacked my elbow on the steering wheel, I pulled away.

"Back seat," I said, hearing my own intention in my voice and not caring. I could have sex with Ronan in a car, I reasoned. That didn't mean we were serious. It meant we couldn't keep our hands off each other, that was all. That was allowed.

We climbed out of the front and into the back, where I lay along the bench seat behind the driver's side, pulling him down with me.

"Wait." Ronan shook out of his fleece-lined denim jacket and tucked it behind my head like a pillow.

Damn it.

He was too good. Too considerate, while I was trying to keep this meaningless car sex. I gripped his T-shirt and kissed him roughly. He lay over me again, his body wondrously heavy and hard. His hand slid under my shirt, then down, along my left thigh, pushing my skirt up.

"You want to stop, we stop," he said, his voice tight.

I shook my head. "I don't want to stop."

The fire of his kiss nearly undid me. When Ronan had permission, he took it. He was going to take *me*, and I was more than ready to surrender. To give him whatever he wanted. It wasn't like me; this loss of control felt wild and reckless and exactly what *I* wanted.

Ronan thrust my legs apart, his hand sliding along the dampness of my underwear.

I whimpered, my own hands fumbling weakly over his hair, his broad back, down the slope of muscle between his shoulder blades. Then around the front, to the huge bulge in his jeans.

Jesus, he's going to break me in half.

Ronan kissed me hard, his tongue invading my mouth while two of his fingers slipped past my underwear, sinking inside me. My back arched at the fire that licked up my spine, pressing myself into him. His mouth moved to my throat while his fingers stroked and rubbed in perfect synchronicity.

He continued his way down my body until he knelt awkwardly, half on the seat, half on the floor. He pulled my panties off and tossed them aside. In the dimness, his silvery eyes glanced up at me, checking in. I nodded, breath held, waiting for his touch. When it came, I cried out, my back bowing, my hands scrabbling to hold on to something. My entire body tensed, my awareness compressing and flowing to where his mouth met my skin.

I came hard and fast, my cries filling the interior of the Buick.

"You like doing that, don't you?" I asked, panting.

"I could do that all night."

"Come here." He kissed me the same way he'd gone at me—relentless—while my hands grappled with the button and zipper on his jeans. I couldn't free him fast enough, and when I did, I gasped.

He was…

Magnificent.

I wrapped one hand around the huge, hard length of him. He closed his hand over mine, and we stroked him together—our eyes locked, our bodies rising and falling in a rhythm, our breaths coming in the same hard gasps.

"Shiloh," he said, eyes dark, voice rough. "I need to be inside you."

God, the raw simplicity of his want nearly made me come again.

"Condom," I said. I took the pill religiously and wanted nothing more than to feel Ronan and let him feel all of me, but I took no chances.

He retrieved a condom from his wallet and rolled it down. My heart pounded in my chest, my breath coming short. Ronan hesitated, mistaking my need for nerves or fear.

"I'm not a virgin," I told him and was glad that I wasn't. Not only because Ronan was so damn huge but because I needed to remind myself this wasn't special. It was fucking in the back seat of a car. Nothing romantic or monumental about it.

Right?

"Doesn't matter," he said. "If it's too much, you tell me."

Everything about Ronan Wentz was *too much*.

He's going to ruin me. Right here. Right now.

I reached for him. Needed him. Wanted him so badly I could hardly breathe. Ronan read my face, felt my body waiting beneath him. He poised himself over me in that tight space, and I reached to guide him inside me. Slowly, inch by inch, Ronan pressed in, and my eyes fell shut as my mouth opened in a soundless cry.

"Shiloh?"

"Don't stop," I breathed. "Oh my God…"

My fingers scratched at his shoulders, struggling to hold on as our hips met, Ronan filling me completely with his hard heaviness. He grunted and drew in tighter, eliciting another cry from me.

"Shiloh, look at me."

I opened my eyes. All I knew or saw or felt was Ronan. On and over me. Inside me. His mouth brushed mine, our foreheads touching, his gaze locked on me, silently commanding me not to look away.

I obeyed, surrendering to him. My eyes widened as he pulled back, and I whimpered as he pushed back in.

"Oh God, Ronan…"

He held me captive in his gaze, moving slowly in and out of me. There was just the intensity of him and the pleasure building from where we were joined. He angled his head, trying to kiss me, our mouths bumping to the rhythm of his thrusting hips. It was too much, staring into his eyes, but I couldn't stop and didn't want to.

He moved faster, his biceps straining to hold him over me on the seat. And then he hooked his right arm under my left leg. I cried out as the angle changed, hitting me somewhere deep I'd never known existed. Ronan watched my reaction, his eyes hooded and dilated. Then he bent his mouth to mine in a shallow kiss—licking and biting, his hot breath gusting over my lips.

The shards of tingling pleasure coalescing between my legs were growing into a heavy pressure, deeper and more intense. My hands flailed for something to hold on to as his thrusting intensified, my palm smearing the fogged glass of the window.

Like Kate Winslet in Titanic, came the random thought, since my rational mind was breaking apart, leaving logic and reason behind. All that remained was how good this was and how I never wanted to leave this world that was just him and me.

Ronan's thrusts were merciless, pinning me to the car seat. I hooked my leg around his waist to lock him to me, to steady my body that was at the mercy of his, while my breasts bounced under my sweater. A drop of sweat trickled down his cheek and dripped off the blade of his jaw, landing in the hollow of my neck. The space was hot and cramped, and there was still too much clothing between us. I wanted to see him naked. I wanted every inch of his body—sweaty and hard—touching mine, because Jesus, if he could do this to me in a car, what could he do in a bed?

That fevered imagining broke apart too as the pressure deep in my core raced toward combustion.

Ronan's mouth took mine, his thrusts relentless, stoking me to the edge and then over. I cried out as every nerve ending in my body fired, a beautiful chaos of sensation that ripped through me, pulsing hard between my legs where he was still driving in and out of me. The tension tapered as the orgasm flowed and ebbed, and I let him have me.

"Take me, Ronan," I whispered dully, drunk with him and the pleasure that slid through my veins like warm syrup. "Take me however you want."

His eyes flared, and somehow his hips drove in deeper, harder when I thought he'd given me all I could take. It was raw and almost dirty how I let my legs fall open as far as they could go, giving him everything while kissing him almost serenely, completely relaxed as my core throbbed.

I felt him tense, muscles straining.

"Yes," I whispered in his ear. "It's yours. All yours…"

Ronan grunted and shuddered, and then a sound deep in my chest rumbled with his release that I imagined spilled deep in *me*, condom or not. It was mine, that release. The sounds he made as he came, the sexiest I'd ever heard. Also mine.

The little voice came back, whispering that we belonged to no one. This was just sex. Casual, messy, back-seat-of-the-car sex. Yet my arms wrapped around Ronan, holding him close, my hands in the damp softness of his hair as he breathed hard against me. His chest was pressed to mine, his hardness cushioned by my softness. My embrace a refuge for him. Every part of him welcome inside me.

Finally, his breathing slowed, and he raised his head from the crook of my neck. His hair was a mess where my hands had been in it, his face drowsy with orgasm.

"You good?" he asked.

"I'm *really* good. You?"

"Yeah. I'm good."

Something in his tone felt heartbreaking. Like it had been a long time since he'd been able to say that.

He kissed me softly and then gently withdrew from my body. He disposed of the condom with a Kleenex from the box I kept on the floor of my car while I smoothed down my skirt. My underwear was lost somewhere. *I'll have to find it at some point*, I thought as the real world returned with a vengeance. I didn't want to go.

Reluctantly, I gave Ronan his jacket back. Reluctantly, he took it.

He climbed out of the back seat. I did the same on my side, and he was already there, helping me out. My legs were wobbly and pleasantly loose. My entire body felt as if I'd slept for ten hours straight.

"Always a gentleman."

"Not always."

He kissed me deeply, holding me close, letting me know I wasn't going to get away with business as usual so easily. I sagged into his embrace, reveling in the feel of him. His mouth—God, his mouth—and the strong solidity of him that made me feel so safe. When Ronan kissed me, I couldn't imagine anything could hurt me.

"Would you mind driving?" I asked. "I don't trust my legs to work properly right now."

He almost grinned. "I'll drive."

The journey back to Santa Cruz went by in a night-darkened blur outside my window. I stole glances of Ronan's profile now and then, his gaze focused on the road in front of him. He had no idea the effect he had just sitting there, his inked forearms too damn sexy as he held the wheel.

He drove to my house and parked in the driveway.

"Wait…how will you get home?"

"I'll walk," he said.

I hated that. Hated that he had to try to outlast the nightmares that chased him.

"If you're sure."

"I'm sure."

In front of the car, he encircled me in his arms but didn't kiss me. Instead, he studied me by the light of the streetlamp.

"Tomorrow night," he said. "The shack."

I arched a brow. "Are you asking or telling?"

"Telling. I want you there."

And I knew what he was doing. Making sure I wasn't going to freak out and ghost him again. His eyes were hard, but beneath, his doubt was the same as mine.

It's better to be the one who leaves.

He was placing his trust in my hands and asking me not to let it fall, not to throw it away. I had to do the same. Be brave.

"I'll be there."

The tension in his body loosened. He kissed me again and then waited as I walked up to my front walk.

Our first date.

I waved to him from the porch. He didn't wave back but nodded his head as I slipped inside. I slumped against the door and let out a shaky breath.

"So that happened."

Quietly, so as not to wake Bibi, I crept to the hall bathroom—my bathroom—and started the shower. I stripped down while hot water ran, steam filling the room. My reflection in the mirror, naked, was the same as yesterday, but I felt different. More than the night I lost my virginity. My smile was softer, my eyes lit up. My skin seemed to vibrate under the surface everywhere Ronan had touched me. I didn't want to wash him off me.

"Silly," I murmured as I stepped into the shower.

But it didn't feel silly. It felt like falling.

PART III

PART III

TWENTY-TWO
RONAN

MAY

"Well, gentlemen." Holden stretched like a cat. "What kind of trouble shall we get into tonight?"

I squeezed the bottle of lighter fluid. A stream arced into the bonfire, making it roar.

"Arson," Holden mused. "An interesting option. We haven't tried that one, but I'm game. Stratton?"

Miller strummed his guitar and sang, "All my friends are heathens, take it slow…"

"Indeed," Holden said. "I am the psychopath sitting next to you. Or is that Wentz?"

I smirked. "You're in a good mood."

"Is that allowed? Or do the Lost Boys have to be tragic and *lost* every minute of every day?"

I exchanged amused glances with Miller, but inwardly, I was glad. Lately, Holden had been sticking to beer instead of vodka, and the smile plastered to his face wouldn't quit. I guessed things were going good between him and River Whitmore, though I wondered if it would last.

And if I'd have to kick Whitmore's ass if it didn't.

Miller smiled a lot more too. Violet wasn't here that afternoon, it was just us, but she and Shiloh were regulars now. Holden never brought River, who was barricaded in the closet behind his king-of-the-jocks rep, so the five of us hung out most nights, laughing, talking, and listening to Miller play.

He strummed a few more bars of "Heathens."

"Who is that again?" I asked.

"Twenty One Pilots. It was on the *Suicide Squad* soundtrack. I think it's our theme song."

"I prefer Suicide Squad to the Lost Boys," Holden said. "Would I not make an *exceptional* Joker?"

He tugged on the lapels of his expensive winter coat. The weather was growing warmer by the day, but he was still bundled up. I guessed that meant things with River weren't perfect. But what was ever perfect? They hid their relationship at school, same as Shiloh and me.

Shiloh and me.

It'd been weeks, and that phrase wasn't close to getting old. I hid a smile behind my beer so the others wouldn't see it and give me shit.

Holden settled into his chair with a satisfied sigh as the sun began to dip below the horizon. "This, gentlemen, is a rare moment of tranquility." He looked to Miller. "You're on the cusp of stardom and—even more miraculous—Wentz here hasn't been suspended in more than a *month*."

They both applauded, and Miller whistled through his teeth.

I chuckled. Assholes.

"And for the time being, I'm…what's the word?" Holden snapped his fingers, pretending to think. "Starts with an H?"

"Heathen," Miller put in and strummed a few chords.

"Yes, but that *other*, more elusive H word."

"Happy," I muttered into my beer bottle. The word tasted foreign to me too, but for the first time in a long time, it was starting to fit.

"Bingo." Holden beamed, but I saw how fragile his happiness was in his eyes. Whitmore still had plans to go away to college and play football, leaving Holden behind.

But things are good now. They might stay good.

Like they were with Shiloh and me.

I felt like shit keeping us on the down-low at school when I wanted to show her off. Kiss her in front of God and everybody, claiming her as mine. But she was okay with the secrecy for different reasons. Trying to keep her shields up. I couldn't blame her; she'd been burned hard, but day by day, she was letting them go. For me.

I felt richer than Holden.

"And I have news," he said. "It concerns a certain rapey football player whose pristine white Jeep was given a new paint job by our own resident vigilante."

I sat up, my pulse kicking. "What did you hear?"

"I heard that said paint job made the local news."

I frowned. "That shit went down months ago."

Holden shrugged. "Seems Kimberly's friends weren't satisfied with her having to leave town while Mikey struts around school, suffering precisely *jack shit* in the consequences department."

"So what's the deal?" Miller asked.

"Michael 'Douchebag' Grimaldi has been booted from the football team," Holden said, tossing one end of his scarf over his shoulder. "More of a symbolic gesture, given the season's over, but he's losing his letter and—word has it—his ticket to Texas A&M has been revoked."

Miller stared. "No shit? *Good*."

"Where'd you hear that?"

He gave me a knowing look. "I have a connection on the football team."

I sat back in my chair, considering this. On the one hand, fuck Grimaldi. On the other, he and Dowd were friends…

Nah, fuck them both.

I sipped my beer, content. Miller frowned, wearing his usual worried expression.

"What?"

"You think he knows it was you?"

I shrugged. "He might."

"But even if he does, he can't prove you tagged his ride." Holden grinned. "Fucking with jocks is high on my list of favorite things." He shot me another knowing look. "Right after actually fucking them."

I got the message, loud and clear.

Whitmore, I swear to God, take care of him.

My phone chimed a text.

Bibi made lasagna. Come over.

My damn heart felt warm. Shiloh hadn't asked me over to dinner since that day back in September.

She's letting me in.

Time?
Dinner's at seven but u can head over any time.
On my way.

I stood up, tucked my phone in the back pocket of my jeans, and drained my beer. "I'm out."

"What?" Holden screeched. "Where are you going? It's early."

"Where do you think he's going?" Miller coughed into his fist, "*Pussy whipped.*"

Holden snickered.

"I think I hear Evelyn Gonzalez calling, Stratton," I said, putting on my jacket. "She has some hair gel options for your next video."

Miller laid his middle finger to his cheek. "Look into my eye…"

We exchanged grins, and I strode out, Holden calling after me.

"Have fun! Use protection! And don't do anything I wouldn't do! Actually, that doesn't leave much. Don't do anything illegal! Nope, that doesn't work either."

I chuckled and shook my head, and then the sound of the ocean washed him out as I walked to Shiloh.

I arrived a little after six. Bibi was on her way out the front door with another elderly lady. She hugged me and smacked a kiss on my cheek.

"Ronan Wentz, this is Esther Morris. She's taking me to visit a friend down the street. Shiloh's in the back, working. Lasagna's in the oven, still baking. I'll be back in twenty minutes, so don't you bother with it."

"Sure thing."

She smiled. "So happy to have you, sweet boy."

I jammed my hands in my pockets. "Thanks."

Esther gave me and my tattoos a quick once-over, then guided Bibi out the front door.

I found Shiloh in the shed, sitting at her table. The night was warm; she wore a sundress in deep blue. A lantern hung above her in the twilight, making her skin glow. Her expression was tight with concentration.

Fuck, she was too beautiful. Too much for a poor

bastard like me. Yet when she felt me watching her, she lifted her head, and her face lit up, became more beautiful.

Then she caught herself and turned her tone casual. "Hey, you."

I joined her in the shed, sitting on the other side of her. I watched as she pressed a plate of silver about the size of a playing card onto a small anvil that was attached to the table with a bench pin. The silver plate was etched with a rose design, and Shiloh was using a jeweler's saw—its blade as thin as string—to cut it out.

"I feel you watching me," she said with a faint smile, not looking up as she sawed and turned the plate, the blade following the lines of the rose exactly.

"Fucking amazing."

Her deep-brown eyes flickered up to me, then back to her work. "Don't say things like that. I'll mess up."

But she didn't. The last piece was cut away, and she was left with a silver rose as large as the palm of her hand.

"You're just going to watch?" she asked as she picked up her hand torch and soldered a tiny loop of silver to the back.

"For now."

Shiloh's lips parted in a little gasp. "Damn, Ronan…"

My blood heated, and I waited, my hands itching to touch her. To strip her naked in the twilight and spread her over the table. No, not a goddamn table. Or her car. Or the shack. In the last month, we'd never fucked in a bed. Never been fully naked. I couldn't take her to my place, and Shiloh hadn't offered hers. Our way of trying to slow things down.

Stupid.

I was all in. And if I thought about it, I'd gone all in for this girl the first damn minute I laid eyes on her.

"Nearly done." She took up a string of smoky quartz beads and held the rose against them. "The backing needs to cool before I can string it, but not bad, eh? I kind of like how it turned out."

She glanced up to see me watching her, drinking her in. Her eyes flared, and she carefully set the necklace aside and moved around the table to sit in my lap. Her hands went into my hair. I loved her hands in my hair. She'd changed hers a few weeks ago—the microbraids were replaced by thicker ones she called box braids.

More for me to grip.

"Bibi went to visit a friend down the street," I said. "We have twenty minutes."

Shiloh's fingertips traced my lips. "Mmm, you can do a lot of damage in twenty minutes. Shut the door."

She stood up while I did as she asked, and then we reached for each other in the dim space, the lantern casting a yellow light. I took a handful of thicker, soft braids and gently pulled her head back, exposing her throat. Her pulse was a flickering beat in the hollow of her collarbone. I put my mouth there, savoring the taste of her that was salty and sweet.

"God, Ronan... How do you do that?"

"Do what?"

"Make me want you so bad."

Her fingers raked through my hair, cradling my head, and she moaned as I worked over the delicate skin of her neck, biting, grazing, licking, until I was at her mouth again. I kissed her deep, my tongue exploring every corner, tasting her until we were both out of breath.

Our eyes met, and she nodded.

I spun her around and held her to me, my mouth on the delicate skin behind her ear, biting. She gasped and braced herself on the table.

"Please, Ronan. Hurry…"

I slid my hands down her back and hiked up her dress, a lacy thong the only thing between me and what I wanted.

"Take that off," I ordered, reaching for my wallet in the back pocket of my jeans and retrieving the condom.

"Bossy, aren't we?" she breathed and stepped out of the thong.

"You wear a lot of skirts," I grunted, freeing my rock-hard erection and rolling the condom down.

"You're just now noticing? I don't own a single pair of jeans."

"Don't start," I said and pushed myself inside her.

Shiloh moaned, and her entire body shuddered. "Oh God. So good. So good…"

I took hold of her hips, trying to restrain myself, though I wanted to take her hard. To try to do the impossible and satiate my hunger for her.

"Harder," she breathed. "Make it rough."

Her words fueled me, driving me senseless. I ran my hand up her spine, over the bunched material of her dress, until I found skin. I gripped her shoulder and pulled, arching her back and holding her there, halfway out of my mind with how good it felt to be inside her. Sometimes, I thought Shiloh letting me into her body was the only salvation I had.

"Yes…" she managed, and I moved harder, faster. She began to moan, then cry out at each thrust.

"Your neighbors will hear…"

Shiloh glanced at me over her shoulder. "Then you'd better do something about it."

My hand moved to her mouth, covering it and stifling her cries. She whimpered, and then I felt the hot, wet softness of her tongue sliding between my fingers.

Fuck.

I held her pinned, one hand on her hip, the other clamped on her mouth, yet Shiloh was fucking wrecking *me*.

We came almost together, my hands falling away to brace myself on the table, my chest molded to hers as we shuddered.

"Jesus Christ," Shiloh breathed.

She slumped over the table, her cheek on the smooth wood, her back rising and falling beneath me. I lay over her, nuzzling her neck, still inside her, still trying to catch my breath. She kissed the teeth marks she'd left on my finger, then her hand briefly cupped my jaw before sliding into my hair. I kissed her slow, taking my time, showing her that sex was only one part of what I wanted from her.

All of her. I want all of her.

Slowly, I stood, disposed of the condom, and tucked myself back in my jeans while she pulled on her thong and smoothed her rumpled dress.

"Well." She moved into my arms. "Hello to you too."

"You good?"

"Better than good." She smiled. "You don't have to ask, but I love that you do."

I kissed her softly, but it deepened quick, the emotions still hanging in the little shed pulling us back to each other.

"Damn, Ronan," she said breathlessly and put her hands on my chest to push me away. "Bibi will be back. We need to show a little restraint."

"I suppose."

She laughed. "Her lasagna is to die for. You hungry?"

"I am now. What's the occasion?" I couldn't imagine it was all for me. I hoped it wasn't.

"No occasion," she said. She kissed my chin, then moved to pack up her tools. "Except, well…miracle of miracles, that little place I showed you in the fall? The laundromat? It's still available. The rent is scary, but not as bad as it could be because of the size."

"That's great. Are you going to make a bid for it?"

"I still have a lot of hurdles to jump through. A bank loan would be nice. But…" She shrugged as if to keep her hope in check, her smile radiant. "We'll see."

The meal was one of the best I'd had. Bibi treated me like a long-lost son without making me feel weird or self-conscious. Instead of feeling like an intruder, like I had that first day, I felt welcome. Like I had a normal life.

After dinner and a dessert of tiramisu from a local bakery, I helped clean up the kitchen and said good night to Bibi. She took my face in her hands and gave me a little shake.

"Good night, Ronan." She kissed my cheek again and then whispered quickly, "She's so happy. You did that. Thank you, sweet boy."

She let me go, and I stepped back, a little stunned.

"Okay, what's with all the whispering?" Shiloh asked with a small laugh.

"I was telling your man that he's welcome for dinner any time he likes. Isn't that right, Ronan?"

"Yes, ma'am."

Shiloh rolled her eyes. "I'll bet." She took my arm. "I'll walk you out. Be right back, Bibi." On the front porch, Shiloh pursed her lips. "*My man*, hmm?"

I shrugged. "You going to argue with your grandmother?"

Shiloh peered up at me, her eyes soft. "Guess not." Then she caught herself and straightened the collar of my jacket. "Bibi says my future shop needs a name. To put it out in the universe and make it real. But I'm stumped."

My hand skimmed up the smooth skin of her back, over her dress, thinking of the piece she'd made earlier. A mix of stone and metal, the elements flowing and blending naturally. Unique.

Rare Earth.

I nearly said it, but this was Shiloh's shop. Hers to name.

"You'll think of something."

"You're a big help." She kissed me and then wrapped her arms around my waist and rested her head against my chest. "I love listening to your heart."

I didn't speak but held her as tightly as I dared and basked in the warmth that emanated from Shiloh's slender body into mine.

Happy, I thought. *I think this is what happy feels like.*

We kissed until time started to slip away, and then I left her and walked home, stupidly thinking I could hold on to that feeling forever. I should've known better.

I was halfway across the parking lot at my complex when they got me.

I heard a shuffle behind me and instinctively ducked. A club meant for my head glanced off my shoulder, and I spun around. Two figures in ski masks—one big, the other skinny—had slunk out of the shadows from behind a van. The skinnier one had the club, and it took zero seconds to recognize the eyes that stared at me.

"Dowd," I seethed, backing up slowly as they both circled me. I jerked my head at the bigger one. "Grimaldi."

Fuck me.

In that instant, I went over every time I'd been with Shiloh in the last month, praying we hadn't been careless. That no one knew.

This can't touch her. I won't let it.

"You're dead, fucker," Mikey Grimaldi bellowed from beneath his mask. "Fucking dead. I know it was you who tagged my Jeep. I *saw* you."

"You saw me tag it, or you saw me the night you violated that girl?" I asked, my voice low and steady while inside, the fire was simmering, ready to ignite.

"Fuck you!" Mikey spat. "You didn't see shit. But A&M canceled my scholarship. My mom can't even look at me. You ruined my life, asshole!"

I wondered if he spared a thought for Kimberly's life and guessed not. Frankie was moving behind me, jumpy, his breath loud through the mask.

I cracked my neck from side to side. "What are you waiting for?" I asked, deadly casual. "Let's go if we're going to do this."

Mikey's eyes flickered at something behind my shoulder, and I spun in time to catch Frankie's club—a police baton—coming down. It whacked my palm, and I closed my fist around it and yanked it easily from his grasp. I sent a left hook to his face, connecting square, and he reeled.

"Fucker!" he shrieked, staggering back, clutching his masked cheek with both hands. "Not this time. This time, we got you. *We got you.*"

From behind, Mikey lunged. I spun again, swinging the baton. He danced out of reach and jabbed a punch to my kidney. The baton dropped from my nerveless fingers as pain rocketed up my side. I took a fist to the cheek and saw stars but let instinct take over. I put the pain somewhere else and delivered a heavy blow to his gut. He bent in half, the breath gushing out of him, leaving him wide open for my fist to smash into his jaw. Blood and teeth flew. Pain crackled up my knuckles, but I hardly felt it. I lifted a boot and kicked him in the side, sending him sprawling.

Frankie was trying again, reaching for the baton. I kicked it away—it skittered across the cracked pavement and into the shadows—and gripped him by the collar, driving my knee into his gut. He made a hitching sound, and I shoved him roughly. He fell on his ass, clutching his stomach.

Too easy.

I stood between the two of them, my gaze going back and forth, wanting it to be over while the dark place in me hoped for more.

"Well?"

"Fuck you!" Frankie sounded like he was crying. "I'm not done with you. I'm not…"

I leveled a finger at him. "*You* are fucking done. Stay down." I looked to Mikey. "How about you? You want to go again, or nah?"

He got to his feet slowly, muttering a curse and holding his gut, but his eyes through the mask showed second thoughts.

Then came a voice from behind me, turning my blood to ice.

"Sniveling little pussies, the both of you."

I whirled around. A bigger guy in a ski mask stepped from behind the van. He wore jeans, a polo shirt, and a blue windbreaker I recognized instantly.

"Two of you can't take him?" Mitch Dowd snorted.

There was a flash of yellow, and then something jumped out of the dark and bit me.

Instantly, every muscle in my body seized, each one gripped tight in its own clenching pain. My head swam, darkness faded in and out, and the ground rose up to slam into me. I convulsed, racked by agony, my vision blurry but just clear enough to see the two coiled springs trailing out of the Taser in Mitch's hand, its teeth buried in my thigh.

"Suck on that, fucker," Mikey sneered, suddenly full of confidence again.

The steely, metallic electricity coursing through me vanished, taking the pain with it, but my body felt loose. I could hardly move. Mikey delivered a hard kick, and agony exploded in my ribs. I tried to curl into a ball, but my limbs wouldn't cooperate. The blows came again and again, as if there were ten of him instead of one.

After what seemed like a lifetime, I was dimly aware of Mitch looming over me. He put out his arm, pressing Mikey back like a referee. "You're up, son," he said to Frankie. "Show him what we do to snitches."

Through one swollen eye, I saw Frankie had the baton again. He danced around me but didn't take his shot.

"What the fuck are you waiting for?" Mitch snarled.

"Give it to me," Mikey seethed, hand out for the baton. "I'll fuck him up good. Fuck him up like he fucked up my life."

Frankie hesitated and then flinched as a shouted voice—high-pitched and shaky—came from my building, cutting across the night.

"I called the police, and I'm recording this!"

Maryann.

Fuck, no.

I craned my neck and saw her in front of her door, twenty yards away, her phone up.

"Fuck." Mitch jabbed a beefy finger at his son. "Go get that phone."

Frankie jerked his head. "N-no…"

"Get it, asshole!" Mikey shouted. He sounded panicked but made no move to do it himself. "*Fuck*. Oh fuck…this is bad."

Mitch muttered a curse. "Frankie, you goddamn shit-stain. Go get that phone!"

"No, Dad. No."

"Little bitch," Mitch spat. He yanked the Taser's claws out of my leg, tearing flesh. "I'll do it myself, but this isn't over, Franklin. You and I are going to have words about what it means to be a coward in this family."

He started for Maryann.

Using every ounce of will I could muster, I forced my muscles to cooperate and snaked my hand out. I gripped his boot, tripping him. With another curse, Mitch went down flat, smacking the pavement, the air *whooshing* out of him.

I hauled myself to my hands and knees, scrabbling to hold on to Mitch as he made to get to his feet. I managed to get him in a weak choke hold that would last only until he caught his breath. I grasped blindly, shakily, as if all my muscles had gone to sleep. My fingers snagged on the eye holes of his mask, and I ripped it off his head.

"Bastard!" Mitch took hold of my arms and flipped me to the ground.

Hard, unforgiving pavement slammed into me. Pain radiated from between my shoulder blades. Sirens—faint but growing louder—rang in the distance. Even then, with my body screaming in agony from a thousand places, the sound woke up every memory of that day ten years ago, infusing me with terror.

Mitch towered over me, breathing hard, his face ruddy in the streetlamps.

"Dad..." Frankie whimpered. "Let's go."

Mitch ignored him. "You're a snitch, Wentz. You ruined a good boy's life. For what? A piece of ass?"

"Dad..."

"Fuck you," I croaked, muscles shuddering and clenching.

Mitch brought his foot up and then down again, a stomping kick. I heard a *crack*, and then pain flooded my face along with the blood that poured from my nose.

"Mr. Dowd..." Mikey sounded scared.

"Let's go," I heard Mitch say. "I'm not done with you."

I didn't know if he was talking to me or Frankie.

Their footsteps scrambled away, and another set hurried to me. Maryann's arms went around my shoulders as I sat up, the sirens growing closer.

"Jesus Christ," she breathed. "I got him. On my phone. His face. He's done."

"No..." I struggled—and failed—to stand up. "Don't. He'll hurt you too."

Shiloh.

Now the terror pushed me to my feet.

"Don't get up," Maryann said. "Wait for the ambulance."

"No…ambulance. No cops." I staggered out of her grip, reeling.

"Ronan, stop. Come inside."

"I'll scare the girls." I peered around in the dark night, trying to get my bearings.

Shiloh. Fuck.

"Where are you going? You have to make a statement."

"No." I rounded on her. My face must've been a horror show. She recoiled, her eyes wide. "Maryann, listen to me. Listen to me. He'll come for you."

He'll come for Shiloh, I thought drunkenly. *He's going there now.*

"He's not coming for me," Maryann said, incredulous. "He's going to jail for what he did to you."

"No," I said, my voice slurry. "Please leave my name out of it. Leave it alone. For your sake. Fuck, I'm sorry. I'm so sorry."

The sirens were getting louder. I shoved out of her grasping hands.

"Ronan…"

I ignored her, hurrying as fast as I could.

Not too late. Please, don't let me be too late.

TWENTY-THREE
SHILOH

As I pulled the Buick into my drive, the headlights lit up a dark figure sitting slumped on our steps.

"Oh my God."

I slammed to a stop and killed the engine. My fingers fumbled to yank the keys from the ignition, and then I tore out of the car, leaving the milk and eggs from my grocery-store run on the seat. At the front walk, I stopped, my blood thrashing in my ears.

Ronan sat hunched over on the middle step, chin to chest, arms resting on his thighs.

"Ronan?"

He raised his head, and both my hands flew to my mouth to keep a scream from bursting out.

"Jesus Christ!"

One of Ronan's eyes was swollen shut, a shiny mess of blue and purple. Blood stained his chin; his nose was horribly broken. He peered at me through one eye, confused. As if he were drunk.

I hurried to his side and wrapped my arms around his shoulders. He winced, and a groan of pain issued from his throat. I jerked my hands back.

"My God, what happened?"

Panic was lighting up my veins, and I fought for calm while my heart felt a sensation I'd never known—to see him in so much pain.

"Shiloh?" His voice was a croak. He sat up a little, looking around. "Where…"

"You're at my house. You don't remember? God, I'm calling an ambulance—"

"No!" He tried to get to his feet and sat back down. Fear lit up his good eye. "Are you okay?"

"*Me?* Ronan, who did this to you?"

He didn't hear me or wasn't listening. He looked around blearily. "I shouldn't have come here. I thought they might… No. Fucking stupid. I shouldn't be here." He got to his feet, his body hunched over and wincing in pain. He looked around as if unsure what to do next. "I have to go."

They hurt him. They hurt him so bad.

I gripped his arm through his denim jacket as gently as I could while still keeping hold of him. "You're not going anywhere. You're coming inside. Right now."

I guessed he was too weak or confused to argue, because

he let me take him inside. Bibi was in her room, her door closed. I longed for her help and advice but didn't want to scare her as badly as I was. Quietly, I led Ronan to my room. He leaned heavily on me, his steps stumbling. I sat him on my bed where he slumped over in the dim glow of the rainbow lights.

"Stay right there," I told him, though he looked like he could hardly lift his head.

I hurried to my bathroom, keeping my focus on my task so my mind wouldn't spin out into outright panic. I grabbed a towel and the same first aid kit I'd used to clean his cut all those months ago, then hurried to the kitchen. I took an ice pack from the freezer and filled a bowl with warm water from the sink.

In my room, Ronan was in the same position I'd left him. I set my supplies on my dresser, not knowing where to begin. With a shaky hand, I touched his bloody chin and gently lifted his head.

Tears filled my eyes. "Oh, baby."

"Shiloh, I'm sorry."

"Don't say that," I said, sucking in a breath, willing the tears back. "I'm going to take care of you. But, Ronan, your nose is broken. Badly. You need a doctor."

"No doctor. I'll fix it."

He tried to take off his jacket and winced. I helped him out of it, scared to death at what lay beneath his T-shirt, and Ronan hauled himself to his feet. In the bathroom, under the harsh fluorescents, he looked even worse. His skin was pale where it wasn't bloody, his puffed eye a rainbow of purples and blues, his nose flat against one cheek.

He raised his head and looked at his reflection. Beneath the blood and swelling, his expression was heartbreakingly sad. Hopeless. He propped himself up on the sink with both hands for a moment, head hung.

I wrapped my fingers around his arm and carefully rested my cheek on his shoulder. "It's okay," I whispered weakly. "We'll make it okay. I promise."

He inhaled, steeling himself, and then stood straight. Stoic. "You might want to look away," he said dully.

"*No*," I said, my voice hard. "I'm right here with you."

He nodded and then turned back to the mirror, mentally bracing himself. He huffed three breaths in rapid succession, gripped his nose, and set it with an audible *crack*. A hoarse cry issued from his throat, and fresh blood spattered the white porcelain sink. His nose was now more or less straight, though it was too swollen to tell.

"I'm sorry," he croaked. "The mess…"

"Doesn't matter. The only thing that matters is making you better, okay?"

I opened the bathroom door and peered down the hall. Bibi's door was still closed.

"Go," I said, gently pushing him back to my room. "I'll be right there."

He went, and I rinsed the sink out, cleaning the spatters

of blood off the faucet, the tears threatening again. In my room, Ronan was back on the bed. I shut the door and knelt in front of him.

"Who did this to you?" I asked as I unlaced his boots. "Tell me."

"Grimaldi."

"And?"

"No one else."

"I don't believe you. You could take Grimaldi one-handed."

"He got the jump on me."

"Ronan…"

"Doesn't matter, Shiloh." His voice was stronger now. Clearer. "I shouldn't have come here. I thought…"

"What?"

He didn't answer, and I let it go. For now.

"We'll talk about it later. We need to get you cleaned up, and you need to sleep."

I stood and carefully lifted his T-shirt—the first time I'd seen him with it off despite everything we'd done over the last few weeks. Being naked was my last holdout against intimacy, though I'd wanted desperately to see him and touch him. Put my mouth on his skin and the magnificent body I felt under my hands.

But not like this. Not like this.

Ronan was covered in bruises—dark shadows in the dim light—except for one angry splash of reddish purple on the left side of his ribs.

"Oh God." I swallowed hard and pushed the panic down and worse, the terrible agony that squeezed my heart to see him in so much pain.

I dipped the end of the towel in the bowl of warm water and held Ronan's face gently in my hand. I wiped the blood off his mouth and chin, being careful not to bump his nose. Then I cleaned around his eye carefully. He took my wrist.

"You don't have to do this. I never wanted this. To bring this ugliness to you…"

"And I told you. You could never be ugly to me."

I held his face in both hands, the towel cradling his cheek, and kissed him softly on the lips. His good eye fell shut, relief sighing out of him, and my heart broke all over again.

I gently swabbed the cut around his swollen eye with antiseptic, then laid him down on my pillow. He let out a half sigh, half groan—more relief to be lying down than pain, I hoped.

I sat beside him, my back against the headboard, and held the ice pack on his eye while my fingertips softly grazed his scalp. My gaze trailed over his shirtless body, rigid with abs and the perfect broad planes of his chest. The compass pendant glinted against the tattoo on his right pec—a quote that was upside down from where I sat and unreadable in the dimness. Beneath it, there was another tattoo I hadn't known about. A sketch of a man in medieval clothes with huge wings, barbed and webbed like a bat, his face turned up in despair. He looked to be falling or flying away from something that chased him.

But it was the bruises that colored Ronan's skin that absorbed my attention.

"I think your ribs might be broken."

"Probably."

I winced at his matter-of-fact tone. As if cracked ribs and setting his own smashed nose were ordinary, everyday occurrences. "I don't know what to do. You should go to a hospital."

"I can breathe okay," he said. "They're just fractured. Nothing to do."

"This has happened before?"

He didn't answer.

"It's late," I said. "Do you need anything else? Water? Aspirin?"

He nodded faintly.

I left him holding the ice pack and rushed to get a glass of water from the kitchen and the bottle of Advil from what Bibi called our medicine basket on top of the fridge. I helped him sip water to wash the pills down and then moved to pull the blankets over him. That was when I saw the bloodstains on his right thigh and the rip in his jeans. I tore the hole wider and found two small, ragged gashes, as if a snake had bitten him and dragged its fangs down half an inch, tearing his skin.

"What the hell is this?"

Ronan shook his head from under the ice pack, and again I had to keep from bursting into tears.

"We're talking about this tomorrow," I said as I cleaned

the fang-like wounds and dabbed them with antiseptic. "All of this."

I quickly threw on pajamas—soft pants and a loose T-shirt. Then I tied up my hair in a scarf and climbed into bed with Ronan.

He took me in with his good eye. "What's that?"

"Headscarf," I said. "For my braids."

"I like it," he said tiredly. "Something I didn't know about you."

My chest felt heavy, and I trailed my fingers over his right pec. "This is something I didn't know about you." I read the quote tattooed there. "*The mind is its own place and in itself can make a heaven of hell, a hell of heaven.*"

"John Milton," Ronan said. "*Paradise Lost.*"

"And is this an angel or a demon?" I asked of the winged person beneath it.

"Both," he said. "It's Satan being cast out of heaven. He was an angel first."

"What does it all mean?" I shook my head. "Never mind. Tell me tomorrow. Sleep now."

He set the ice pack on the floor, and I curled up next to him as gingerly as I could. My eyes started to droop, the adrenaline having run its course, leaving me drained. I started to doze, my thoughts drifting and scattering, but jerked awake at the vision of red blood in the white sink.

I looked up to see Ronan staring at the ceiling.

"What are you thinking about?"

"Nothing. Everything."

"Close your eyes, baby," I said, the word slipping out again. "You need to rest."

"I can't."

I frowned, remembering. "The nightmares? They come every night?"

"Every night."

I tried to imagine lying down to sleep every single night of my life, knowing the horror that was waiting for me on the other side.

I bit my lip, thinking. "Not tonight. I'm going to… stand guard."

"What?"

"You sleep, Ronan. I'll stay awake. I'll watch you, and if they try to get you, I'll talk to you. Maybe talk you through them. If they get too bad, I'll wake you up, and we can try again."

"You would do that?" His jaw clenched, and then he shook his head. "It won't work, and besides…" His voice grew hoarser. "I scream, Shiloh. I wake up screaming, and it's bad. I'll scare the shit out of you. And Bibi."

Jesus. The thought horrified me. Not for me or Bibi but for him. What he suffered every night, never complaining.

I waited until my voice was steady. "We're going to try it. Okay?"

He wanted to protest, but he was too tired, his eyes already closing. I put my arm across his chest and snuggled as tightly to him as I dared without hurting him. I felt him settle into the bed, into my embrace.

He inhaled a breath and sighed it out. "I love you."

The words were spoken so softly, I thought I misheard. But my heart heard them plain as day—seized them and drew them in where they sank in deep. It felt fuller than it'd ever felt. As if my chest couldn't contain it.

"You don't have to say it back," Ronan said, eyes still closed, voice drifting. "I don't expect…anything. I just wanted you to know that."

I swallowed hard. Disbelieving. Within moments, he was asleep, his breathing even. And I still couldn't move.

He's delirious and exhausted. He doesn't know what he's saying.

Except Ronan never said anything he didn't mean. Never wasted a word. But before I could process it or what those words were doing to my insides, to my heart, the nightmares were already coming for him.

His shoulders twitched, and his brow furrowed. "No…" he breathed. "No, don't."

I held him tighter and put my mouth to his ear. I had no idea what to say but let the words come.

"Ronan, listen to me. I'm here. I'm right here. Listen to my voice. Come with me. Come away with me."

His body relaxed, and his face smoothed of tension. I eased a breath, relief so great that he might have a peaceful sleep after so long without.

But it took all night.

Again and again, he jerked and writhed, calling out for someone to stop. For someone else to stay. Each time, I talked him down, soothed him, ran my fingers through is hair. Once, I had to wake him before the screams came. He jerked awake, his breath coming hard, not knowing where he was.

I reassured him, held him, and he slept again. And sometime late in the night, he went under deep, and the nightmares stayed away. I stayed awake, never ceasing my vigil until dawn's light began to creep in my window. I knew then he was okay. He'd made it.

I curled into him and slept too.

My alarm went off for school. I silenced it and heard Bibi bustling around in the kitchen. Ronan hardly stirred. I slipped out of bed quietly so as not to wake him and went to find her.

"Bibi…"

She turned in her housedress, the pot of coffee burbling beside her, her face soft but drawn with concern. "Oh, honey."

I rushed into her arms and let her hold me, the fear and horror of last night shuddering through me.

"I thought I heard something last night. Tell me."

"Ronan," I said, pulling away before I fell apart completely. "Someone hurt him. Badly. He's in my room. I tried to help him, but his ribs are cracked, and he doesn't want to go to the hospital. He'll hate that I'm telling you. He doesn't want anyone worrying about him."

"That's too bad for him. He's part of this house now, whether he likes it or not." She patted my cheek, squinting at me. "You're tired, honey. Go back to him. I'll let the school know you're not coming. Him too. When he's ready, we'll get some food in him and hear the story." She chuckled softly. "I dated a rabble-rouser once too. Always getting himself into all kinds of fixes."

I hugged her again, feeling as if the reinforcements had arrived, and then climbed back into bed with Ronan.

An hour or so later, I woke to him stirring. He blinked open his eyes—his left eye already much less swollen—and glanced over at me. If he remembered what he'd said last night, he didn't show it.

Because it wasn't real. He was half asleep.

"Hey," he said, his voice hoarse.

"Hey. How are you feeling?"

"Like shit." He frowned. "But the nightmares… Did I…"

"No. You got some sleep. Which you desperately needed."

His brows furrowed. "You stayed up all night?"

"I told you I would."

"Christ, Shiloh, I don't even know what to say but thank you, and… I'm sorry—"

I silenced him with a soft kiss. "If you say sorry one more time… How're the ribs?"

He inhaled deep and winced. "Okay."

"I told Bibi. She's going to want to feed you until you're better."

He gingerly sat up to lean against the headboard. "She doesn't need to deal with this. I shouldn't have come here. I was so out of it, I thought…"

I sat up beside him. "What happened last night? Tell me the truth."

He sighed. "Frankie Dowd and Mikey Grimaldi. Payback for the Jeep. Mitch Dowd was there."

"Frankie's dad? He's a cop, isn't he?" Then what Bibi had told me about him at the beginning of the year came rushing back to me. "*He* did this to you?"

"When I had Grimaldi and Frankie beat, the fucker tased me." He jerked his chin at the bloody tears in his jeans.

"My God. That *asshole*."

"I don't remember much after that." He frowned. "Something happened that stopped it, but I don't know what. I remember thinking I had to get to you before they did. Like they were coming here next."

My heart clenched, thinking of Ronan, bleeding and stumbling, having been *tased* for fuck's sake, but thinking of me.

Because he loves me.

I took the thought and buried it deep.

Later.

"The next thing I remember was sitting on the steps of your house with you."

I bit my lip, thinking. "The bruises you had the first time…back in the fall. Those were from Mitch too, weren't they? It's him you're afraid of. Not Frankie or Mikey."

He nodded. "Not afraid for me. For you. If he fucks with you to get to me…"

"He's not going to. Bibi knows everyone in town. She's friends with a cop. A *good* cop. There are more of those than there are of him."

"Maybe," Ronan said. "But my mom needed the cops too. She needed them a lot, but the system kept failing her. Dad would do a night in lockup, then come right back. Restraining orders meant shit. A judge didn't put him away. So when the sirens come…" He shook his head. "It doesn't remind me of help. It reminds me of the last time they came, too late. They arrested him, locked him up in prison with a life sentence, but so fucking what? She was already gone."

I rested my cheek against his bare shoulder and twined my fingers in his.

"Don't let Bibi get dragged into this," he said after a minute. "Last night was bad enough for you."

"I told you, I'm in this all the way." I cleared my throat. "And besides, if you're really afraid Mitch might come here, Bibi is our best defense. Her police friends will take care of us. So please try not to worry, okay?"

He nodded reluctantly, and his eyes fell shut again.

"You want to sleep some more?"

"I could try. But…"

"Then I'll sit with you."

"Shiloh…"

"I told you, Ronan. I'm not going anywhere."

Ronan napped. Only once did a nightmare try to sneak in, but I talked him through it. He twitched and cried out, but I whispered soothingly into his ear until he settled again. He woke at noon, his stomach growling.

"Bibi and I will get lunch, and then we can figure out what happens next."

"What happens next?"

"Mitch goes to jail."

He tried to protest, but I silenced him with a kiss, then kissed him again gently on the side of his nose and on his temple above his eye.

"Put a shirt on," I said with a grin. "And that is likely the first and last time I will *ever* say that."

Bibi and I fixed grilled cheese sandwiches with tomato soup. Ronan, moving slowly and stiffly, came into the dining room.

"Hey," he said, self-conscious and unsure.

"Oh, my sweet boy." Bibi's hand went to her throat. Tears filled her eyes, and suddenly I was on the verge of a breakdown too, to see how much she cared for him. She recovered quickly and gestured to a place setting. "Sit. You must be starved."

We all sat at the table, Ronan beside me and Bibi across from us.

When we'd eaten, she wiped her mouth and tossed the napkin on her plate. "Tell me, honey."

Ronan told Bibi everything, including how Mitch had paid him a visit in the fall after his fight with Frankie at Chance Blaylock's party.

Bibi pursed her lips, her eyes slightly unfocused but angry. "Shameful," she snapped. "Using his authority like that. Ronan, you need to press charges."

"He'll just deny it. Frankie and Mikey will vouch for him. There's no proof..." Ronan stiffened, his eyes widening.

"What is it?" I asked, alarmed.

"Maryann... Oh shit, I remember. She had her phone..." He tore from the table. "I have to go."

Before I could stop him, he hurried back to my bedroom. I found him pulling on his boots, grimacing in pain.

"Ronan?"

"Fucking stupid. I'm so fucking stupid."

"What are you talking about? Who's Maryann?"

"My neighbor. She's the one who stopped it. She recorded the whole thing on her phone. And Mitch knows it."

"Okay, so?"

"I need to get back. Make sure she's okay. Have Bibi call her friend. Tell him to help Maryann."

"Ronan, you're panicking. Just take a breath—"

He stopped, and the look on his face chilled my blood. "I couldn't save her, Shiloh. Do you get it? I couldn't save her. I was too late."

I nodded, my heart breaking when I was sure it'd already been shattered to pieces.

"I get it," I whispered. "I'll drive you. Don't argue. It'll be faster, and you can hardly walk."

He nodded with gratitude and gingerly pulled on his jacket.

"I'm taking him home," I told Bibi when we came out. "I'll be right back."

She heard in my tone that this wasn't over and nodded.

I drove Ronan to his apartment complex. All looked quiet. He leaned over to me and kissed me quickly.

"I'll wait here," I said. "Until I know everything's fine."

"No, Shiloh," he said, his voice hard. "Go. I'll call you."

"Absolutely not. I'm not leaving you alone."

"But I need you to."

His tone was grave. Simple. I remembered the stricken look on his face in my bedroom. What Ronan had been through was almost too much for me to comprehend. All I could do was support him, however he needed me to.

I bit my lip. "I don't like this. *At all.* But…call me later. Call me as soon as you know anything."

"Thank you, Shiloh. For…everything. What you did for me…" He shook his head.

I wanted to do it every night. Stand guard over his dreams so nothing could hurt him.

He kissed me again, and I drove away, hating to see his image grow small in my mirror.

I got a text as I pulled back into my driveway.

All good. Maryann's at work. Found her number

in my uncle's files. Going to rest and wait until she gets back.

There was a pause, and then the rolling dots that said he was typing returned. I stared at the phone, breath held.

I ran out quick. Tell Bibi thank you.

I exhaled.
What did you think he was going to say?
I didn't answer that. I texted him that I would, then went inside. I slumped on the couch beside Bibi, drained and exhausted, and rested against her shoulder.
"How are you doing, honey?"
"Tired. Last night felt like a million years long."
"Being scared for someone you love is draining, isn't it?"
I stiffened. "I don't… I mean…"
Bibi's shoulder shook a little as she chuckled.
"What's so funny?"
"Not funny so much as joyful, honey. I was remembering something you said in the fall about Miller and Violet. That it was so obvious they belonged together that *not* being together didn't make sense. And I said I was going to remember that and hold it against you."
I peered up at her as she peered down at me.
"So this is me, very gently holding that against you. I'm so happy for you."
"Happy for me? Last night was awful."

"Things got pretty scary, but you didn't back down. I'm proud of you, Shiloh. Your heart is open for that boy, and it's beautiful to see. Just beautiful."

I started to protest, but sleep was coming for me. And she was right. I'd crossed over a line and could not go back. Could no longer imagine a life without Ronan Wentz in it.

That, I thought as I drifted to sleep, *is my nightmare.*

TWENTY-FOUR

RONAN

Maryann had said she'd be home by six. I lay on the ratty couch watching ESPN and icing my eye with the same bag of peas she'd given me the first time Mitch Dowd had shown up. My body felt like it'd been hit by a truck, but I was more awake than I'd been in a long time.

Shiloh did that.

She stayed up all damn night, keeping the nightmares from taking hold. The kid in the kitchen watched his mom being murdered, but Shiloh took him by the hand and led him away.

And I told her I loved her.

It was too much to put on her after all that shit with Dowd, but I'd been half drunk with pain, and the blood and violence of the night left me wondering if I'd see tomorrow.

I didn't want it to be too late.

At six fifteen, a knock came. I hauled my aching body off the couch, wincing at the pain in my ribs, and opened the door to Maryann. She whispered a curse under her breath at the sight of me and stepped inside.

"Where are the twins? Not alone?"

"At a friend's until seven. They're safe, Ronan."

I nodded, and we sat at my kitchen table under the lone bulb.

"I sent the video to the police," she said. "Anonymously. But it clearly shows his face. Especially that last kick," she added, tears shining in her eyes. "But it's too dark to see you."

"Good. I'll stay home the next few days. Make sure he doesn't come back."

"He's not going to come back, Ronan. That was assault and battery. He's going to jail."

"I'll believe it when I see it."

She sighed. "Let me see your eye." I moved the peas, and she winced. "Damn it, this is bullshit. Do you feel well enough to go back to school? You need to graduate, young man."

Despite everything, I *was* going to graduate. My grades weren't great, but they were enough.

I did it, Mom. Barely.

"I'll go back in a few days."

"What will you do after? College?"

"Manage this building, I guess."

"You can do more than that, but you don't want to leave us high and dry, do you?"

"Maybe. I like it."

That was the truth too. I liked taking care of the building

and the tenants. I liked the idea that I was helping—in a small way—to provide a decent home when I'd had none.

"You've been good to us," Maryann said and rummaged in her purse. She slid an envelope across the table. "It took me too long to save it up, but this is yours."

I set the peas down and peered in the envelope. Two one-hundred-dollar bills lay inside. I immediately closed it and shoved it back across the table.

"No."

She laughed a little. "Just…no? This is the partial rent you covered for me. And don't bother denying it. Your uncle has never been in a good enough mood to let two hundred dollars slide."

"I'm not taking this, Maryann."

"You are, Ronan. For me. Because you can't leave me feeling like shit. I worked hard to earn this, so you're going to take it." She slid the envelope back and crossed her arms, a single eyebrow arched.

I nodded once.

"Lord, you're a stubborn man. But a good one." She rested her chin in her hand. "If only you were twenty years older. Don't take that the wrong way. I'm not a…what do they call it? A cougar? But you'd make an amazing dad for my girls. They love you."

I sat back and quickly returned the peas to my face to cool the strange rush of warmth that flooded me.

"You've never thought of yourself that way?"

"No."

"You have a lot to offer, Ronan. More than you think." Maryann got up from the table and came around to me. "Get back to school as quick as you can." She pecked the top of my head. "And for God's sake, take care of yourself. We need you." She touched the pendant that lay against my shirt. "I'll bet she does too."

After Maryann left, I lay stretched out on my couch and called Shiloh.

"How are things?" she asked.

"Good, I guess. Maryann thinks Dowd's going to jail."

"Maryann is right. Bibi talked to her detective friend. *Someone* sent in a video that clearly shows Dowd attacking an unknown victim. He's been arrested and will most likely face jail time. And he's been kicked off the force, effective immediately."

"Even without my testimony or pressing charges or whatever?"

"I asked about that too. Apparently, the victim is basically just a witness. They don't have to press charges if there's another witness. Like a video."

"What about Frankie?"

"No word. Bibi says Mitch isn't talking, which is weird. He seems like the kind of guy who'd rat out his own son."

"He hates snitches," I said. "Told me personally. But… he's in custody now?"

"He is. So you can rest easy, okay? Everyone you want to keep safe is safe."

I let out a breath and sagged deeper into the couch.

Safe. They're all safe.

I wondered if my mom knew that too.

"You know there is an upside to all this madness," Shiloh said in my ear.

"What's that?"

"We don't have to hide at school anymore."

My eyes widened. "I thought you hated people being up in your business."

"I do, but no sense in pretending if we don't have to. Right? I haven't been a…girlfriend to anyone. Ever. But I want to try."

Girlfriend. Holy shit.

I felt her holding her breath, waiting for my reply. I knew it took a lot to show this side of her—the side that was unsure and unguarded.

"I've never been anyone's boyfriend," I said.

A small sigh came over the line, and I heard her smile. "What do you think? Want to give it a go?"

"Yeah," I said. "I do."

Days later, Shiloh met me coming out of the parking lot at Central. She wore a white sundress that highlighted the deep black of her hair and made her skin glow in the bright May light. Her smile when she saw me was fucking stunning.

"Hey, you." She fell in step beside me and took my hand. "It feels weird, doesn't it?"

"Yeah," I muttered. It felt really weird to have a girl like Shiloh beside me—my *girlfriend*—willing to show the world she was mine. As if I'd gone to sleep in my old shitty life and woke up in a brand-new one.

"Maybe we should do something about it," she said. "Get it over with. Like tearing off a Band-Aid."

We were crossing the quad, and Shiloh pulled me to a stop right in the middle and kissed me. In front of the whole school.

"I have to admit," she said when she pulled away. "PDA is much less annoying when I'm the one doing it."

I chuckled and spied Frankie Dowd watching us. He looked like hell—skinnier, his face pale—as if he hadn't slept or eaten in days. He sneered and flipped me the bird but without any real fight. I sort of felt sorry for him.

I put my arm around Shiloh and steered her in another direction, shooting him a glare that warned of pain if he fucked with her. He slunk away quickly, but part of me wondered if I couldn't drop my vigilance just yet.

"Prom is in the air," Shiloh said, nodding at a huge poster strung between two poles. *The Pogonip Country Club is proud to host this year's senior prom—A Night Under the Stars! Get your tix now!* "Word on the street is that my very own Violet will be crowned queen."

I looked down at her. "You want to go?"

She stared. "Are you asking me to prom?"

I thought of the two hundred dollars Maryann had given me. I hated taking it, but if I spent it on Shiloh, maybe it wouldn't be so bad.

"If you want to go...then yes. I'm asking."

"I told you, dances aren't my thing. And I didn't think they were yours either. Are they?"

"Fuck no. But I want to do what you want."

She slipped her arms around my waist. "Maybe we could do our own thing instead."

"Like what?" I asked, and then it hit me all at once, like a vision from the future. "Never mind. I have it."

Her brows rose. "Care to share?"

"No."

"I don't get a say?"

"No. Leave it to me."

"He says to the type A personality," Shiloh said, laughing. "I've planned all my own birthday parties since I was six."

"You're going to have to sit this one out." I bent and kissed her. "It's what boyfriends do for their girlfriends."

TWENTY-FIVE
SHILOH

THE SUN WAS STILL HIGH IN THE SKY AT FOUR O'CLOCK ON prom night when Ronan knocked on our door. Bibi answered while I gave myself a last once-over in the bathroom mirror.

My dress was an off-the-shoulder in muted yellow, covered in outlines of flowers in black—like sketches—every few colored in bursts of white or red. The loose layers flowed to my shins in the front, my ankles in the back, and gathered at the waist. I'd tied half of my braids away from my face, the rest flowing between my shoulder blades. I slipped a few silver rings on my fingers and bangles on my arms, but Ronan had told me not to get too fancy. Maybe because he wasn't exactly rolling in cash. Not that I cared. We could eat at McDonald's and then go bowling, so long as I was with him.

You are so gone, girl.

My heart skipped a beat as I heard Ronan's low voice

and Bibi's higher one as she crowed over him. I blew air through puffed cheeks and headed out. I got as far as the dining table and stopped.

Oh. My. God.

Ronan was in all black. Black T-shirt, black jeans, black boots, and a black bomber jacket that I'd never seen before. His hair was darker too, slicked back from his face from a shower, and his eyes were as silver as the necklace around his neck. He wore it against his shirt now instead of tucked under. His injuries had healed, returning his face to its usual beautiful perfection—sharp angles and full lips. High cheekbones and thick brows.

"And he's mine…" I murmured, the words falling out of my mouth before I could stop them.

"There she is," Bibi said, her throat thick. "Oh my, aren't you the most beautiful girl and most handsome man in all of Santa Cruz?"

"You have to say that because you're my great-grandma," I said, crossing to them. I smoothed the lapels on Ronan's jacket. He smelled like shower soap and the burned wood from a bonfire at the shack, as if he carried the fire with him. "There should be a law that requires you to wear all black, every day, for the rest of your life."

Ronan didn't seem to have heard. "You look… I mean… *Holy shit.*" He shook his head. "Sorry, Bibi."

She chuckled. "That's okay, honey. I like that reaction just fine."

So did I.

Ronan held a small bouquet of wildflowers. They looked delicate and feminine in his large hands.

"Are those for me?"

He handed them over, adorably awkward and self-conscious.

I plucked a few yellow flowers and tucked them into my hair where the braids were tied back. "How's that?"

"Good," he said, then scowled at himself.

Bibi took a few pictures, though Ronan looked about as uncomfortable as he could get.

"That's plenty," I said. "We need to arrive at…wherever Ronan's taking me while the sun is still up. Don't we?"

"Yeah. Better head out."

"Just one more," Bibi said. "I need photographic evidence for the gals that my great-granddaughter is participating in a mushy and romantic rite of passage, or they won't believe me."

I rolled my eyes, laughing. "We're taking the beast, right?"

Ronan nodded. "Open the garage, and I'll meet you."

He went outside, and I kissed Bibi's cheek. "Don't wait up."

She chuckled. "I wasn't planning on it."

I opened the garage door and popped the Buick's trunk so Ronan could stow a cooler, a blanket, and his backpack that looked bulky and heavy.

"What's all this?" I asked. "You still haven't told me—"

He slammed the trunk shut and hauled me to him, kissing me hard. Deep. His tongue was deliciously rough and sharp-tasting from harsh mouthwash, the only alcohol I could ever taste. But I didn't need booze; Ronan's kiss left me delirious.

"I've been wanting to do that since the second I saw you," he said gruffly.

"Me too," I said. "If you say we're spending prom in a hotel room, I'd be okay with that."

"Don't tempt me. You look incredible."

I traced the line of his lower lip. "So do you. Look incredible." The thought that this man was mine came over me again like a pleasant chill.

"Keys," he said, holding out his hand.

"So bossy."

I loved it when he was bossy. Commanding. I'd prided myself on being the kind of girl who didn't fall for that stuff, but *God.* Ronan was on another level of masculine virility.

I don't stand a chance.

Ronan drove us eastward, the coast glistening gold as the sun started to descend toward the ocean. We passed a sign for the Natural Bridges State Beach Visitor Center and pulled into the lot.

"Crazy enough, I've actually never been to this beach," I said.

"We're not going to the beach," Ronan said, his eyes on the road. He maneuvered the car into a parking space in the empty lot, which was odd since the day was perfect and warm. "You good to walk in those?" he asked with a nod at my sandals as he unpacked the trunk.

"Yep. I remember your instructions. Are we hiking?"

"Not exactly."

We walked up to the visitor center where a sign plastered to the darkened window explained why we were the only ones there.

"That fucker," Ronan muttered under his breath, then laughed a little, shaking his head.

Natural Bridges Monarch Trail is CLOSED due to a private event. Welcome, Shiloh and Ronan!

I stared. "Did you do this?"

"I wish I could take credit. I told Holden my plan to make sure it wasn't totally stupid or…not good enough for you." He jerked his chin at the sign. "So he bought the damn place out."

"To make sure we're alone," I said, smiling up at him. "He's a good friend."

Ronan didn't say anything, but I could tell he was touched.

"What's the Monarch Trail?" I asked as we started up the wooden plank path around the visitor center. "And how have I never heard of it?"

"You'll see."

He led us up to the trail entrance where a park ranger checked that we were Ronan and Shiloh, then welcomed us in.

Ronan carried the backpack on his shoulder, the cooler

in one hand. I carried the blanket. We crossed a long wooden bridge into a forest of pine and eucalyptus trees. The planked path continued for another few minutes and ended on a wooden platform in the midst of a grove of just eucalyptus. Sunlight poured in, giving it an ethereal quality. The kind I tried to capture in my jewelry.

"What is this place?"

Ronan set down the cooler and backpack and pointed toward a tree.

I looked up and drew in a little intake of breath. A bough of green eucalyptus leaves was positively dripping with orange-and-black monarch butterflies. So many that it appeared the tree's leaves were made of them. Their wings opened and closed slowly, like breathing. I turned and there was another. And another. Thousands of them, clinging to the leaves or flitting here and there.

"Ronan…" I gripped his arm, staring.

"Is it okay?"

"*Okay?*" I moved to the wooden railing, to the closest cluster of butterflies hanging a few feet above me. "I never knew this was here. Never seen anything like it." A handful of butterflies took flight and then settled again. "This is the most beautiful thing I've ever seen."

Ronan stood with his hands in his pockets, a strange, soft smile on his lips. His eyes were full of me. "I know what you mean."

God, this man.

I admired the butterflies, delighted when one of them

landed on my wrist for a few seconds and then rejoined its family.

Ronan unpacked the cooler while I laid out the blanket. "I don't cook. I hope this is okay."

The spread was from a gourmet restaurant downtown. He opened containers of grilled lemon chicken, pasta salad, mashed potatoes, and little mason jars of yogurt berry parfait—all foods that were obviously chosen with me in mind. For drinks, he had two bottles of beer and two bottles of sparkling water.

He popped a water and handed it to me. "Okay?"

"You keep asking me that, as if it could be any more perfect."

"I've never done something like this before."

"You're *slaying* this boyfriend stuff." I leaned over the picnic blanket and kissed him. I tasted his potent fire, stirring places deep inside me that were hungry, and not for food.

We ate as the sun began to sink in a blood-orange sunset. Ronan opened his backpack and pulled out eight small metal torch-looking devices with stands, each no more than a foot tall.

"There's more?" I asked.

"That was dinner," he said. "This is prom."

He ringed the wooden viewing platform's railing with the little torches and turned on their flickering orange LED lights. They glowed from within metal cups, each cut with flame-like designs to give the appearance that real fire burned within.

When they were set up, the entire space glowed, the orange light illuminating the orange wings of the butterflies that looked as if they'd gone to sleep.

"I figured—*hoped*—this place wouldn't be busy at night," Ronan said as the last torch was lit. "But thanks to Parish…"

"You would have done this anyway? With an audience?"

He pulled me to my feet and held me close. "Only for you."

We hovered in that moment, our lips inches apart, his eyes boring into me, smoky and hot. He leaned in, brushing that mouth of his against mine, sending sparks dancing down my neck.

But he didn't kiss me. Instead, he pulled his iPhone from the back pocket of his jeans. "Music."

My eyes widened. "Are we dancing?"

He made a noncommittal sound and showed me the phone. "I made a playlist of stuff I thought you might like."

My heart…

He pressed the first song, and Dua Lipa's "Physical" played over his phone at a medium volume. "Don't want to disturb *them*," he said with a nod at the butterflies.

For a second, all I could do was stare at this man who was miles deeper than anyone knew. Considerate and kind beneath his hard stare and black ink.

Then I smiled as joy—running on the currents of the music—poured out of me. I danced on the platform, letting the song and euphoria carry me where they wanted to go. I took Ronan's hands and tried to get him to join me, but he shook his head and pulled out of my grip.

"I don't dance."

"You're just going to watch?"

"*Yes.*"

God, how he could load one syllable with so much sex was beyond me.

Ronan crossed his arms and leaned against the railing, and I could feel his heated, hooded gaze watching me as the night sky darkened to dark-blue velvet.

The song ended, and "Umbrella" began. I closed my eyes and let Rihanna's voice take me too. I thought I'd feel self-conscious with Ronan watching me, but instead, I felt electrified. Uninhibited. I moved to him, turned my back to him, pressing myself against him. His hands came up and took hold of my hips.

"Fuck," he gritted out, his lips near my ear, his hands sliding up my waist to my breasts.

I slid out of his grasp and tossed him a coy smile. "If you want to touch me, you have to dance."

He started to shake his head when the song ended and Maroon 5's "She Will Be Loved" came on. A softer, slow song. I pulled him to the center of the platform.

"Now you can touch me."

He wrapped his arms around my waist and pulled me close, hardly moving. My arms went around his neck, my hands sinking into his hair. He pressed his forehead to mine, and the world disappeared. Just him and me, sharing a breath, his eyes locked on me. The playful sexiness mellowed and deepened, and I drew in a breath at the potency of the moment. What I felt for him. *How* much I felt for him.

So much. God help me, it's so much.

Ronan's lips brushed mine, and then he kissed me. Shallow and soft. Then harder, his tongue delving into my mouth. The fullest, most complete kiss of my life, the sucking pull drawing everything from me, and I let it. The kiss took over, and there was no more dancing. Only the song's lyrics floating over us among the sleeping butterflies.

On your corner in the pouring rain…

A moan fell out of me, and my arms around him tightened. The moment swelled in me and crashed over, so strong it scared me.

"Ronan?"

"I know," he breathed, his hands sliding up my back, holding me tight to him as if he'd never let me go. I hoped he wouldn't.

"Take me home," I whispered. "Your home."

He didn't protest like I thought he might. He only nodded and kissed me a final time. Wordlessly, we cleaned up and packed the lights away but for one to lead us back.

The night was thick and warm; summer was fast approaching. Ronan took the wheel and drove us to his apartment complex. In the parking lot, he killed the engine but didn't get out.

"I don't live with my uncle," he said in a low voice. "I

only said that so I wouldn't seem weird. A high school guy who lived alone. But I do. I live alone."

"I know."

"You do?"

"When you were hurt, you never mentioned an uncle who might be worried about you. But I think I suspected even before that. You never talk about him."

He faced forward, his lips drawn.

I reached over and sank my fingers in his hair at the back of his head. "It's okay. I don't like it, but I don't think it's weird."

"You don't like it?"

"I don't like that you're alone."

He looked to me, his gaze drinking me in. "I'm not tonight."

Ronan led me to the upstairs corner unit with OFFICE marked on the door.

"It's not much," he warned, letting me in and flipping on the light.

He was right—the place was small and simple but clean. What struck me most was its emptiness. No pictures on the wall, no photos of anyone on the coffee table. No sign that anyone lived here. As if I could look in the closet and find Ronan's suitcase still fully packed.

The loneliness of it broke my heart but hardened it too

with fierce pride. More evidence that Ronan was pushing through the horror of his past the best way he knew how—suffering in silence to keep it from touching those he cared about.

"Show me the rest."

He led me to the bedroom with a tiny attached bathroom. The room was sparsely furnished—a bed with a plain dark comforter, a nightstand, a dresser. No art on the walls, no photos.

I turned at the foot of the bed. He was at the door, waiting for the verdict.

"Come here."

He crossed to me in two long strides. His mouth found mine while my hands gripped him at the waist and pulled him close. He unzipped my dress in the back, and I pushed the jacket off his shoulders. His shirt went next as my dress pooled at my feet. Down to my bra and panties, I wrapped my arms around Ronan and was enveloped in the heat of him. If there was a heaven, this was it. His warm skin, his hard muscle, and his heart beating against my ear.

I pressed a kiss there, then over his tattoo. The owl on his shoulder watched me with orange eyes. But I was no longer a stranger.

Ronan unclasped my bra, pulling it off my shoulders while we kissed with shallow, wet, licking kisses. His eyes drank me in, his hands on my breasts—they fit perfectly in his palms. He bent, and his hair tickled my chin as he put his mouth to one hard nipple.

I moaned as he bit and sucked, sending shivers dancing up my chest and down my back, between my legs. My panties were already damp.

When my breasts were aching and heavy from Ronan's relentless mouth, I pushed him away and fumbled at the button and zipper on his jeans. His erection strained against the denim, and I reached inside to grip him. To stroke him while his mouth blazed a trail of wet kisses up my neck to my ear.

"Ronan…" I breathed. "I need…"

I needed him naked. I needed to *be* naked beneath him. Or on top of him, nothing left between us. No more rules or labels. Just him and me.

Ronan lifted me up and wrapped my legs around his waist to take me down to the bed. He settled himself over me, bracing himself on his forearms while his groin dug into mine, the stiff denim hard between my legs.

"Take those off," I breathed. "Take everything off."

Then I lay back and watched him strip down to nothing. He tugged my panties off and tossed them aside and ground his hips down. Mine rose to meet them, straining, the urgency tightening in me like a knot, needing and wanting him so badly I could hardly think.

He reached for the nightstand drawer.

"Don't," I said, pulling him back.

"You sure?"

"I'm on the pill. And have a clean bill of health. You?"

He nodded. "Had a workup before I left Wisconsin." His gaze deepened. "And there's been no one but you."

"Same," I said. "I want to feel you inside me. And I want you to feel me." I hardly recognized the woman saying these things. But this was the first time I'd been in his place, the first time in his bed, the first time we'd been naked together. "I want all of you."

His brows furrowed; his expression looked almost pained as he kissed me. The entire vibe in the room changed. Downshifted from something raw and heated to slow and intense. Ronan positioned himself over me, blanketed me with his body, so perfectly heavy. Perfectly *masculine* in every way. He kissed me deeply, thoroughly, his hands holding my face, and he settled deeper into the V of my body.

"Oh God," I moaned, arching into that first perfect thrust. Ronan was so big, so heavy and hard, touching places inside me. The feel of him without anything in the way made me dizzy.

"Shiloh, fuck..." He bent to kiss me, still holding my face. "You feel so good. Christ, so good..."

His hips rolled, undulating like a wave, slow and deep. Our skin, naked and sweat-slicked, touched in a hundred places. I felt myself begin to unravel. The slate gray of Ronan's eyes and the beauty of his face became one reality while the heavy ache he stoked where we were joined became another. Every touch, every thrust drew me tighter, the ache becoming sharper, glassier, and stronger than anything I'd felt before.

He kissed me until kissing became impossible, and then it was just his eyes on mine and our bodies moving somewhere below, automatically rising and falling, my hips lifting as his came down.

The beauty of the night—the butterflies and the lights, the food and the dancing, and now this…*him*. Ronan was right there, giving himself to me.

All I could do was let go, the last of my reservations and protections crashing down as the orgasm swelled up. I pulled him tight to me, wrapped my arms and legs around him, our bodies moving like one entity, the two of us burning in one fever.

I cried out as I came, unraveled completely, delirious and lost in the best way.

Ronan came hard moments later. I clutched him to me, my core throbbing, my body humming everywhere.

A few more erratic thrusts and he collapsed on top of me, his face in the crook of my neck, his body shuddering with the last of his orgasm. His hard chest pressed against my breasts, his heartbeat pounding with mine.

I wanted him to stay there forever.

"Too heavy," he murmured and rolled away, only far enough that we still lay tangled in each other.

He slept, and I kept my vigil over him until my eyes drooped, then I slept too.

And there were no nightmares.

TWENTY-SIX
SHILOH

Early the next morning, I woke to feel the bed dip as Ronan climbed out and drew on his clothes.

"How are you even moving?" I stretched under the sheets. "I'm not going to be able to walk for a month."

"Miller needs me. Holden and I are going to help get rid of his mom's asshole boyfriend."

"What does that mean exactly?"

"Tenant eviction," Ronan said with a wry smile, drawing on his boots. "I won't be gone long. Stay here. The coffee maker is ready to go if you want coffee. There are doughnuts on the counter and fruit in the fridge... I wasn't sure what you might want."

"You have all that waiting for me? Did you plan on me coming here?"

"I hoped that you would." He smiled a little and went to the top drawer of his dresser. "I would have given this to you sooner, but we didn't do much sleeping." He turned, and my heart swelled to see a silky headscarf in red and orange. He handed it to me. "If you want to sleep more."

"Ronan..."

"If you want to shower, there's shower gel for you, a toothbrush, and a shower cap. And I got a bottle of conditioner, like the kind you have in your bathroom."

My jaw fell open. "When..."

"I might've peeked when I was at your place the morning after all that Dowd shit went down." He bent swiftly over the bed and kissed me. "I gotta go. Be right back."

He left me staring after him, dumbfounded. I wrapped myself in the comforter and dragged it to the bathroom to pee. Sure enough, he'd stocked up on everything I needed to spend the night. He even bought the same flowery shower gel I used.

"Ronan Wentz..."

Last night came back. All of it. The enormity of what he'd done for me was overwhelming. Hard to believe it was all for me.

I fished around in his drawers for a T-shirt. It came down to my thighs and smelled like him, like having him next to my skin all over again.

In his simple but tidy kitchen, I hit the button on the coffee maker, then drank a cup with a jelly doughnut from the same place I'd taken him to in downtown Santa Cruz. My body felt pleasantly heavy and lazy. I climbed back into bed and tied up my braids in the scarf, then settled in to wait for him.

I must've dozed off. Some hours later, when the clock said it was midmorning, Ronan returned, a dark expression on his face. I came fully awake instantly and scanned him for injury.

"What happened? Are you okay?"

"I'm fine," he said. "We did it. Chet won't be bothering Miller's mom ever again."

"Then why do you look…almost sad?"

Ronan was quiet for a minute. Thoughts swam behind his eyes that looked like the gray before a storm.

"I hate that I sort of love it," he said finally. "The fight. The adrenaline rush. The violence. Even the pain. It's everything I want to keep away from you."

I reached for his hand; his knuckles were swollen and red. "But, Ronan, you only ever fight when it's to help. Miller and his mom. Kimberly…"

"The part of me that loves it is *him*."

"Your dad?"

He nodded and tapped his chest where the Milton quote was inked into his skin. "That's what this means. We were in hell, my mom and me. A hell that Dad made. But the devil is me. I was cast out of a good life, and I worry sometimes it's turned me into something bad. Something like him."

"You're not anything like him."

"I wanted to fight this morning. I wanted to make Chet suffer for hurting Miller and his mom. It reminded me of my family. Like I was being given another chance to save her." He flexed his knuckles; his voice was low and stony. "I wanted to hurt him."

"But you didn't, right? Not badly?"

"Scared him more than anything."

"And that's the difference between you and your dad," I said. "You stopped. He didn't."

He said nothing, and I could see he was still struggling with it. I didn't know what else to say. My phone on his nightstand rang into the quiet.

"It's Bibi." I hit the green answer button. "You okay?"

"I'm sorry to interrupt you and Ronan on what is surely a morning of sheer bliss…"

I clapped my hand to my eyes and shook my head. Ronan raised an eyebrow.

"An envelope has arrived from a bank," Bibi said. "The one where you applied for a start-up loan. It feels thick."

"Holy shit." My chest tightened, my heart clanging. "Bank application came back," I said to Ronan's alarmed stare. "My loan…"

"Esther is here," Bibi said in my ear. "She can read it for me if that's okay with you."

I wasn't exactly excited about sharing potentially bad news with Esther Morris from up the street, but I couldn't wait either.

"Okay. Open it."

I gripped Ronan's hand and waited an eternity as the ladies chatted and mumbled and rustled the phone in my ear. Then I heard Esther say, "It looks like she got it. Oooh, fifty thousand dollars. That's nothing to sneeze at."

My mouth fell open, and I stared at Ronan, shaking my head. "I got it. Fifty thousand…"

"Baby!" Bibi cried in my ear. "Did you hear?"

"I heard." Tears threatened. "Oh my God. Oh my God," I said over and over, disbelieving as my future unrolled in front of me. My own business. The responsibility of it… The *potential* of it…

"Wait." I held still. "Bibi, you didn't put up the house, did you?"

"No, honey, I promise," she answered. "This is based on the strength of your Etsy shop and your business plan. *Your* hard work."

"Holy shit."

Ronan stood at the end of the bed and began tugging the blanket off me. "Tell her you'll call her back." His voice was low and gruff.

"Um…Bibi, I have to go." I smothered a laugh as Ronan crawled on all fours over me. "I… I'll call you back."

I hung up as Ronan bent to kiss me, slow and deep.

"What are you doing?" I breathed.

"You got the loan," he said matter-of-factly. "Good job."

Then he climbed back into bed to *congratulate* me in a very Ronan Wentz type of way.

We finally finished celebrating until I was sure I couldn't have another orgasm for at least a month. But Ronan was shirtless as we sat at his kitchen table, eating fruit and doughnuts. The look in his eyes when I licked powdered sugar off my lip had me doubting if that were true.

The man is a walking orgasm machine.

"What do you want to do today?" he asked.

"I have to get home at some point to celebrate the bank loan with Bibi. I still can't believe it."

"Fifty K is amazing, Shiloh."

"It's not bad," I said. "I've done the math a thousand times in my head. The space is seven hundred and seventy-five square feet. At forty-two dollars per square foot, that's about thirty-three thousand dollars per year. Divided by twelve months means fifty grand will cover eighteen months of rent. That's just to lease the property. Doesn't include insurance, interior design—"

"I'll help," Ronan said. "Whatever I can do. I'll build whatever you need."

I shook my head. "You are too much. Last night. This morning…"

Because he loves me.

The moment you know your life is about to change forever hits like a sledgehammer, the weight of it heavy and monumental but exhilarating. I felt it when Bibi told me I got the start-up loan for my business. I felt it again in that kitchen, looking at Ronan Wentz.

I love him. I'm helplessly, hopelessly in love with him.

I opened my mouth to let the words come out when his phone on the table between us rang.

"Yeah?" His eyes widened; his face paled. "When?"

My pulse sped up as I watched confusion, alarm, and then something worse play over his features.

"Okay," he said. "Okay, I'll be right there." He set the phone on the table and stared at it. "Nelson is dead."

"Oh no," I breathed, my hand flying to my chest. "Oh God, Ronan, I'm so sorry. What happened?"

"Not sure." Ronan's voice sounded hollowed out by shock. "That was a tenant in the building he manages. Said he found him this morning. I have to go over there."

He stood, and I stood with him.

"I'm going with you."

"You don't have to."

"Ronan." I took his arm, gazed up at him. "You are *done* facing these things alone. Okay?"

He nodded and then let out a breath. "Okay."

We arrived at the complex called the Bluffs just as the coroner was preparing to leave. The apartment building was in terrible shape—looking to me like it was on the verge of being condemned. On the ground floor, corner apartment, yellow tape had been strung across the open front door.

Ronan stared blankly as a gurney with a body shrouded in white was loaded into a van. My hand slipped into his, and he held on tight as we approached the coroner.

"Hey," Ronan said. "I'm here for Nelson Wentz."

"Are you next of kin?"

"I'm his nephew."

"I'll have some paperwork for you," the guy said, peering at a clipboard through thick glasses.

"What happened?"

"Looks like cardiac arrest. Won't know until the autopsy."

I squeezed Ronan's hand at the coroner's cool, businesslike tone. He had Ronan fill out his information, clearly eager to go.

"We'll be in touch."

"Can I go in?"

"Suit yourself."

Ronan turned to me. "You don't have to…"

I held on tighter. "If you want some privacy, I'll stay here. Otherwise, I told you. I'm not going anywhere."

He smiled thinly, gratefully, and we went inside.

The place was a mess, with garbage and stacks of papers everywhere. Ronan had given me a pair of flannel sleep pants to wear before we left. I'd tied the drawstring tight and rolled up the legs, but they were in danger of falling down and dragging in the trash and refuse that littered the floor. The TV was on, the chair facing it draped with a sheet.

"The tenant said he was in that chair," Ronan said dully. "He wasn't well. I tried to ask him about it, but he brushed me off. I talked to him on the phone, but I haven't seen him face-to-face in weeks. I should have. I should have checked in more. Made sure he was okay."

"Don't think like that," I said softly. "I'm sure there was nothing you could have done."

"Maybe not. But what if there was?"

I had nothing to say to that.

Ronan took a last look at the apartment, then shut the TV off and went out. He strode into the parking lot alone and stood with his back to me, hands on his hips. I gave him a minute and then slowly approached.

"Ronan?"

"He was an asshole," he said, his voice tight. "My dad's brother. Looked like him too. He was terrible to his tenants and tried to teach me to be just as bad. A real prick." He shook his head, a muscle twitching in his jaw. "Yeah, he was a real prick. But he was my uncle." Tears stood out in Ronan's eyes now, turning them molten silver. "He was all I had."

Ronan turned away, his shoulders shaking silently. I moved to him, burrowing into his front and wrapping my arms around him. He held me tight, his face buried in my hair, his big body trembling.

"He's not all you had," I said, my voice wavering. "You have me, Ronan. I love you. I love you so much, and I'm sorry it took me so long to say it."

He pulled back, his cheeks streaked with tears. His expression was heartbreaking, struggling to believe he'd heard right.

I moved closer, held him tighter.

"You told me you loved me that horrible night Mitch attacked you. And I was too scared to say it back. I tried to minimize it and pretend like I didn't feel the same. But I do. I can't control my feelings or manage them like I try to manage everything else. I love you. And I love how it feels to love you. I've never been more scared, but never happier either. Loving you feels better than anything I've ever known."

His brows furrowed. "Shiloh…"

When he said nothing else, I had a horrible moment of doubt. Maybe he had been delirious when he told me he loved me. Maybe he didn't mean it.

Maybe he wasn't even talking to me.

Then he took my face in his hands and pressed his forehead to mine. He held me close, eyes squeezed shut, his voice a whisper as if he were afraid the fragile moment would shatter. "You're the best fucking thing to ever happen to me."

"Does this mean you love me too?" I asked, my heart in my throat. In his hands. "I didn't dream it, did I?"

He shook his head, still holding me close. "I love you, Shiloh. I can't believe you're real. Christ, I keep waiting to wake up to learn it was all a fucking lie. A cruel joke."

"It's not. I'm here, and I'm yours, Ronan," I said, and then he kissed me, and the rest of my words stayed locked in my heart.

Forever. I'm yours forever.

TWENTY-SEVEN

RONAN

"Holden's not answering," Miller said and hung up his phone. The flames of the bonfire lit up his worried expression. "He's been a mess since prom."

"Can you blame him?" I said, thinking of how my night with Shiloh had been fucking perfect in every way, while Holden's night with River had been a nightmare. He hadn't even told us how bad it was the morning after when we kicked Chet to the curb.

"He's leaving the country," Miller said. "Did he tell you that?"

"No," I said, a sudden, heavy weight settling in my chest. "He fucking did not."

That hurt more than I expected. That hurt a lot.

Miller shook his head and strummed his guitar absently. You wouldn't know by looking at him that he'd signed a deal with a major label and was gearing up to move to Los Angeles to record his first album.

They're both leaving.
That hurt too.

The hour grew late. Shiloh and Violet had gone out for a girls' night. Graduation was coming up, and Violet was going to school in Texas a week later.

"Everyone's scattering to the winds," Shiloh had said the other night in my bed. "Except you and me."

Damn straight. I wasn't going anywhere. I'd promised to watch over Miller's mom until he could move her to LA, and a lawyer had contacted me to say he was sorting out Uncle Nelson's shit. I'd keep taking care of the Cliffside apartments until then, but I was probably going to have to find a new place to live. Get a job and think about my future.

I couldn't see what was in it, except Shiloh.

Eventually, Miller called it a night and packed up his stuff.

"You staying?" he asked.

"For a while."

"Text me if you hear from Parish."

"I will. Same."

We clasped hands, and he took off. I sat in front of the fire, in no hurry to go. Watching the flames and listening to the ocean crash. Despite my worry for Holden, I felt more content than I had in years. Shiloh's love had sunk in deep, quieting that gnawing hunger that had plagued me for years. For the first time since Mom died, I felt closer to what I wanted to be instead of living in the shadows of *him*. Even the nightmares had backed off a little. I still woke up now and then drenched in sweat, my throat hoarse from a scream, but they were coming less and less frequently. And never when Shiloh slept over.

I settled deeper in my chair and had started to doze when I heard a muttered curse.

Holden appeared, looking pale, his usually perfect silver hair a mess. Dark circles ringed his eyes; his expensive clothes looked slept in.

"Ocupado," he muttered. "I was hoping for some alone time, Wentz."

I sat up. "Tough shit. Where have you been?"

He slumped against one of the boulders that ringed the bonfire. "Busy. Very busy. Lots of plans to make, plane tickets to buy, vodka to drink."

He took a long pull from his flask as if to prove his point.

I turned away quickly and put my own beer to my lips. "Were you ever going to fucking tell me? Or just split without a goddamn word?"

"Does it matter?"

I glared. "Yeah, it fucking matters."

He recoiled, guilt in his eyes. And shock. As if he still couldn't believe he meant something to me.

"I leave in a few weeks," he said. "After graduation. I have to have the damn diploma in my hand before the walking pus bags known as my parents relinquish my trust. Then I'm gone."

"Where?"

He shrugged. "Paris, maybe."

"You going to say goodbye to River or just ghost him too?"

"I said goodbye to him. At the hospital."

"And that was enough?"

His silence answered for him.

"Fuck," I muttered into my beer.

"Oh, you have thoughts on my situation, do you?" Holden spat, pushing unsteadily to his feet. "Tell me, o wise one, how you, who up until a few weeks ago had never been in a relationship that lasted longer than the time it took you to finish, are suddenly an expert."

"At least I'm trying," I said darkly. "I'm doing my fucking best, and I'll keep trying to do right by her. You're giving up."

Holden sagged. "I tried too. I failed."

"Try harder."

He smiled wanly and pushed himself off the rock. "Tough love from Ronan Wentz. You're one of the good ones. The best. I hope Shiloh knows how lucky she is."

He gave me a little salute and wandered back the way he came.

"Holden, wait."

But he was already slipping into the night. I thought about following him, but then what? Lock him up in the shack until he listened to reason?

"Shit." I tossed my beer bottle into the fire and pulled out my phone.

Just saw H. Doesn't look good.

Miller's reply was almost instant. What do we do?
I had no clue, hating how hopeless I felt.
But doing nothing wasn't an option.

On the last Wednesday of school, I hunted the quad for River Whitmore. I found Frankie Dowd first. Or he found me.

He stepped in front of my path—at a safe distance—looking like shit. Unwashed, stained clothes, eyes red-rimmed, like he hadn't slept in weeks.

"You happy, fucker? My dad lost his job thanks to you. He's *going to jail* thanks to you."

I crossed my arms. "Good."

"Good?" Frankie cried, drawing looks from students passing by, most with yearbooks tucked under their arms. "They gave him a year. What the fuck am I supposed to do?"

"Not my problem," I said.

A year wasn't forever, but it was long enough. I pushed past Frankie.

"We're not done with you yet," he screeched after me. "You hear me, Wentz? You'll pay. In the way that hurts you the most."

I spun around and gripped Frankie by the front of his dirty T-shirt. We had onlookers now. A ring of students, some with cell phones out.

"I'm done fucking with you, Dowd," I said, my gaze boring into Frankie's pale-blue eyes. "You come near me or anyone I care about, and I will *fuck your shit up*. You get me?"

He nodded frantically, his eyes wide.

I let him go with a shove. "Now fuck off. You stink."

He stumbled and slunk away, muttering to himself, and I spied Whitmore walking with Violet across the quad. His left arm was in a sling, and he had a bandage on his temple but otherwise looked okay. I strode to them, leaving a trail of whispers behind me.

"Hey," I said to Violet. "I need to talk to Whitmore. Alone."

"Sure." She pecked his cheek. "See you soon, River. And tell your mom I'm thinking of her. Always."

"I will," he said. She left, and he jerked his chin at me. "What's happening?"

"It's Holden."

"I figured. What about him? Is he okay?"

"He's a mess. He'd already be in Paris or fucking who knows where, except he's waiting on some cash. Then he's gone."

Whitmore's jaw clenched, his eyes flooding with pain. "Just like that? No saying goodbye?"

"He told me he said goodbye to you at the hospital."

"That doesn't fucking count."

I agreed. "Look. I know him. He needs…help. Or I don't know what. He needs you."

Whitmore nodded. "I need him too. Just as much."

"Show him."

"How? He won't talk to me. He won't answer my calls, and my mom is sick. I can't be camping out on Holden's goddamn porch for hours." He cursed with frustration. "I want to do whatever he needs but…*fuck*. My life's about to have a bomb dropped on it."

I knew how he felt. Losing a mother *was* like a bomb dropping, blasting the life you knew to little pieces.

"There's a parking lot near the cliffs," I said. "Not much to it. A utility shed at the west end. Go there today. Four o'clock. And keep out of sight."

"Dude, I don't have time for some cloak-and-dagger bullshit—"

"Do you want to see him or not?" I snapped. "Be there. I'll handle the rest."

After school that day, I walked with Shiloh to the student parking lot. I'd squeaked out a C-minus in history, though I suspected Baskin hadn't wanted to give me that much.

"He's an ass," Shiloh said, fingers twined in mine. "Your last paper on the Cold War was brilliant."

"Don't know about that."

She kissed my chin. "I typed it, so I do." We arrived at her Buick, and she ran her hands up my chest. "I have a free afternoon, if you catch my drift. Want a ride to your place?"

"Can't. Tonight?"

"A man of few words. Tonight will have to do." She kissed me softly. "Love you."

"Love you," I said and watched her go, still trying to believe that girl was mine.

I started for home while typing a text.

Meet me at the shack. 4 o'clock.

I waited and walked, praying Holden would answer. Relief gusted out of me when he did.

Why?

I hesitated over a response. It had to be good. Holden was too fucking smart; he'd see through bullshit immediately.

I have something 4 u.
Sounds romantic.

I rolled my eyes. It's important. And if you don't take it, I'll never speak to you again.

Too late, I realized that might be exactly what Holden wanted.

I see what you did there, he replied. I don't need new boots.

Just come. Please.

Please? Is this still Ronan Wentz, or did someone steal his phone?

I bit out a curse and was typing something a lot worse than *please* when another text came.

I'll be there.

I sighed again. *Christ, he's more work than Shiloh.* The thought made me smile, and then it faded instantly because the fucker was leaving.

But I'd done what I could. I didn't know if it was enough, but it wasn't nothing. That was something.

I walked home and arrived at my complex to see a thin old guy in a gray suit outside my door. He knocked, peered in the side window, and then started for the stairs to leave.

"Hey," I said when he came down. "Can I help you?"

"Are you Ronan Wentz?"

"Yeah." I crossed my arms, tensing.

"I'm Joel Barker, your uncle Nelson's attorney. We spoke on the phone."

"Oh, right."

"Can we go inside and talk?"

"Sure."

We went into my place, and I offered him a seat at the kitchen table. "Beer?"

"Thank you, no." Joel Barker was a short guy, bristly

gray mustache, rumpled suit. He pulled out a worn briefcase and set it on the table. "I'm very sorry to hear of Nelson's untimely passing. I've represented him for years. Can't say he was a friend, but… My condolences."

I sat down across from him as he unlatched the briefcase. "Did they find out what happened?"

"Pulmonary embolism," Barker said, withdrawing some papers. "Fortunately, they don't think he suffered."

Maybe not, but he died alone. That was the part I hated.

"I am the executor of your late uncle's will," Barker was saying. "He made modifications to it back in March. You are his sole beneficiary."

"Meaning what?"

"Meaning he left you everything." Barker put on glasses and peered at the will. "'I, Nelson Kenneth Wentz, being of sound mind and body, do hereby bequeath to my nephew, Ronan August Wentz, all of my earthly belongings to be disposed of, sold, or kept as he sees fit.'"

I thought of the mountain of shit in his apartment that I'd now have to wade through.

"'Also bequeathed to my nephew, the residential complexes, Bluffs and Cliffside—'"

My head shot up. "Wait, hold on. He left me the buildings?"

"Indeed. May I continue?"

I sat back in the chair, my thoughts going a mile a minute.

"'I also do hereby bequeath to him all liquid assets in my

bank accounts, personal and business, in amounts totaling $63,976.'"

I stared. "*Dollars?*"

He smiled. "Cold hard cash."

I thought about the state of Nelson's apartment, how miserly he was with the tenants and his own well-being.

"He has that much?"

"Had," Barker said. "It's yours now. Just sign here. The check will be issued to you within thirty business days. As for your uncle's remains, he has requested to be cremated."

"And then what?"

"He did not specify." Barker adjusted his glasses. "Business with the apartment buildings is a bit more complicated. I'm in contact with the city and will help officiate the transfer of property deeds, permits, and so forth into your name." He folded his hands. "That's quite a big responsibility. I'm sure the city would be very eager—especially in the case of the Bluffs complex—to purchase the land from you."

"And do what with it?"

"Knock the buildings down and turn them into condos, I'd imagine. The land is valuable. That would be another rather large windfall, young man, if I may say. Congratulations."

I nodded vaguely, thinking the tenants who would have to move out wouldn't see it that way. But *holy shit*.

I signed where Barker needed me to sign, and he shook my hand. "We'll be in touch."

I sat in the quiet of my kitchen for a long time—until the shadows started to creep across the floor—thinking about what Nelson had done. I replayed every conversation, every phone call. There weren't many and few that had meant anything.

Except one. When I'd demanded to know where he'd been while I was rotting in foster care. His response echoed in my head.

We're here now, aren't we?

He was right. Because *right now* was all anyone was guaranteed…and the easiest thing to forget.

PART IV

TWENTY-EIGHT
SHILOH

JULY

Bibi knocked on the bathroom door. "You ready, honey?"

I stared at my reflection in the mirror.

Am I ready?

I'd been preparing for this night for years. All those late nights, working by a single light bulb in the garage until my muscles ached and my eyes burned. Countless trips to the post office to mail off orders, saving every penny...

I let myself smile. A little one. "I'm ready."

I smoothed down my bright-yellow dress and gave my hair one last inspection. Letitia was a wizard. She and the rest of the family had arrived a few days ahead of the grand opening, and she'd spent an afternoon giving me boho braids—small, less polished, loose ends, with strands of color woven in here and there. I loved it. I loved that she was here with me to see this. Letitia had opened her own shop too; she knew what tonight felt like better than anyone.

I let out a shaky breath and went out.

Except for Violet who was at Baylor in Texas, everyone I loved was gathered in the living room. Uncle Rudy, Aunt Bertie, Letitia, Bibi, and Ronan, who looked devastating in charcoal slacks, a fitted white button-down, and a dark blazer. His uncle had left him a pile of money, and he'd bought some new clothes. He hated shopping but said it was worth it to make my night as perfect as possible.

"I don't need anyone thinking I'm the bouncer," he'd said.

"That's ridiculous," I'd teased. "You'd obviously be my arm candy."

My family, each dressed up for the occasion too, burst into excited—and excessive—crowing and cooing over me when I stepped out of the bathroom. Ronan stood quietly among them, the look on his face worth a thousand compliments.

"I'm so glad you're all here," I said, hugging and kissing them. "You too, Mama."

My mother smiled thinly from her seat at the dining room table, apart from everyone else. She looked beautiful in a deep-maroon dress, but her eyes were glassy. When they'd arrived this morning, I'd bent to kiss her cheek and thought I smelled alcohol. And when I'd introduced Ronan as my boyfriend, her face had frozen, a million thoughts behind her eyes. She'd only been courteous to him since.

"Let's get on now before I burst with excitement," Bibi said. My grandmother looked beautiful in a purple dress with bright-yellow flowers and was wearing her favorite wig—the one she said made her feel like Oprah.

"Yes, let's!" Aunt Bertie said. She beamed at me. "I am dying to see all your hard work come to life, sugar."

"Two entrepreneurs in the family," Letitia said and high-fived me. "Black Girl Magic, for real."

My smile was so wide, I thought my face would split, the happiness trying to burst free, but I couldn't let it. I was still scared to feel so much. As if that were tempting fate.

A few days after high school graduation, I learned that the city was going to lease me the laundromat space. The next weeks passed in a flurry of activity, remodeling it and getting it ready. I had my start-up bank loan but quickly learned that $50K sounded like a lot more money than it was.

Ronan wanted to spend his uncle's money on me, but I refused. I compromised by letting him design and build the displays for my jewelry and help me with the remodel. Turned out my backyard work shed was only a small example of Ronan's skills. I would've spent a small fortune for the work he did with just as much expert care and precision.

I met his eyes across the room. *And he picked the name.*

Uncle Rudy clapped his hands together. "Come on, ladies. Let's roll."

We stepped out into the late-afternoon twilight. I'd been at the shop all day preparing with the event planner and had come home to change and bring the family early before the crowds came.

If the crowds came.

Ronan's hand found mine, and he gave it a squeeze. "Hey. It's going to be perfect."

"Thank you for saying that. I feel like I'm going to puke."

He bent his tall frame down to me. "That dress," he said gruffly. "Is it expensive?"

"No, it only looks that way."

"Then you won't care when I tear it off you later."

"Don't say stuff like that right now. I can barely think straight as it is." I laughed. "And only you could think of sex right after I mention puking."

Ronan got behind the wheel, and Bibi sat beside him in the front seat of the Buick. I sat with Letitia in the back while Uncle Rudy took Bertie and Mama in the black Cadillac they'd rented.

We drove downtown, and my heart tried to climb out of my throat at the sight of the little shop. My shop.

The *Rare Earth Jewelry* sign was made out of gold-painted bamboo-looking bars set against the clean lines of plain glass with smoked glass edging. I smiled and glanced at Ronan.

"There it is! There it is!" Letitia clapped her hands. "*Girl...*"

My heart felt ten sizes too big. *There it is.*

Ronan parked, and my family all congregated at the front

of the shop. A local paper had done a write-up of me as one of the city's youngest entrepreneurs, and Ronan had taped it to the glass on the front door. Bertie and Bibi clung to each other as my aunt read it out loud, both streaming tears, while Rudy rocked back on his heels, hands in his pockets as he took in the shop. "Will you look at that?" he kept saying over and over.

Mama peered into a window, her face unreadable. I tried not to watch her too closely. Tried to tell myself it didn't matter if her face lit up with pride or not. I'd done it. This shop was for me, not her. But still, when she only smiled faintly and nodded, a little piece of my heart broke off, and I didn't think I'd ever get it back.

June Seong, my event planner, waved at me from inside, pulling my attention. Her services were a gift from Bertie and Rudy. "To give your shop the send-off it deserves," they'd said. June beckoned for us to come in.

I heaved a breath and faced everyone. "I just want to thank you all for being here tonight. Each of you has helped make this happen, and I'm so grateful for your love and support." I cleared my throat. "Before I get too mushy…" I opened the door. "Welcome to my shop."

They burst into a small round of applause and cheers that threatened to bring me to tears, then filed inside. Ronan lingered behind.

"Whoa," I whispered to him. "That felt…good."

He put his mouth by my ear. "I love you."

I stared up at him, shivers dancing all down my skin, no matter how many times he said it.

"I love you," I whispered back and kissed him. "Thank you."

"For what?"

"For you."

Inside, my family was oohing and aahing. I had to admit, it turned out well on the stringiest of shoestring budgets. My jewelry glinted on the displays Ronan had made—beige velvet stands in geometric blocks in rectangular and square shapes.

Along the right was the cash register, which sat on a huge display cabinet that I'd found at a yard sale and Ronan had restored. It now housed a hundred rings, the gemstones and turquoise bright under soft light. Behind the register was the door that led to the back room—a tiny storage space and bathroom.

On the walls were colorful prints of women from all over the world—South Africa, Tibet, Brazil—wearing the natural stones and metals of their countries. I couldn't make enough inventory on my own to fill an entire store but had contracted with another small company that sold ethically sourced jewelry to keep those displays full. Eventually, I planned to partner with local artisans too and share their work in my windows.

If I can stay in business long enough.

June beamed at me, looking beautiful in deep blue and yellow. "The *Santa Cruz Daily* is sending someone. They're going to want to ask you a few questions. The ads are in place, and invitations to local artists have been sent.

At least two have called me already, eager to talk collaboration." Her phone chimed an alert. "Aaaand the caterers are here."

"I'll go let them in," I said, starting for the back, but she stopped me.

"Enjoy this calm before the storm. I'll handle it."

"I love that she thinks there's going to be a storm," I said to Ronan.

He gave me a crooked smile. "She would know."

"Baby steps," I said. "I still can't believe I have *caterers*."

Two weeks before the grand opening, I'd received a letter in the mail with a French postmark. Inside was a fancy gold voucher for Elite Eats and a note.

Dearest Shiloh,

I hope you'll accept this small gift with my congratulations. (I'm only ever allowed to pay for the food.)
I wish you the best and every success.

Regards,
Your Holden

P.S. Tell Wentz I'll never forgive him for what he did and that I love him for it too.

I didn't know what the postscript meant except Ronan had facilitated a meeting with Holden and River Whitmore before Holden disappeared. I hadn't known that there was something between Holden and the quarterback of the football team in the first place; Ronan had kept Holden's confidence about it, which made me love him more.

That night, at the mention of caterers, Ronan's lips drew down. "It means Holden's alive at least."

I tucked my arm in his, wishing I had the words to ease his mind. Holden leaving suddenly hurt him worse than he let on, especially on the heels of Miller's departure for Los Angeles. The Lost Boys were scattered, and it was looking like they wouldn't be reunited any time soon.

Bertie brought Bibi over to me, and my great-grandmother took my arm. "If you'll excuse me, Ronan, darling, I must have a word with this girl."

"Of course."

He moved off, and my heart swelled to see Uncle Rudy and Aunt Bertie take possession of him, peppering him with questions.

Bibi's eyes were shining. "I am so proud of you, I can't stand it. This old heart of mine feels like it's going to burst."

"It had better not," I said, her emotion trying to pull out mine.

She leaned into me, and I smelled her jasmine perfume. "I know Marie is being Marie. And I know a lot of what's happening tonight is because you've been trying to make her *see* you. But don't let her dim your shine, baby. Tonight is your night. We all see you. *I* see you, Shiloh. And I know that's not the same as a mama's love, but I hope it can make up for what you're missing."

"God, Bibi," I breathed, hugging her fiercely. "None of this would have happened without you. So long as you're proud"—I swallowed hard—"nothing else matters. Nothing."

Bibi dabbed her eyes with a Kleenex from her pocketbook. "Now look at me. I'm a mess."

"No, you're perfect," I said. "And you always have been."

From beside me, June delicately cleared her throat. "We're ready."

I turned to see that night had fallen and that there was more than a small crowd of nicely dressed people gathered outside the shop.

"Are they..." I cleared my throat and tried again. "Are they here for me?"

June beamed. "Shiloh, you are open for business."

The grand opening was everything I'd hoped it would be and better than I'd imagined. The crowds flowed in and out, sampling the exquisite appetizers and sipping wine circulated by a waiter on a tray. The store was tiny, but people seemed happy to congregate outside, eating and drinking, then coming in as others left. Bibi and Bertie sat in folding chairs on the sidewalk, catching up, while Rudy took my mom for a walk downtown.

Amber and some other friends from school stopped

by to congratulate me, and a journalist interviewed me between customers, though I hardly had time to talk. Letitia turned herself into a saleswoman, engaging customers with so much enthusiasm and charm, they could hardly resist her. Ronan replaced sold items with inventory from the back so none of the displays were empty for long.

Hours later, the last customer left, telling me she thought this shop was just what Santa Cruz needed. "The tourists are going to leave here with something earthy and beautiful to remember the city by."

Hope swelled to help mute the anxiety that was starting to creep in. Not every day would be a grand opening. I was going to have to work my ass off to stay afloat.

But I'm ready for that too.

I thanked June and the caterers, locked up, then drove with the family back to Bibi's for a little private after-party. The talk flowed, and Letitia's laughter filled the house while Shirley Bassey played on Bibi's ancient record player. The women sipped champagne while Rudy and Ronan stuck to beer. I wished I could've had just one glass of the bubbly to celebrate.

But then I will *puke and no sexy times with Ronan*, I thought, then giggled, giddy from the night. *On the other hand, he probably wouldn't care.*

My laughter faded when I saw Mama drain a glass of merlot and pour another. I'd lost count of how many she'd had at the shop. I frowned and went to the kitchen to get her a bottle of water.

Ronan joined me. "When can we leave?" His voice was low and rough with the promise of sex.

"You're not having a good time?" I said, hiding my smile in the fridge and letting the cool air waft over my face.

"I'm having a hard time keeping my hands off you."

I turned, a bottle of water in one hand. I filled my other with Ronan's groin. "Me too, as a matter of fact."

He leaned in to kiss me when a voice rose in anger from the living room. We both froze as Bertie said loudly, "Oh no, you don't, Marie. Don't you *dare*."

Bibi, Letitia, and Rudy were on the couch, my cousin holding tight to Bibi's hand. Bertie stood in the center of the room, her black velvet dress rippling with anger as she leveled a finger at Mama, who was clearly drunk.

"I have to tell her," Mama said, swaying, spilling merlot on the carpet. "She's eighteen. She's...old enough."

"Tell me what?" I asked, though I knew. Of course I knew.

"Nothing, baby," Bertie said quickly. "Your mama's just done a little too much celebrating. We're going back to the hotel. Rudy..."

My uncle jumped off the couch and spoke soothingly to Mama, but she pushed him away, spilling more wine. "No. I have to do this. I tried before. I can't...keep it in another minute. Not one..."

"Now?" Bertie cried. "You got to do this now? On her night?"

Ronan's hand slipped into mine. I held on tight, my mind reeling.

"Yes," Mama said and spun to find me, one eye shut to keep from seeing double. "Shiloh, you need to know. You needed to know a long time ago."

"Marie..." Bibi's voice was low and tremulous. "Not *now*."

"Yes, now."

"Yes, now," I echoed.

Five pairs of eyes came to me, but I needed to hear it, even if it ruined the perfection of the night.

"I'm starting a new chapter in my life, and I want to know who I am. No more lies. No more secrets." I looked to my mother, hardened my voice. "Tell me."

She briefly held my gaze, and I saw the hesitation—the fear—behind her eyes. For a moment, I thought she was going to do what she did last time and try to flee. Instead, tears spilled over, unheeded, down her cheeks.

"They don't want me to tell you who your father is," Mama said, flapping a hand in Bertie and Bibi's direction.

My father. The words seemed alien and strange.

"I should've done it a long time ago. But I was scared. And wanted to protect you. But it hurt you instead. My weakness hurt *us*. Because I look at you...and I see him. And I can't..."

She half sat, half fell into the dining room chair. I rushed forward and knelt in front of her, even as fear sank cold knives into my chest. "What happened? Tell me now."

Mama's head lolled; she was so drunk. "I loved him, but he didn't love me the same way. He couldn't have. He *couldn't* have."

"Mama, who?"

"No one," she answered, her smile sad. Resigned. "He's no one now. He has no name anymore. He's just the man who raped me."

I stared, her words slapping me across the face, brutal and harsh. That word, the ugliest, heaviest word, carrying with it a lifetime of pain.

"That's all he is," Mama said. "All he can ever be. Except...he's not. No matter how I try to make him nothing, he can't ever be nothing." She raised her tear-streaked face to mine. "Because he's your father."

The ground tipped out from under me, and I fell to the carpet. My heartbeat had slowed to a heavy clanging in my chest, blood rushing to my ears.

"No, I..." I glanced around vaguely, not seeing. My mouth had gone dry. I couldn't breathe. "It can't be. He loved you. You said he loved you."

"I thought he did too," Mama said sadly, the sorrow emanating off her in waves. "But I told him I wanted to wait." She shrugged, horrible in its finality. "He didn't."

The implications filled me, the cruel truth hollowing me out and leaving me empty.

Because what am I? The product of a nightmare. Mama's nightmare in the flesh.

I don't know how long I sat there, but voices surrounded us until the room felt suffocating. Bertie and Bibi and Rudy, all scolding or comforting. Letitia was kneeling next to me, speaking softly in my ear. I wanted to get up and run. I wanted to curl up in a ball right there on the floor.

Then strong arms wrapped around me, and I burrowed into Ronan. Sought refuge in him, clinging to him and wishing I could crawl inside him and be safe.

"Ronan…"

"Shh." He sounded angry. He *felt* angry, his body vibrating with it as he held me.

He'd started to lift me, to get me out of there, when the doorbell rang. The house that had been bustling with raised voices suddenly hushed.

Rudy opened the door, and I heard men's voices, indistinct. Then Ronan tensed around me all over again, holding me tighter.

"Shiloh." Uncle Rudy's voice was trembling. "These officers are here to see you."

He stepped aside, and I saw two uniformed policemen in the doorway. A chill ran through me, leaving me numb. With Ronan's help, I stood on stiff legs. Bibi had her hand to her mouth. Letitia's eyes were wide.

"Shiloh Barrera?"

"Yes." My voice didn't sound like mine.

"Are you the owner of Rare Earth Jewelry?"

I felt the sledgehammer poised to fall again, about to change my life forever.

"Yes."

Both men looked grim. Apologetic. "We're going to need you to come with us."

TWENTY-NINE

RONAN

The second trip to Rare Earth was fucking light-years from the first, and I could hardly believe they both happened in the same night.

Bertie and Bibi stayed home with Shiloh's mother, who'd begun sobbing after spilling her secret and hadn't stopped. The rest of us followed the cop car downtown. Rudy and Letitia took the Cadillac. I drove the Buick, glancing at Shiloh beside me. She sat silently, staring at nothing; her beautiful face was blank, shocked numb. Her perfect night, ruined. I gripped the steering wheel tight.

The streets were empty, and the store was dark. The front entrance looked the same except for the police tape that ran across the front door and the squad car parked directly in front.

"It looks okay," Shiloh said in a strange, small voice that made my stomach clench. "It looks okay."

I gritted my teeth.

"There's been an incident..." the cops had said back at the house.

I wanted more than anything for it all to be okay, but my gut told me it was bad. Real fucking bad.

I followed the cops around to the back parking lot, trying to bury my own rising nightmares at the sight of the red and blue lights. My only goal was to get Shiloh through this and then fix whatever the fuck needed fixing. All of it. Whatever it was, I'd make it right for her somehow.

In the back lot, we climbed out of the car, and I went to Shiloh's side. She didn't look at me or anyone else but walked tall and silent behind the cops to the rear door of the shop, to the first sign of damage. The wood around the lock had been pried away with a crowbar and the knob itself smashed off.

"They got in here," said one officer—his name tag read Tran—leading us in. The lights in the back room were on; everything looked intact. He nodded at the boxes of inventory—Shiloh's life's work. "Did they take anything?"

Shiloh shook her head. "Looks okay," she said in that same strange voice. A flicker of hope lit up her eyes, but Tran shook his head.

"I know this is hard, but you need to see the rest."

She nodded again, and we followed him into the shop that was dim.

"Responding officers made their initial inspection and dusted for prints, though to be honest, there wasn't much to dust." He looked at Shiloh with a kind, sympathetic expression. "Brace yourself."

He flicked on the light, and Shiloh made a sound I hoped to never hear again as long as I fucking lived. Her hands flew to her mouth, and she stared.

Letitia let out a little cry, and Rudy threw his hands up. "Good goddamn."

I said nothing, the rage burning me from the inside out. I could hardly breathe, never mind speak.

Motherfucking sons of shit-licking assholes…

Glittering under the pot lights Shiloh had installed during the shop's renovation was an ocean of shattered glass. Every single display was smashed, including the front-facing glass on the cabinet that served as her cash register desk, the rings glittering with shards. The walls and floors were tagged with black spray paint in random zigzags and lines, the faces of the women in the artwork blacked out, and what was left of the display boxes was marked with haphazard sprays.

Shiloh had been so careful with every penny of the start-up business loan, keeping costs down and using her own talents to make simple things beautiful. She let me pay for a fraction of what I wanted to spend of my inheritance, insisting on doing as much as she could by herself.

And now she stood in the center of the rubble of her dreams that had, a few hours ago, been perfect.

I moved beside her, glass crunching under my boots, not knowing what to say or do.

"Who would do such a thing?" Rudy asked.

"That's what we're hoping you'll be able to tell us,"

the other cop—Murray—said, his notepad out. "Did you remove all your items from the window displays before close of business?"

She nodded. "Yes."

"Anything else look taken?"

She stared blankly at the jewelry in the smashed and sprayed displays, covered in glass, some pieces shattered too.

"Don't know," she said dully. "Don't think so."

He frowned. "Not a robbery then. Just straight mayhem. Whoever the perp was, they only wanted to cause damage."

And then a ball of pure ice seemed to slam into my chest, making my blood run cold.

We're not done with you, a voice screeched in my memory. *You'll pay. In the way that hurts you the most.*

I looked at the woman beside me. Hurting Shiloh was how to hurt me the most.

Fuck. Oh fuck, no.

"How did this happen?" Shiloh said, looking and sounding so damn lost. "I have security. Cameras and a company. They're supposed to call me…"

"I grabbed your phone," Letitia said, rummaging in her bag. "Thought you might need it."

She handed it to Shiloh, who stared, disbelieving, at the screen. "I muted it. I took a few selfies behind the register and of the crowd…and then I went to work."

Over her shoulder, I saw a bunch of missed call notifications from the security monitoring company she'd hired.

"I wouldn't blame yourself for that," Tran said. "Typical smash-and-grab. They're usually long gone before we show up. Can I take a look at your security footage?"

Shiloh nodded absently as she pulled up the security camera app, and we gathered around to watch.

The lights were out and the shop shadowy, but enough street light came in to see a skinny, hooded figure in a ski mask rampage through the store, a crowbar in one hand, a spray can in the other. I felt sick.

Frankie Dowd. Though it may as well have been me under that fucking ski mask.

I did this. I brought this to her, just like I knew I would.

Shiloh made a choking noise and shoved the phone at Tran, then stepped away to touch the jagged edge of a display case.

"Any clue?"

"That's Frankie Dowd," I said.

The officers glanced at each other. "As in Mitch Dowd's son?"

"That's what I said."

Murray made notes on his notepad, and Tran frowned.

"What is it?"

"Mitch Dowd was released from prison a few days ago," Tran said.

"The fuck? I thought he was serving a year."

"He was *sentenced* to a year," Tran said. "He appealed, and the judge commuted his sentence to six months of house arrest."

"You think his kid did this?" Murray asked. He looked hesitant to follow up. "You can't ID a face on that video."

"I don't need to see that fucker's face to know it's him."

The officers conferred, and Tran said, "We'll head over and ask him a few questions."

"And then arrest his ass."

"We need probable cause," Murray said. "The video alone isn't enough to make a positive ID."

Tran held up his hand when I started to protest. "Take her home, okay?"

I sucked in a breath and nodded.

Tran took Shiloh's information, and the cops left.

Rudy and Letitia were huddled together, watching Shiloh move through the wreckage of her shop.

"Get her home," I said. "I'll clean up here."

Shiloh shook her head. "No, I can't… I can't leave…"

I moved to her and took hold of her shoulders. "Shiloh, look at me."

She turned her brown eyes up to mine, not really seeing me, and my heart ached. She was still in shock, numb.

"Go home, baby," I said. "Rest. I'll clean this up."

"You can't clean this up," she said, frowning as if I were crazy. "It's too much. Too much."

"I'm going to get started, and then I'll be there, okay?"

She nodded mutely and let Letitia take her out the back.

Rudy stood in front of me. "Thank you, son. For being so good to her."

He patted my shoulder and left, and I wanted to scream.

This is my fault. Mine.

Rage flooded me, burning through my veins like fire. I grabbed a broom from the back and gripped it as if it were Frankie Dowd's fucking throat. I concentrated on the work, cleaning up the shattered glass and smashed displays as best I could, extracting jewelry from the mess.

I couldn't do anything about the spray paint, but I wanted to. I wanted to paint over everything so that when Shiloh saw her shop again, she wouldn't feel so undone.

It was nearly two in the morning, and I'd done all I could for the night. I loaded all Shiloh's inventory into the Buick's trunk and back seat, then jerry-rigged a way to lock the door with a chain and padlock.

I drove to her and Bibi's house. Rudy had taken Shiloh's mom and Letitia back to their hotel. Bertie and Bibi were still awake, sitting on the couch, drinking tea and talking in hushed voices.

"Oh, honey," Bibi said, tears coming. "Rudy told us everything. Is it as bad as that?"

"Yeah, it's bad. Shiloh's asleep?"

Bertie nodded. "The poor child. First Marie, bless it all, and now this?"

"I'm going to check on Shiloh," I said.

"Thank you," said Bibi. "Thank you, sweet boy, for all that you've done."

All that I've done.

I strode down the hallway to Shiloh's room. The rainbow

lights were on—dim but enough to see immediately that her bed was empty.

Okay. She's in the bathroom. Or outside in the shed, working to try to make up for tonight somehow.

The bathroom was empty.

"Ronan?" Bertie called as I went through the patio door to the backyard. The shed was empty. I checked the garage. Empty.

I came back inside, forcing myself to sound calm so as not to freak the women out.

"Did she lie down in your room, Bibi?" I asked carefully.

She frowned. "I don't think so. Bertie?"

Bertie hurried to Bibi's room and peeked her head in. "She's not there," she said, her hands twisting now.

I whipped out my phone and called Shiloh's number. Her cell phone came to life on the dining room table, right next to her purse.

Shit.

"Oh no," Bibi breathed. "Oh no. Where… Where could she have gone? When?"

"I'm calling the police," Bertie said. "I know they'll say it has to be twenty-four hours, but after all that's happened tonight…special circumstances…"

Bertie got up to rummage for her phone in her bag. Bibi looked small and helpless on the couch.

"I'll find her," I said, striding out the front door.

"Ronan…"

"I'll find her, Bibi," I said. "I'll bring her back."

If it's the last fucking thing I ever do in this world.

I drove the Buick back to Rare Earth for the third time that night. It was dark, my makeshift lock untouched.

"Fuck, Shiloh," I said, pacing the dark parking lot, thinking. "Please, baby."

I got back behind the wheel and pushed the Buick as fast as the heavy engine could take to my place. Maybe Shiloh needed me at home, and I wasn't there, so she went looking.

My place was dark, quiet in the early hours, the parking lot empty but for tenants' cars. So was the back storage area.

Fucking stupid. Why would she come here? You did this to her. She doesn't want you. She won't want you ever again.

I shut up the incessant voice long enough to think. Violet was at college. Who else did she know? Amber?

And suddenly, I knew. The one place to go when the rest of the world was fucked.

Wheels squealed as I tore the Buick out of my complex and headed toward the coast. I screeched into a spot in the parking lot and ran as fast as I could along the beach path, tripping over rocks in the dark, slamming my knee into a boulder.

I saw the light of the bonfire first, and then there she was.

Thank Christ.

Shiloh was sitting in one of our beach chairs, three of my beer bottles sticking out of the sand around her feet, a fourth in her hand. Blearily, she watched the fire and lifted the bottle to her lips. I couldn't blame her. I wanted to get plowed and pretend like this night never happened too.

Except she can't drink.

"Shiloh?"

She swiveled her head, and it was obvious she was wasted. She could hardly keep her eyes open, swaying in her seat.

"Ronan…" she said and then pitched to the side and puked.

"Fuck."

I hurried to her, held her hair out of her face as she retched up all the beer. Her body was shaking from the cold and the allergic reaction she was having to the alcohol.

When she finished, she lay back against the chair, eyes closed and shivering.

"Hold on, baby," I said. "Just…hold on."

I hurried to the shack for the small stash of blankets we'd collected over the winter and grabbed one.

"Who am I?" Shiloh asked, her head lolling as I wrapped a blanket around her shoulders. "I'm a mistake. No. Worse than a mistake."

"You're not a mistake," I said, kneeling in front of her, face-to-face. I pulled the blanket tight around her. "You need to get home."

"A mistake at least isn't *violent*. What I am…" She shook her head. "I'm a *violation*."

I clenched my teeth to hear the pain in her words.

"Shiloh, look at me. You're not...*that*. You're..."

Everything good and beautiful in my life.

But I'd ruined hers. I clenched my jaw. "Come on. We have to get you home."

Shiloh shuddered, her face flush, and retched again, dry heaving and gasping for air.

"I'm empty," she said when she caught her breath. Her bleary brown eyes met mine, tears shining in them. "There's nothing in me because there's nothing *in me*. I'm... nothing."

"Stop talking like that," I said, lifting her from the chair. "The last thing you are is nothing."

You're everything to me, and I fucked it all up.

"I'm sorry, Shiloh," I said, holding her tight to me. "So fucking sorry."

But she'd already—mercifully—passed out, so I began to walk.

THIRTY
SHILOH

I don't remember walking to the shack. After chugging the beer I found in the guys' mini fridge, the night turned hazy. As if I were submerged in a dark pond, wading through the murk. A million times better than the sharp, piercing light of reality. Images burned in my eyes—the glitter of broken glass, like diamonds. The black slashes of spray paint. The horrified expressions on my family's faces. The pity.

And lurking beneath all that, Mama's truth.

Better to drown.

I vomited at the beach. At home. Someone gave me water, and I vomited again. I lost track of the hours. Lost track of where I was. I lay in bed, and Bibi put a cold cloth to my face. The next instant, I was in the bathroom, kneeling at the toilet.

The hours ebbed and flowed around me in that murk. Ronan's deep voice spoke to me in hushed undertones. Bibi soothed. Both tried to get me to look at them. To talk to them. Both tried to tell me it was going to be okay. When I wasn't sick, I lay curled away from them, facing the wall, shudders running through me. The alcohol poisoned me but not nearly as bad as the rest.

Mama...

Finally, my body had purged itself to the point of exhaustion, and I slept.

Sunlight was coming through the windows in my room the next time I opened my eyes. Midday maybe. Ronan was sitting on the floor against my bed, head down. I watched him for a few moments, the rise and fall of his chest.

God, I loved him. It felt impossible I could love him as much as I did. But how could he look at me now that he knew the truth?

Ronan stirred, and I rolled away again, curling up tight.

"Shiloh..."

I squeezed my eyes shut, and after a while, he gave up. I slept.

When I woke next, the light was honey-colored twilight, and Ronan was gone.

He left me.

In the deepest part of my soul, the thought didn't ring true, but *I* wanted to leave me. I wanted to crawl out of this skin and into someone else's body. Someone who was created with love out of partnership. Being an accident, like I'd been raised to believe, was better than this. Anything was better than knowing I was the product of my mother's nightmare.

I sat up and hugged my knees to my chest. I was in my

underwear, the dress for my grand opening hopefully in the trash. Or burned. The alcohol was out of my system, and the murky drunkenness was gone, leaving me alone with my thoughts, clear and naked.

My shop…

I sucked in a breath, unwilling to let the torrent of pain come flooding out. If I cried over my shop, my mother's revelation would follow, and then I might not stop.

A soft knock came at my door, and Bibi poked her head in. "Shiloh?"

"I'm awake," I said, my voice a hoarse croak. "You must have a sixth sense."

"Of course I do. You're my girl." Bibi sat on the edge of my bed and cocked her head. "How we doing, baby?"

I shrugged. "My store is ruined, and my father's a rapist. That's how I'm doing."

Bibi sighed and took my hand. "Oh, honey."

"I don't want to talk about it," I said. "I don't know *how* to talk about it. Or what to think or feel except…*horrified*. Disgusted. Dirty. I feel so dirty, Bibi."

"Now don't you talk like that. There's nothing you did wrong. Nothing wrong with *you*. Not one thing."

I was too exhausted to argue, and it was useless anyway.

"Where is everyone?"

"They're back at the hotel, ready to come over the minute you feel up to it."

I was already shaking my head. "Tell them to go home. Tell them thank you, but they should go home."

Because how can I ever look them in the eye again?

"Come on," Bibi said. "Let's get you a shower. Get some food in you. You need to eat. Then you'll feel better and can think more clearly. When you've rested up, we can work out what to do about your shop—"

"My shop." I scoffed. "There is no shop, Bibi."

She pursed her lips, her expression harder than I'd ever seen it. "Now you listen to me, Shiloh. What happened last night was bad. Very, very bad. And you're allowed to feel all kinds of ways about it. But you *cannot* give up. Do you hear me?"

Giving up sounded really good right about then. All the work I'd done—years' worth—was teetering on the edge of a high cliff. Barely hanging on.

"My insurance is bare-bones," I said. "It covers customer safety and theft, not vandalism. And the repairs, the cleanup…" I shook my head with a sour laugh. "It's fitting, isn't it? I worked my ass off for that shop to prove to Mama that I was worth something, that I could create something beautiful, and it was smashed and ruined and painted black, just like Mama's life was that night. She was vandalized too."

Bibi squeezed my hand tighter. "One step at a time. We're going to get all this sorted out and made better. But first things first. Shower and food."

I relented and stood on trembling legs. "Where's Ronan?"

"He went back to the shop," she said.

"God," I muttered. "He'd better not spend his money—"

"*Shiloh*," Bibi said sternly. "That boy loves you and wants to help. Let him."

Tears welled in my eyes. "How can he love me, Bibi? Now that he knows… How can anyone love me?"

"Oh, honey."

The enormity of it tried to get me, but I couldn't let it. Not yet. It was too much. Terrifying.

Bibi helped me into the bathroom. I brushed my teeth and showered. After, she handed me a towel and walked with me back to my room. She'd laid out clean underwear and a short nightgown I wore in the summer. My sheets had been changed.

I dressed and climbed back into bed. Bibi brought a bowl of homemade black-eyed peas and collards soup.

"Had to keep myself busy and thought the soup would be easy on your stomach."

"Thanks," I said, taking the bowl. For Bibi's sake, I had a few bites, and she was right, I felt slightly stronger. Strong enough to ask what I didn't want to ask.

"What happened with Frankie? Was Ronan right?"

"I spoke with Detective Harris this morning. The police questioned him last night."

"And?"

"Harris said they didn't have probable cause to arrest him. He had an alibi—at home with his father all night."

The soup wanted to come back up. I set the bowl on my nightstand.

"Shiloh…" Bibi said as I slunk under the covers and curled in a ball.

"I'm tired. I just want to sleep a little more, okay?"

I heard her sigh, and I hated that she worried about me but not enough to sit up and eat her soup and pretend like my life wasn't falling apart.

The bed dipped as Bibi left. The tears threatened again, but I dove into sleep before the grief could find me.

When I woke next, it was dark, and Ronan was where I'd seen him last—sitting on the floor as if he were waiting for me.

"Hey," I said softly.

His head came up instantly, and he unfolded his tall body to sit at the foot of my bed. "Hey. How do you feel?"

"That's a loaded question." I sat up, toyed with the coverlet. "I'm having a hard time not wallowing in self-pity, honestly. Part of me wants to get up and go to the shop and work. Work even harder… But part of me wants to curl up under the covers and not come out."

"I know."

"Bibi said Frankie wasn't arrested."

"No, he wasn't." Ronan's voice was still and dangerous, like black water.

"But you're sure it was him?"

He nodded.

I sighed. "Guess it doesn't matter. It's done."

"I'm handling it," Ronan said.

Something in the way he said that made me shiver. "You don't have to—"

"Yes, I do. It's my fault."

"Yours? How?"

"Doesn't matter."

I plucked at the cover. He was down at the foot of my bed, and I was at the head, and he wasn't touching me. He wanted to leave; I could practically feel it vibrating off him. And then I couldn't take any more. Losing him…

"You don't have to stay," I said, the swell of emotion beginning to rise like a river threatening to overrun its banks. "In fact…" I swallowed the tears, but they gathered behind my eyes with a hot, achy pressure. "If you don't want to see me anymore, I'll understand."

His head whipped up to look at me. "What?"

I shook my head, my gaze on my hands. My hands that were like my mother's but with *his* blood flowing underneath. "After what Mama said… I get it. I can hardly stand myself right now."

Ronan shot off the end of the bed to sit beside me. His hands gripped my shoulders, then slipped up over my cheeks, holding my face. "Fuck, Shiloh, no."

I shook my head, the first tears spilling over and running down to his fingers. "I think I knew. I think I always knew, somewhere down deep. So I tried so hard to prove I was…more. That I had a purpose here." The sobs were in my chest now, stealing my breath, tearing my voice to tatters. "But she could never stand to look at me, and I… I get it now. My whole life…it's her pain. That's what I am. I'm a walking, talking reminder of that night… Half of me is *him*. A monster."

The dam burst, and the sobs poured out. Racking, choking sobs I'd been holding in for years. Stagnant and poisonous. Ronan's arms went around me, and he pulled me into him. Held me tight so that I could collapse. At long last, I fell apart. I cried like I'd never let myself cry, and he held the broken pieces of me together.

"You're not," he said gruffly into my hair. "You're so fucking beautiful, inside and out. And brave, Shiloh. So brave."

"I'm not brave," I cried against his chest. "I'm scared. I don't know what to do."

"You don't have to do anything right now," he said, his voice rumbling in my ear. "I got you. I'm going to fix things, Shiloh. I swear it."

"Do you…still love me?"

He sucked in a shocked breath. "Shiloh…*yes*. Christ, of course I do. But what happened to your shop—"

"It happened. I don't want to think about it right now," I said. The sobs had emptied me out, and I felt like a shell that could collapse or blow away. I needed something—him—to anchor me down, to keep me from fading away altogether. "I need you, Ronan." I kissed his chin, his lips, pulling him to me. "Please… I need to go away with you for a little while."

"Shiloh, wait."

"Please." I kissed his neck, my hands going into his hair. "Bibi's asked me a thousand times what I need. This is what I need. You. Please."

I found his mouth with mine and kissed him, the tears burning up in heated desperation.

He relented for a moment, kissing me deep, and then stiffened and took me by the shoulders. "Shiloh...I can't. You're upset."

"Yes, I'm *upset*," I said fiercely. "But I know what I'm doing. What I want. I want you, Ronan. I want...us."

The truth of it reached him. More than anything, I needed to know we were okay. If Ronan could still love me, then I might have a chance of surviving this. I could get out of bed in the morning and get back to work.

He held my face in his hands, his silver eyes boring into mine. "I love you."

Now that I'd cried, it seemed the tears didn't want to stop. "I love you. I love you so much."

We fell into each other then, kissing with increasingly heated need, last night receding with every touch of his skin on mine, with every kiss. I sank deep into his intense gaze—my reflection a shred of evidence that I wasn't merely an ugly remnant of a terrible night. I was beautiful in Ronan's eyes, and his eyes never lied.

My self-worth didn't live or die with Ronan, but that night as he held me, kissed and touched me, as he entered me with the heavy solidity of him, I took the first step to reclaiming myself. With his love, he gave me something I could believe in.

Quietly, Ronan brought me to release, a swell of pleasure against a tsunami of pain. I held him tight to me as he grunted against my neck, spilling his own release deep inside me, warming me from the inside out. Filling the emptiness in me with him and the essence of him.

After, he held me for a long time, lying on his back with his arm around me and my head on his shoulder. But his expression grew more and more grim, clouding his eyes.

"What are you thinking?" I asked, running my fingertip in the worry lines between his brows.

"I'm thinking about what you said earlier. *Half of me is him.*"

I nodded.

"I said something like that to you. About my dad. And you told me that I was nothing like him."

I smiled sadly. "And you didn't believe me."

"No," he said. "And I know you won't believe me if I say the same about you."

"It's hard. Impossible even."

He nodded against my hair. "Yeah. But maybe..." He paused, and I felt him struggling to sort his thoughts, to say exactly what he meant. "We're supposed to trust each other, right?"

"Yes."

"So...maybe we need to do that now. Trust me when I tell you, Shiloh, that the last thing you are is ugly. Or empty. Or...whatever you're feeling about what your mom said. You're still you. You're perfect."

My eyes filled. "I'm not. I'm so far from perfect, Ronan."

"You don't get to decide that." He glanced down at me gravely. "You have to trust me. And I'll try to trust you too. That's all we can do, right? Trust and keep going."

I nodded against his chest, and my eyes grew heavy. They burned from the tears that I'd finally let go, but it was purifying. The hollow feeling inside me was refilling slowly, with determination to do what Ronan had said—trust and keep going.

I slept, and when I woke, it was to the rustle of Ronan putting on his clothes. I glanced at the clock that said it was a little after eleven.

"Where are you going?"

"Out." He drew on his boots.

"Now? It's late."

"I have something to do."

I sat up, drawing the sheet around me. "What? Where?"

"I told you I'd fix things."

"What does that mean?"

"It means what it means."

The room was dark, and it was hard to see more than his eyes, glittering silver in the dim light.

"Ronan…"

He bent and kissed me hard. Then he left.

I stayed up for a long time, watching the minutes become hours. Only because I was still somehow exhausted did I fall asleep. When I woke up at eight the next morning, Ronan wasn't there.

He went to his place to rest or shower. That's all.

Feeling like I'd been turned inside out and back again, I slowly got dressed in sweatpants and an old T-shirt—clothes I didn't mind getting dirty. My mother's revelation slammed into me several times as I went about my morning routine. Each time, my stomach churned, and I wanted to be sick all over again. I realized this was my life now. I'd carry this knowledge with me forever—the dirtiest of secrets no one could ever know. Not Amber, not Violet... God, *Violet*.

What could I say to her? How?

I understood now why Bibi, Bertie, and the rest of the family wanted to keep this from me. You can't unknow something once it's known. The shame would haunt me forever, and I'd spend the rest of my life looking in the faces of men on the street and wonder, *Is that him?*

I gave myself a shake and went to the kitchen, ready to do what I always did—focus on work to keep me sane.

Bibi was stirring a pot of grits. Eggs and bacon were on the stove, fresh coffee in the pot.

Thank God for Bibi.

I put my arms around her from behind. "I love you."

"Oh, baby girl, I love you to pieces. And my old heart is bursting with joy to see you up."

"I'm going to the shop."

"Attagirl. Eat first, please. You need to get your strength back."

We filled our plates, but despite my hunger, I picked at my food. "Have you seen Ronan this morning?"

"Not this morning." She sipped her coffee. "Are you worried?"

"No, but something he said last night…" I waved a hand. "Nothing. I'll call him after breakfast."

We ate, and I did the dishes. The last few nights had to have taken their toll on Bibi. She went to her room to take a nap, and I called Ronan's number as I headed to the garage.

No answer.

I texted. Where are you?

I drove the Buick to Rare Earth. Still no reply. The message was marked *unread*.

I went to the back entrance and stopped. It was an entirely new door—heavy and industrial—with a new dead bolt lock.

"Ronan…" I murmured with a small smile, then realized I couldn't unlock it. On a hunch, I checked my key ring, and there it was: a brand-new key I didn't recognize. I tried it in the door, and the dead bolt *clicked*.

That man…

I went through the back room, mentally bracing myself for the damage up front. I still had some paint left over from the reno; I could spend the day cleaning up the glass, then repaint tomorrow. One step at a time…

My thoughts fell apart as I stepped into the main room. The glass was gone, as were all the smashed displays. A tarp was laid on the floor with a ladder and several buckets of paint. The room smelled of acrylic, and all the black streaks were gone. Ronan had repainted every wall, except one that was still in progress. The horrific damage from opening night was muting into a bad memory.

My hand went to my heart, and tears flooded my eyes and spilled over. I couldn't stop them anymore and wasn't sure I wanted to.

"Oh, baby," I breathed. "Thank you."

I retrieved my phone and called him again. It went to Ronan's curt voicemail: *Leave a message.*

I hung up and texted, the good feeling in my stomach fading and turning into worry.

"He's fine," I muttered to the empty shop.

Because he has to be.

I set up the ladder and finished the wall Ronan had started. I was nearly done when a rapping came at the front door. I peered through glass and metal mesh gates to see a tall man in a suit. He waved what looked like a badge at me.

I climbed down on shaking limbs and unlocked the door for him.

"Yes?"

"Shiloh Barrera? I'm Detective Harris. I'm a friend of your great-grandmother's."

"Yes, hi." I stepped aside to let him in and shut the door behind him. "What can I do for you?"

"I've been assigned to your case and need to ask you some questions."

"I have a case?" I asked, my heart thudding loudly in

my chest. "The other night, the officers made it sound as if there wasn't much they could do."

"Circumstances have changed in the past twenty-four hours," he said. He wore an unreadable expression. A detective's poker face. "There's been an arrest."

A sigh gusted out of me. "Oh, thank God. Frankie Dowd—"

"Is in the hospital in critical condition. Ronan Wentz was brought in for questioning and has been arrested."

The floor dropped out beneath me, and I sagged against the door. "For *what*?"

"Attempted murder."

THIRTY-ONE
RONAN

"I THINK YOU'RE GOING TO PRISON FOR A VERY LONG TIME."

Detective Harris backed off, and Detective Kowalski got up from behind the desk in that claustrophobic holding room that grew smaller and smaller with every passing second. He pulled a set of handcuffs from his belt.

"Ronan Wentz, you have the right to remain silent. Anything you say can and will be used against you in a court of law…"

They read me my rights and took me to processing where I was booked and fingerprinted and had my mug shot taken along with photos of my bruised and swollen knuckles. A bus was waiting to transport me to the county jail, where I was strip-searched, given an orange jumpsuit, and tossed in a cell with a scared-looking skinny guy. He flinched when I looked his way.

I lay on the bottom bunk, staring at the mesh wiring

and torn mattress of the bunk above me, one thought running through my mind.

I'm not like him. I have to trust Shiloh. I'm not like him.

But I was *behind bars*. After going through the humiliating process to get here, those words were flimsy and weak.

I'm sorry, Mom. I'm so sorry.

That afternoon, a guard came to tell me my public defender was here. I was handcuffed and taken to the visitors' room where a tall guy—maybe forty—with a receding hairline and glasses was sitting at a table with a file in front of him.

"Mr. Wentz? I'm Forrest Perry, your court-appointed defender."

I sat across from him, my handcuffed hands in my lap. Just like my dad had once.

Perry shuffled through the papers. "To be perfectly frank with you, this doesn't look good."

"I didn't touch Dowd," I said. "I found him at this place he hangs out, and I warned him to leave Shiloh alone. That's it."

"Because you think it was him who trashed her place."

"I know it was him."

"How?"

"He all but told me a few weeks back, before graduation. And the security footage—"

"Shows a guy covered head to toe in black. No prints. No DNA."

"It was him. And when I confronted him, he confessed and said he was sorry."

Perry's brows rose above his glasses. "So you admit to confronting Dowd that night? He's currently at UCSC Medical in intensive care and said it was you who put him there."

"He's lying. That night, I told him to lay off, and I walked away."

"If that's true, who beat the hell out of him?"

"Don't know."

Perry met my gaze for a minute, then waved a hand. "Never mind. It's not our job to prove who did, only that you didn't. But I'm going to be honest, Mr. Wentz, this is an uphill battle. Looking at your files...your history with Dowd..."

Your father's bloody crime...

"I didn't do it," I said. "That should count for something."

The words sounded stupid and weak in my own ears.

Perry rapped his fingers on the file. "You want to fight this? Enter a not-guilty plea at your arraignment? Because I can talk to the DA and see about cutting a deal. Otherwise, you could be looking at twenty-five years behind bars. Maybe more if the charges stick and the judge decides you intended to kill Frankie."

The possibility of a life spent in prison made my chest so tight I could hardly breathe. But I had Shiloh. I had tenants who needed me. For the first time, I had something to fight for. The system had ruined my mother. Maybe this time would be different.

"No deal."

Perry studied my face for a moment, then nodded. "Okay. Tell me what happened."

My arraignment was the following afternoon. I was bused to the courthouse and marched into a hallway with a dozen other inmates there for the same reason. Shiloh had tried to contact me at County, but I couldn't stomach the idea of her seeing me there. Or at the hearing, which I knew she and Bibi would show up for. The orange jumpsuit was a uniform of humiliation and degradation. They had called me a criminal at Central High School, and now that was what I was, guilty or not. Less than human. A kind of animal that had to be restrained, caged, and guarded. The cuffs felt like they weighed a thousand pounds.

Finally, the side door to a courtroom opened, and we were shuffled in, the chains connected to my feet and handcuffs rattling. I kept my head down, but there was no avoiding it. Shiloh was there, in the front row, between Bibi and Maryann Greer.

Fuck.

Shiloh was so beautiful—light-years from the sick, sobbing girl I'd seen a few days ago.

Because she's so damn strong.

And if she could be that strong, maybe I could be too. I lifted my head and nodded at her, my gaze full of apologies.

Tears filled her eyes, and she nodded back, her support unwavering. I felt like crying too.

On the other side of the courtroom sat Mitch Dowd. Beside him was Mikey Grimaldi, both come to watch me go down, I guessed.

Forrest Perry sidled up to me as the inmates in front of me were read the charges against them. Each entered a plea, and the judge moved on to the next.

"Second thoughts?" Perry murmured.

I leveled him a cold stare. "You giving up already?"

"No, no." He held up his hand. "I just need to know the score before we enter a plea and this all becomes really real."

News flash, I wanted to tell him. It was already *really real*. Being locked up, watching your back in the yard or in the showers or at mealtime was *really fucking real*.

Perry leaned in to me and nodded at the older man with a head full of white hair at the front of the courtroom. "Judge Jack Norman. He's a tough old guy. No nonsense but fair. Could've been worse."

"Docket number 29575," the clerk said. "Ronan August Wentz."

I was unshackled from the line of waiting inmates, and Perry and I moved to stand at the defendant's table, our backs to the crowd. At the other table was the district attorney—a severe, sharp-looking woman in an expensive suit, her blond hair tied up in a tight twist.

"Lydia Wells," Perry muttered. "This isn't going to be fun."

Judge Norman read over the file and then peered down at Perry. "Before a plea is entered, I believe there is an issue of probable cause?"

"Yes, Your Honor," Perry said, getting to his feet. "My client was brought in for questioning without the presence of an attorney, and the grounds for his subsequent arrest are purely circumstantial. In fact, the allegations rest solely on the word of Franklin Dowd, who has a well-documented history of animosity toward my client and whose father—formerly of the Santa Cruz Police Department—still has friends on the force. Honestly, Your Honor, this entire situation feels like a classic setup, and we move to dismiss the charges entirely."

I let out a breath. Smart to bring up my history with Frankie before the prosecution could do it. But I never pressed charges against Mitch. If I had, I might've had something to fight back with.

Fucking stupid.

Judge Norman thought this over. "Ms. Wells?"

"Your Honor, it's laughable for the defense to reduce the accusations against Mr. Wentz as hearsay or a conspiracy among law enforcement when the defendant has a clear history of violence and criminal behavior and who has, in fact, assaulted Frankie Dowd in the past."

Perry shook his head. "A typical high school fight, Your Honor, is hardly grounds—"

"However," Wells interjected, holding up a hand, "if the accusation from the victim himself—rendered from his hospital bed in the critical care unit, no less—isn't sufficient, prosecution is prepared to submit an eyewitness. Michael Grimaldi."

Someone in the audience gasped. Shiloh, I thought. Mikey got to his feet, looking like a Boy Scout in a suit, hands folded in front of him. Mitch caught my eye, his expression smug.

Beside me, Perry stiffened. "What's this?" he whispered.

"Bullshit," I hissed back.

Wells smiled calmly. "Mr. Grimaldi will submit to deposition and stipulate that he was there on the night of July thirtieth and can attest that Mr. Wentz did indeed perpetrate the heinous attack that left his friend clinging to life."

Perry cleared his throat, regaining his composure. "The arresting officers made no note of any testimony from Mr. Grimaldi that would give them probable cause."

"Mr. Grimaldi will testify that given the severity of Mr. Wentz's attack on Frankie, he feared for his own life and fled the scene. But after visiting his friend in the ICU, he knew he could not remain quiet."

"Is there an affidavit?" the judge asked, annoyed. "Or are we just having a conversation?"

"Here, Your Honor." Wells handed a document to the bailiff. "With regard to probable cause, I respectfully refer Your Honor to the detectives' report that clearly gives motive. Mr. Dowd will plead no contest to the vandalism of the Rare Earth Jewelry shop, the owner of which is romantically attached to Mr. Wentz."

Judge Norman set the affidavit down. "It is the determination of this court that probable cause has been sufficiently rendered."

"Your Honor—"

"Mr. Perry, do you wish to go forward in entering a plea? Or perhaps you'd like to talk it over with your client?"

Perry adjusted his glasses and stood straight. "In light of Mr. Grimaldi's affidavit, I ask for time to consult with my client."

"I thought you might. This arraignment is hereby postponed to the day after next." Norman banged his gavel.

I was shuffled out of the courtroom, hardly able to catch a glimpse of Shiloh.

In the hallway, Perry asked the guards to back off. "I need to confer with my client." He leaned against the wall beside me. "So that wasn't ideal."

"They're lying," I said. "Grimaldi wasn't there. I tagged his car a few months ago. This is bullshit. It's vengeance."

"Which we'd have to prove." Perry glanced up, and I followed his gaze to Ms. Wells, who'd entered the hallway surrounded by her assistants. "I hate surprises. Let me see what we're up against."

He conferred with her for a few minutes, his expression growing grimmer by the second, while she wore the look of someone who held all the cards.

Perry rejoined me, loosening his tie.

"Well, this just gets better and better," he said dryly. "They have cell phone footage taken back in June. You're shown telling Frankie that you will 'fuck his shit up' if he messes with your girlfriend. They have photos of your bruised hands from the night in question, they have an eyewitness, and they have the victim's *own word*. If this goes to trial, they're going to go for attempted murder in the first degree. That's a life sentence, Ronan."

Like father, like son.

"But if you take the deal, they'll reduce the charges. Second degree attempted murder or even aggravated battery and injuring with intent to cause grievous bodily harm. You could get ten years instead of twenty-five. Behave yourself, and you're out in half that."

I stared at him. "You want me to plead guilty to a crime I didn't commit so I can spend ten years in prison instead of the rest of my life."

I'd lose everything. Shiloh. She is everything.

"The case against you was already strong, but you add Grimaldi..." Perry shook his head. "That changes the game. If you want to plead not guilty, that's your right. But it's a risk. A long shot. If we lose..."

If I lose...

I closed my eyes and thought of my mom. How she tried to go through the system and how it failed her. Again and again until she was dead.

The rest of the inmates had finished rendering their pleas, and the guards motioned it was time to get everyone shackled back up and moved out.

Perry put a hand on my arm. "I know it's a tough call,

but this is what we're up against. Think long and hard about it."

That night in my cell, I thought about it. I thought about handing over five or ten or fifteen years of my life to prison because that was my best bet. But the raging anger at the unfairness of it all burned out, leaving bitter ashes of regret. This was my fault. I was Russell Wentz's son. His blood was in my veins, and it didn't matter that I tried to do right and protect those I cared about. The poison corrupted and corroded me.

I flexed my bruised knuckles in the dim light.

My fault. Because I like it too much.

But Shiloh... Christ, how could I not fight for her? For us? Ten years in prison wasn't the torture—it was ten years without her. That was unsurvivable.

The night grew late. The sounds of other inmates coughing, cursing, or snoring echoed in the hollow hallways. My cellmate cried himself to sleep, as usual.

Sometime deep in the night, I was still awake when footsteps approached and stopped outside my cell.

"Hey, Wentz."

I held up my hand as a guard shined a flashlight in my face through the bars.

"Mitch Dowd is a friend of mine. A good friend."

I tensed all over, my chest tight.

"He wanted me to pass on a message about your little girlfriend's shop." He leaned against the bars, his voice low. "It won't stop until you do."

THIRTY-TWO
SHILOH

I showed my ID at the window and passed through the metal detectors, feeling like I was trapped in a bad dream that began the night of the grand opening, and I couldn't wake up. A corrections officer led me to the visiting room, my stomach twisting in knots. The room smelled sharply of musty sweat and vending machine food.

Ronan was already there.

I moved on numb legs to the table and sat down across from him. He looked as beautiful as always but different somehow. Maybe it was the orange county jail jumpsuit or the fact that we were surrounded by armed officers and inmates, but he was less like himself. Right there in front of me but far away too.

"Hi," I said, my throat dry.

He looked up, his expression softening to see me, and then it shut down again. Turning hard.

"How's Frankie?" he asked. "They won't tell me."

"Not great, but he's going to live."

I reached for him, and a CO barked at me, "No touching."

I jerked my back, feeling small and helpless. "How are you?"

"I'm okay," Ronan said and then set his hands on the table between us. The clank of the handcuffs seemed louder than it was, the bruises on every knuckle jumping out at me.

"What happened?" I asked, my voice small.

Ronan knew what I meant. He rubbed the fingers of one hand over the other. "Doesn't matter." He leaned over the table to me. "Listen…"

"*Doesn't matter?* Of course it matters." I stared, incredulous, ignoring the twinge of doubt that nipped at me. "We can still fight this. Go to trial, but you have to tell me—"

He was already shaking his head. "Shiloh, listen to me. We don't have a lot of time." He nodded at a corrections officers stalking the visitors' room. "No matter what happens, I'm going to take care of you."

"What does that mean?"

"The money from Nelson. I have a lot left. Almost all of it. It's yours now. Rebuild the shop. Or save it for tough times or…whatever you need."

I crossed my arms, a cold feeling settling in the pit of my stomach. "This sounds like goodbye."

"Because it is."

"No!" I smacked my hand on the table, drawing the

eye of the CO. I lowered my voice to a hiss. "If you didn't do it..."

I checked myself, hearing the doubt in my voice again. My gaze couldn't stay away from his bruised knuckles while his words from the other night, *I'll take care of it*, echoed in my mind.

No! I have to trust. Trust and keep going.

"You have the truth on your side," I said.

His expression was grim. Resigned. "Truth and justice aren't always the same thing."

"So that's it? What about us?"

"There is no more us, Shiloh," Ronan said, the words slamming into me like hammer blows. "No matter what happens, I'm going away for a long time. You need to move on."

"What? Move on? *No.*"

"This is humiliating," he seethed. "I hate you seeing me like this. I can't fucking stand it, Shiloh. If I have to do this for ten years... If *you* have to do this shit for ten years... Metal detectors and collect calls and two-hour drives for thirty-minute visits..." He shook his head gravely. "I won't do that to you. I can't."

"You can't just...cut me off," I said, disbelieving. "You *can't.*"

"I have to," Ronan said, his voice thick. "For your safety. They'll keep going. Harassing you. I made it worse. I brought this to you."

"No, Ronan."

"Promise me, Shiloh. Promise me you'll live your life. Don't wait for me."

"No, I'm not going to promise that. I can't."

"You have to." He swallowed hard. "I'm letting you go, Shiloh. You have to let me go too."

I stared, agony clawing at my heart. "No. *No.* I will not let you do this. I will *not…*"

Right before my eyes, the love fell out of Ronan's expression. Turned ice-cold. Stony. His gaze flattened; his tone emptied of humanity. "I did it. I beat up Frankie. I wanted to kill him for messing up your shop."

I sat back, pushed by the sudden danger emanating from him. "You're lying."

"I'm going to take the plea deal."

"No. You can't. You're just saying this to push me away. It won't work."

He rubbed his bruised knuckles as if drawing my attention to them. "I couldn't protect my mother, Shiloh. I can protect you." He tilted his chin up, the dead tone in his voice sending shivers down my spine. "Frankie won't bother you again."

"Ronan…"

A CO stopped behind him. "Time's up, Wentz."

"No, not yet," I said, panic rising in me.

This cannot be how it ends. It cannot.

"Time's up, Shiloh," Ronan said gruffly, the emotion he'd been trying to hide seeping through the cracks. "End of the road."

Quickly, he looked away and let himself be taken from me.

I sat, stunned and unable to move, a sick, heavy feeling settling over my chest—years of being without Ronan, pressing me down.

"No."

It was a tiny whisper, lost in the muted conversations of the county jail visitors' center that faded away to nothing.

The next day, I sat in a Santa Cruz Superior Courtroom, wedged between Bibi and Maryann Greer—one of Ronan's tenants. They squeezed my hands, held me up as Ronan entered a plea of guilty. The judge's words would jolt me from sleep in a cold sweat for a hundred nights after.

"Ronan August Wentz, for felony aggravated battery resulting in great physical injury and injuring with intent to cause grievous bodily harm, you are hereby sentenced to ten years at San Quentin State Prison."

It was so simple. Over so quickly. With one slam of the gavel, the judge snatched ten years from Ronan's life and ruined mine. Before I could even begin to process it, a guard was walking him out.

Ronan looked back at me, and for a split second, the hard exterior he'd shown me in the jail cracked. His eyes revealed everything—the agony in their smoky depths.

They said goodbye.

Someone let out a sob, and I realized it was me.

The following week, I tried arranging another visit, but Ronan wouldn't take my calls. Then I tried showing up and found out my name wasn't on the approved visitor list.

"What do you mean?" I asked. "Who approves the list?"

The woman behind the glass smiled pityingly. "The inmate, honey."

A few days later, after Ronan had been transferred to San Quentin, I tried there too. I got the same response. Ronan had meant what he said about me moving on and living my life. Not waiting for him.

Except he *was* my life, and waiting for him or not wasn't a choice I could make.

I called Violet, crying, and told her the whole sordid story. She cried with me and said she'd see if Miller could get through to him. But Ronan had cut him off too. Probably Holden as well, though he was still MIA.

The Lost Boys were broken, when that had seemed impossible.

I visited Maryann and her girls at the complex, hoping she'd had better luck.

"He won't talk to me either," Maryann said, making us some tea, and my heart sank.

"Who won't, Mommy?" one of the twins asked.

"Ronan?" asked the other. They were both suddenly on the verge of tears.

"Yes, Ronan," Maryann said, stroking their hair.

"Are you his girlfriend?" one asked.

"You're so pretty," said the other.

"Oh! You're the one who made that necklace he always wears."

"Yeah, I made that," I said, my throat thick.

For when you're adrift.

Now that pendant was locked in some prison storage room, and I was adrift.

"He hired a management company to take care of us," Maryann said.

"From prison?"

She nodded. "Apparently, his uncle owned both complexes free and clear. Ronan's company has orders to keep the rent the same no matter how long he's gone and to use every penny of our payments to make repairs as soon as an issue comes up. No scrimping."

Maryann's eyes filled, and she reached across the table to take my hand.

"I'm on the verge of a breakdown over him," she said. "I can't even imagine how you must be feeling."

Sick. I felt sick at the idea of a life without Ronan.

I left Maryann's place with hugs from her twins and a promise from her that we'd stay in touch. In the parking lot, I looked up at the corner unit, the window dark.

I ducked inside the car just as a torrent of sobs racked me.

At home, Bibi was knitting on the couch, Ethel and Lucy curled around her ankles.

"Hey, honey," she said. "Hungry? I have some chicken with biscuits and gravy cooking. Maybe some basil mint lemonade?"

The idea of food made my stomach twist. "Maybe later."

I sat on the couch beside her and opened my laptop. The shop had been closed, losing money every day. I still had repairs to make before reopening, though it all seemed so tedious. Too much work to do, and I didn't have the energy—the fire—to do it.

I opened my banking app to see what I had left in savings and saw that Ronan had made good on his word. My account was more than sixty thousand dollars richer.

A little cry fell out of me, and I shut the laptop.

"What is it?" Bibi asked, alarmed.

"He gave me his money, Bibi," I said, the tears flowing. "All his money."

"Oh, honey." Bibi drew me to her and held me against her bosom. My tears dampened the lilac of her housedress. "Then he wants you to have it."

"I can't. It feels like…he died and left it to me like his uncle did. Because he won't talk to me, Bibi. He's cutting me out of his life, trying to force me to move on."

"I know," she said with a sigh. "I was afraid of that."

"Doesn't he get it?" I cried. "Doesn't he understand how much I love him? I can never *move on* from him."

Bibi shook her head, her voice heavy. "The boy was shuffled from home to home for ten years after his mama died. He has no idea that good things can stick. That people can care about him for longer than a month or two. In his world, *moving on* is what people do, so he's doing what he thinks is the best thing for you."

"Joke's on him. *He* is the best thing for me." I sat up, wiping my eyes with the heels of my hands. "He told me he did it. His hands were bruised, and he confessed to beating up Frankie."

"Do you believe that?"

I didn't have to think about it; the answer rose up from the deepest part of me, a lone truth in an ocean of grief.

"I know he didn't." I looked to her, pleading. "But what do I do now, Bibi? Just what the hell am I supposed to do now?"

Bibi faced forward, thinking for a minute. "Ronan has been pushed around by life so hard… I suspect he's given little pieces of his heart to those he trusted and watched them walk away with them. Now something like this happens, and I worry there's nothing left."

I raised my head. "Is there?"

"You have the last piece of his heart, Shiloh. For good or bad. Silence or no silence. One year or ten. It's in your hands." She gave my fingers a squeeze. "And it's up to you what you do with it."

PART V

THIRTY-THREE
SHILOH

THREE YEARS LATER

APRIL

My eyes burned as I focused on the delicate filigree on my current piece—a silver ring with multicolored gemstones—the kind of work that required more than four hours of sleep at night. I kept hoping I'd get used to this new schedule, but three years in, and I was only more exhausted with each passing day.

Each day without him.

I'd put a small workstation in the back of Rare Earth's showroom so I could create jewelry and man the store at the same time, not an hour wasted.

I set the ring down and stretched. It had taken an entire month to get the shop reopened after Frankie Dowd had his fun with it. One month of lost revenue and one month of rent I still had to pay. Now it was nearly what it had been before, except without Ronan's displays. I had to purchase new ones because he wasn't here.

The store had been perfect. We'd been perfect in our own imperfect way.

My cell phone rang with Violet's number.

"Hey, you," I said, trying not to sound as tired as I felt. "By my calculations, you're back in town in T minus three months. *Do not* tell me there's been a change of plans."

She laughed. "No change. I'll be there before you know it. I cannot wait to hug you again and be *home*."

Violet had struggled through three years of school at Baylor while stardom had kept Miller insanely busy, recording and touring. But that lifestyle had taken its toll with his diabetes. He and Violet were moving back to Santa Cruz so he could rest and she could finish her undergrad at UCSC before embarking on God knew how many years of medical school.

"I can't wait." I forced a laugh to cover the cracks in my voice. "Literally."

"You okay?" Violet asked. The woman missed nothing. "I mean…*okay* is relative, given everything that's happened, but you sound extra tired."

"I'm okay. Hanging in there."

"Shi, you don't have to pretend with me. If you're having a hard time, you can tell me."

Tears stung the corners of my eyes. "It is hard, Vi," I admitted. "All of it. And Bibi has been so great—as usual—but I don't want to worry her. Or Mama." I pulled myself together and huffed a breath. "I'm counting down the days till you come back so I can dump my problems in your lap instead. Or at least grab a coffee with someone my own age."

Violet laughed. "I am ready to be dumped on. Wait... that came out weird."

I smiled, and then a figure passed by the front of my shop. I could've sworn I'd seen the same gray coat, the same hunched shoulders earlier this morning.

"How is everyone?" Violet asked.

"Good. Except Bibi's getting up there. Her blood pressure isn't great, and her vision is all but gone. Being away from home to sit at a shop that's empty half the day feels like I'm failing in all the ways."

"You're not failing. You're taking care of everyone, and you're doing it beautifully. But wait... Business is slow? I thought you said you had a great winter?"

"I did, but it ebbs and flows with the tourists. That's just the business. I need to keep adjusting, calibrating, and working to keep up. But damn..."

"I know," she said softly. "But the summers are usually busy, right?"

I smiled. "Thank you for reminding me of the good stuff. It's easy to forget when I'm missing him so damn much."

"Do you want to talk about him?"

"There's nothing to say. He's on year three of a ten-year

sentence and still won't let me see him." I shrugged as if the heavy burden pressing down on my heart could be reduced to that casual gesture. "I miss him, Vi. That's the bottom line. I miss him with every particle of my body. But I'm also so *angry* at him for shutting me out. In my worst moments, I'm tempted to do what he said—let him go and move on with my life."

"But…"

"But that's impossible. And I wish he knew that," I said, tears pricking my eyes again. "More than anything, I wish he understood what he means to the people who love and need him."

"I know," Violet said. "Miller doesn't talk about it much, but he's hurting too. Both Ronan and Holden disappeared in their own way, cutting him off."

"God, I haven't even asked how Miller is doing," I said, quickly wiping my eyes. "Better, I'll bet, now that he has you with him."

I heard Violet's smile over her words, happiness infusing her voice. "He's going to be okay. No more touring until he's rested, and even then, no more arena shows."

"Good. I—" I stopped as I caught sight of the same figure in gray skulking outside my window, only this time, I caught a glimpse of hair too. A furtive glance, then he was hurrying away. "Vi, I'm sorry. I have to call you back."

The figure was halfway down the sidewalk when I tore out of the shop.

"Hey!" I called sharply. "Stop right there!"

THE LAST PIECE OF HIS HEART

The guy jerked to a stop and hunched deeper in his ratty coat. Then, slowly, he turned around, and I tensed all over, the air catching in my chest as if I'd been punched in the gut.

Frankie Dowd was almost unrecognizable. Pale, sickly, nearly emaciated, with one eyelid permanently drooping from the beating he took three years ago. He shuffled toward me, limping, as if he couldn't control his left leg very well.

"Hey, Shiloh," Frankie said, his hands jammed in the pockets of an old windbreaker that might've once been blue and was five sizes too big. His jeans were ripped, and his Converse were filthy, the laces held together with knots.

I glared at him, trying to ignore how my heart sort of ached to see him like this, so wretched and sad. I'd never seen a person completely without hope before, but Frankie was close.

Then I remembered how hopeless and undone I felt the night my shop was vandalized. How *Ronan* must've felt when he had ten years taken from him for something he didn't do. I hardened my voice.

"What do you want? Why have you been skulking around my store all morning? Casing the joint for your next attack?"

He winced, but truthfully, the guy looked like he couldn't lift a crowbar now to save his life.

"I need to talk to you."

"I have nothing to say to you."

"But I have something you want to hear."

His sad, plain tone caught my attention. I crossed my

arms. "After all that's happened, why should I give you the time of day?"

"You shouldn't," he said. "I don't blame you for hating me, but you're going to want to hear this. Please."

I crossed my arms tighter. The urge to scream at him, to rage and rail and try to inflict a fraction of the pain on him that I'd endured—that *Ronan* had endured—in the last three years was fierce but fading until I just felt sorry for him. And the fact that he was here, talking to me, sparked a little flicker that it wasn't going to be the same hopeless day as every other day over the last three years.

"Fine. Let me lock up first," I added pointedly, and Frankie hung his head in shame, like a whipped dog.

My lone employee—Luisa—was off that day. I grabbed my purse from the back room, put the *Will Return Soon* sign up, and joined Frankie Dowd on the sidewalk.

"You want to get a coffee?" I asked. "Something to eat?"

He shrugged one shoulder. "If you want."

It was obvious he was hungry. Even more obvious he didn't have any money.

Am I going to buy Frankie fucking Dowd lunch?

It seemed that I was. He looked as if he hadn't eaten in a week.

"Order what you want," I told him as we sat down at the Hill Street Café, a little diner I frequented sometimes on my lunch breaks from the shop.

"Thanks," he said, hardly a whisper, and ordered the soup and sandwich combo of the day.

"Just coffee for me," I told Lucy, the waitress.

Frankie looked sheepish. "You're not eating?"

"My stomach is twisted in so many knots right now, I can't possibly think of food." I folded my arms and leaned toward him. "Do you know how much I *hate* that I'm sitting here, desperate to hear what *you* have to say? Because for three years, I've had nothing. No hope."

"I know. I'm sorry, Shiloh. For so much."

I braced myself, my heart pounding in my chest. "Well? Let's hear it."

Frankie toyed with his napkin, not looking at me. "My dad is dead. Heart attack. A few days ago."

I sat back, absorbing this. "Forgive me if I have a hard time offering condolences right now."

"Don't bother. He wasn't a good man."

"Was that what you wanted to tell me?"

That can't be all. Please.

Frankie's eye twitched, and he pressed the napkin to it. "Sorry, it does that sometimes. My leg doesn't work so great anymore either. The doctors say it's brain damage from that night." He looked at me with one eye, clear and blue. "My dad did this to me. It wasn't Ronan."

The café faded away, and all I knew or felt or thought was hope, blooming wild and huge in my chest.

I blinked hard, unwilling to let Frankie Dowd see me cry. "What happened that night?"

Frankie heaved a breath, his eyes on the napkin in his hands as he spoke. "I was at the parking lot behind the

Burger Barn, hanging with Mikey and some people from school. Mostly Mikey. No one else liked me much. Everyone left, but I didn't want to go home." He hunched deeper into his jacket. "My dad was supposed to do a year, but they put him on house arrest. Then things got real bad. So bad my mom left, and she didn't take me with her."

I nodded. His pain was palpable, emanating from him like the stink of his unwashed clothes.

"Dad was stuck at home with no job. Nothing to do. He *loved* his job. Not the *protecting and serving* like it says on the squad cars. It was the power he loved. He was mad all the time. Beating up on people he thought were 'criminal scum' made him feel better."

The waitress came back and dropped off a coffee for me and a three-bean soup and ham sandwich for Frankie. He didn't seem to see the food, his mind somewhere besides this café.

"That night, I was alone in the parking lot, sitting on the hood of my car. Then Ronan walked up, like out of nowhere. His face was…scary. I was sure he was going to kill me. I tried to drive away, but I couldn't get the keys in the ignition, I was shaking so bad. He tried the door, not saying a word. Which was almost worse, how quiet he was. I'd locked the door, so he smashed his fist into my window, hard enough that it cracked. Then he threw a right and *shattered* it."

"The bruises on his fists…" I said, almost to myself.

Frankie nodded. "That crazy fucker." He cleared his

throat at my sharp glance. "Sorry. But he actually *pulled me out of the car* through the broken window."

"Holy shit," I murmured, envisioning it all perfectly: Ronan—deadly calm and quiet—taking care of business. To protect me and my shop.

I'll handle it, he'd said.

A shiver ran down my spine, and I had to refocus on Frankie, who was looking at me through remorseful eyes.

"Ronan knew it was me who trashed your place. I'm sorry for that, Shiloh. My dad... He told me to do it. And I admit, I was happy to at first. Things were so bad at home, I needed to break shit. But after it was done, I was sorry."

"Why?" I asked. "Why would he tell you to do that?"

"Dad wanted revenge on Ronan for getting kicked off the force. When he got an idea that you were an enemy, that was it. He wouldn't let it go." He shifted in his seat and glanced down, his voice low. "I was the one who told him you two were together. How hurting you was the best way to get to him. The plan was to keep hitting your store. Throw a rock or tag it. Constantly. Just wear you down until it closed."

My stomach clenched. "Go on. Or go back. What happened when Ronan got you out of the car?"

"He slammed me against it and told me to leave you alone," he said. "He told me that his life meant nothing, that he wasn't afraid of me or my dad. He said he'd do whatever it took to keep you safe."

Oh, baby. "Then what?"

Frankie looked away. "I pissed my pants."

"You *what*?"

"Ronan wasn't fucking around. I could see it in his eyes." He smiled a little. "And did I mention he'd just yanked me out of a car window he'd smashed with his fists? I got the message loud and clear, and I didn't want to go along with Dad's plan anyway. Ronan made me swear to him I'd leave you alone, and I did."

"And then?" I asked, breath held.

"He let me go."

"He just...let you go?"

Frankie nodded. "He walked away, and I went home."

The implications of what Frankie was telling me were starting to seep in.

Ronan's innocent.

In my deepest heart, I knew that, but not having a reason for his bruised knuckles or Frankie's injuries always lingered at the edge of my thoughts, whispering doubt. Hearing the truth out loud brought hot tears to my eyes. Ronan had fought so hard to not be the monster his father was. But he ended up in prison anyway, suffering the same fate, the same public perception—that he was a criminal.

He was never a criminal. Never.

"I tried to sneak past my dad on the couch, but he caught me," Frankie was saying. "He saw I'd pissed myself and..." He hunched his shoulders. "Dad hated cowards more than anything. Said it was the worst thing a person could be and something his son could *never* be. He called me names and asked me what happened. I told him that I was done messing with your shop. I remember that first punch, and that's about it. I woke up in the hospital."

"Jesus."

"When I came to, Dad was there. He looked a little bit scared about what he'd done to me. Then Mikey visited me in the hospital. They came up with a story to pin it on Ronan."

"Mikey Grimaldi?"

Frankie nodded. "Because Ronan spray-painted that word on his car. Mikey wanted revenge too, even though he really did…do what he did to Kimberly. So he lied for my dad."

The ramifications were filling me up, lighting me up from the inside, erasing my bone-weary exhaustion and filling me with hope. And anger. Years' worth of anger, pain, and longing. Missing Ronan with every breath.

"Frankie, Ronan has served three years in prison for the lies you told. *Three* years. He won't speak to me. He's cut me off because he thinks we're better off without him." My voice was shaking. "You *ruined* us."

Frankie nodded. "I know. I'm sorry. I really am. But after I got out of the hospital, I was messed up. I can't think so good, and I get these headaches. I can't hold a job, so I had to live at home. Once Ronan was put away, Dad's temper got worse. Like he had nothing to fight against anymore except me." He picked at the tablecloth. "I wanted to come clean so many times. But I was too scared of him to say anything. But he's gone now, and I'm ready to talk. To get Ronan out. I know that's a chickenshit way to do it, and I'm sorry. I'm really sorry, Shiloh. For everything."

I stared, the full weight of his story sinking in. I wanted to grab Frankie by the collar and drag him to the police station, but he was fiddling with his spoon as if waiting for my permission to eat.

"Finish your food, and then we go to the authorities, okay?"

He smiled gratefully and dug in. I couldn't stand the thought of Ronan being in prison for one more minute, but Frankie wolfed down his sandwich and drained his soup bowl, and we went outside to call an Uber—I wouldn't have him in my car alone.

We waited in the bright April sun for our ride to arrive. Any minute, I expected Frankie's cackling laugh that said I'd fallen for his sick joke. Then I took a closer look at his drooping eyelid and shuffling gait and knew he was telling the truth.

At the station, I was directed to the Investigations Division where I asked to speak to Detective Harris.

The detective's eyes widened as he walked up. "Hello, Shiloh…and Frankie Dowd."

"Can we go somewhere and talk?" I asked.

Harris stared at Frankie as if he'd seen a ghost. "Sure."

He led us to a small room—white walls, a table with a chair on either side, and a two-sided mirror. I wondered if Ronan had been questioned in this room before he was arrested for the crime he didn't commit.

Frankie sank into one of the chairs; Harris took the other. I remained standing like a guard in case he decided to bolt. "Tell him what you told me."

Frankie took a breath and told Harris everything. The detective's face remained impassive as he listened, but his eyes widened more than once.

"You're willing to put this in writing, Frankie? Because making false allegations—especially allegations that lead to a wrongful conviction—is a serious crime. You could do real time."

Frankie shrugged his skinny shoulders. "I'll have a roof over my head anyway."

Harris studied him a moment, and I held my breath, but Frankie didn't back down.

"Okay. I'll make some calls. Frankie, stay put for a bit. I'll have a few more questions for you. Shiloh?" Harris motioned for me to step outside with him.

"When?" I blurted when he shut the door. "When will Ronan get out? Because this changes everything, right? He's innocent. He's always been innocent."

Harris held up a hand. "It's a process. There will be a hearing before a judge. Frankie has to swear an affidavit, and I'll have to haul Mikey Grimaldi in for making a false police report. He might put up a fight. But Frankie's willing to risk jail time by coming forward. If he recants and says Ronan didn't do it, that holds a lot of weight—more now that we have the full history between Mitch and Ronan."

I nodded, absorbing every word, then tensed up all

over again when Harris rubbed his chin, frowning. "What is it?"

"Shiloh, I've been friends with your grandma for a long time," he said. "All of us here at the station love Bibi. But we can't let friendships interfere with doing our jobs."

"Okay…"

"But sometimes the job *becomes* everything. You get a suspect in the room; he's got a history of violence with the victim. He's got banged-up knuckles…" He shook his head. "You get excited that you nailed your perp, case closed. And nine times out of ten, you're right. It's Occam's razor: the simplest explanation is the best and almost always the truth."

I crossed my arms, my voice low. "Not always."

"Not always," he agreed grimly. "As soon as I saw you come in here with Frankie Dowd, I knew. I knew this was the one time in ten that we'd made a huge mistake. I'm sorry I didn't dig deeper, especially considering what I knew about Mitch. I'm sorry about that, Shiloh."

I swallowed hard. "Thank you, Detective Harris. But if that's the case, I would appreciate your help now. If there's any chance the judge believes Mikey or wants to keep Ronan where he is…"

He smiled gently. "I'll do whatever I can."

I left the station and went back to Rare Earth but only to

secure the inventory, lock up for the day, and drive home. I parked in the garage at our house and came in through the kitchen. Antoinette, the day nurse, was making a pot of tea.

"Hey, Toni," I said. "How's it going over here?"

She smiled her megawatt smile. "You're home early. Bibi's taking a nap and—"

A playful squeal sounded from the living room.

Toni grinned wider. "Someone else is *not* taking a nap."

I hung up my sweater on the back of the kitchen door. "You can cut out early if you want. I'll take it from here."

"You sure you don't want to steal a few winks yourself? I'm on the clock for another three hours."

I smiled. I couldn't sleep if I wanted to. Not then.

"Nope, I'm good."

"You got it. This tea will keep for Bibi when she wakes up, and I think Marie said she'd be popping in later too."

"Great. Thanks, Toni."

I followed her to the living room where she bent down to ruffle the soft halo of baby curls on the toddler who was sitting on the floor amid a mess of toys, stacking and knocking down blocks.

"Goodbye, little man," Toni said. "I'll see you tomorrow."

"Bye-bye," he said, then spied me. His little face burst into a smile that never failed—no matter how tired I was—to warm my heart and remind me what it was all for. "Mama!"

"Hey, baby boy," I said, the tears already flowing. I

picked him up and sat with him on the couch. "Did you have a good day today?"

He nodded, then cocked his head and touched a chubby little finger to the tear that trailed down my cheek. "Mama sad?"

"No, baby. I'm not sad. I'm happy. I'm so, so happy."

I held my son—August Barrera-Wentz—hugging him tight as the tears fell in earnest.

"Your daddy is coming home."

"Shiloh? Come on, honey. You gotta eat."

I curled tighter on the bed.

"Shiloh, I'm not playing," Bibi said. "It's been two weeks." She sat down and brushed the braids, which were getting rough-looking, out of my face. "It's time."

"For what?" I croaked.

"To try again."

Just the words made me tired. It'd been two weeks since Ronan had been shipped off to San Quentin, taking my will to "try again" with him.

I rolled over and sat up. "I have tried, Bibi. After Mama's secret, I'll never look at myself in the mirror the same way, and my shop was trashed. But I kept going. I went back to work and 'tried again.' Then I lost Ronan." I shook my head. "It's too much."

"Now, now, giving up isn't allowed, remember?" Bibi's tone was firm, but her hand on my shoulder was gentle. "You've

been knocked all the way down, but it's time to get back up and return to life."

The idea of life without Ronan made me sick.

Literally.

I pushed off the bed and ran to the bathroom. I barely made it to the toilet before the half a sandwich Bibi had coaxed me to eat that afternoon came back up. Kneeling at the toilet, I stared up at Bibi at the door. She stared back.

"No..." I breathed. "No, no, no."

"Could it be?" I didn't miss the glint of happiness in her hazy eyes.

"No. Impossible. I'm always so careful. We used condoms, and I'm on the pill..."

Except that Ronan and I had stopped using condoms months ago, and I got drunk the night the shop was wrecked. I puked up everything in my system until there was nothing left. The next day, I was a mess. Not thinking. I couldn't remember taking my pill that day.

"But I slept with Ronan," I murmured. "That I remember." I clapped a hand to my mouth. "Oh my God."

I pulled myself together enough to drive to the drugstore. When I came back, I locked myself in the bathroom with the little stick and waited. But I already knew. My sense of smell was insanely strong, and my stomach felt queasy whenever I stopped crying long enough to notice.

The five minutes was up. I picked up the stick, and there was the little pink plus sign. It fell into the trash, dropped from nerveless fingers.

"Just like Mama," I whispered.

Except I loved Ronan. The night we slept together was beautiful—a flicker of warmth in a cold storm.

Bibi was waiting on the couch. "Well?"

"I'm pregnant."

Christ, saying the words out loud sent a shiver of fear down my spine.

Bibi smiled to herself, then scattered the cats and patted the cushion next to her. "Sit. Let's talk."

I dropped beside her. "There's nothing to talk about. I can't have this baby, Bibi. I can't run a business and have a baby. I can't."

"Well, the fact that you're talking about running your business is an improvement, since as of three hours ago, you wouldn't get out of bed. Already this baby is motivating you."

"I'm serious. Ronan is gone. For ten years. He won't even talk to me. I can't even tell him he's a fa—" The word stuck in my throat. "I can't do this alone."

"You won't be alone." She held up her hand. "I know, I'm an old lady, but Ronan gave you a bunch of money—"

"That I can't bring myself to spend."

"You can if it's to take care of the child you two made," she said, and that glint of happiness was back.

I shook my head. "It's not the money, Bibi. Or the work even. I can't be like Mama. Keeping a baby and then resenting him or her. Making them feel worthless their entire life."

Bibi leveled me with a harsh look. "You honestly believe you would do that? After everything you've been through? Because I don't."

"No," I admitted. "But I can't know the future, except how impossibly hard it's going to be. And if I do manage to keep my head above water, people won't see the work. They'll see a single mother with the father in jail. I'll become a statistic."

"I'm not going to hear you talk like that, Shiloh," Bibi said sternly. "That's small thinking. Behind every statistic is a human being with a story. Like your mama. She told you her awful secret but not how hard she struggled after."

"But you know the whole story, Bibi. You've always known. They all did. Why didn't you or Bertie or someone *tell me*?"

"Because Marie made us promise. She swore she'd do it her way, in her time."

"Drunk, in front of everyone? In front of Ronan?" Shame wanted to curl me back into a ball.

"Her way and her time were all wrong, obviously. And over the years, I wanted to break my promise and tell you proper. But you know why I didn't?"

I shook my head.

"Because it didn't matter." She reached to touch my cheek. "You are a treasure to me, Shiloh, and have been since the moment you came to live here. I knew telling you would only make you question your worth. Instead, I tried to raise you to believe in yourself. To let your value come from within. And I think I did a pretty darn good job. You know how I know? Because you love Ronan Wentz with your whole heart."

I nodded. "I do. I love him so much."

"It's very difficult—impossible even—to love another with your whole heart if you can't find any of that love for yourself."

I shook my head. "I still feel dirty now that I know. I am Mama's pain, walking around in a flesh-and-blood body."

"Once the shock of it loosens its hold, you'll be able to think more clearly. And if you sit down and actually talk with your mama, you'll have the whole truth. Understanding unlocks doors, child."

I bit my lip, thinking. Bibi was right in that I needed to talk to Mama. Really talk. I couldn't think about my own situation until I did. They were bound together, and I couldn't make a decision about my future until I fully understood my past.

I hugged Bibi, kissed her cheek, and booked a flight to New Orleans.

When I arrived in Louisiana three days later, I took an Uber straight to Mama's little shotgun house on Old Prieur Street in the Seventh Ward. My heart in my throat, I knocked on the door.

Mama answered, a look of shock registering on her face for a moment. Then she nodded as if she'd been expecting me all along.

"Come in." She offered me a seat in her small living room, neatly and colorfully furnished. "You look…different. Radiant."

"That's a word for 'scared shitless' I haven't heard before," I said and heaved a breath. "I'm pregnant."

Mama's eyes widened, and for a moment, I thought she was going to hug me or cry. Or both. But she bottled herself back up and indicated for me to sit on her neat couch in her neat living room.

"Ronan's?"

"Of course," I said stiffly.

"The one who's now in prison?"

I crossed my arms. "Yes. For a crime he didn't commit."

Mama pursed her lips as if she'd heard all that before. "Would you like some water? Something to eat?"

"I'm fine."

"Are you going to keep it?"

The question caught me off guard, whacking me in the chest. "And they call me direct. Must've gotten it from you."

She arched a brow.

"I don't know," I said. "I don't think so. I can't imagine trying to get a business that already crashed and burned back on its feet while raising a baby alone."

"So you came to me?" Mama shook her head, her curls falling around her face softly. "I have no advice. I've done nothing but make mistakes. Starting that night with your father."

"You didn't make a mistake that night, Mama. What he did to you…that wasn't your fault." I shifted on the couch. "But I have to know… Why did you keep me? You had every right not to."

"Because I thought I could do it," she said. "I was like you. Strong. Driven. Ambitious. I wasn't going to let anything stop me. Not my broken heart or the violation of my body by someone I thought loved me. So I pushed through. I tried. For four years, I tried, but every time I looked at you, instead of seeing the beautiful child you are, I saw him lurking beneath." She shivered and hugged herself. "Pushing through didn't work. I couldn't keep you, and I hated myself for giving you up. I've been stuck in that purgatory for years."

"And now?"

She looked at me, her dark eyes heavy. "Does it matter? There's nothing left of me."

"That's not true," I said. "But, Mama, did you ever get help? Talk to someone professionally?"

"I never told anyone what happened until the day I gave you to Bibi."

"Why not?"

"It was humiliating and degrading, and I'm already a private person. I don't like anyone in my business. I try to work hard and take care of myself."

I sat back, marveling to hear my words come out of my mother's mouth.

"You could have been talking about me," I said. "I'm private and a workaholic. And…closed up." My hands went to my belly. Until Ronan.

"I'm sorry, Shiloh," Mama said. "For ruining your grand opening. For not being there for you. For failing you so badly."

I moved to sit next to her and took her hand. Mama stiffened, then clutched mine back as if, now that she had it, she didn't want to let go.

"You didn't fail, Mama. You never had help. There are certain things we just aren't made to face alone."

I thought about Ronan in prison, how he believed being alone was the best thing he could do for me.

"It's hard, asking for help," Mama said. "I was so lucky to have Bibi."

"I am too," I said, smiling gently. "She's…everything."

"I'm assuming she knows about your situation?"

"Of course. I think she wants me to keep it."

"I'm sure she does."

"She wants to help," I said slowly. *"And I have the money Ronan gave me."*

Mama's hand in mine tightened. "And...you have me. If you want."

I glanced up quickly. "What?"

"I have a lot of work to do. Healing, I guess. But I'm your mama." She brushed my braids off my face. *"I think it's time I acted like it."*

Tears flooded my eyes. "Can I...hug you?"

"No," she said, her own eyes shining. *"I'm going to hug you."*

Mama pulled me into her embrace, and I sank in, reveling in her softness, the scent of her...different from Bibi but familiar too.

"But I don't know for sure if I'm keeping this baby," I said when we pulled apart, wiping my eyes. *"It's still so scary and... daunting."*

But a vague vision of the future came to me, with my shop where it had been before it was vandalized. And there was a little person waiting for me at home while I worked to create a life for Ronan to come back to.

Maybe I can do this. Maybe.

"No matter what you choose," Mama said, *"I'm going to try to be better for you. I can't promise I won't make mistakes, but I'm going to try."*

I didn't know what Mama trying might look like or if I

could count on her, but when all is said and done, that's all you can hope for. To trust and keep going.

On the flight back to California, my hands couldn't leave my stomach alone, cradling a roundness that wasn't there.

"You're his too," I whispered to the baby that wasn't even a baby yet. Just a collection of cells—his and mine. But I knew without a doubt in my heart that Ronan would make an amazing father. That he'd love our baby with all that he had, fiercely, just like he did me.

And maybe I'd be a good mother too.

I had a chance. My heart was wide open.

THIRTY-FOUR

RONAN

It happened fast.

One day, I was facing down seven more years of my sentence. The next, Forrest Perry was in the visitors' center at San Quentin, telling me I was getting out.

"Frankie recanted," he said, his eyes lit up behind his glasses. "He admitted it was Mitch who put him in the hospital." He rummaged in his briefcase and pulled out a few documents, then held them up one at a time since I wasn't allowed to touch them. "Frankie's affidavit…and this is the judge's order for your immediate release and expungement of your record." He folded his hands on the table. "Mikey Grimaldi has been sentenced to a year for obstruction of justice and filing a false police report, and I've already taken the liberty of filing for your restitution."

"Wait…release?" I said dumbly. I hadn't heard much after that. "I'm getting out?"

"Yes, and with some start-up cash to boot. The State

of California is going to give you one hundred and forty dollars for every day you've been wrongfully imprisoned. Your release is set for eight days from now, which—by my calculations—means you're looking at roughly $145,000."

I stared. "I'm getting out in eight days?"

"Yes indeed. I wish it were immediate, but there's some paperwork. Isn't there always?" He chuckled until he read my expression. "I'm sorry, Ronan. I know this is a lot to take in. But in eight days, you'll be a free man and with a nice chunk of cash to get you back on your feet."

I hardly heard him. The money didn't mean shit. Nothing mattered except...

Shiloh.

But I'd cut her off so that she'd move on. I'd only served three years instead of ten, but it was still too long to wait, to have a woman like her put herself on hold for *me*.

Four days later instead of eight, a guard came to my cell and told me to pack up my shit. I said goodbye to my cellmate, Marcus, and to some of the guys I'd befriended out of survival necessity. I was walked to processing, where my intake three years ago happened in reverse. I was given the clothes I was arrested in—jeans, boots, a T-shirt, and my denim jacket. I changed in a small room, ditching the dark-blue sweatpants and the light-blue shirt that looked like doctor's scrubs. The CO behind the counter slid me a small manila envelope. Inside was my wallet, the keys to my apartment, and the compass pendant Shiloh had made for me. I slipped it on and put the pendant against my skin, over my heart.

I could keep that at least.

The restitution cash hadn't processed yet, but they gave me fifty bucks and a bus ticket to Santa Cruz, my last place of residence. The management company I'd hired to take care of Nelson's apartment buildings said repairs to maintain the Bluffs complex were too costly and not enough; it was on the verge of being condemned. I figured I'd handle all that, make sure the tenants at both buildings were taken care of, and then…

I didn't know what. Start over somewhere else maybe.

You could fall at Shiloh's feet and beg her to forgive you.

Nope. Too fucking selfish. I couldn't shut her out and then show up and take it all back. Too late. It was too late…

I stepped outside into a bright April afternoon. The sun felt different, shining in a different sky than the one we had over the prison yard. Air, sun, food…none of it was the same on the inside—given in bits and pieces and taken away just as easily. Suddenly the entire fucking world was available to me.

I'd give it all for Shiloh.

Fuck, I had to shut down these thoughts. My entire body ached for her, my heart screaming for her. But even if I wanted to undo it all, she probably hated me. Hopefully she did exactly what I wanted and moved on.

There was a sleek black SUV in the prison visitor parking lot. Two guys in dark sunglasses—security, by the size of them—stood at the front and rear. A driver sat behind the wheel, but the tinted windows darkened the back.

I started to walk past but stopped short when a door opened and Miller Stratton stepped out. My chest tightened so quickly, my eyes stung. He looked good. Bigger, healthier. He wore his usual jeans and T-shirt, but they were money now.

He slammed the door and leaned against the car, arms crossed. "You asshole."

"Hey to you too," I said, keeping my voice hard and pretending I hadn't missed the fuck out of him.

We faced each other in that parking lot like gunslingers about to draw.

Miller opened his mouth, then snapped it shut. He jerked his chin at the SUV. "Get in."

"What for? You kidnapping me?"

"If I have to," Miller said. "To make sure you get where you're supposed to go."

"I know where I'm supposed to go. I got shit to handle in Santa Cruz, and then…"

"And then? Does this *shit that you need to handle* include seeing Shiloh?" He read my silence and scowled. "Fuck that, man."

"Stay out of my business, Stratton," I said and started to walk.

He moved in front of me, put a hand on my chest, and shoved me.

"That's not going to work anymore," Miller said, getting up in my face. "You always kept your shit to yourself, and I respected that. Same with Holden. But he disappeared, and you shut everyone out for three fucking years."

"I had my reasons."

"They're shit reasons."

"What the fuck do you know about it?" I asked, shoving him back, my voice rising. "You know what it's like to spend three years in a place like this?" I stabbed a finger behind me. "To be locked up like an animal—*with* animals—the guys who actually murdered or raped or beat the shit out of their victims? When I wasn't on constant alert for a shiv in my back or a beatdown, there was the fucking humiliation of it all. Maybe you'd have visited once or twice, but when the years on my sentence really sank in, you'd see it too. That I wasn't an actual person anymore. I was Inmate #339033."

"That's not what would've happened," Miller said, his voice low.

"No? Until four days ago, I was in for ten fucking years—"

"And I'd have stuck with you, no matter how long it took," Miller raged back. "You don't fucking get it, man. You and Holden, you're my brothers. You don't get to take a time-out from my life. I need you in it. I fucking need you."

I hated how his words were seeping in through the cracks of the walls I'd built in prison. You don't survive one minute on the inside unless you pack yourself in cold, unfeeling armor that is miles thick. Ten minutes free, and Miller was already tearing it all down.

"And Christ, *Shiloh*..." Miller shook his head, and something in his expression scared the shit out of me.

"What's wrong? Is she okay?"

"She's okay, but I'm not saying another word," Miller said. "You want to know how she is, then you go see her. You *have* to see her. I'm not fucking around."

"She's not going to want that."

"As if you would know?" Miller scoffed, then his voice softened slightly. "Come on. Get in the damn car. My security is going to think we're having a lovers' spat."

"You sound like Holden."

"Someone should."

"You haven't heard from him at all?"

"Nope. But he wrote a book. His first book, so naturally it hits number one on every list and wins every award under the sun."

"Good," I said. Not for the awards but because it meant he was still alive, somewhere out there. He hadn't disappeared completely.

At the SUV door, Miller stopped. "You good? I mean… San Quentin can't be a fucking cakewalk."

"Not like selling out arena tours."

He snorted. "They got TMZ in prison?"

"You're a big deal, Stratton." I smiled a little. "No one doubted that but you."

Miller met my gaze for a moment and then put his arms around me, clasping me tight. It was the first time in three years I'd had physical contact with anyone that didn't have violence lurking beneath it.

"We gotta get going," Miller said, pulling back. "I'm under strict orders to deliver the package straight to Shiloh."

"Whose orders?" I asked as we climbed into the leather interior of Miller's car that reeked of money and was configured like a limo with seats facing each other. "How did you know I was getting out today?"

"Selling out arena tours has its privileges," Miller said, taking a seat across from me. "And that's all I'm saying. Whatever you need to know about Shiloh, you have to hear it from her." He handed me a beer from the car's mini fridge and popped one himself. He clinked his bottle to mine. "Happy birthday."

"It's not my birthday."

"You turned twenty-one in there," he said as the car rolled smoothly out of the parking lot. "You're legal now."

I'd had three birthdays in prison, but it could've been ten. I was twenty-two years old and free instead of almost thirty. The first cold swallow of beer hit my tongue. I nearly groaned.

Miller smiled. "Good?"

Good didn't begin to describe it. I was free, sitting with my best friend, drinking a beer.

"Doesn't feel real."

"I can't imagine it."

"You look good," I said. "Healthy."

"Took a while to get there," he said and told me all about his life postgraduation.

"You're moving back to Santa Cruz?" I asked when he'd finished.

He nodded. "Until Violet finishes her undergrad. Then

I'll go wherever she wants to go for medical school. San Francisco probably. She doesn't want to leave the Bay Area, and I'm not leaving *her*, so…"

He shrugged like it was the easiest thing in the world. I toyed with the label on my beer bottle.

"Hey," he said. "It's going to be okay."

I shook my head. "I did what I thought was best for her. And you."

"I know, but you screwed up, Wentz. What's best for us is you."

The two-hour drive from San Quentin to Santa Cruz was both the longest and shortest of my life. Miller wasn't fucking around—he drove straight to Rare Earth Jewelry and parked out front. Through the tinted glass, I could barely make out Shiloh at the rear of the store. My stomach clenched until I thought I'd puke up the two beers I'd drunk.

"Does she know?"

"She knows you're getting out. That's it."

I heaved a breath, and we clasped hands.

"See you later?" I asked.

"If there's anything left after Shiloh gets done with you." Miller chuckled, and then it mellowed into a strange smile. He jerked his chin at the shop. "Go on. It's been long enough."

I climbed out, but the SUV stayed, likely to make sure I didn't take off. Miller didn't have to worry. Now that I was less than twenty feet from Shiloh, I had to see her. Even if she raged at me. Or worse—if she didn't care one way or another. If I could just breathe the same damn air as her for a minute...

I stepped inside the shop.

It smelled of incense, or maybe a scented candle was lit somewhere. Everything was what it'd been before Frankie had trashed it—classy and beautiful like its owner. A soft chime announced my arrival.

"Be right with you," Shiloh called, bent over her work, and Christ, her voice... Rich and smooth and going straight to my head like a hit of something potent.

She slid off her stool and started toward me. "How can I—" Her words choked off in a little gasp. She gripped the side of a worktable, knuckles pale, her mouth falling open.

My girl.

Fucking beautiful—more beautiful than I remembered, though I didn't know how that was possible. A white sleeveless dress with yellow flowers draped her body, highlighting the glow of her skin and curves that were rounder than they'd been three years ago. Half of her braids were piled on her head, and the other half fell down around her shoulders, drawing my eye to the perfection of her neck, her jaw, her lips...

"Ronan..." She swallowed, and she was staring too, her eyes soaking me in as if she couldn't believe I was real. "I thought...you had another week."

I fought every urge to stay on the opposite side of the shop instead of rushing at her, grabbing her, taking her…

She's not yours to take.

"Don't know how it works," I said, my throat dry. "Perry made it happen fast, I guess."

She nodded faintly, moving slowly to me, then stopping. "Lock the door, and turn the sign. If a customer walks in right now, I'll lose my mind."

I did as she said and faced her. "Shiloh…"

"Don't say a word." She shook her head and held up a hand, trembling. "When it was official that you were getting out, I had a million things planned to say to you, and now I can't remember any of it. You're here, and I can't…"

Tears flooded her eyes, and she grasped the edge of a display case, her legs giving out.

I was there in two long strides, catching her before she fell. Once my hands touched her, I couldn't help myself, I was so fucking greedy for her. I gathered her in my arms, holding her tight. She relented, her body collapsing against me.

For long seconds, I held her, and she was holding me just as tight.

"I can't believe this is real. You're here?" She lifted her head, and her eyes roamed my face, her fingertips tentatively touching my chin, my lips, my cheeks.

"I'm here," I said gruffly.

She shook her head, her hands curling into fists and hitting me weakly in the chest. "No. *No…* I can't…" she cried. "Goddamn you."

But I couldn't let her go. My arms slid around her slender back, then into her hair, my fingers tangling in her braids. Three years of not having her crashed over me, demanding erasure.

"Ronan..." she breathed, tilting her head up, our lips brushing. "God."

She was trembling against me, and my body was vibrating with need until I thought I'd combust. Slowly, I bent my head to her, a brief kiss...short and shallow. But that was all it took. One touch, and we fell into each other. Her mouth opened for me, and I invaded hard, taking back the time we'd lost, reclaiming her. My tongue tasted every corner of her mouth until she moaned and kissed me back, just as demanding and desperate. Our hands roamed and grasped, tugging at clothes to find skin. My hand slid up her thigh to her ass and the lacy nothing of a thong.

"Fuck, Shiloh," I gritted out, mauling her, devouring her while she pushed my jacket off my shoulders, then slid her hands under my shirt.

"We shouldn't," she whispered between kisses. "This isn't right. I'm so mad at you." But she didn't stop kissing and touching me and grasping at my clothes. When she feverishly whispered, "Back room. *Now*," I instantly obeyed.

I hefted her easily. She wrapped her legs around me, and I carried her to the back room and pinned her against the wall. I held her with one arm while yanking down the strap of her dress. I bent to suck and bite while she cried out, her hands clawing at my shirt.

"The desk," she breathed.

I carried her to the small desk, swept everything off the surface, and set her down. She lifted my shirt off. I could've fucking cried to feel her hands on me, her mouth pressing hot kisses on my chest. I gripped her hair, my mouth on her neck, while she tore at the button and zipper on my jeans.

"Condom?" she whispered.

I nodded, praying there was one left in my wallet. I found the lone packet and tore it open. We kissed—raw and biting—as my hands slid up her thighs and came back down with her thong. I tossed it aside and thrust her knees apart.

"Slow," she warned as I bent over her, needing to be inside her like I needed air. "Go slow. It's been three years."

"No one? You've been with no one?"

"God, Ronan," she breathed. "You have no idea."

Then she reached between us and guided me inside her. Her body tensed beneath me, and she hissed in pain. I froze.

"I'm hurting you."

"Don't stop," she gritted out, her brows furrowed but her mouth open, sucking air in little gasps. "Don't stop. Not now."

I let her draw me in at her own pace until our hips were touching. My eyes fell shut. "Christ, baby."

"Kiss me," she said, pulling at me desperately. "Kiss me, Ronan."

I kissed her and she moaned, but the pain was leaving, her body softening under me. I moved a little faster, but still held myself back with every bit of self-control I had.

Shiloh hooked her legs around my waist, clinging to me. "Yes," she breathed into my neck. "God yes, now. Harder…"

Relief surged along with the hot, naked lust that burned through me. I braced one hand on the desk, the other at the small of her back, holding her into my thrusts, each one driving a cry from her throat. When I didn't think I could contain myself for another second, she tensed against me, and I wanted to stay there forever. Because there wasn't going to be another woman after Shiloh. If she kicked me out of her life after this—and she had every right—I'd still be hers.

Only her. Only Shiloh, for the rest of my fucking life.

She gave a little cry and then clamped her teeth on my neck—the pain like a fuse shooting down my spine and igniting my release. I came hard, my hips jerking, erratic, until she pulled me tight, as deep inside her as she could take me.

For long moments, we held still, her face buried in my neck, her fingernails gripping my shoulders while I bent over her, sweaty and gasping.

Eventually, like I knew they would, her hands went to my chest and pushed me back. I withdrew from her, disposed of the condom, and tucked myself away. She pulled her dress strap up and pushed her skirt back down.

"This is what we do," she muttered, shaking her head. "Sex first, conversation after." She raised her eyes to me, liquid and dark. "Goddamn you, Ronan."

"Why did you wait for me?"

"Why? *Why?*" She scoffed a harsh laugh. "As if I had a choice in the matter. Like us just now. As if I have a say. As if I'm not hopelessly *yours*."

Her words sank into my heart. Maybe I still had a chance. Maybe, by some miracle, I hadn't lost her.

"I thought I was doing ten years," I said quietly.

"Well, you didn't," she snapped, her voice trembling. "And it doesn't matter anyway. You could have served all ten years or one week, and I'd still be waiting for you. Because I love you, Ronan. I never stopped loving you."

I swallowed hard, wanting to touch her but not daring. We'd just fucked, and she said she loved me, but there was something else between us. Something in her that wasn't there before.

"The shop looks good," I said slowly. "Is it doing okay?"

"I'm surviving. Thanks to the money you left me."

"Good."

She shook her head. "It's been hard, Ronan. So hard, you have no idea."

Tears spilled over, but her voice was strong. *She* was stronger somehow, when she'd already been the strongest girl I'd ever met. But my heart cracked to think of her struggling for any reason.

"They're giving me a bunch of money for the time I did," I said. "A hundred and forty-five K. It's all yours if you need—"

"Jesus Christ, stop!" Shiloh jumped off the desk and

shoved at my chest with both hands. "I don't want your money. Don't you get it? I want you. I've only ever wanted you."

"They put me away, Shiloh," I said, catching her wrists, my voice barely controlled. "It was all I had to give."

She shook her head, tears falling freely now. "No, it wasn't. There was *you*."

"Behind bars? A two-hour drive?"

"*Yes*," she cried. "At least then I could see your face. Hear your voice. Even a little piece of you is better than nothing." She broke down then, her slim shoulders shaking.

I pulled her to me, my mouth against her hair. "I'm sorry. I thought it would be better that way. For you. For me too."

She cried against my bare chest, her tears hot on my skin, burning me with guilt and regret.

"I know you did," she said. "But you're wrong. It wasn't better for me. I needed you. *We* needed you." She pushed away from me and wiped her eyes. "Come on. We have to go home now. It's been too long, and every minute that goes by is another minute that…"

Her words trailed, sudden nervousness flooding her. I put on my shirt and jacket while she locked up and set the alarm. On the sidewalk, she called an Uber.

"Where's the Buick?" I asked, wondering if the old thing had finally died.

"At home, in case they need it," Shiloh said but didn't elaborate.

I made a vow to buy her a new damn car—something she could use for her business—whether she wanted me to or not.

"Bibi is going to be so happy to see you," Shiloh said on the way to her house. "And yell at you." She smiled a little. "Or not. She loves you too."

"How is she?"

"Perfect. Getting up there but still herself."

I eased a sigh of relief. A selfish one. Because I realized I loved Bibi too, and if something had happened to her while I was locked up, I'd never have forgiven myself.

The Uber dropped us off, and I followed Shiloh up the front walk. Her hands were trembling as she unlocked the door.

"What's wrong?" I asked.

"Nothing. I just… I've been waiting for this moment for a long time. We both have."

I thought she meant Bibi, but when she opened the door, the first and only thing I saw was the little boy—maybe two years old—standing in a playpen in front of the couch. Soft black curls framed his face, and large brown eyes watched us come in. He broke into a smile to see Shiloh and held his arms to her.

"Mama!"

I was dimly aware that Bibi had come in from the kitchen and stood at the dining room table, her hands clutched tightly with Shiloh's mother, Marie.

My blood was thrashing in my ears, and my heart

crashed against my ribs again and again. Shiloh picked the baby up and set him on her hip.

"Ronan," she whispered, her eyes flooded. "This is August."

I stared at the little boy, then at Shiloh and back again, a thousand emotions flooding me, more powerful than any I'd ever known.

"He's…"

Shiloh nodded, her smile hopeful but scared too.

"Your son."

THIRTY-FIVE
SHILOH

I watched, my heart in my throat, trying to read Ronan's reaction. What if he never wanted a kid? What if this was too much? What if…

He put his hand on his chest. "Mine?"

That word, in his broken voice, broke my heart too. "Yours."

Ronan nodded vaguely. His gray eyes went between us, and then he turned and walked back out the door.

A gasp came from the dining room.

I looked to my mother. "Mama?"

She rushed forward to take August out of my arms, and I hurried outside, fear flooding me that Ronan was walking away from me. From us.

But he was sitting on the bottom step, hands dangling off his knees. He shook his head, staring at nothing. I shut the door behind me, gathered my dress, and sat beside him.

"Talk to me," I said. "Please."

"How did this happen? When?" he asked, still not looking at me, his voice low.

"The last night we spent together. I'd been sick and not thinking after Mama dropped her bomb on me. I didn't take my pill, and you didn't ask if I had."

"You were upset that night," he said. "I'd have done whatever you asked to make you feel better."

"I know," I said gently. "I'm saying we're both responsible. We made him together, and he's not a mistake that someone needs to take the blame for. But it was hard, Ronan. You not knowing…"

"I'm glad."

"What? You're *glad*?"

"Mostly, I'm fucking wrecked, Shiloh," he said, his voice cracking. "But part of me is glad, because I'd have gone insane knowing what you were going through when I couldn't be there. Watching him grow up through prison bars…his first memories of me as a criminal, like my dad. That would've fucking killed me."

"You're not a criminal, Ronan. I knew the truth before Frankie made it real, and I've been telling August about you since the beginning. About what kind of man his daddy is. How you always do whatever you think is best to protect those you love." My voice wavered. "Even if it means you had to be away for a long time. Even then…"

"Fuck, Shiloh."

"It wasn't your fault," I continued. "They saw what they wanted to see. But you're here now, and that's all that matters."

"Whatever you need," he said roughly. "You and him… I'll take care of you both. You won't have to do this alone."

"I didn't do it alone," I said. "I had help. Mama and Bibi and the money you gave me. The only way I would spend it was to take care of August and to make sure the business stayed afloat to support us. To build something for you to come home to."

He shook his head, years of regret still hanging heavily over him. "You're so brave, Shiloh. So fucking brave."

"I hardly ever feel brave. I think scared shitless and exhausted are my default settings." I laced my hand in his. There was a scar on one of his knuckles that hadn't been there before. "I just did what I had to do. Like you." I kissed the scar and pressed his fingers to my cheek. "How bad was it?"

"I did what I had to do," he said with a shrug that told me it was harder than he'd ever let on. "I got a degree."

"You did?"

"They have adult education programs at San Quentin. I got an AA in business management. It didn't make sense, even as I was doing it. I thought I was serving ten years and that you and I were…done."

"Impossible."

"Something told me to keep going. To get the degree and not give up."

"You were building something to come home to too."

"Home," he said, like he didn't know what the word meant.

"Yes, home. You and me and Bibi and our little boy. You have a home now. A family, if you want it." I swallowed hard. "Do you...want that?"

Do you want to be his daddy?

A muscle in his jaw ticked as he struggled to contain the emotion I could feel rising in him.

"Christ, Shiloh," he said tightly. "I thought having you back would be the best thing that could ever happen to me. But seeing him..." He heaved a shaky sigh. "I had no idea I could feel like this."

"Like...happy?"

"So fucking happy, it doesn't feel real."

A little sob erupted from my throat, and Ronan's arms went around me and pulled me in, letting me feel the solidity and permanence of him for the first time. I sagged in relief so strong, it left me weak while the purest joy rushed in. I clung to him, my Ronan, who gave everything and asked for nothing in return. Who'd lived his entire life in an empty void so that he didn't trust the love that was his or believe he deserved it.

He kissed me then, the sweetest, best kiss of my life. The kiss that sealed our promises and tears that washed three years away and let us start again.

"Come on," I said, tugging him to his feet. "You need to meet your son properly."

"You keep saying those words, and my heart explodes."

"Wait until he calls you Daddy for the first time."

"Christ."

We stepped back inside the house. Bibi was bustling around the kitchen. Mama sat with August on her lap on the floor, the two of them going through a huge picture book.

"Is that them?" Bibi called, sounding nervous. "Are they back?"

"We're back," I said.

"Hey, Bibi. Marie," Ronan said in a low voice.

"Hello, honey," Bibi said, shuffling into the dining area. Her hands twisted in front of her like she didn't know what to do with herself, and I realized she'd been waiting for this day just as much as I had been. "Aren't you a sight for sore eyes. How are you doing? Big day, isn't it?"

He nodded, his gaze glued to August. "Yeah," he said faintly. "The biggest."

"I believe I'm in your spot, Ronan," Mama said with a smile. She set August down and stood up, giving Ronan's hand a short squeeze.

Ronan sat on the floor with August and me, still looking a little shell-shocked.

"He's all you," he said.

"Not all me," I said. "He's got a lot of you in him."

August studied Ronan with his big brown eyes solemnly. "Mama, who dat?"

"Do you remember how I said your daddy had to be away for a long time?"

He nodded.

"Well, he's home now. What do you think of that?"

August considered this. "Daddy home now," he said, more curious than wary.

"I'll stay somewhere else," Ronan said to me. "Take it slow."

I hated the thought, but he was right. And the fact that Ronan was already doing right by his son…

My poor heart isn't going to make it through this day.

Ronan cleared his throat and picked up the picture book. "You reading this book? Hey, that's a lot of trucks."

August studied his father for a moment more, and then my heart nearly burst when he toddled over to him and situated himself on his lap.

From the couch, Mama clapped a hand to her mouth.

"Truck!" August said, pointing at a yellow dump truck on a page of trains, cars, and construction vehicles.

"And what's this?" Ronan asked, his finger on a freight train.

"Train!" August said. "Dis a fire truck," he said, pointing. "An' dis right here, dis a race car."

"Sure is." Ronan looked at me, his eyes full. "Smart kid."

They finished the picture book and moved on to a book about a grouchy caterpillar, and then Bibi announced from the kitchen that it was dinnertime. The scents of beef stroganoff and warm bread filled the house.

"You ready for dinner, little man?" I asked.

August nodded and held his arms up for me. I picked

him up as Ronan got to his feet, and the three of us stood for a moment together. August's chubby fist wrapped around a handful of my braids, his large eyes still on Ronan. Then he put his hand on Ronan's cheek.

"Dis my daddy," he said like a proclamation.

Ronan and I looked at each other.

"Now it's official." I smiled through tears. "Guess you're stuck with us."

"Guess I am," he said and smiled back—the real, genuine smile I'd been waiting years to see. So beautiful. So much *him*.

"You're staying for dinner, right, Ronan?" Bibi asked, then snorted and muttered to herself. "What am I saying? Of course he is."

"Stay," I whispered. "For always."

He leaned in and kissed me softly. "For always."

I closed my eyes, letting the bliss wash over me, filling in all my broken pieces, making me whole.

We moved to the dining room, and Ronan went to Bibi.

"I didn't get a chance to say hello," he said, his voice thick.

"You were a little busy getting acquainted," she replied. "Oh, honey."

I watched as he bent his tall, powerful frame to hug her. I watched how she closed her eyes against his shoulder, holding him tight. And how she seemed bigger than him somehow—his shelter from the storm, like she'd been for me my entire life.

My battered heart rejoiced and finally knew peace because my beautiful man, who'd been lost and cut adrift, was safe at last.

"My darling boy." Bibi took his face in his hands and kissed his cheek. "Welcome home."

EPILOGUE

1: SHILOH

SIX MONTHS LATER

"Don't wake our boy," Ronan whispered into my ear.

Ronan nuzzled my neck, nipped my ear, and his hands began exploring and caressing…

I laughed. "How are you ready again? I need a few minutes to recharge."

"If you insist."

"What's with you tonight anyway?" I reached up to sink my fingers in his hair. "You're in an unusually virile mood." Actually, there was nothing unusual about it. Ronan didn't have an off switch. He'd been known to wake with only a kiss and be inside me a minute later if that was what I wanted. "Are we celebrating something?"

"Nope," he said. "Oh, except that Hector and I got the bid."

"You did?" I screeched, and we both glanced fearfully at the baby monitor on my nightstand.

Ronan had built an addition on to Bibi's house—August's room—where my work shed used to be. It took up most of the backyard, but leaving Bibi alone to get our own place would break her heart, and I couldn't bear the thought of leaving her anyway. We were a tight fit but too happy to notice.

The monitor remained quiet, and I turned my arched brow on Ronan.

"Why didn't you tell me?"

He pulled me on top of him so that I lay flush with his warm, broad chest, his smile lazy. "I'm telling you now."

I rolled my eyes, laughing. "Well, damn, that's amazing news. But what does that mean exactly?"

"It means we are now the proud owners of that rotting little cottage down on Beachside."

"God, Ronan, I'm so happy for you," I said, kissing him and marveling at how fast life moved.

The Bluffs apartments Ronan's uncle had lived in had been condemned. As much as Ronan hated to unhouse the tenants, there was nothing he could do. The best option was to sell the land to the city, then use the profit to upgrade the apartment complex at Cliffside. He hired a contractor, Hector Morales, and together they put in a new HVAC system and a new roof and upgraded the fixtures, all without raising the rent one penny. It was imperative to Ronan that he provide decent homes for people without strangling them financially.

Throughout the process, he and Hector hit it off and decided to use Ronan's restitution money from the state to start their own construction business…with a bestselling author and a Grammy-winning rock star as key investors. The only way Ronan would allow Holden or Miller to give him any money was if they were going to get it back once the business took off. Which it would, because I knew Ronan would work his ass off to make sure he let no one down. Just last week, he and Hector had put in a bid to buy the "rotting little cottage on Beachside" that they planned to flip and make beautiful. Make a home for someone. A family maybe.

"I was thinking," Ronan said, settling beneath me and brushing my braids away from my face. "We're going to need some help with the remodel on the cottage. Neither Hector or I have the first damn clue about backsplashes or lighting fixtures or…whatever."

I grinned. "You want me to choose the design elements? Or…whatever?"

"You're the artist," he said as if it were the simplest thing in the world.

It was total, how much he believed in me. And with Ronan being back in our lives and taking his share of the stress off my shoulders, I'd been able to make my shop what I wanted—attending craft fairs, advertising, and reaching out to other artists for collaborations and showcases. For the first time since its second grand opening, Rare Earth turned a profit three months in a row.

"Sounds like a challenge," I said. "I'm in."

"Yeah?"

"I'd love to. Anything to help. We'll be like the house flippers on HGTV. But let's be more Chip and Joanna, less Tarek and Christina."

Ronan stared at me blankly. "I don't know who any of those people are, but...sure."

I laughed and lowered my mouth to his. He kissed me back with intention, but I still couldn't feel my legs. I slid like butter off his hard, warm body and cuddled against him.

"Not yet, you beast."

"Water?"

Without waiting for an answer, he drew on his flannel sleep pants and padded out to the kitchen. He returned with a glass of water, handed it to me, then stripped naked again and climbed into bed.

I laughed. "You're insatiable."

"You're naked," he said. As if that explained everything.

I took a few sips, then curled into the warm solidity of him. His fingers played in my hair while mine trailed over his skin, his tattoos. The owl watched me, and I smiled. Ronan had explained it was for his mother. The owl symbolized wisdom and vigilance and was her favorite animal. He got the tattoo so she could watch over him and make sure he always did right by those who needed him. To trust and keep going.

She'd be so proud of him, a thousand times over.

"Maybe, just maybe, after you and Hector get that house flipped and after the Boardwalk Crafts Fair, we can take some time off," I said. "I think we've both earned a vacation." I frowned. "But hold up. Do I remember what that word means? I think I do…"

"Where do you want to go?"

"I don't know. France maybe." I ran my fingertip over his luscious lips. "You can kiss me under the Eiffel Tower."

"Sounds like mushy romantic shit. The kind you hate."

"Maybe I'm changing my mind about mushy romantic shit. I blame you. The prom night you made for us with the butterflies and the lights… I was helpless to resist."

"We'll go wherever you want," he said.

I pressed my cheek to listen to his heartbeat. "Paris might be a bit much for a two-and-a-half-year-old, and I don't think I can be that far away from August just yet."

"Me neither."

Ugh, this man.

"A long weekend in San Francisco maybe?"

"That works too." Ronan nuzzled my neck. "I'd settle for anywhere I can make you come until you scream without worrying about waking up toddlers or grandmothers."

"Amen to *that*," I said, listening to the rain and reveling in the feel of Ronan in my arms. In my bed. Back in my life after three years of excruciating absence.

"Speaking of France," I said after a minute, "I got a very interesting order from Paris last week on the shop's website."

"What kind of order?"

"For a wedding ring. Do we know an Albert Bernard?"

"Don't think so."

"He's a lawyer—and an artist on the side apparently, because he designed the ring himself, and it's…"

"Ugly as hell?" Ronan supplied. "Tacky? Ridiculous?"

"Just the opposite. It's stunning. Mixed metals, which I love—silver with gold edging and an asymmetrical configuration of three stones. An aquamarine, a blue topaz, and a diamond in the center."

I frowned, something nipping at the edge of my awareness again, like it had when the order first came in.

"Those are our birthstones," Ronan said just as it came to me. "Yours, mine, and Augie's."

"That's true," I said slowly. "How do you know that?"

"I've been around you long enough to know about the magical powers of gemstones and birthstones and crystals…"

"*Magical powers.*" I laughed and rolled my eyes. "But isn't that funny? It's a truly beautiful design. And so romantic. The email said he's going to surprise the love of his life with it, the lucky girl. It's going to be hard for me to part with it."

Ronan was silent, and the weird feeling didn't leave me but grew into something like suspicion…

"Ronan?"

"Marry me."

I froze. My heart, the only part of me that was moving, beat hard in my chest. "What did you say?"

I raised my head to find his brows furrowed, doubt painting his features.

"Fuck, I'm sorry," he said. "I'm doing this all wrong. I have no plan. No ring. Just…blurting it out like a jackass. But this talk about other people's wedding rings and Paris… I want to give it all to you right this fucking second."

My breath caught. When I thought I couldn't love Ronan more, my heart expanded and made room, letting it all in.

"There's never going to be anyone else, Shiloh. From the moment I laid eyes on you, a part of me knew you were it for me." He took my left hand and kissed my ring finger. "I love you. I love our boy. I love this life that we're making. That you've given me. Will you marry me?"

"Yes," I whispered, then louder, "Yes, Ronan. I want nothing more than to marry you."

He shook his head, disbelieving, like a man waking up from a dream. I took his face in my hands, wanting to obliterate any doubt once and for all.

"You opened my heart and then filled it with everything I could possibly want. Filled it with everything I didn't *know* I wanted and now can't imagine living without. I love you, Ronan, and I'll love you forever."

His gray eyes turned smoky, and he kissed me softly, then deeper. We sank into the kiss that was rich with love but burning hotter with every passing second. My body came wide awake, wanting to celebrate all that we'd endured and all that we'd face together, from that moment through all the years left to us.

Ronan rolled me onto my back, his mouth making a slow migration.

"Can't argue with that."

The rain lashed the window, and through the baby monitor, August fussed. We both froze, eyes on the door that led to his room, attached to ours, waiting to know if it was a one-time fuss or something more.

August whimpered again, sounding scared. Ronan shot off the bed, instantly vigilant.

"I'll get him," he said, drawing on his flannel sleep pants.

I put on his T-shirt and my underwear and listened to Ronan talk to his son through the monitor.

"Hey, buddy. The storm waking you up?"

"Yeah," August said tearfully.

"Don't be scared. I got you. I got you."

I got you.

Watching the two of them grow close over the last few months had been one of the greatest joys of my life. August accepted Ronan faster than any of us expected, asking for him when he was away at work or when he was trying to give August space.

August didn't want space. He wanted his daddy.

Ronan's apartment at Cliffside had been rented out by the management company he'd hired, so when he wasn't spending his nights here, he crashed with Miller and Violet in the house they rented while Violet finished school. But after only a few weeks, it was clear August wasn't going to put up with that. Ronan had moved permanently into my little room in Bibi's house and begun plans for the addition that same week.

I worried that we might be too much for Bibi, that instead of staying with her for her sake, she'd rather have peace and quiet. But from the moment she suspected I was pregnant, she'd fallen in love with August. And Ronan…

She might've loved him before I did. Or before I could name what I felt for him.

Ronan reappeared, carrying our son. August wore a white onesie with cartoon trucks all over it and lay against Ronan's bare chest, his head tucked under his daddy's chin. His large, dark eyes were open but sleepy.

"Hey, baby boy," I said as Ronan lay down with him between us. I kissed his soft baby cheek. "Can't sleep?"

He shook his head, his little fingers reaching for my braids. I scooted closer to him, and he curled tight into Ronan with a handful of hair, bringing both of us into his cocoon. He was asleep in moments.

Ronan kissed his son's head and looked to me, his eyes soft under my rainbow lights.

"*I love you*," I mouthed.

"*Love you*," he mouthed back, his own eyes looking heavy. I grinned as he began to drift—he who had been ready for another round mere minutes ago.

I studied Ronan's beautiful face as he slept, his arms a protective circle around August and me. The demons in him had been laid to rest, and he was determined to keep them buried. He strove to be the best father for August—the kind of father he never had. And I knew he'd never stop working for us, to make his entire life a fulfillment of his promise to his mother.

The owl on his shoulder watched me. My own eyes were growing heavy, but through my sleepy haze, it looked like she was smiling.

II: SHILOH

SIX MONTHS LATER

"There," Mama said, adjusting the delicate sprigs of baby's breath in my hair. "Beautiful. Just…beautiful."

I turned to look in the mirror in the bride's dressing room at the Highland House, tucked deep in the redwoods. My reflection looked back—a daughter, a great-granddaughter, a niece, a friend, a business owner, a mother, and soon, a wife. And in that moment, I realized that all those things weren't me; they were reflections of the love I had in my life. That was who we all were—reflections in the eyes of those who loved us.

I looked to my mother. With Bertie and Rudy's help, she'd moved to Santa Cruz before August was born. She found an apartment and got a job as an assistant manager in a bank. Aside from helping me prepare for August's arrival, she used her marketing skills—those she had set aside for so long—to help me promote the store. And once she was settled, she went to a therapist twice a week. I joined her for half of those visits, and together, we healed.

It was a slow process, but I learned to stop thinking of myself as walking evidence of my father's depravity and to start thinking of myself as an embodiment of my mother's strength. I stopped looking for him in the faces of strangers, because he didn't mean anything to me. He wasn't a reflection in that mirror.

I clasped my mother's hand and looked to Bibi, sitting on a sofa with Bertie. To Letitia, chatting with Violet and Luisa by the window, where the sunshine streamed in. I had everything I needed.

I heaved a breath and smoothed down my dress. It was pale-pink satin, sleeveless, and tightly fitted around the bodice with a tulle overlay. Floral embroidery in periwinkle, lilac, and sage green cascaded over the full skirt. Letitia had pulled my natural hair into a loose, elegantly messy bun with tendrils falling softly to frame my face.

"Do you think Ronan will like the dress?" I asked the room. "It's not exactly conventional."

Bibi cackled from her seat. She looked beautiful in red with a lightweight beaded jacket over her shoulders. "Since when have you two been conventional? Doing everything backward from the get-go."

"She has a point," I said, grinning at Mama in the mirror. "Wearing white wouldn't fool anyone. We have a toddler."

I smiled, thinking of that toddler, who was currently on the men's side of the building, readying for his role as our little ring bearer.

"Girl, that dress is stunning," Letitia said, looking pretty stunning herself in her lilac bridesmaid dress.

Violet nodded, coming to stand with me. My maid of honor already had tears in her eyes. "Gorgeous," she agreed. "Mostly because you look so happy."

"I am. I never thought…" I shook my head. "I'll cry and mess up my makeup."

Luisa, my employee turned friend and third bridesmaid, rushed over with a tissue. "That's my Bat-Signal."

I laughed. Luisa Coelho was an artist in her own right—doing makeup tutorials on YouTube—and had lent her services, giving me a subtle look that complimented the softness of my hair and dress.

I looked at the assembly of amazing women in my life, marveling at how blessed I was. How it seemed like too much happiness for one person.

A knock came at the door, and Holden Parish stuck his head in, covering his eyes.

"Is it safe?"

I laughed. "You're good."

He peeked open one eye, then both, and clutched his heart. "The sheer volume of beauty in one room is rather excessive, don't you think?"

Aunt Bertie chuckled. "What a charmer. Where did you find him, Shi?"

"No one found me, my dear lady," Holden said. "I sprang full blown from Ronan and Miller's imagination."

I exchanged grins with him, and he winked.

After graduation, Holden had disappeared, leaving River Whitmore to wait for him like I had with Ronan. Holden had been all over Europe, killing his own demons, purging them and putting them between the pages of an award-winning novel.

Now he was back and was one of Ronan's groomsmen, along with Miller and Hector. He looked devastating in a soft-gray suit, no tie, the top buttons of his white dress shirt undone. A sprig of pale-purple, yellow, and baby-blue wildflowers—a miniature version of my bouquet—was tucked in his lapel.

"The coordinator is busy with some flower emergency." Holden flapped his hand. "I've been sent to tell you...*it's time*."

I blew out a breath, butterflies taking flight in my stomach.

"That's our cue." Bertie, resplendent in deep purple, helped Bibi to stand. They kissed my cheeks—Bibi's eyes full, seeing me like she always had. Straight into my heart. She said nothing but patted my cheek, and I pressed into her hand, the love for her overflowing.

The other gals hugged me, and everyone slowly made their way out, Luisa shooting Holden—her partner up the aisle—an appreciative smile.

Holden leaned into me. "Since rehearsal dinner last night, that girl can't stop making eyes at me. Not that I blame her."

"It must be such a burden, being as beautiful as you are."

"It really is," Holden said seriously, his green eyes twinkling. "If it gets worse, I'm going to have to jump River in the middle of the ceremony to show I'm spoken for."

"Pretty sure you were going to do that anyway." I laughed and gave him a kiss on the cheek. "Shoo. Behave yourself."

He shot me another wink and went out, leaving me alone with Mama.

She faced me and took a steadying breath. "You sure you don't want Uncle Rudy walking you down the aisle? Or Bibi? There's still time to get her back. I know she'd be honored."

I shook my head and slipped my hand in hers. I'd thought about it, but Bibi and I had talked it over.

"A parent gives the bride away. There is no better way to show Marie that you see her than to let her do this."

I agreed.

"You're my mama," I said with a teary shrug.

She felt the weight of everything in those three words, her eyes shining too. "Thank you, Shiloh." She hugged me close.

"You don't have to thank me."

"I do." She pulled away, her smile beautiful. "I know a second chance when I see one."

June Seong, my wedding planner, rushed in and delicately cleared her throat. "Excuse me, ladies."

She'd done such an impressive job with the grand

opening of my shop, her name was the only one on my list to handle the wedding. As I knew she would, June made it the beautiful, somewhat rustic event I'd dreamed of. Unfussy, set in the backdrop of the forest, with just enough touches to give it an understated elegance that wasn't too fancy, nor too casual.

"Crisis averted," she said. "Your flower girls showered your ring bearer with all their petals, much to his delight, but everything is ready now."

I grinned. While Ronan was incarcerated, Maryann Greer had been promoted at her work and moved from the Cliffside apartments to a better place, but we never lost touch. She and her twin girls were frequent visitors at our home, Cami and Lily treating August like their baby brother.

"You both look gorgeous," June said, sizing us up. "Ready?"

Mama and I nodded and followed June outside. The day was warm but with a breeze rustling the leaves in the trees to keep it from being too hot. I couldn't see around the corner to the flower-laden awning in the clearing amid the redwoods that served as our altar, but I could hear the soft sounds of Miller's guitar as he accompanied the procession down the aisle—Cami and Lily, then August, then our bridesmaids and groomsmen.

The music changed to Wagner's "Bridal Chorus," and I heard the rustling of fifty guests as they rose from the white folding chairs that faced our little awning. I laced my hand around Mama's arm, and she gave it a squeeze. Then we walked.

I'd already seen the wedding preparations, of course, at the rehearsal yesterday. But seeing the finished product, with everyone Ronan and I loved in the world gathered together, stole my breath.

And Ronan...

My heart ached to see him standing there, devastating in the same soft-gray suit, no tie, his hands clasped in front of him stiffly. His eyes widened to see me come down the aisle, and his jaw clenched, a muscle ticking in his cheek.

I had to bite the inside of mine to keep the tears in check. We arrived at the end of the aisle, and the officiant—Eleanor Hutchins, a friend of Bibi's from one of her church groups—smiled down at me from her small podium.

My mother gave me away, placing my hand in Ronan's, and when I looked up into his eyes, nothing could stop the tears from blurring my vision.

"Shiloh..." he whispered gruffly.

I knew how he felt, the overwhelming perfection of the moment washing over me too. I squeezed his hand, and he squeezed back, anchoring us to the present, sharing our strength. I felt the power of our partnership that had seen us through so much together and that had carried us through when we were apart.

Eleanor began the ceremony, giving a little speech about the power of enduring love, and then had us repeat the traditional vows. It would have been too much to ask Ronan to write his own to be recited in front of fifty people—it wasn't his way. Ronan made vows to me every day: in the work he did to help create our perfect life, in the way he loved our son, and in the grasping embraces in our bed at night. The intensity of his gaze when he looked at me held all his promises, and I knew deep in my soul that this love was going to last forever.

"And now the rings," Eleanor said, and the entire congregation *awwwed* as August, in a miniature version of the men's suits, climbed off Mama's lap and toddled up.

"Hi, Mama! Hi, Daddy!" he exclaimed loudly, setting the crowd off again and making my eyes shine.

"Hi, baby," I said, taking two boxes from his hands and passing them to Eleanor. "Thank you, sweetheart."

"Okay, bye!" he said, job done, and rushed back to my mother's lap.

I exchanged a grin with Ronan, but nerves twisted my stomach. We'd both wanted to keep our rings a secret until this moment.

"Ronan," Eleanor said, handing him one of the boxes. "If you will take your bride's ring."

My heart pounded as he opened it, and inside lay the silver-gold ring with our birthstones, glinting up at me in the brilliant sun.

I stared. "You? You made that order?"

He nodded, taking the band from the box. He jerked his thumb over his shoulder. "This one helped."

Grinning proudly, Holden twiddled his fingers at me, and then I knew why the Parisian order had felt familiar.

I shook my head, marveling, as Ronan leaned in. "Is

it tacky that you made your own ring?" he whispered. "I just couldn't imagine giving the job to anyone else. But...I designed it. If that counts for anything."

"You designed it," I whispered back. "That counts for everything."

We locked eyes, and I nearly kissed him before it was time. Eleanor cleared her throat; we were holding up our own wedding.

We straightened, and Ronan took my hand and repeated the words, "With this ring, I thee wed," then slipped the ring over my finger. It fit so perfectly; I couldn't imagine how I'd lived twenty-two years without it.

Then it was my turn to reveal the ring I'd made for Ronan—a wide band of hammered black gold with a vein of twenty-four-carat gold gleaming down the middle. To me, it represented the heart of gold that beat inside the chest of the man standing across from me, whose love and goodness shone brightly, even through the darkest of nights.

I opened the box, and Ronan's jaw tightened again. He shook his head at me. "It's perfect," he whispered. "It's..."

His thought trailed, and I was glad when Eleanor had me recite the words to Ronan so that he could recover.

"By the power vested in me by the State of California, I now pronounce you husband and wife." Eleanor turned to Ronan. "You may kiss your bride."

Ronan took my face in both hands, his eyes meeting mine for a split second—speaking volumes—before he leaned in to kiss me, the crowd erupting in sniffles and cheers.

"I love you," he whispered against my lips. "God, Shiloh…"

"I love you," I whispered back. "I love us."

I felt a tug at my dress. August was there, reaching for us. Ronan scooped him up, and the three of us walked down the aisle together, my husband carrying our son, pieces of my heart existing outside my body, yet I'd never felt more whole.

III: FRANKIE

ONE YEAR LATER

Behind closed eyes, I heard the shuffle of footsteps, heavy ones, against the noise of the street traffic. The damn headache pills had put me to sleep again, and the hard concrete made my ass numb. Someone was close. Without opening my eyes, I shook the plastic Big Gulp cup. The rattle of coins sounded lighter than they had earlier that morning. Someone had probably ripped me off. I almost cared.

"Spare change?" I muttered, giving the cup another shake. Fuck, something stank. Then I realized it was me.

"Hey," said a deep voice. One I recognized.

A sliver of fear slid down my back, and I came wide awake.

Ronan Wentz was crouched on his heels in front of

me, the busy downtown streets behind him. He looked good. His jeans were paint splattered, but they looked new. Like his work boots. His T-shirt read *Wentz & Morales, Contractors*. The shirt was tight around his huge fucking arms—arms strong enough to punch through glass and haul a guy out of his car window.

"What do you want, Wentz?" I muttered, sitting up. My stomach growled loudly. I was used to it; hunger was a part of life now, like my limp or the way my eyelid drooped. But Ronan frowned and stood up.

"Come with me," he said.

I snorted. "I got nowhere to go. No place to be."

Nothing to eat. Nowhere to live. Nothing. I have nothing.

Ronan rubbed his hand over his jaw. Behind him, I could see the sign for Rare Earth Jewelry. Of all the places in downtown Santa Cruz to sit and panhandle, near Shiloh's shop was my favorite. Not so close that she could see me but close enough that I could watch the steady stream of customers come in and out, most leaving with little white bags with gold writing on the front. Knowing her store had survived was the only thing I had going for me.

And it wasn't fucking much.

Ronan nudged my falling-apart Converse with his boot. "Come on, Frankie. Get up."

I scowled. "What the fuck for, Wentz? I did my time. We got nothing to say to each other."

He cracked his neck, deadly casual. "Yeah, we do. Unfinished business."

Shit.

If Wentz wanted to break me in half, he could. I guessed spending a year in the clink for making a false accusation wasn't enough. I'd been out for three months, living on the street. Maybe Shiloh had seen me after all.

I got to my feet, struggling with my left leg that always felt like it had fallen asleep and was just waking up. Pins and needles, all goddamn day. Nerve damage, the docs had said. Dad had fucked me up good.

I grabbed the trash bag that held everything I owned in the world and followed Wentz to the Pizza My Heart.

He pointed at one of the wrought-iron tables out front. "Sit."

"I'm not your fucking dog, Wentz," I said but sat down anyway. Mostly because I hadn't eaten in two days.

Ronan ignored my comment. "Pepperoni?"

I shrugged. If he was going to feed me before he beat my ass, may as well let him.

"My last meal," I snickered tiredly.

Ronan returned a few minutes later with two large sodas and two slices of pepperoni pizza each. He slapped a plate down in front of me, but it was the soda I went for first. Cold, sugary, fucking heaven. I drank until my forehead ached, then dug in to the pizza.

Ronan ate too, not saying anything, confident and strong, while I felt pathetic and weak. But I was used to that feeling. Ever since I was a kid and my dad saw I wasn't going to be a big football player like Chance Blaylock or Mikey

Grimaldi, who, last I heard, had finished his six months for filing a false police report and was working at the gas station down by the highway.

No more football for him.

I polished off my first slice and started on the second, slower now, to make it last.

Ronan, already done, balled up his napkin and tossed it down. He reclined in his chair, his gray eyes—eyes like a shark, back in the day—studying me. I noticed the wedding band on his left hand—black with a vein of gold down the middle.

"Congratulations," I said, taking a bite of pizza. "Shiloh made that, right?"

Ronan nodded. "Of course."

"She's good."

"She's the best," Ronan said, and I knew he wasn't talking about rings.

"Listen, man—"

He cut in. "Drugs?"

"Huh?"

"It's noon, and you were sleeping. Are you high?"

"Do I look like I can afford dope?" I asked, indicating my stinking worn-out jeans, shirt, and Dad's old windbreaker, so faded now it was gray instead of blue.

Ronan shrugged. "You panhandle for money, use the money for drugs. Or?"

"Do other things to score?" I shook my head. "I stay away from that shit."

I rolled up my sleeves to show him my arms, skinny and

white but free and clear of tracks. I didn't know what the hell I was trying to prove to Wentz anyway. Or why.

"The meds for my headaches make me tired. That okay with you?"

Ronan considered this. "No drugs?"

"No drugs."

He nodded and jerked his chin at my food. "You done?"

"Almost."

I took my time finishing my pizza, my stomach feeling stretched from food and sloshy with soda.

When I was done, Ronan threw our empty plates in the trash and gestured to my bag. "Get your stuff. Let's go."

"Where to next?" I asked, shuffling after him. "There's a Ben and Jerry's up the road if you're springing for dessert before my beatdown."

"You're not getting a beatdown, Dowd," he intoned.

"Then what the fuck do you want with me?"

He stopped at the curb where a black pickup truck with the same *Wentz & Morales* logo was parked. The flatbed was filled with buckets of paint, stacks of wood, and a bunch of tools.

"You going to put me to work?" I snorted. "Make me dig my own grave?"

Ronan opened the passenger side door. "We'll see."

I had nothing better to do than see where the hell all this was going, so I climbed in.

"Goodbye, cruel world," I snickered, waving at the streets I called home.

Ronan drove us to an apartment complex. The sign in front of the newly paved parking lot read *Cliffside*. My stomach clenched. The complex had had a makeover since I'd seen it last—it looked new and pretty decent, but I recognized the place where Dad had driven Mikey and me to whale on Wentz for spray-painting Mikey's car.

"Look, man, I told you," I said. "I confessed. I apologized to Shiloh. I did my time."

"Relax," Ronan said, putting the truck in park. "I want to show you something."

I must be crazy, I thought as I grabbed my bag of shit and followed Ronan to the complex. We took a set of stairs up to the second floor. The building had new cement, fresh paint on the doors. The corner unit was marked OFFICE.

Ronan unlocked the door from a set of keys and went inside. I followed more slowly. The place was small but clean, and the sink and appliances and shit looked new. The furniture too. Simple but nice.

Ronan jerked his chin past the living area that had a TV and everything. "Bedroom and bathroom down there."

I frowned and checked it out. The bedroom was furnished, and the bathroom had shampoo and soap and all that. Not like anyone lived here but all new.

A strange feeling tightened my chest, making my eyes water. My heart started to pound. I came back out. Ronan was leaning against the small counter, arms crossed, his face blank.

"What is all this?" I demanded, hearing the whine in my voice—the tone that pissed my dad off so many times.

"First food and then…this place. What are you playing at, Wentz?"

"I need a manager," he said. "It's an easy job. Mostly collecting rent. Fielding any requests for repairs and passing them to me. Keeping the laundry room maintained. Helping me handle tenants moving in or out, that kind of thing."

My throat had gone dry, and the pizza and soda threatened to come back up. "You can do all that yourself."

"I can," he said. "But it's better to have someone on-site to stay on top of things. The pay isn't much, but rent and utilities are included."

I stared. "Don't fuck with me, Wentz," I said, my voice trembling. "What are you saying? Are you…giving me a job?"

"And a place to live." He leveled a finger at me. "But I have to protect these people, Dowd. I swear to fucking God, if you put them in jeopardy for *any* reason… One *whiff* of trouble, and you're out."

"I wouldn't," I said quickly, my pulse crashing in my chest. "I never would. But, Ronan… *Why?*"

His flat gray eyes lost their hard glint. "Because I know what it's like to have a dad who takes a sledgehammer to your entire life, smashing it to fucking pieces until there's nothing left." His gaze hardened again. "This is it, Frankie. This is your one shot. Take it or leave it."

I looked around the apartment. Four walls and a ceiling. All mine, with no raging monster on the couch you had to sneak around, careful not to breathe too loud so he wouldn't get pissed and take a swing...

I blinked and swallowed hard. "I'll take it."

Ronan extended his hand.

This was a dream. The headache meds torturing me. Any second, I was going to wake up back on the street...

But Ronan's hand was strong and real, shaking mine.

"I put some food in your fridge to get you started. Not sure what you'd want," he said, then nodded at an envelope on the small kitchen table. "That's your first month's pay plus some change if you want to do laundry." He jerked his chin toward a cordless phone unit on the counter. "My cell number is on there. My business partner Hector's too, if you can't reach me. I'll be back tomorrow to start showing you the ropes."

"What does Shiloh think of all this?"

He smirked. "It was her idea." He turned for the door.

"Ronan."

"Yeah?"

I shook my head, the words to thank him sticking in my throat. Small and weak, like how I'd felt for so long. "I won't let you down."

"Good."

He smiled a little and went out, shutting the door to my place behind him. *My place.*

"Not yet," I muttered. What Ronan had done for me went beyond words, and I didn't deserve it. *Not yet.* But I could do a good job and earn it. I'd prove to him I wasn't the worthless piece of shit my dad called me every day of my life.

Because what Ronan had given me was better than food or even a roof over my head and rarer too.

A second chance.

IV: RONAN

"How'd it go?" Shiloh asked as I crossed the sand to where she sat at the firepit in one of six beach chairs. She smiled in the late-afternoon sun.

I bent and kissed her, then sat beside her. "Good. I think he'll be okay."

"I hope so." She shook her head, ringlets blowing across her cheek. "If you'd have asked me four years ago…"

"I know," I said. "So damn weird. But it feels good. It feels right."

Shiloh leaned over and kissed me again. "You're a good man. The best."

"Don't know about that. But you're my wife, so I must've done something right."

Her smile was radiant. Happy. To think I had a hand in that blew my fucking mind. We'd been married for a year, and every day still felt like a dream, one that I never wanted to wake up from.

Voices sounded from down the path that led to the shack. Violet and Miller appeared, him with his guitar strapped to his back and carrying a cooler while helping his very pregnant wife along.

"I think I remember how to walk on sand," Violet teased, then laughed as Shiloh and I hurried over. "You guys are too much," Violet said after Shiloh hugged her and helped her to her chair. She was at least six months along but looked about ready to burst.

"I remember lugging one around in there," Shiloh said. "I can't imagine two."

Violet laughed. "Neither can I. Neither can *he*." She jerked a thumb at Miller, who looked more tired and harried than his wife.

Shiloh beamed at Miller. "Because he's taking the best care of you, aren't you?" She kissed his cheek.

"I'm trying," Miller said.

"He's doing more than *trying*," Violet said, smiling fondly at him. "He's amazing."

"The both of you are," Shiloh said warmly.

About six months ago, Miller and Violet adopted a foster child through the charity Miller's last concert supported. Sam was a sweet, quiet kid who loved photography. They hadn't planned on adding to their threesome so soon, but sometimes life had a way of making plans for you.

Miller and I clasped hands, and I relieved him of the cooler that was filled with hot dogs, buns, chips, and marshmallows. "Sit."

He sank gratefully into the chair. Miller was a natural worrier, but I didn't blame him. I'd missed Shiloh's pregnancy. I'd missed so much that she'd endured alone. I envied Miller his worry; I'd have taken all of it from Shiloh had I been there.

But as Bibi liked to say, wallowing in regret was like choosing to drink from a poisoned well. We can never go back and fix our mistakes, only learn from them.

I glanced at Shiloh, my thoughts full of second chances.

I got the fire going as the sun began to sink into the ocean. More voices approached. Holden strode up, River Whitmore following, both carrying more coolers of food.

They stopped just outside the ring, Holden wearing an expression I'd never seen. Unsure. Nervous.

"Hey," he said. "Everyone, you all know River."

River gave a small wave, and it was so good to finally see him here.

Now we're complete.

Violet gave a little cry and struggled to get out of her chair. Miller helped her to her feet, and she flew at River, hugging him and kissing his cheek.

"So happy you're here!" She turned to Holden and smacked a kiss on his cheek too while River shook hands with Miller and me. Then Shiloh took her turn kissing Holden and welcoming River into our circle.

"How you doing?" I asked Holden with a grin. He looked dumbstruck, watching River with our friends, here at the shack, talking and laughing.

"Oh, shut up," Holden said tightly. "You know exactly how I feel."

"Like you're so happy, your fucking head is going to explode?"

He nodded, sniffed. He looked at River the way I looked at Shiloh, the way Miller looked at Violet. Like he couldn't believe something so good was his.

"He looks perfect here, right? Like he belongs."

"Because he does." And because I'd had a really good day, I pulled Holden in for a hug.

Holden sagged against me for a minute, then stiffened and shoved me away. "That's enough out of you, Wentz. I'm already on the verge. I'm relying on you to be your usual unpleasant self or I'm going to lose it."

I smacked my hand on his back. "How about this? If you ever fucking disappear again…"

He snorted. "You're one to talk. But fear not. My disappearing days are over." He flashed his left hand, the setting sun glinting off the silver band—a ring River had commissioned from Shiloh a few months ago. "River has made an honest man out of me."

"I doubt that."

Holden's mischievous smile returned. "He loves to try."

I rolled my eyes as he joined the group, taking charge of the food and barking orders at everyone.

River approached me, and we clasped hands. "Where's the little guy?"

"Home with the grandmas," I said. "Congrats, by the way. You guys set a date?"

"Not yet," River said, rubbing the back of his neck.

"After Holden's book tour, I guess. Tomorrow, we leave for six weeks. I'd rather stay put, but if he doesn't travel now and then, he'll go stir-crazy. Compromise. That's what it's all about, right?"

I nodded, and we both looked at Holden, drinking from a bottle of sparkling water and saying something that had Violet clutching her belly with laughter.

"He looks good," I said. I met River's eye. "You did that."

"Nah, he did that," he said, referring to Holden's time away, when he wrote his book and got himself dried out. "He worked his ass off. I'm really fucking proud of him."

"He worked hard for *you*. He's happy because of *you*. Thank you for that."

River smiled, glanced down. "Well, it goes both ways—that happiness. It runs deep."

Holden sidled over. "The last thing I need is you two palling around together. Next thing I know, you're BFFs." He steered River away. "Ronan's the most dangerous of us all. Knows all my secrets."

I chuckled and rejoined Shiloh in the chair beside hers. The night's hours flowed in laughter, music, and food. Holden had us all clutching our sides at some of his stories, and then Miller would play, his voice carrying across the night, seeping into our bones.

Shiloh leaned into me, her cheek on my shoulder.

Violet sat with Miller in the sand, tucked into his embrace.

River and Holden did the same—Holden wrapped in River's arms. He wasn't sleeping, but his eyes were closed, his expression purely content.

"I'm so glad they're here together," Shiloh whispered to me. "Now we feel complete."

"I had the same thought," I said, except something nagged at me. I watched Miller run his hands over Violet's belly and knew what it was.

Shiloh felt my eyes on her. "What is it?"

"I want to take you home and put a baby in you."

Her eyes widened, her face flushing. "I wish you'd say what you really mean," she teased. "You're serious? You want...another baby?"

"And this time, I'm going to be there with you every step of the way. From the moment you find out you're pregnant to the day she's born."

"She?"

"Or he. Or them. I can't go back and be there for all August's firsts..."

"No, but you'll be there for his everything else's," Shiloh said.

I nodded. "Like the day he becomes a big brother."

Her eyes flooded, and she leaned over to kiss me; I tasted the salt of her tears and her happiness.

"Okay," she breathed. "I want that too. I want everything with you, Ronan. Everything this life has to give." Her smile fell, and I knew her thoughts went to Bibi. "And what it will someday take away."

"Someday," I said, brushing the curls off her face. "But not yet."

She smiled, so goddamn beautiful. "Not yet."

I pulled her into my lap and held her close until the time came for us to go. Miller and Violet would be heading back to San Francisco where Violet was set to complete her residency and Miller was finishing his next album. Holden had his book tour and was taking River with him. No way to know when we'd all be together again or at the shack. It felt like one chapter was closing and another opening for all of us.

We said our goodbyes, hugging and kissing cheeks, the women smiling through tears and reminding each other that San Francisco was only a few hours from Santa Cruz.

"You coming, Wentz?" Miller asked as the last of the coolers and chairs were packed up.

"You guys go ahead. I'll put out the fire."

The group filed out, and I remained, staring into the flames that were the same as the first time I'd been here. The beach was the same, the same ocean crashing against the shore, the place giving the same sense of belonging like it had all those years ago. Only I was different now. Made better by this place and these friends.

I looked up to see Miller approach, a small, crooked smile on his lips. "Hey."

"Hey," I said. My voice was gruff. "Stupid. I can't fucking put it out."

He nodded. "I know."

More footsteps. Holden stepped into the ring of light beside Miller.

"Gentlemen," he said, his voice thick too.

Miller put one hand on Holden's shoulder, the other on mine. Miller Stratton, our anchor. The homeless kid who'd once pawned his guitar so his mom could eat. The center of us. Our North Star, keeping us from going adrift.

Holden moved to clasp my shoulder, and I gripped his, making the circle complete.

"Guys…" Holden whispered.

"Yep," Miller said, and I nodded, unable to speak.

No one said another word. No one had to explain or finish the thought. We each felt it. Bone-deep gratitude and love that ran deeper than words.

They'd called us the outcast, the vampire, and the criminal. The Lost Boys. But we were bonded by something stronger than blood or friendship or circumstance. We were soulmates.

And not lost anymore.

THE END

AUTHOR'S NOTE

This book deals with heavy issues including that of sexual assault and a woman's right to choose. The choices made by the women in this book serve the needs of this story alone. They are not meant to be a statement or judgment on the real-life choices women are faced with every day—choices that are becoming increasingly restricted as resources are being legislated away. If I have any "agenda" here, it's to increase awareness and empathy and to foster understanding that behind every statistic is a human being with her own story.

RAINN Sexual Assault Hotline: rainn.org/about-national-sexual-assault-telephone-hotline
Planned Parenthood: plannedparenthood.org

And one more thing… In this novel, Ronan takes Shiloh to the Natural Bridges Monarch Trail in Santa Cruz. That is a real place, and thousands of monarch butterflies flock to it each year…in October. Not June. I may have fudged a little on the great migration so Ronan could create some magic for Shiloh. To all the entomologists out there, my apologies, but anything for the romance. ;)

though-provoking, well researched and written that it captured the hearts of many. His passion for writing has aimed throughout his life and he is both an inspiration and

WANT MORE EMMA SCOTT? READ ON FOR A SNEAK PEEK AT *LITTLE PIECES OF LIGHT*

Chapter 1

XANDER, AGE SEVENTEEN

PRESENT DAY

"Hey, Dad, we're here," I said, pulling the Buick onto the driveway that led to the little house. What was once smooth cement was now bursting at the seams with weeds. I grimaced as our car—already overburdened by the U-Haul container attached to the roof—hit a pothole.

But neither my words nor the jolt shook my dad out of his thoughts. Or stupor. Or wherever he'd gone—deeper into the intricate, twisting tunnels of his own mind. The entire drive up from Maryland, he'd stared out the passenger window, muttering to himself. Figures, mostly, for an equation that had no end.

He's not getting better.

I faced forward, observing the house through the grimy, insect-splattered windshield. It looked smaller and more run-down than it had seven years ago. The area was pretty, at least.

Our house was tucked into a corner of forest along the bend in the land that created the Bend. The Bend was an entire neighborhood, but you wouldn't know it. The forest, the road, the silence...it felt as if no one were around for miles. Which was good. There was no one to see how the house was falling apart.

Our only house now. The last stop.

I glanced over at Dad, who had yet to realize the car was no longer moving and sighed.

Mom's leaving wasn't a Big Bang that created a brand-new reality. Instead, it had opened a wormhole to an altered version of the same universe. The same reality on the surface, saturated with all the same painful memories. But if you dug just a little deeper, you'd find an alien landscape.

Dad and I'd become reluctant explorers, discovering little artifacts of Mom's absence every day. Here is the first breakfast she's not here to make. Here is my first day at Langdon School with no one to kiss my cheek in the morning. Here is an empty house after the bus drops me off in the afternoon. Here is Dad, alone in his bedroom, alone in his study, alone at the dinner table while I cleaned up remnants of TV dinners or takeout. Alone, alone, alone.

Mom said it wouldn't be forever, but it'd been seven years. My childhood was all but finished. So was Dad's career. She wasn't going to come back, and if she did, it'd be too late.

Dad was still waiting.

He talked frequently about himself and Mom in their early days. "We were in grad school when I first laid eyes on her," he'd tell me, his eyes distant. "I fell helplessly in love with her in that first moment, but she left me anyway."

I knew exactly how he felt.

Seven years after Mom left, things fell apart. Without her salary, Dad had to work full time with no breaks. We were no longer able to spend summers in Rhode Island, and all that sadness had taken its toll. I'd witnessed the slow erosion of his mind long before a pair of his supervisors from the NIST paid a visit a few weeks ago.

"He's had a breakdown, son," one of the suits had told me in our house in Gaithersburg. "He's increasingly forgetful. Long stretches of blankness…" He cleared his throat. "It's necessary that he retire and begin collecting his pension."

The other suit had been more direct. "We think he might benefit from a therapeutic setting."

I read between the lines.

"Don't let them put me away," Dad had pleaded that night. "I'm onto something. Something big, and they're jealous. They've always been jealous."

"They want to help, Dad."

"I don't need help." He offered a small, heartbreaking chuckle. "Don't put your old man out to pasture just yet. I'm not that far gone. Quite the contrary. My mind has never been sharper. Never have I felt this clarity." He clutched my shoulders. "I'm close, Xander. I'm so close."

Dad insisted he was on the brink of accomplishing what every physicist on the planet was striving to accomplish: to reconcile quantum theory with general relativity and arrive at a unified Theory of Everything.

"I just need to work alone, without all the noise and interference. We could go back to Rhode Island!" Dad cried, hope flaring in his eyes. "You can go to school in Castle Hill and be a regular kid for a change. Go to a normal high school and do all the things normal kids do. Trust me, Xander, you want that. Stay safe a little while longer, because once you get into the field, they'll try to tear you apart."

I *wanted* to be in the field, to keep my brain occupied with practical facts instead of impractical feelings. But Dad needed to be in the Rhode Island house more.

It was decided I'd do a senior year of high school at Castle Hill Academy. A gap year, in which my father would either recover or fall into the cracks of his own mind. He'd spend his days working on his equations and I'd play pretend at the high school. CHA had a robust program of academics, STEM classes, arts, and "elite" sports: gymnastics, lacrosse, water polo, and row. They were even magnanimous enough to allow poor Bend kids to attend.

I already had three degrees from the University of Maryland; the last thing I needed—or wanted—was more high school, but the rowing team was a selling point. I'd been on the Langdon crew, and the physical exertion saved me from drowning in my mother's abandonment and all those empty mailboxes.

The downside to this grand plan was the high probability that Emery Wallace would also be attending the Academy. Unless she'd moved away. That might explain her silence, but I doubted it.

For years, I'd written to Emery. A humiliating and pathetic number of letters, considering that every single one went unanswered. Like my mother, it seemed Emery had changed her mind about wanting to know me. Two years ago, I'd sent the final letter. A confession straight from the heart that left no mystery as to how I felt about her.

No answer.

I'd given up on whatever we might have been. But even so...

Even so, sitting in the drive of our ramshackle house seven years later, my heart thudded at the idea of seeing Emery again. How beautiful she must be now that she'd grown up...

I cleared my mind that wanted to populate with images of Emery. Years of pouring my thoughts and feelings into letters she never bothered to answer had carved the wound in my heart even deeper. A canyon now, a canyon that echoed with emptiness because there was zero probability I'd ever let anyone in again.

"Come on, Dad," I said, gently nudging him back to reality. "We're home."

Dad rushed into the living room like a little kid on Christmas morning. The house was too small for a proper office, so years ago he'd made a workstation out of an old rollaway desk in one corner of the living room, now almost entirely buried under books and papers.

"Yesss," he sighed, sinking happily into the creaky chair. "I'll finally be able to do some real work."

I let the duffel bags—mine and his—drop to the shag carpet and glanced around. The house was 1,500 square feet of clutter, only now all that clutter was covered in seven years' worth of dust and cobwebs and sprinkled with rat droppings. The front door faced a set of stairs that went up one floor, a ratty maroon couch and chipped wooden coffee table were positioned in front of a stone fireplace, and under the front window sat an old piano. Dad had been pretty good back in the day, and I'd taken lessons. We used to play duets—the one thing that Mom seemed to enjoy—but I couldn't imagine either of us playing again.

Every inch of it—except for my loft—was cluttered with mess. Not filth, just *stuff*. Too much stuff, and now I could see it through my mother's eyes. A claustrophobia-inducing wreck of a house presided over by a wreck of a man and his bitter son.

No wonder she left.

I dismissed the excuse. She had her reasons—maybe a hundred of them, big and small, but all of them had been more important than me.

When the first day of school arrived two weeks later, I rode my bike—it was less embarrassing than the Buick—into the student parking lot of Castle Hill Academy. True to its name, the school sat like an ultramodern castle on a hill—all white planes, sharp angles, and glass. The lot was filled with Mercedes, Teslas, and BMWs with a few junkers sprinkled in. Other Bend kids.

I didn't see any of my people, but plenty of Richies, sitting on hoods or gathered in groups, talking and laughing. Everyone was dressed for the humidity: the girls in short skirts or cut-off shorts and tight, revealing tops. The boys wore jeans that didn't have holes in them like mine did. Their shirts were designer label polos, while mine was a thinning T-shirt bearing a faded image of a Radiohead—my favorite band—logo.

I locked my bike and shouldered my backpack. I felt the stares as I walked past a clutch of students leaning against a Range Rover. Its back window was soaped with the words *Bow down to your SENIORS!!!*

"What's up, Bender?" someone called.

I rolled my eyes behind my glasses and kept walking. "Bender." How original, not that "Richies" was the paragon of creativity. I wondered—not for the first time—why I was subjecting myself to this experiment.

Tell the truth, a voice whispered. *You're here for her.*

I couldn't help it. I had a masochistic urge to see Emery Wallace, to reopen every single scar on my heart by confirming that she was alive and well and had *chosen* to ignore me.

As I crossed the green expanse of grass that fronted the enormous school, every blond head of hair, every girlish laugh, drew my eye and made my heart jump. I'd nearly made it across the lawn, wondering with equal parts dismay and relief, if Emery had moved away.

And then there she was.

Statues of lions—the school mascot—sat regally on short pillars on either side of a white staircase that led up to the school's front doors. Emery Wallace was perched on one of the pillars, next to a lion's paw, surrounded by a group of Richies. She swung her legs like she had when she was a little girl, beside me on our rock. But she was no longer a little girl.

God help me…

Her legs were tanned and muscled like a dancer's or gymnast's. She wore fashionable, chunky white sneakers, ankle socks, and short shorts. So short, they revealed the flawless expanse of her thighs. A tight-fitting top strained to contain the…*evidence* of her maturity.

I dragged my thoughts away from primal, objectifying observations and studied her face. Emery's blue-green eyes were framed by long, dark lashes under a fringe of bangs. Thick, golden hair poured down her back in loose curls. My knees literally weakened. In seven years, she'd gone from beautiful to breathtaking.

Any second, she'd see me. I wanted the light of her recognition and dreaded it. A rejection in the flesh instead of in the silence of unanswered letters.

I was still yards away when a tall, blond hulk of a guy hooked an arm around her waist. He effortlessly lifted her off the pillar and spun her around. When he set her on her feet, I calculated Emery's height to be hardly over five feet. Her boyfriend, by comparison, was a giant.

Then recognition hit.

Tucker.

The bully who'd thrown water balloons at us with his friend while our backs were turned. What more did I need to know about Emery if this guy was now her boyfriend?

Tucker bent to kiss her, and his hand went straight to her ass, grabbing a handful of flesh through her shorts. She broke the kiss and shoved at his chest, laughing. But when he turned away, her smile collapsed like a wave function once it's been observed.

Observed by me and no one else.

But maybe I was only imagining—*hoping for*—her annoyance, because in the next instant, she was smiling again. Haughty. Imperious. No trace of the warmth I'd known. None of her innate, luminous magic that had erased my loneliness for a few, fleeting moments.

Because there was no such thing as magic. Only facts. Logic. Science.

And these were the observable facts: Emery Wallace was queen of the school, surrounded by adoring drones, with a Prom King of a boyfriend, while I was a poor, pathetic Bend kid who'd clung to a single afternoon long after she'd let it go.

I ducked my head and trudged toward the stairs. I was nearly past Emery's group when she brushed a lock of hair from her eyes and her gaze found me. I felt it in my chest, where it struck me like an electric jolt. Emery's eyes widened in shock, and I could have sworn she lit up, her mouth wanting to smile...

But it must've been my imagination, because her full lips formed a grim line—almost a sneer—and she looked away.

It was no more than I expected yet it hurt. We'd shared only a short, golden collection of minutes seven years ago, and it still fucking hurt.

ACKNOWLEDGMENTS

A huge thank you to my gal Friday, Melissa Panio-Petersen, who is the perfect example of found family. Love you so much for all that you do but especially for all that you are.

To my incredible sensitivity reader, Korrie Noelle. I will forever cherish our discussions and you for sharing a piece of your heart with me to make this book what it needed to be. Shiloh can't help but be a reflection of your beautiful spirit.

To my beta readers, Joanne Louise Weightman, Marissa D'Onofrio, and Joy Kriebel-Sadowski. You both do so much to keep a nervous author sane and are the bringers of happy tears. Thank you for sharing your thoughts (and screenshots) with me along the way. Much love.

To Officer Elon Kaiserman of the Los Angeles Police Department. Thank you so much for sharing your professional expertise and answering countless questions on police procedure and the ins and outs of courtrooms, departments, and prisons. Any mistakes are liberties I took for the sake of the story, but thanks to your generous input, there weren't many.

To my agent, Georgana, and the amazing team at Bloom for sending my Lost Boys out in the world with so much care and support. I'm blown away every single day by how lovely this group of people, how kind, and how supportive everyone is. Thank you all for making my dreams come true.

To Robin Hill, who made this book possible from day one to the last chapter, through a once-in-a-lifetime winter storm, through power outages and empty pipes and sick doggies… Through it all, she carried this book from the muck of the first draft to the final copy, taking my rough collection of words and making them shine. I will forever be indebted to you, not just for this book (or all those that came before it and those to come), but for giving me the gift of knowing that through my own mental hardships and grief bombs, my work is cared for so that I can share it with the world. Thank you, with love.

And lastly, to my readers. These novels are about belonging, finding one's place in the world, and making family where there wasn't one before. It has been a joy—and a few tears shed—being in Miller, Holden, and Ronan's world. I'm forever grateful to you, my readers, who have taken these boys into your hearts and who have given me a community to call home no matter where I am. Thank you and much love to you all.

ABOUT THE AUTHOR

Emma Scott is a *USA Today* and *Wall Street Journal* bestselling author whose books have been translated in five languages and featured in Buzzfeed, Huffington Post, *New York Daily News*, and *USA Today*'s *Happy Ever After* blog. She writes emotional, character-driven romances in which art and love intertwine to heal and in which love always wins. If you enjoy emotionally charged stories that rip your heart out and put it back together again with diverse characters and kindhearted heroes, you will enjoy her novels.

Visit: emmascottwrites.com
Subscribe: bit.ly/2nTGLf6
Hang Out: facebook.com/groups/906742879369651
Follow: facebook.com/EmmaScottwrites
Contact: emmascottpromo@gmail.com